Southern Fried Women

Stories

Pamela King Cable

For Michael

In Memory of Mom
Roberta Sue (Burns) Rossi

Lynn Andreozzi ~ Many thanks for your incredible attention to detail and professionalism in designing the re-release cover of *Southern Fried Women*. We are truly grateful.

Julie Murkette ~ Thank you, friend and mentor, for your tireless work in book design, and for being there for us, once again.

Kathy Savoy, my loving and devoted sister, and Debbie Shircliff, dear friend ~ Thank you for your time and encouragement. I adore you both.

Judith Lyon ~ Aunt Judy, few of us match the beauty of your steadfastness, your love for our risen Savior, and your countless prayers for my life's work. I am forever grateful.

Table of Contents

No Time for Laura

I originally wrote **NO TIME FOR LAURA** in 1985. Inspired by my best childhood friend, Laura, sweet memories of her are now immortalized in words and a few old snapshots.

In this story, my desire to find the true meaning of friendship begs the question: How far will a person go for the love of a best friend?

Through the years, the character of Laura remained steadfast in her appearance and personality. She refused to allow me to change her.

Laura, my faithful friend, born on February 22, 1954, died tragically on July 8, 1968. There is a special place in my heart I can always find her, and I dedicate this story to her.

ightning flashed near Macon, Georgia the afternoon I drove my truck down a red dirt road to Mamaw's funeral. Thunderstorms rolled through the county for days as I boxed up her belongings. Rummaging through her old-lady junk drawer, I uncovered a Polaroid picture, discolored and cracked with age. Mamaw titled it at the bottom, "Laura and Patsy with Popsicles–July 1968."

Laura—a neglected piece of my past. I had no siblings; we were sisters by default, hooked-at-the-hip best friends.

I imagined God laughing, loading a kinky mass of sweet potato-orange hair on Laura's head. At twelve, red freckles blanketed every inch of her baby fat while thick black glasses slid down her adult-sized nose. By the time we experimented with makeup, Laura announced she was the long-lost sister of Bozo, the clown. Peering into my mouthful of perfect teeth, she hissed through her braces, "At least I can tune into the radio." We busted up laughing. Life was a joke: we laughed at everything along with God.

"I want to be the skinny blonde in the Mamas and the Papas," she said.

I stared at her large, wobbling head. "You can't be serious."

Laura snorted and wiggled all over. But deep down, Laura knew what she was. Cass Elliot and Pippi Longstocking rolled into one. A face only her grandma loved, but I loved her too.

Laura's dirty fingernails scratched and scraped at the label on the empty mayonnaise jar. "The perfect size," she said. Satisfied, she plopped it on my lap.

I shrugged. "We use this jar for lightning bugs, but I suppose it'll work."

We launched our latest summer project, a haphazard tent made with old quilts pitched over Mamaw's rusty clothesline. Reveling in our accomplishment, we sat in the tent, watching the sky yawn and stretch in the twilight. Weekly sleepovers turned brilliant ideas, like tents and time capsules, into adventures. I thought up the tent. But the time capsule was all Laura. A memento for the Star Trek alien in the future who would dig it up and learn about the two most groovy girls who walked the planet.

The next afternoon, I dug a hole up to my knees by the climbing tree. "That'll do," I said, shaking tiny pebbles out of my Keds. I laid the jar stuffed with paper and shiny trinkets into its hiding place and covered it with red Georgia dirt. After placing the hole's grassy hat on top, I gazed up to find Laura dangling from a tree limb by her legs. She giggled as gravity gathered her shirt around her armpits, revealing her flat chest. The sun blinked around her and through the leaves of the tree.

That was over thirty years ago.

Staring at the old photo, I felt guilty for not missing her. Except for the raging storm outside, Mamaw's house grew quiet, and I sat alone with my memories. Had I forgotten Laura on purpose? I closed my eyes, recalling our perfect childhood and the anticipation of a most excellent future.

But there would be no future for Laura.

"I'm off to the new Dairy Queen in Macon with Aunt Jean; wanna come?"

"I'm grounded. Take notes," I said. "I'll talk to you tomorrow."

"Later, Tater," she said. Her deep, throaty chuckle burned into my memory as she hung up the phone. It was the last time I would talk to my best friend.

Nobody wore seatbelts in 1968. Speeding down a wet highway, her aunt lost control of her Volkswagen Beetle. The car rolled like a bowling ball. Aunt Jean broke both legs. But Laura's neck snapped like a chicken bone, and the black hand of Death claimed her in one fell swoop.

At thirteen, I had not learned the art of taking life seriously. When I staggered into the funeral home, her grandma's weathered face wailed in grief. She reached for me, and Mamaw nudged me to hug her, but I could not. I was utterly unprepared. My arms hung limp at my sides. I moved my legs, but the rest of me felt strangely numb. Creeping forward, I glared into the casket and swallowed hard. Laura did not look like herself, more like a doll with too much makeup. No tears came. I had shut her out. How dare she leave me to face my future alone? Enraged, I hurled myself outside to the faint sound of her laugh on a chilled breeze.

Trudging through the rainy afternoon, I finished packing Mamaw's kitchen. When I picked up the photograph again, lightning flashed and cracked outside the window. The electricity popped and went off. But in that blinking instant, grief showed up. I knew what I had to do. Find her. Tell her I was sorry.

In the near darkness, I bolted to the garage. After grabbing a flashlight and a well-used pick, I ran to the old tree, ignoring the sheets of freezing rain stinging my skin.

Three unsuccessful attempts at digging in the mud resulted in incredible frustration. Refusing to quit, I shouted into a rain-filled sky. My voice hoarse and unrecognizable even to myself, I refused to give in to the night's stranglehold on my grief. "Where'd we dig, Laura?!" *The lilac bushes—further to the left.* I moved and dug faster. *Clink.* I hit something. The heavy pick made digging difficult, and my rain-soaked body ached to stop. *Clink.* Murky shadows surrounded me like a black cloak as I tunneled through more cold March mud. Excavating with my hands and feeling the jar, I probed around it. Tender tugging gave way to the sucking sound of muck as I pulled it up.

I rushed into the house, lit a candle, and bathed the jar in Mamaw's kitchen sink. After a couple of hard twists, a labored grunt, and a loud moan, I felt the jar open. Rust from the lid fell on the carpet.

Our *valuables* slid out first. The adjustable decoder ring I found in our church parking lot. Next, Laura's contribution slipped into my hand and around my fingers. A string of plastic pop-together pearls. I smiled, dropped them into my pocket, then pulled out papers that had yellowed over time. Secret lists, newspaper clippings, and pages of nostalgia. Our favorite TV shows, food, teachers, boys we liked, and the current events of that glorious year.

I reached deep into the jar for what remained. Essays we had kept top-secret, even from each other. First, mine read of more sweet rhetoric of the time in which we lived and played. Finally, I pulled out Laura's essay, opened it, and gasped. It was a letter.

Dear Patsy,

I think someday you might dig this up. So, I'm writing to you, not to some dumb alien Klingon.

Do you still watch Peyton Place? How old are you now? Do you have kids? Are you married? To Paul McCartney, I hope. Are you rich and famous?

I have so many questions. Are we living side by side as we promised? Am I fat and wrinkled with gray hair, and do I look more stupid than I do now? Maybe I'm prettier than you and have bigger boobs. Ha Ha. I can't picture myself as a grownup. I think adults are goofy.

You are my one true friend. I hope we will always be together, but I don't think I'll get old. Not like you will. If you read this and I'm not around, remember you are my best friend forever. Wherever I am, I'll never forget you.

A bushel and a peck and a hug around the neck.

Laura, 1968

I crumbled to the floor with Laura's letter in my lap, holding it. Holding her. I pressed it to my heart. I said I was sorry she died, and that I didn't cry at her funeral. My lost tears found their way to my heart, and I sobbed to the depth of myself.

The lightning flashed in the darkness. In some strange Star Trek cosmic fashion, I felt her there. She accepted my apology.

Vernell Paskins

VERNELL PASKINS spoke to me in ways I never dreamed a character could.

Years ago, I discovered a tiny town on a North Carolina map called Needmore. Nothing more than a crossroads, Needmore intrigued me. Not living far from there, my husband and I drove to that beautiful little spot in the country. As I suspected, there was not much to see, and the place needed more to be called a town. Still, the name of the locale stirred a story within me.

What type of person lives in Needmore, and do they—need more?

Over the next several days, a character popped into my head, and I placed her in Needmore with a dose of humor, hopes, dreams, and tremendous disappointments. Although she struggles to make a way where there seems to be no way—living paycheck to paycheck like so many women I know—she is a product of her environment with the deck stacked against her.

VERNELL PASKINS is a character study, a profile, a deep dive into the life and thoughts of a southern woman with little education or work experience. But neither her twangy speech nor the people who call her "low life" or "White trash" can diminish her strength.

I explored two questions that simmered beneath the story's plot. Does God forgive ignorance? Will God love us despite the way we speak and our unintentional sins?

I gaze up at the sky and wonder if it's rain or pee from Victoria's diaper dripping on my leg. I hold my one-year-old grandchild on my hip and pull out a nice, rosy-colored quilted bag to show my next customer.

The clouds that've rolled in this afternoon look like handfuls of dryer lint from a load of blue jeans. I hate stormy weather because I don't make money when it rains. I'll have to dip into my savings next week for the rent. I got money from Floyd's employer when I sued them for exposing my husband to asbestos, and it's dwindling.

Victoria rubs her eyes and kicks her feet into my side. Her legs have rolls—they're bitable. So damn cute. I call her Mamaw's little tubby tuba. Still cutting them back teeth. Got a touch of diarrhea and a raw bottom. I need to rub Jack Daniels on her gums when I get her home. Maybe stop at the drugstore for Paregoric. Help her sleep. Hell, help us both sleep. She smiles up at me; I imagine she's done forgot her momma by now. She looks like Vernise, and I choke back tears. What'd I do wrong? How'd I end up 40 and raising a baby again? Mmm-mmm.

Two women stop at my table. Typical city gals. They talk in circles and say things like, "Carolyn, I can make these same purses and sell 'em at our Christmas church bazaar!" Opening my handmade bags, they check out the double knot stitching. Damn haughty women come to waste my time asking stupid questions. Ain't about to buy a blasted thing. Not a stitch of their padded blazers, linen trousers, or leather loafers comes from Walmart, that's for dang sure. Real gold rings squeeze every one of their fat fingers. But they sure smell better than me, and their freshly permed hair reminds me of Sue Ellen Ewing on Dallas. They'll head over to the next booth and bother Flossie if I'm lucky.

These days I worry more about my daughter, Vernise. She up and ran off with that low-life redneck Lenny I-cain't-remember-his-last-name. I wish I could've hog-tied her to the trailer's hitch. After Vernise had herself a baby, she couldn't keep her job at Eckerds Drug Store. They fired her after three weeks. Flossie said she'd heard Lenny about drove Vernise nuts. He'd show up at the store, act like a crazy man—stalk her up and down every aisle. Good God Almighty.

Ain't no wonder Eckerds kicked her butt out after she and Lenny fought in the health and beauty aid aisle. Flinging boxes of Band-aids and Kotex at each other, screaming louder than a pissed-off preacher, Flossie said.

One evening she came home all lovey-dovey, kissed Victoria, and packed her bags. I'll be damned if she didn't leave me a note in the middle of the night.

> *Dear Momma,*
>
> *I got to go with Lenny. I can't live in this place no more. Please take care of the baby. I'll come back to get her when I've found a job and a place to live.*
>
> *Love, Vernise*

That was five months ago. Ain't heard hide nor hair from her since. And I ain't got the money or the energy to go looking for her either. *Humph.* Vernise is a grown woman. She's making her own bed right now, I guess.

"For ten dollars, this here purse will make a nice present for your Momma," I say and watch the Saturday crowd meander past; their eyes peer down at my tables and seldom see me. They hear my voice but never bother to acknowledge my existence. I'm used to it. Sometimes a nice old lady stops and chats. But mostly, it's tourists or folks out for a drive or yard sale hoppin'. They see the sign for the flea market and end up here, buying things they don't need, trash they end up selling in their *own* yard sales. A few folks hope to find a rare antique. But ain't many antique dealers here. Just junk dealers and crafters like me. Years ago, my daddy collected ashtrays and yardsticks and sold them here. God only knows why. I still collect and sell them—in his memory.

I've rented a booth at the I-85 flea market for the past ten years. Folks call it Spencer's Garbage Dump, and I don't care what they call it long as they see the sign at mile marker 82 and stop.

My name is Vernell Paskins, and I make purses and bags from old, ragged quilts I buy cheap from estate sales and thrift shops. My friend, Thelma, works over at the Jesus is Lord Thrift Store in Salisbury. She keeps an eye open for quilts and calls me when folks donate them to the store. Thelma lets me buy them cheap. My bags usually sell out over the weekend.

I live in Needmore, North Carolina. In the land of doublewides. It's about twenty miles from the interstate and the flea market. The town's name fits perfectly because everybody here needs more. I raise my youngest daughter and granddaughter in Tub's Trailer Park, not far down Pot Neck Road. My friend Flossie calls me the mobile home queen of Needmore. I suppose that's because I've lived in one all my life. First, with Momma and Daddy in a single-wide that's done rusted and hauled to the landfill. Then later, my husband Floyd and I rented the doublewide trailer where I still live.

I tended bar in Statesville when Floyd worked construction until he died in '69. Wounded in Vietnam, Floyd suffered from headaches that knocked him flat. Headaches and night sweats. But asbestos is what killed him. I'm still trying to get over it all these sixteen years later. My oldest daughter, Vernise, was four when he died. Vivi, my youngest, was a baby.

I make do. The money I earn from the flea market keeps a roof over our heads and food on the table. I ain't complaining.

Flossie says I should pray about my Vernise. I don't pray. I don't believe in using God as a wish book or a cosmic errand boy. When I lived with Momma, I'd flip through the JC Penny catalog and make a wish list the length of my leg for things I couldn't afford. I think that's the way it is with most folks and God. Always wishing, never getting. I've heard my whole life He supplies our needs. I guess He figures the girls and me don't need much.

Flossie Muldaney rents the booth next to mine. She pedals her handmade jewelry, washcloth slippers, and crocheted doll toilet paper covers. The dolls' eyes open and close and come in all colors of yarn and hair. In the summer, Flossie sells peaches when her trees are in season.

Lin Wang, a Chinese woman, has a booth on the other side of my tables. She cain't speak a lick of English. Sometimes I worry a customer is taking advantage of her. But old Lin knows American money. She sells paperweights and silk shirts embroidered with dragons and little Asian kids. Once, I tried to tell her she priced her stuff too high.

Flossie butted in, as usual. Her dangly earrings shook with her head, and she burrowed her fists so deep into her hips they disappeared. "Leave that Chinese lady alone, Vernell. Them people think they know ever'thing."

So, I gave up until one day, Lin's granddaughter stopped by my table and spoke perfect English. Her name was Ming, I think. Friendly gal and more amiable than her grandma. I told Ming to tell her granny if she lowered the price of her shirts a dollar, she'd sell more. I'll be damned if the old lady didn't do it. The next weekend, she sold a right smart many. She smiled and gave me a nod at the end of the day. We been friends since.

It makes Flossie mad. She'll get over it.

Victoria is heavy on my hip again; her diaper's soaked. I see the kind of woman I despise from the corner of my eye. She tries to be friendly, like the hypocrites from the Baptist church who meander into the flea market on Sundays and pass out them Bible tracts, trying to make us feel bad because we work on the Lord's Day. But this lady doesn't wear gold-tone shoes or a floral dress with a big white collar. No. This woman wears a cotton print shirtwaist dress with a crooked zipper that hangs below her knees: clothes only Pentecostal women wear. She teased her chestnut hair and stacked it high, like a Country-Western singer. Staring at me with enormous brown eyes, they appear liquid and pour themselves through her thick eyeglasses into mine. Her teeth are a little crooked, and her smile—is weak.

"That your baby?" she asks.

"No, my granddaughter, Victoria Jean. Excuse me. I've got to change her." The dense, molasses-like strands of my drawl become obvious compared to her soft Scarlett O'Hara tone. I'm hoping she'll move on to Lin's tables.

"Pretty child. Pretty name, Victoria." The woman reaches over the table to stroke my grandbaby's chubby legs. "Are you old enough to have a grandchild?"

"No. I ain't. You interested in buyin' a bag? I make each one myself. Made this bag here with a quilt what come from Tennessee. An elderly widow lady stored it in her attic. The material's in great shape." I move the baby from my left hip to my right. She's fussy.

"Where's her mother?"

"What?" My reply is a bit distracted as Victoria pulls my hair, wanting down. Baby girl makes a swiping pass for my sunglasses. I lightly smack her chubby hand, kiss her forehead, and then put her dolly in her fat little fist instead. She throws it to the gravel lot and cries.

"Your grandchild's mother?" she asks a second time.

I stare at the woman. Now, is that any of her business? Nosy people have asked me these questions before. Maybe Child Services sent her. Then again, most women can spot a needy woman a mile away, especially if you've been one yourself. So, I lie. Try to hide my need and not spout off. "My daughter's out of town; she's job huntin' in Raleigh. I take care of my granddaughter."

The woman smiles at me. Again. "My name is Rosalyn Boudreaux. Pleased to meet you." She offers her hand.

I shake it but hesitate before I turn on my smile. Now I remember. The tent revival is back in town. "I know who ya're."

"Yes, well, my husband is the Evangelist Jimmy Boudreaux. We're in town from New Orleans and having a tent revival in Lexington all next week."

"I seen your tent." I shift from one foot to the other like I'm four instead of forty.

"I'd like to invite you to the Say Yes for Jesus Crusade. We've had big crowds, and the Burger King is letting us use their parking lot."

"Well, ain't that just super," I say. "I suppose I can say yes to Jesus and grab me a Whopper on the way out."

Rosalyn won't wipe her sinner-radar grin off her Pentecostal face. She ignores my ignorant statement and says, "We set up a nursery in a nearby trailer. You're welcome to bring the baby."

"Yeah?" I feel my holier-than-thou-self shift into high gear. "You sellin' any tambourines, T-shirts, bumper stickers, or them King Jane Bibles?"

She doesn't flinch. "No." She smiles again. "We don't even sell Jesus. We give Him away. If you get the chance, come on over next Sunday."

"Sure." I laugh. *Like I'd give up a day to sell my bags for a pencil stick evangelist to shove religion in my face.* All smart-alecky, I point to Lin Wang. "Why don't you ask Missus Wang over there to come to your tent meetin's. Now there's a soul who needs savin'. She's one of them Buddha worshippers." Inside, I laugh harder at the thought of this evangelist's wife trying to speak Lin's language.

She stretches her neck toward old lady Lin's tables like she's looking for Buddha himself. Then she says, "I'd love to speak to her, and I'll take the rose-colored bag. By the way."

I mentally stuff my fist in my mouth and bag up my sale. Then I watch Sister Rosalyn stroll over to redneck Chinatown. I decide Flossie would enjoy watching this religious woman make a spectacle of herself. I nearly knock over my table, rushing to find her.

Flossie is an ample woman who laughs from deep in her belly. She can be downright imposing when she chooses. She's also a woman with no filter between her brain and tongue.

"Hey—Flossie!" I am plum out of breath with excitement. "Flossie!"

"What now, 'Nel. I'm busy. Maynard just brought in a truck full of peaches."

I point to Lin's booth. "See that woman in the dowdy dress? That's the tent preacher's wife, solicitin' for revival."

Flossie smirks. "I already heard what revival foolishness is fixin' to take place over there in Lexington."

"You gonna go shout with all them Holy Roller do-gooders next week?" I ask.

"Lord, no. You crazy?" she fires back at me. "Why would I carry on with a bunch of damn fools playin' with snakes, fallin' on the floor, and foamin' at the mouth? I got enough to do around here ever'day," she says as she plops between two peach crates on a rickety board that sags with her weight. Flossie raises herself slightly and tucks her housedress under her legs. Her ankles swell beyond the tops and sides of her shoes. "It's too damn hot today; that's what it is. This dress is a stickin' to me." She fans her chest, then dips her hand into the opening at her neckline to adjust her bra strap and droopy left breast. She sighs, then grumbles. "My thighs are gaulded in this heat. I'm 'bout to burn up or have me an itchin' fit."

"Well," I say, "that preacher's wife is 'bout to get a lesson in Chinese."

Flossie cain't resist. At that, she stands and leans over her tables, staring down the row. "Hmm. Looks to me like they's either carryin' on a conversation or the preacher gal is speakin' in tongues." Flossie points as if I don't know where to look. I'll be damned if Rosalyn ain't talking Chinese to Lin Wang. "She must've been a missionary," Flossie says.

"Yeah. Must've," I say and watch old-lady Wang accept Rosalyn's Bible tract. I cain't imagine that Chinese woman agreeing to attend any tent revival. "She's probably thrilled she's got somebody who can speak her language."

"Uh-huh." Flossie's response tells me she's no longer interested. I turn around. Maynard has carried in a crate of peaches. Flossie's counting and shoving them into little bags.

⌁⌁⌁

Victoria is bawling, and I feel bad about her full diaper. "C'mon, little tuba, Mamaw's gonna get that nasty thing off you. Where'd I put the zinc ointment?" I find I'm down to two diapers.

I kiss my granddaughter's fat cheeks, smooth her fine corn silk hair out of her baby blue eyes, and then lay her in the playpen. I change her, but she kicks and screams when I sprinkle cornstarch between her little legs. After I put a fresh plastic bottle of cold milk in her mouth and cover her with a light blanket, she settles. "Take a nap, young'un. Mamaw has to make you some milk money." I point to her toys. "Look at your Pooh bear; he's takin' a nap, too." Victoria's playpen is under my makeshift tent. The humidity is climbing, and she's fussing again. I sit in my lawn chair and pat her backside until she's asleep.

I could blister Vernise's butt for taking off and leaving her baby like this. I knew Lenny knocked her up her senior year. She hated high school but graduated with the minimum amount of credits—a miracle. Nine months pregnant at graduation, Vernise made it half-way across the stage when her water broke and trickled down her legs. Principal Walker handed her a diploma and hollered for a mop. I laughed. The prissy Valedictorian got the wind blown out of her sails. There was no time for her speech. Instead, Vernise stole the show.

But the following week at the Food Lion, I overheard two old biddies gossiping in the dairy aisle. "It was awful," the one said to the other. "A whore gets all the attention, and a hard-working student like Debbie Fairchild cain't finish her speech."

It broke my heart. Vernise is a little misguided, is all. She's no whore. She was looking for somebody to replace her daddy when she started dating Lenny. I'm sure of it. Unlike my youngest daughter, Vivi, Vernise remembers her daddy. She had her choice of men. At five foot eight, one hundred twenty pounds of legs, breasts, blonde hair down to her butt, and blue eyes that'd burn a hole through your heart, Vernise could've picked any military man from Camp Lejeune, Parris Island or Fort Bragg. Hell, I'd have paraded her naked around the Naval Academy to keep her away from Lenny. Damn it.

But she chose that Lenny. A man ten years older than her and divorced twice; I'd heard he'd sired three of his own and never daddy'd any of them. Then he sweet-talked Vernise into opening her legs and promised to take her away from the world I raised her in. She figured she had found a man to love and care for her. It's the only way I know to explain it.

At the end of a twelve-hour day, I pack my goods and carry my granddaughter and boxes of unsold bags to my Ford Fairlane. By myself. No man around here will help me unless he's expecting an invitation to follow me home for a beer and a night of passion. Ain't interested in passion. Not with a grandbaby in a crib next to my bed and a teenager in the next room with hormones already moaning.

No man's been in my trailer since Floyd died, except Daddy. And Roger Moultrie, a handyman and long-distance truck driver who lived in the doublewide at the end of my street. Roger's gone now. Moved to Arkansas last time I heard. Seems all the good ones are dead, married—or driving a truck in Little Rock.

I lay Victoria in her car seat; she's asleep. The trunk's full of yardsticks and boxes of ashtrays I cain't sell. People ain't smoking much in 1985. Not like they did when I grew up. Lord, I wish I could quit. But it's the only thing I enjoy these days—besides that little girl sleeping in the back.

I see my reflection in the car window. My skin's brown from baking in the Carolina sun three days a week for the past ten years. The heat's turned my once-soft skin into a leather consistency, and lines from smoking two packs of Camels a day have formed around my eyes and mouth. My teeth appear white in my brown face, but I know they're a little off-color. Ain't no tar on my heel; it's all on my teeth. My hair is thin and sun-bleached but cut off neatly at my shoulders. I suppose I ain't half bad to look at. Don't weigh much. Puckered and sagging, my biceps flap a little when I wave, and I sense the weight of gravity pulling on my smile. I've been feeling my face fall lately. So, I fight back and try to smile more. Even when I'm pissed off, and that's a good thing. I think it's helped me sell my bags and purses.

⌒⟋⟍⌒

"Good Lord, it's eight o'clock." The trailer's like an oven. I roll over to see Victoria sitting in her crib, naked except for her full diaper. The room stinks like a small animal died and rotted next to the bed. It smells terrible enough to knock me over. The night air didn't cool things off much. Baby girl holds something in her little outstretched hand and says, "Momma." My room's so tiny I can reach out and touch her without leaving my bed. I look at her messy little head; so beautiful. I miss Vernise, and I wonder if she's missing her baby.

"What you got?" I open her chubby fist.

"Momma," she says again.

Great. A little poop ball. Must've rolled out of her Pamper. She squishes it between her fingers. I grab her up fast before she puts it in her mouth, rip off her diaper, and stick her messy bottom in a warm tub. Sitting on the toilet, I watch her splash. I run my hand through my hair and peek at my tired face in the mirror.

It's Sunday, and I've got to sell the rest of my bags today to break even. "Damn you, Vernise. You need to be here takin' care of your baby."

I spend the morning cleaning up and preparing to go to the flea market. I work Fridays, Saturdays, and Sundays. The rest of the week, I plug away under a slow-moving ceiling fan on my enclosed front porch. It's where I cut, stitch, and sew material into tote bags and purses. I've had a love affair with my Singer sewing machine for the past ten years. It's all I know to do to keep us alive. I suppose I could get a part-time job serving drinks at the Crow's Nest again. But I swore to Floyd I'd never tend bar while raising our girls.

Coffee is perking on the stove. Vivi parked our only portable fan on the coffee table and pointed it directly at her head. Like most selfish teenagers, she doesn't think maybe I'd like a cool breeze blowing my way. She curls up tighter into a ball on our fat blue recliner. A chair that our dog chewed the stuffing out of the arms. The damn chair never did tilt back. An unwieldy floor lamp looms dangerously over Vivi's head. I walk over and shove the glass-top coffee table back with my foot, anchoring the lamp against the wall. Vivi ignores me, pulls her housecoat down around her knees, and flips through the pages of her Teen magazine.

Sixteen, bony, and knocked-kneed, Vivi has some growing up to do. I gave her stringy brown hair a perm last week. Wants to be like Madonna, she says. "Not on my watch," I say. Floyd used to say that a lot. My Marine husband also used to shout, "Death before dishonor!" I've quoted it a time or two to Vivi. Especially since the night Vernise hightailed it out of town in Lenny's Dodge pickup. I'm determined my Vivi doesn't give me another grandchild to raise.

Problem is, Vivi draws boys like a fresh cow patty draws flies. She inherited her chest from my momma. Viola wore a double D, and Vivi is nearly there. Her face is like a young Marilyn Monroe. Flossie told her she could change her name to Norma Jean and get away with it. She's a beauty, I admit.

Vivi clenches her fist and holds her housecoat tight against her collarbone. Her hair is wet, and I see goosebumps march across her arms. She turns the fan toward me now. She lets go of the collar, and the fabric remains molded by her damp palm—it reminds me of how we mold our lives before we even know we've done it. Vivi tosses her magazine to the floor and smiles. Victoria has crawled to where she is.

"Hey, baby girl," she says. Vivi loves babies. It scares me to death.

I groan at the pile of dirty dishes drowning in my stainless-steel sink. Coffee grounds and sticky jelly from breakfast cover the kitchen counter. My floors need sweeping, and our garbage cans overflow with dirty diapers. I sigh, reach for my checkbook, and pay past-due bills and one shut-off notice. After a cup of strong coffee, I wash the dishes and smoke. It calms my nerves, and I'm less apt to snap at Vivi again. I pinch my cigarette with a sudsy hand and flick the ashes into an ashtray on the window ledge above the sink.

"Vivi, I expect this place to be spic and span by the time I get home. I mean it."

"Can't, Momma; I promised Missy I'd go to the movies with her."

"Ain't no money for you to waste on movies. Have your friend come here and make popcorn. I bought a box of Chef Boyardee Pizza mix last week. It's is in the cupboard. But you ain't goin' to the movies."

"You're gonna run me off like you did Vernise! Nothing changes!"

"You're right 'bout that. Nothin' changes 'round here, but the size of my ass and the number of dependents I can claim on my taxes. Behave, Vivi. I'm off to work." I fill my travel mug with coffee, put a little hat on Victoria's head, and hope she keeps it on.

Vivi sneers at me. I smile back and blow her a kiss goodbye. She can sass as good as Vernise, I swear. But if I go mining for the truth, I'd have to say I have no more to offer Vivi than I did her sister. She may take off one day too—leave me a note. I cain't think about that now.

The baby's car seat gives me fits. It's second-hand from the Salvation Army, and you'd think broken in by now. But I find it harder than hell to buckle in my screaming twenty-five-pound grandchild without pitching my own hissy fit. Once I strap her in and calm her down, I grab my Camels, tap the bottom of the new pack, pull off the cellophane, and light up. The nicotine hits my bloodstream just in time.

Old man Deeter waves as I drive by. That man is ugly as a hairless goat. He rents the trailer next to mine. His Christmas lights stay hooked to his awning all year, and sometimes he turns them on in the summer. Keeps his dog chained to the cement block on his patio. I wave back with my cigarette in my hand. That's the extent of my neighborliness in this place.

I recall Roger Moultrie as I exhale and steer toward his abandoned residence. He was so smart. Handsome too. I had high hopes he'd be my knight in denim armor. I heard he graduated with a degree in Transportation. Anyway—that's what Flossie said. The first time he spoke to me, he said, "Ma'am, you sure have a pretty baby." I quickly corrected him, pointing out my relationship with Victoria. Don't matter now. But I think about him from time to time.

Flicking my ashes out the window, I drive slowly past his trailer. I know it's empty. A trailer has an unmistakable look when it's no longer inhabited. Last winter, Roger came to my place when my pipes froze and showed me how to use my hairdryer to thaw them out. I invited him to stay for a beer and a barbeque sandwich. Of course, Vivi was there. I think she liked him, but she never said. We started waving to each other after that. Then one day, I heard he had moved on. Some woman in Little Rock's making goo-goo eyes at him now.

Maneuvering through Needmore takes all of five minutes. Only a crossroads makes up this place. Calvary Baptist Church sits on the corner with their Vacation Bible School sign that reads, *Seventy-five years of celebrating Jesus.* The rest of Needmore includes a one-woman beauty shop, a ceramics shop, a run-down filling station, and little frame houses squatting among weeds. This morning I notice one house with a sign in the yard—Notary Public. I wonder if a Notary Public makes decent money. I jot down a mental note to inquire in Salisbury the next time I drive in for groceries and needles for my sewing machine.

Arriving at the flea market, I see Flossie barreling toward me with a pile of yardsticks in her hand. "Got cha' some yardsticks, 'Nel. From an estate sale."

I shake my head. "I'll give you a dollar for the lot, and it's the best I can do."

"Sold," she says and wobbles back to sell a toilet paper doll to a customer.

"Thanks, Flossie," I yell after her, "but I still need to sell the ones I bought from you last week."

I unpack my car and park Victoria in her playpen. It's been quiet this morning so far. Sunday morning customers who've skipped church wander in. For some reason, I take a hard look around me. This flea market is White boy heaven. You can buy cheap gun racks for your truck. The man at the end of my row sells every size of Confederate flag imaginable, along with turquoise jewelry, Budweiser neon signs, belt buckles, and little homemade outhouses with half-moons in the doors. When you open them, there's a little old man with his pants down reading the Sears and Roebuck catalog.

Vendors sell every kind of NASCAR paraphernalia you can imagine inside the pole building. I heard there's a raffle next week—if you put your name in the Dale Earnhardt hat and they pull your ticket, you win a free paint job and two tickets to Bristol Raceway. I ain't a race fan, but it'd be a way to get out of town for a day or two and get my Fairlane painted.

They sell meat on a stick down the way. Always a line, though. Nobody knows what kind of meat, but the out-of-state people love it. None of us will eat it. The stand next to it sells pork skins and lemonade. And once a month, the Lexington barbeque trailer sets up and sells a large tray of chopped barbeque, slaw, and a side of hush puppies for two dollars and fifty cents. I usually get enough to take home for supper.

The afternoon drags on. I look over, and Flossie is fanning herself again. This time under her triple chin. I hear her flip-flops smack the bottoms of her heels, making her way to my table. Pink powder has gathered in the wrinkles of her plump face as she leans over and points like a bird dog. "Look out, Vernell; here comes Dot."

Dot Bickham is the owner of Dot's Antiques and Emporium. In her store on Main Street, she sells used furniture. Laminate kitchen tables with missing chrome chairs or a couch with a hole chewed out of the back by somebody's dog. But if you're hard up and need to furnish your place, it's the place to shop. Dot is the woman to see for pure American junk. She'll give you a good deal on boxes of overstocked and chipped tableware she buys wholesale from a once-a-year trip to factories up north.

Dot scours the papers for the best yard sales. The day before the sale, she knocks on the door and asks the folks if she can get first dibs, which usually works. Every other weekend, Dot hauls her pickup full of furniture, antique picture frames, and boxes of old books to the flea market, where she wheels and deals enough to make ends meet.

The old gal sleeps on a cot in the back of her store, cooks on a hot plate, and once a month, she washes her clothes at the Laundromat. I invite her to Thanksgiving every year. Dot has no family. She thinks I'm her family now.

I watch her cross the gravel drive, lean over the chain-link fence, and spit a tiny stream of tobacco juice into a rusted trash barrel. She taps the side of a Skoal can pulled from her back pocket, then tucks a fresh pinch into her lip. I can smell her. She reeks of gasoline and egg salad. She yanks at her Esso ball cap to cover her eyes from the bright sun. I don't think the woman has any sense to buy a cheap pair of sunglasses. Her eyes are wrinkled from squinting. I guess she's in her fifties, but nobody knows. We all took a stab at guessing Dot's age once or twice.

Flossie shakes her head resentfully. "No wonder she ain't got any relatives. Who'd claim her!" I swear, Flossie and Dot—they don't gee-haw very well. They're like a pitbull and a fat fluffy poodle. Get too close, and somebody's going to get bit, and usually, it's fluffy Flossie yelping in the end.

Flossie turns and huffs back to her tables. Her rear end sways back and forth like the rump of a Holstein heading to the barn. Flossie's threadbare housedress, hitched above the creases behind her fleshy knees, does nothing for her sizeable bottom. And Lord knows, Flossie shouldn't talk about family. I've seen her unmentionable relatives. Her nephew's a bone hound who works at the Waffle House and plays Hank Williams and Porter Wagoner on the jukebox all night. Nothing to be proud of, for sure.

Thing is, Dot's not afraid to work. I heard she pumped gas at her daddy's Esso station for twenty years to buy her store in '69. She's okay in my book. Dot smiles at me with tobacco-darkened teeth. I can tell it tickles her to watch Flossie run from the confrontation she's sure to get if she sticks around.

Dot's husky voice, laden with sin, yells loud enough to wake the dead. "At least I run better'n that Flossie Muldaney!" Her colonial-blue eyes and angular jawline hint at beauty once upon a time. For an older lady, she's muscular and toned. Dot removes her ball cap and fans away summer flies.

"Vernell. Look at my new hairdo. What in tarnation happened? After I went to bed, I guess I wallered it to death. Your beauty shop girl fixed it purty last week. Now, look at it. What am I supposed to do with this?"

I'm about to bust up laughing. I smother it. Lord, my dog's hair looks better than Dot's. "When's the last time you washed it?" I ask.

"I ain't washed it since the beauty shop girl cut it."

"Dot," I say slowly, "when you go home tonight, shower, and wash your hair with the shampoo I bought you, not a bar of soap. Rinse it, then comb it with a clean comb. Let it dry before you go to bed. Wash your body while you're at it."

"That'll make my hair purty again?"

"Yes." I turn, roll my eyes, and wait on my next customer, offering to pick out a pretty bag to match her dress.

⌒ℓℓ⌒

That evening I drive home with my car windows rolled down. I stop at a light next to the tent revival and hear the faint tune of *Are You Washed in The Blood* echoing out to my car.

I look over to the cars parked in neat rows on the blacktop. A couple of stray women and children run in as the music plays. I sit at the light, the music swells, and another familiar praise song floats in on a breeze. I recall the words, *Jesus on the main line, tell Him what you want.* Quite vividly, it all comes back to me. . .

. . . I never measured up to church or my momma and daddy. Viola and Elmer walked down that sawdust aisle more times than I could count. I remained on my metal chair, ate butterscotch Lifesavers, or pretended to sleep. They hauled me to revivals every summer. Weeklong

meetings where they both rededicated their life to holiness in front of an evangelist in an all-white suit, sporting a red pocket-handkerchief.

Pounding on a pulpit, he screamed sermons about fire and death, the book of Revelation, and the judgments reserved for those who abuse their "temples of God" with cigarettes, drugs, and alcohol. Those tent evangelists waged war against slow dancing, television, movies, card games, homosexuality, makeup, and rock and roll. They wailed that all liars, whoremongers, thieves, murderers, and backslidden Christians were doomed to a lake of fire. And if we didn't walk the aisle that night, we'd surely get in a car wreck on the way home, die, and open our eyes in Hell. Or worse, miss the rapture and burn forever.

The most terrible fear we knew was missing the rapture. It hung over our heads like a lit match by a gas pump, and God was liable to drop the match at any minute.

I tried not to allow evangelists to heap any more fear on me than the psycho in the Alfred Hitchcock movie. I watched Momma and Daddy get saved every summer. They praised the Lord for about two weeks after the revival was over. The house remained peaceful for those two glorious weeks. Then, one night, without warning, they wouldn't come home until early morning. All liquored up; they'd been out all night at the bars, roadhouses, and honky tonks where, in the hot, steamy Southern nights, yearning, excitement, and the desperate attempt to hold on to their secret desires for all they were worth surfaced once again. It went thataway until the following summer when revival came back into town.

In the meantime, Momma prophesied over me plenty before she died. "Vernell, you'll end up like me, livin' in a trailer with six snotty noses screamin' at yer feet and dust coverin' the diapers and T-shirts you hang on your clothesline. Sure as my name is Viola Pauline Truvey." She was wrong. Were only two baby girls in my future, and Floyd bought me a Hotpoint washer and dryer the year before he died. I never believed in prophecy. Especially Momma's.

But the terror of fire and brimstone plagued me with every visiting evangelist who came to town. Even as a young woman professing to *be an agnostic, I dreamed about screaming preachers and an eternity of torment.*

One night I woke in a sweat on my bed. Hoping for sleep to overtake me, I confessed my sins and tried to pray. But just as I nodded off, I heard what I thought was the archangel's trumpet to rapture the saints. My heart raced, reaching for my radio. Expecting to hear the news report that I'd been left behind; a damn blasted train whistled in the distance. Not a trumpet. After a sigh of relief, I left the radio on for diversion, wishing to God I'd been born in some jungle in South America and never heard about religion.

Years later, I married Floyd and got busy raising my girls. I swore I'd never put my young'uns through that nonsense. I figured if I focused on them, I'd no longer fear Hell. No longer stay awake, wondering if a demon shared my bedroom.

The traffic light changes, and it feels like warm oil poured over my head. I recognize it. The feeling I heard my momma tell of; the sensation right before you decide to rededicate your life.

Somebody painted a sign on the side of the semi that hauled the tent and equipment into town. *Ask, and ye shall receive.* I turn into the lot and park next to Burger King.

I find the nursery and, like a coat check, hand Victoria over to a sweet lady who sticks a ticket in my hand, identifying me as the owner of the child. Victoria cries for a moment, then sees a trailer full of toys and children and is eager to get down and play. I sneak out and walk to the pay phone near the filling station on the corner.

I'm tired. What am I doing here? I can hardly hold my eyes open. I call Vivi.

"Where you at, Momma?"

"I'll tell you later, don't worry; we'll be home in a couple of hours."

I hear a *click* and then a dial tone. Vivi doesn't care.

Inside the revival tent, a trio is leading a song. I see Rosalyn and her preacher husband are part of the trio. He doesn't look so scary. He's wearing a nice-fitting blue suit, a white shirt, and a red satin tie. His hair looks stylish, much better than his wife's. From where I sit, I see him put his arm around her. I like that. Regular churchgoers stand around the walls of the filled-to-overflowing tent and spill out onto the asphalt lot. An occasional cough and the crackle of candy paper cuts the silence between songs. I sit in the back row and watch Evangelist Jimmy Boudreaux step up to the microphone with a big black Bible.

The congregation grows quiet, and I hear the rustle of fans, young'uns fussing and told to hush, and the low talking of people in the parking lot. It sounds like the preacher is talking in tongues. The organ music swells again to no song in particular, and I decide to stick it out and concentrate on the sermon he eventually starts to preach. It's not as bad as I remember from my childhood. Brother Jimmy doesn't seem hard-core Hell, fire, and brimstone. He's preaching about love and renewed mercies more than anything else. I like him.

But then he jumps and shouts, "Revival!" Swaying from side to side, he raises his hands high. The organist hits the keys again. The air is seductive. "Revival, brothers and sisters," he says, "is for those washed in the blood, but through carelessness, temptation, covering their light with a bushel, and plain lack of devotion, have fallen away. Revival isn't just for the unsaved. Revival is for the backslider!"

He drones on; his voice grows louder and more compelling. After he's been at it a few minutes, ghosts from my past loom in front of me with special punishments reserved for blasphemers. People either amen him or, like me, become agitated and shift in their seats.

The longer Brother Jimmy speaks, the louder the Holy Rollers shout, and the more I feel sick. My eyes throb, and by the end of the sermon, I want to crawl under the piles of sawdust.

He finally gives the altar call, inviting us to receive Jesus. I find myself in the aisle, walking toward redemption the same way Momma did. This time I step on sawdust over asphalt instead of dirt. Hoping my decision will make a difference in my life, I catch a glimpse of Rosalyn praying with Lin Wang. I cain't believe it. I kneel in the dust beside Rosalyn. Her desire to save me is a burning passion smoldering under her plain cotton dress and pointy eyeglasses.

"The wages of sin are death, Vernell," she says. *She could've said, nice to see you, Vernell; remember me?* But she gives me a look as if she's caught me with my hands in a cookie jar. "Are you sorry for your sins and reprobate mind? Do you want to be baptized in the Spirit?"

"Yes, I do."

She prays with me, and I see the sweat beaded on her forehead and neck. I smell it. It's mixed with her perfume. She ends her prayer and then looks into my eyes again and says, "The Lord loves you. Do you believe that?"

"I don't know. I've seen little evidence lately."

"Then ask Him. Ask Him to show you a sign. What is your greatest need or your heart's desire? Jesus says, behold, I stand at the door and knock. Ask Him to do more than supply your needs; ask Him to grant your greatest desire."

I swallow hard and wish she'd stop talking.

But then she puts her arm around my shoulders. "Oh, Vernell." I hear a change in her voice, a tenderness. Like she rocked her words in a baby cradle down in her throat. "Just let Jesus into your heart."

So, I fold my hands and cock my head toward heaven, hoping, wishing, and praying to hear the Lord's voice.

Lord? You still up there somewhere? I'm sorry. Sorry I dodged You all my life. I know I ain't got any right to ask, but my rent payment, it's due next week, and I've no idea how to pay it. I cain't keep dippin' into my savings. It's 'bout gone. Unless I sell a shit load, oh sorry, a bunch of purses, I'm gonna be broke and homeless. I got a child named Vivi, and she needs things. I have a little grandbaby to take care of. And my daughter, Vernise, I don't know where—

I cry. Rosalyn stuffs a tissue into my hand. The congregation sings, Just as I Am.

True, I ain't followed You as I should have. I wish I knew more 'bout the Bible and religion, except it still scares me to death. Never got saved as a child. If I had walked the aisle with Momma, maybe I wouldn't be in this mess. Maybe I wouldn't have lost my husband.

I cry harder. I miss my husband.

Anyway, dear Lord, I been stuck in a trailer park since I was four. In Needmore. Well, hell, You know where I dadgum live.

I feel the splintery sawdust dig into my knees. I sound like a hillbilly on steroids. My prayer hits a wall, and I stand. I'm not sure anybody's listening. I bend over, whisk wood chips off my legs, wipe my eyes, and walk out.

"Openin' beer bottles is easier'n this." An usher hears me mumble and shakes his head in disgust.

As I drive home, the sky is bright with stars and a full moon. Rural as far as my eyes can see, it appears as if I could drive off the edge of the earth. There's no artificial light other than the car's headlights. No traffic. I stop on a gravel road and turn off the engine. Dust from the road behind me floats across the field on a breeze. It looks like a lone cloud sparkling in the moonlight. All is quiet. The baby is asleep in her car seat. I ease the door shut after stepping out into the night air. I hear the chuff and cough of deer in the distance and a raccoon or two. The faint stench of skunk and cow manure from the plowed field reminds me of where I am, near old lady Weber's farm. Sitting on the hood of my car, feeling its warmth, I lean back on my elbows and gaze up into the vastness of space. *Where are you, God?* I'm not afraid when I hear His still, small voice.

"You can find Me anywhere," He says.

And all this time, I thought I had to look for Him in revival tents and buildings with steeples. The night is alive with signs and wonders that follow me, as I believe for the first time in my life. Peace floods my insides. A shooting star startles me for an instant, and I wave as it passes overhead. "My turn," I say—amazed.

I watch a televangelist on the PTL Club. He drives divine words down the back of my throat, and I choke on my tears again. Since visiting the revival, I have cried often. I suddenly realize God is not small. He didn't need me to clean myself up before accepting me, just as I am. He doesn't care how I speak or if I act like church people think I should. Maybe it's true; the *last shall be first.*

"Oh, sinner, reach out and touch the Lord as He passes by. You'll find He's not too weary to hear your heart's cry. He's passing by this moment; your *needs to supply*—"The tall, good-looking man with slicked-back hair, shiny black shoes, and a sweat-soaked shirt shakes his Bible and wails his message through pearly white teeth. His tie bar glitters as the TV camera suddenly pans the inside of his tent revival. The small-town congregation gawks like wide-mouthed bass, ready for the deep fryer. I try to guess the color of his tie on my black and white Zenith. Color TV ain't something I can afford. At least not now.

The healings begin as he touches people's heads, and they fall to the sawdust floor. Women and children walk the makeshift aisle as I did a month ago. But between rows of metal chairs, a woman looks like she's having convulsions. Her hairdo shakes loose, and ushers try to calm her.

The phone rings, and it startles me. Vivi runs to answer it. "Momma! For you!"

"Hush," I say. "He's 'bout to cast demons out of that woman."

The organ hymns mount. The faith healer lays his hands around the woman's neck and prays. "Come out, Devil!" The woman shakes harder and falls to the ground. The evangelist's chin quivers so fast you can see it on the TV. "Thank you, Jesus. Yes, Lord! Praise Him, people!" He starts hopping on one leg.

Vivi hangs up the phone and folds her arms in front of her. "They all look drunk to me."

"They are. Drunk in the Spirit." Vivi's right; there is a resemblance to the liquored-up drunks at the bar where I used to work. A bar where I may have to beg for my old job. "Oh nuts, we're losin' the signal. Need new rabbit ears."

Vivi giggles. "Ah shoot, Mommie, you're missing the begging for money part."

"Ain't got any to send him this month, anyway." I sigh. "Shit. I'll miss the blessed cloth special." I smash out my cigarette butt in my favorite ashtray. "But I got my pressed flowers from Bethlehem last month. I suppose I could use them if I need to."

"Need to what?"

Pray for money. "Never mind. Who called?" I ask.

"Dot. She said to drive over to her store. Right away, and she said it's important."

"Is she sick?"

"How would I know? I didn't ask; she didn't say."

"Watch the baby; I'll be back in an hour."

I grab my cigarettes and hope my Fairlane starts. It's been acting up the last few days. I worry about Dot. Sometimes mean people poke fun at her. Mostly young punks. Big, unpredictable, and cruel young men. It's not Dot I should worry about, though. Last year, a young man from a neighboring high school found himself with a bottom full of buckshot for taunting her because she smelled bad. She got a week in jail. Old Dot didn't mind. She asked to stay a few more days; she said the food tasted better than the slop she cooked. Lord, help us all.

When I arrive, I see Dot run toward my car. She's clenching a toothpick between her lips. I never saw her move so fast. A half-dozen mixed-breed dogs follow behind her, barking and wagging their tails. I jump out of my car and meet her in the alley. She cain't get a decent breath between the smell of fried okra wafting from her kitchen window and her snuff.

"You—you, 'member that box of old books you gave me to sell for ya?"

I haven't thought about that box since I gave it to Dot. "Yeah, so?" Staring hard at Dot, I see her mouth move, but I hear only the voices in my memory.

Rosalyn Boudreaux came to the flea market the day after they packed up their revival tent. She carried a box of mildewy old books and said, "Vernell, I bought these books at a church rummage sale in Broken Arrow, Oklahoma. We met local pastors for breakfast the morning of the sale, and then I found these at a table marked five dollars for the box. Pastor Jimmy searched through and took out books written by Dwight Moody and John Wesley, but you can have the rest to sell."

"How much do you want for the box?" I wasn't interested in buying old books.

Rosalyn laughed. "Heavens, I don't want any money for these. I want to help you, Vernell." Then she laid a twenty-dollar bill in my hand, and I shoved it back into her shirt pocket. Can you imagine getting an offering from a preacher? I wouldn't be able to stand myself.

"Please, Vernell, let me help you," she said.

"I'll accept that nasty-smellin' box of books, but not the money. Thanks anyway," I said. That ended our conversation. The next day, I asked Dot to sell my books in her shop. Last week, I heard Rosalyn and Jimmy Boudreaux pitched their revival tent in Beckley, West Virginia.

I repeat my question. "What about the box, Dot?"

Dot is having a tough time finding her words, which is unusual. She pulls me down to sit next to her on two cement blocks she uses to prop the door open on hot days.

"Vernell, you ain't a gonna believe this. But at the bottom of that box lay an old newspaper. Dated back to 1950. Yellered and brittle. I lifted it out, thinkin' I might like to have it, and figured I'd pay you a dollar for it. When I opened it, inside was a picture wrapped in some special blue tissue paper between two thick pieces of cardboard—a real purty painting of a good-lookin' cowboy. I 'membered you said that preacher woman got this box in Oklahoma. I thought maybe I ought to give the whole kit n' caboodle to my friend in Greensboro. This nutty professor-friend of mine. Likes old books. So, I took the books and the cowboy picture to Professor Wendell at UNCG. My alma mater."

"What? Dot—say that again. Did you go to college? Now, wait—I cain't picture it."

"Don't tell anybody down here; it's embarrassin.' I cover it well, don't I?"

"Yeah," I say. I'm in shock.

Dot's mouth tries to keep up with her thoughts. "Anyway, middle of the night, I get a phone call. 'Bout scared the fuckin' shit out of me. It's Professor Wendell askin' me to meet him at his office to talk about that damn picture."

"Dot, please don't use that language. It hurts my newly saved ears." I never saw Dot so flustered.

"Oh. Sorry." Dot stands and holds her hand out for me. "Git up, Vernell. Come inside."

I'm puzzled. But like a foolish puppy dog, I follow Dot to the rear of her store. I see a car parked beside Dot's pickup truck in the dirt lot. I step through the back door to her living quarters. Nothing's changed. It's still a pig sty and reeks of urine and cooking fat. I walk behind her through torn fiberglass curtains separating the back room from the front retail area. Two men, hunched over an antique pool table, take turns peering through a magnifying glass. They've rolled warped pool sticks into a pile to make room for Dot's discovery placed at the end. Open briefcases sit on a glass counter behind them—a counter where Dot displays her junk jewelry.

Dot begins her introductions. "Vernell, this here's my friend, Professor Hal Wendell. And that's Mister Grant Tucker from New York City. Professor Wendell asked Mister Tucker to come to North Carolina, and Grant wants to talk to you about your picture."

I stare at the odd-looking men. Mister Tucker can barely take his eyes off of it. He gives me a brief nod, then folds the magnifying glass and sticks it in his vest pocket, where I glimpse a pocket watch. He reminds me of what Sherlock Holmes must've looked like if such a character had existed.

I shake Mister Tucker's hand first. Then, shaking the hand of the man Dot introduced as Professor Wendell, I notice he could pass for someone around here. He's wearing Levis, a plaid flannel shirt, and boots. His salt and pepper hair match his mustache, and only his wire-rim glasses give him the appearance of a professor.

Mister Tucker motions for me to look at the picture. "Missus Paskins, I work for a reputable auction house in New York City called Sotheby's. Have you heard of it?"

"No, cain't say I have."

"We are experts at finding and appraising rare art, and I was skeptical when Miss Bickham and the good Professor here tracked me down. But I've known Hal Wendell a long time, and he persisted. You have an exceptional piece of artwork here, Missus Paskins. Rare indeed."

By this time, my shock has turned to butterflies in my belly. "Well, you want to tell me about it, or am I gonna have to guess?"

He clears his throat. "Yes—well, you're looking at Charles Marion Russell, his self-portrait. He was born in 1864 in St. Louis, Missouri, on the edge of the flourishing Western frontier. Popular sculptor, and a heck of a gifted storyteller, he also sketched in his free time and soon gained a local reputation as an artist. His firsthand experience as a ranch hand and his intimate knowledge of outdoor life contributed to the remarkable realism characteristic of his style. He completed this painting of himself in 1900."

"In when?"

"1900."

I cross my arms in front of me and bend slightly over the picture. It appears in good enough shape, but what do I know? The only art hanging in my trailer are prints of little birds and flowers or bowls of fruit in cheap silver frames, and I buy them at the flea market or from Dot. But this is a cowboy. With his feet planted solidly on the ground and a tipped-back hat, he's wearing a red sash and high-heeled riding boots.

"There is not much else to say, Missus Paskins. I am a legal company representative and have reported back to them that the painting is the original. I have a check here. Sotheby's has authorized me to pay you two hundred thousand dollars for this painting."

I sit on a nearby folding chair. My legs shake, and my tongue is numb.

"All I want is a finder's fee, Vernell," says Dot.

Today is Thanksgiving, and I am the most thankful woman on earth.

Dot is here; bless her heart. She took a bath and bought a new pair of blue jeans and boots for the occasion. I gave Dot a check for ten thousand dollars and told her to clean up her act. She did. She sold the store and bought a cabin, complete with a washer and dryer. Her new house sits in a meadow near the mountains where she can live how she wants, with nobody around to make fun of her. I never figured out why she went to college. I drive up now and then. The cabin is small but nicer and somewhat cleaner than the store.

I sent twenty thousand to Brother Jimmy after I cashed the check. I figured God deserved His tithe. He and Rosalyn built a church in Raleigh and started a home for wayward girls. They called it The Paskins House. Floyd would be so pleased.

I bequeathed all my handbags and sewing machine to Flossie. She took over my tables at the flea market, started collecting boxes of old books, and learned to speak a bit of Chinese. Now she thinks she's an expert. We still have coffee and talk about Dot. I'm trying to quit my Camel habit, and Flossie gave up biscuits and gravy—at least for now.

I bought a house. My first. It needs some work, but it's mine. There's a park across the street, and I put money into a college fund for Vivi. I bought a new swing set yesterday for the baby. She has her own room, and I painted it blue, like her eyes. I purchased health insurance, life insurance, and a slightly used car. I didn't want to blow the rest at Walmart or the Food Lion. Of course, I understood nothing about investing money, so I called the smartest man I knew. At the advice of Professor Wendell, I invested in stock. Microsoft or some silly name like that.

I saw Roger Moultrie in town yesterday. He's back in Needmore. He said he moved to Little Rock for a while to care for his sick momma. After her funeral, he decided to return to North Carolina. I said, "Good, I missed you." We're having dinner together next week.

Vivi's lounging on our modern recliner, watching the new color TV set next to Victoria's playpen. The baby is asleep, and I think I'll turn in early. Dot's already snoring on the couch.

The doorbell rings, the dog barks, and Vivi jumps up to answer it. We ate our pumpkin pie, but I suppose there might be one piece left for a visitor.

"Hey, Viv." I hear her voice. My eyes pool with tears, and I thank the good Lord quietly. Vernise has come home, and I don't care how or why or for how long. She's here now.

God has breathed life into my past and is blowing it into the present. It feels good for a change.

Punkin Head

Bearing children is not an option for some women. Never having the slightest desire to raise offspring, they lead full and happy childless lives. But when a woman decides to have a baby, nothing and nobody can stop her, not even her mate. The maternal pull of childbearing is nothing short of a miracle, and few men understand that urge.

The story, **PUNKIN HEAD**, originated from the TELEVENGE trilogy. The blind admiration of a mentor, political figure, or family member can wreak havoc. Within the church, it's perilous to irrationally follow a pastor, reverend, evangelist, teacher, priest, prophet, or bishop without a mind of your own. You would think that's common knowledge, but in many congregations today, the preacher's voice is the voice of God.

This story is unusual because most denominations fervently oppose abortion. Yet, a few religious leaders discourage their members from having children. And in cases I am familiar with—they forbid it.

I have spent decades exploring this manipulation and the dark side of televangelism. A natural God-given desire made complicated by religious legalism. There is a fine line between listening to your heart and following what your pastor declares as "the will of God."

I dedicate this story to two special people. Had it not been for their mother's bold determination, they would not have been born.

ndie kept her secret as long as she could. Time to tell him. The morning routine of holding her head over the toilet resulted more from fear than pregnancy. Joe didn't want a baby. Now or ever. Her husband, a dedicated staff member at the House of Praise, announced two months after their wedding that children meant less money, time, and devotion to his job. Andie blamed their pastor for Joe's decision to remain childless. She didn't want to believe Reverend Calvin Artury's *no-children* policy for staff.

But it wasn't a request.

He had instructed her not to bother him when he studied his Bible, but Andie knocked anyway. Joe opened the bedroom door with his foot. Two hours of Wednesday night prayer time took priority over meals, TV shows, or talking with his wife. "This can't wait any longer," she said. "You need to know."

Joe straightened in his chair and lifted his head. His tired eyes blinked in confusion. "What? What is it?"

Andie felt herself shrinking from the coldness in his voice. Her breathing stopped, and her heart pounded in her ears.

Joe's face turned as pale as school paste. "Are you—are you pregnant?"

Twisting her Kleenex and dabbing at tears, she hiccupped sobs back into her throat. She nodded and lowered her soft blue eyes, whimpering a pathetic "yes."

Joe's reaction reminded her of watching werewolf movies as a child, covering her eyes while Lon Chaney contorted into deformities of fur, fangs, and claws, mutating into a bloodthirsty werewolf. Andie felt that same fear trickle down her spine. Joe ran his hand hard through his hair. But with his next breath, he flung his King James Concordance at her head, missing her by a finger-width. His target hung on the wall behind her—their wedding picture. He hit his mark, knocking it to the floor and shattering the glass.

Andie clasped her hand over her mouth and backed against the door.

Joe's eyes flashed fire and daggers aimed at her heart, and he sprung from the chair, lunging toward her. Stopping inches from her face, nose to nose, he grabbed her shoulders and shook her until her teeth rattled like dice in a cup. "You promised me! You agreed, no kids! Didn't we agree, Andie?" Bullets of spit flew into her eyes and hair as his pointed finger jabbed over and over at her chest. "You know how important my future is on the ministry team! How could you do this when Reverend Artury told us—hell, he demanded we never get pregnant! You were there. You heard him!"

Wrangling free, Andie chewed on her reluctant *cult* membership. She raised her chin with a cool stare and stepped toward him. Her brows formed a V, and her eyes narrowed to serpent slits. She gritted her teeth. It irritated her that the Reverend controlled their few private moments together, and she had held her tongue long enough.

Before this moment, she had not met the dark side of her new husband. He'd been a gentle lover and sweet to a fault. Faithful in his ambition to build a better life for them both, Joe and his impeccable work ethic drew the attention of Reverend Artury. But after months of her husband working late nights at the church, she felt him turn his attention more to his pastor than to her. She decided to fight Joe's sudden rage and blind allegiance he mistook for doing the Lord's work with the calm tone of common sense.

"Joe! God has given us a gift," she said, daring to challenge him and the grand poohbah behind the pulpit.

Panting like a rabid werewolf crazy with rage, Joe grabbed his jacket and car keys. "Get rid of it! Give it back to God!"

The Piedmont basked in an autumn sun. Crisp breezes floated down from the north as the late October day waxed bright, invigorating, and cool enough for a light jacket. Wine-colored crepe myrtle, pear, and dogwoods heralded the muted leaves of a North Carolina fall: colors of plum, candy apple red, nutmeg, and rust—and a variety of neon yellows and peach.

Cutout jack-o'-lanterns and ghosts decorated the town's windows. A grinning cardboard skeleton with accordion-pleated legs swung from the entrance of Dr. Eshelman's office.

"I can't tell you what to do, missy. If you choose to have this baby, let me know. You two need counseling, and I can recommend somebody," he said. Andie swallowed her tears and fled the exam room, avoiding her doctor's eyes.

Brittle silence wrapped an icy hand around her throat on the ride home. She needed a distraction. The car radio hadn't worked in months, and she missed it and the Joe she used to know. In the distance, the sun's rays bounced off the tin roof of a produce stand. Indian corn, burnt orange mums, and pumpkins adorned the front. Temporarily blinded by bright sunlight, she pulled into the parking lot and stopped.

Andie stared at a line of perfect pumpkins displayed on a rickety plank of old barn siding shelved between two apple crates. Arguments with Joe replayed in her head. Disagreements as irritating as his scratched Reba Rambo record.

"We can't afford a jack-o'-lantern! You got no business wasting money. Giving to the Lord's work is more important than buying a pumpkin. Besides, those things are of the Devil."

"Pumpkins? God made pumpkins, Joe!"

"I'm talking about the Druids, nonsense people who made evil faces out of pumpkins. Remember Reverend Artury's sermon? Besides, I won't have you contributing to a celebration of the Devil."

"Oh, Joe! Trick-or-treat's just a fun night for kids to dress up and get candy."

"Just the same; I won't have evil sitting on my front porch!"

After counting her quarters, Andie browsed the roadside stand. Yellow and red leaves spun around her head as she took her time to find the ideal pumpkin, one a Druid might like. Daydreaming, she turned and nearly tripped over a little boy with tears resting on his plump cheeks. His skin was as black as her daddy's hunting dog, Pitch. The boy's pouty pink lips appeared dry and cracked. His torn jacket needed washing, and his two sizes too small T-shirt exposed his round belly. Andie crouched down to look into his wide-eyed childish stare. "What's wrong, sugar? Can't you find your mama?"

He nodded his head and wiped his nose on his sleeve. "Mama's over there." He pointed to an old Volkswagen van, smashed in the front, rusted, and on its last legs. Andie shielded her eyes from the sun with her hand, observing several young children crawling over and through the van like ants on an anthill. A muffled yell from the woman in the driver's seat drew customers' attention in the parking lot. The ample woman with pink sponge curlers sprouting from her head attempted to discipline her children.

"Your mama know you're out here?" Andie asked.

"Yes'um. Sent me to get Granny. She be buyin' some beans." Another tear popped out. "I want a punkin head. Mama won't buy one. She say cost too much."

The boy's granny shuffled out the door of the produce stand with her sack of beans. She motioned for him to come. His sad eyes glanced up at Andie, holding her pumpkin. Forcing a smile, she watched him turn and amble back to the van, kicking at dry leaves that cartwheeled and crackled around his little feet. Andie felt the pumpkin's weight as the boy's granny assisted him into the rundown vehicle.

"Wait!" Andie shouted, rushing toward the roar of children. "This is for you." The other kids hushed as she held out her pumpkin to the boy. He grabbed hold, and his face beamed, exposing a bright, toothy smile. "Every child needs a punkin head at Halloween. Make a good one, okay?"

"Thanks, Ma'am."

Andie rubbed his head, then smiled and nodded at his mama. She shot Andie a curious look before hollering again at her noisy kids, "Percy, leave your brother's punkin alone! I gone beat you when we git home!" The van door closed.

The blinding sun reflected off the side mirror of the dilapidated van as it rolled out of the lot. Andie blinked. *No child deserves a beating.* There was only one beat that mattered to Andie. Only one beat she wanted. A beat that could stop time, or a beat to *keep* time to the tune of love songs and lullabies sung by mothers to their infants all over the world. It had a rhythm, and she could dance to it. A simple beat passed down for thousands of generations. A beat that was hers inside. She could listen to the sound of it forever. A heartbeat, the most angelic sound she'd ever heard.

Wild horses from Hell couldn't drag her to a clinic to *give it back to God*. It was time to tell that to the other half of the heartbeat.

At midnight, Joe returned home from church to find a rather huge jack-o'-lantern smiling on the porch. Candlelight flickered through the devilish grin of Andie's punkin head. Cut through the back, the words penetrated the darkness. WE'RE HAVING A BABY.

Cry

CRY is a contrast in extremes.

Living a hair above the poverty line, a young girl struggles with unanswered questions about her past.

Parallel to her story, the abundant life of a televangelist unravels. A national celebrity, the evangelist is a woman. "God's anointed daughter."

The inspiration for this tale of two women came from the first sentence. With church paramount in my youth, I wanted to explore the life of a young girl *not* raised in the church and an evangelist who regrets the choice to become one.

Two different lives—two unique women—merging in the most unexpected place.

~ **Selma, North Carolina, October 1989** ~

 *H*ad I known my mother planned to leave me the day after I was born, I would've fought to stay inside her a while longer. My cousin, Ray Keith Bertram, and his wife, Janey Gay, were my best friends. Janey, who was all of twenty-two, celebrated eight months of pregnancy the same day I turned fifteen. Over time, I watched her belly inflate to the size of Ray's basketball, so perhaps it was no surprise I thought of my mama a lot during those days.

Ray Keith joined the Marines, and we were on our way to the Cherry Point Marine Corps Air Base, Janey Gay and me, when she steered her Ford Pinto into the Walmart parking lot. She said she needed to use the toilet and have somebody fix her glasses. They broke the week before, and the first aid tape wrapped around the nose bridge wasn't holding. Then she mumbled something about needing makeup to cover the zit on her chin and a pair of maternity pantyhose and said if I complained one more time, she'd throw me out on the side of the road.

We planned to drive to Cherry Point and back home in three days. Janey ached for Ray Keith. Her baby was due in three weeks, and she'd cried buckets when we heard Uncle Sam might ship Ray Keith to Kuwait. But I'd not even landed a boyfriend, and I wasn't ready for a crash course in birth and delivery.

After she dropped off her glasses and used the ladies' room, I took her by the hand in a search for the unmentionables aisle. Janey couldn't see a lick without her pop-bottle lenses, which added to the severity of her waddle. It passed like an electric current through her arm into her hand and then flowed right into me. Before I knew it, I waddled like a pregnant woman.

Janey pulled a purple hosiery package off the hook and squinted. Holding it an inch from her nose, she whispered, "Essie, use your pretty green eyes and tell me what it says on the back."

"Queen-size, for women up to 200 pounds."

"Shhh, not so damn loud."

So, I whispered, "Sorry. Queen-size."

Janey leaned against an end rack of tube socks and sighed. "Well, that's me. I'm pregnant in both legs too. Open it. Let's take a look."

Peeking down rows of bras and underwear, I searched for anyone who looked like security. I yanked the fleshy mesh hosiery out of the cellophane. "Good God! Uncle Royal could hang a couple hams in that thing."

"Essie! Keep your voice down! I can't wear this dress without hose; it wouldn't look right in front of all those officers on base." She grabbed the pantyhose and stuffed it back into the package; then, I led her like a puppy dog to the cosmetics aisle. We matched a bottle of Cover Girl to her fair skin, which looked even fairer next to her coal-black ringlets. After paying for the repair of her glasses, we were ready for our road trip.

Almost.

Another hurried stop at a gas station so Janey could fill up her Pinto and empty her bladder—again, but the toilet was nasty. So, we detoured with a quick trip to Aunt Sye's.

❧

Although Aunt Sye scrubbed her home clean inside, she seldom noticed its lived-in look on the outside. The house settled unevenly on cinderblock footings, and a broken-down couch rested where the porch sagged.

Stepping out of the car, I wilted with the humidity, like the dandelions and peonies by the porch that had gone weak-kneed. Two missing screens allowed Aunt Sye's lace panels to billow out at the front windows. I looked around at the weed-choked yard covered with parts of things—car parts, bike parts, old washing machine parts, and a push mower—all rusting between prickly shrubs, warped Pepsi Cola signs, and patches of grass and dirt. Uncle Royal's '67 Dodge, with its tires long gone, corroded behind the house. I'd played for hours in the scruffy yard as a child and loved it.

But lately, living with Janey Gay, I caught a glimpse of the different ways people lived. Sharing her Dream Home Scrapbook with me, Janey cut pictures from magazines and taped them to construction paper pages. Furniture, shiny kitchen appliances, curtains, china, manicured lawns, swimming pools—things she longed for, beautiful homes she dreamed about day and night. We spent hours driving around fancy neighborhoods in the dark, peeking in windows.

Circling open houses listed in the newspaper and touring with other house hunters served as our Sunday entertainment. Janey talked to the realtor like she had enough cash in her pocketbook to buy the place. But I enjoyed snooping in people's closets, drawers, and refrigerators, seeing what they owned that I didn't. Their homes smelled good, like furniture polish and Blue Waltz perfume, unlike Aunt Sye's house, which smelled of bacon and heating oil. Janey carried hand-drawn floor plans in her purse. She even made an appointment with a builder to discuss her dream house blueprint. Her heart's desire. Which raised the question—what was mine?

Walking Up Aunt Sye's porch steps, I realized the house resembled her. Worn and tired. I wondered if Sye ever wanted a dream house, and maybe Janey's dream house was just that. A dream. We were poor as dirt, and not much was bound to change anytime soon. A cold revelation for such a humid afternoon that stung like a mad bee as I ran my hand over the splintery porch railing.

Janey Gay hollered for me to follow her into the bathroom. I giggled as she sat on the commode. Her belly dropped between her legs, and the whole toilet disappeared. I perched on the clothes hamper, thinking God stuffed *two* babies inside her. She opened the package, and I watched her gather the legs of the pantyhose. Janey tried to bend over, but the toilet lid squeaked and slid around on the seat. So as not to embarrass her, I gazed up at Aunt Sye's dotted-swiss sheers on the window above the tub. A smudge of Prell dried on the tile, and I noticed someone had about used up the bar of Zest.

"I need your help." She handed the pantyhose to me. "Once you get them over my feet, I can pull them up the rest of the way. Try not to snag them."

I removed her shoes and slid the silky feet part over her puffy toes, rolling them above her swollen ankles. Janey bent over again, groaned, and grunted, wrestling her pregnant body into her new pantyhose. It was pitiful. It reminded me of Aunt Sye squeezing into her girdle on Sunday mornings.

Janey stood. Her massive stomach filled Aunt Sye's tiny bathroom. I stood too, and for a moment, we had sandwiched ourselves between the hamper and the toilet, blinking at each other. All at once, she grabbed the sink and held on. Sweat beads popped out on her upper lip and forehead, and I saw it was hard for her to catch her breath. Watching her flinch and sweat, I hesitated. I didn't know how to react. Old enough to know how people made babies, I shivered, thinking about the entire process. I'd never known a pregnant woman before. She was the first.

I'd watched Janey's shirt bulge and move a couple times when her baby kicked. She let me feel it. It felt like a kitten squirming under a blanket. The day she told me she was pregnant, I cried. I don't know why; I just did.

"Maybe them pantyhose are too tight," I said.

"No," she took a deep breath. "I'm fine. If you're sure about that shortcut to the base, we can get to Cherry Point in a few hours." Her eyes pleaded with me through her thick glasses.

I smiled and nodded, despite the creepy feeling we needed to wait. "What's one more day? Let's have supper with Aunt Sye."

"No!" Tears filled her eyes until one rolled down each cheek. "I miss Ray Keith something fierce," she said, wadding toilet paper off the roll and dabbing at her eyes. "According to the nightly news, things don't look good in Iraq. Ray called and said President Bush is pretty pissed off, and there's talk on the base of war soon. I remember my mama, pregnant with my sister, when Daddy left for Vietnam. When he died over thataway, she never forgave herself for not watching him ship off. I want to spend every second I can with Ray. Let's go." Janey blew her nose, and I dutifully followed her to the car.

~ Atlanta, Georgia, October 1989 ~

Loretta Lynette suffocated backstage. Her beautician plugged two fans into the wall to keep perspiration from soaking through Loretta's makeup. A backstage monitor allowed her to observe the crowd and her entire team. For the past hour, her ministry leader conducted praise and worship with the quartet and soloists, leading the congregation of over five thousand into the mood she requested: one of heightened excitement and readiness for miracles.

Blessed relief was the word of the day after receiving a last-minute invitation from the Atlanta mega-church. She needed the week-long revival to cover her mounting expenses.

The Atlanta Journal lay at her feet. She leaned over and stared, once again, at the headlines on the Events page. *Loretta Lynette, Preaching Nightly at the Church of the Savior.* The article continued: *This onetime hairdresser heads one of the world's largest television ministries. Taking Jesus To The World expects to bring in $75 million this year.* She cringed. Why do they have to bring up money?

For the past few months, major newspapers reported the

ministry's purchase of her million-dollar home in Little Rock, her two-million-dollar summerhouse on Sanibel Island, and more houses worth another four million for staff. The articles also outlined Loretta's recent personal purchases, which included a $300,000 vacation around the world where she reportedly ministered to the nations but *relaxed in the sun on her days off.*

She'd needed that vacation. Loretta expected opposition to only some degree. But it was a fact: her numbers were down significantly because of recent bad press. Evangelicals everywhere still reeled from the Jim Bakker and Jimmy Swaggart fiascos; the uphill battle of the past two years to bring integrity back into televangelism took its toll. Any additional media mudslinging and her board was sure to demand cutbacks. As it was, religious leaders who made money in evangelism were now held in suspicion by a world of unbelievers.

But Loretta hoped that Bakker and Swaggart's losses become her gain. That, in time, evangelicals left hanging shift their alliance to her. As it stood, even the fallen angels' accusers left her alone for reasons of chivalry or because her ministry appeared squeaky clean, and no one proved otherwise. At least for the moment.

Long ago, Loretta developed the fine-tuned talent of asking for money. A mass of humanity sent thousands of dollars every month so she could take Jesus to the world. Loretta televised testimonies of men and women who acquired blessings due to their seed-sowing faith. Believers who received huge bonuses, unexpected money in the mail, and healing for their children because they had tithed their hard-earned paychecks. Specifically, into *her* ministry.

For Loretta, gathering cash was like finding treasure in a sunken chest on the ocean's cold floor. There for the taking. When she walked out on the platform, her presence fell on hearts like a ray of sun on a prison wall. Resembling the Apostle Peter, even her shadow was a source of comfort and healing to her followers. And oh, how the money flowed in. As easy as Peter pulling tribute out of the mouth of a fish. People gave their last nickel.

Loretta's cutting-edge personality, Southern drawl, and ability to get down on their level—a woman who had once been poor and walked in their shoes—won her the respect and friendship of most Christian women in the country.

It didn't hurt that she was single, either. The women wanted to be like her, and eligible men flocked to her crusades in record numbers. She could've dated a different man every night of the week. But she turned them away, avoiding scandal, claiming she needed to spend time with the Lord.

At thirty-six, she evolved quickly into one of the charismatic greats. Evangelicals often compared her ministry to the ministries of Aimee Semple McPherson and the beloved Katherine Kuhlman. Even Billy Graham endorsed her as "God's anointed daughter."

Loretta stared at the monitor. Her head pounded with strange new thoughts and desires. *Evangelicals all wear the same faces as if righteousness were a mask. No one is better than anybody else.* She needed air.

"Tell the organist to play a little longer," she told her assistant. Edwina collected Loretta's Bible and sermon notes, complete with bullet points for the healing service. Reported cases of the sick and maimed throughout the congregation: where they sat, their infirmities, weaknesses, and possible faith or resistance levels. All information gathered by "collectors." Men and women on Loretta's staff stationed throughout the auditorium as the people entered, greeting in the name of the Lord, acting as ushers, and collecting valuable pre-service information Loretta used on the Lord's behalf later in the service.

Edwina tipped her head and raised an eyebrow. "You okay?" she asked, handing her boss a tissue to dab the sweat from her brow.

"Fine. Fine. I need some air, that's all. Give me another fifteen minutes. Tell Rusty and Pastor Higgins to keep singing."

"Don't be too long; I think the natives are restless."

Edwina was right. Loretta knew if she delayed much longer, the congregation, despite their excitement, would end up impatient, hard to manage, and not open to the Spirit. The people came to hear *her*, not the praise and worship team. A risk, true. But she wasn't ready.

Sweat soaked her navy-blue suit. Her auburn hair, though cut short, dripped beads of perspiration down her neck and spine. Smothered by the heat, she waved to Edwina. "I'll be back soon." Maneuvering around the long backstage hallway, she found her way outside and into the cooler evening air. Loretta slid sideways between her million-dollar buses, tractor-trailers, and the flotsam and jetsam of television equipment. Power cords plugged into the state-of-the-art traveling television studio that followed her to city after city on the crusade route. Pungent diesel fuel nauseated her, and she hurried to find her private bus.

Pulling off her five-carat diamond earrings, she slid them into her pocket.

Recently criticized for her fondness of nice things, Loretta responded to accusers that God blessed her for putting Him first in her life. As a poor sinner, she owned nothing but enjoyed spending her salary as a wealthy Christian. A healthy salary her board awarded her as the ministry grew. So what if she wanted nice things? So what? She had fun buying the $11,000 marble statue of Queen Esther that greeted visitors in her Little Rock headquarters. Loretta's three-million-dollar yacht, docked behind her Florida home, served as her only escape from the world. Her only mode of relaxation. She had to take a vacation at least once a year. Didn't everybody? Thousands of people pulled on her for everything from their paychecks to healing their sick children. To those closest to her and the privileged few who sat in front of her mahogany desk displayed with the Dresden vases, Loretta's tastes ran more toward filet mignon than hamburger.

"Give, and it shall be given unto you." She'd preached it for years; the well-known scripture made her a rich woman. She'd given all, too. More than any of them knew.

Loretta found her bus and motioned for her security man.

"You out here all alone, Ma'am?"

"I'll be fine, Sam; I need my bag off the bus. Go back inside. I'll lock up."

"You sure?"

"Yes, go; I need to pray and get some fresh air. I won't be long."

She waved him on and watched him reluctantly return to his post. A stool inside the loading dock in front of a monitor with a bird's-eye view of their ministry team vehicles. Retrieving her travel bag, she stepped off the bus and grabbed a folding metal chair by a trash barrel behind the mammoth church.

Her bag slung over her shoulder, she carried the chair to the edge of the parking lot, searching for seclusion. All she asked for was another ten minutes. Behind her, the distant sound of familiar praise songs floated out on a breeze. Her singers and musicians would remain on stage, singing their hearts and lungs out because they knew that's what she wanted.

Highway traffic rumbled in the distance. Other than a few muffled voices in the parking lot, she found herself alone next to an empty church van. Feeling safe, she faced a vacant lot full of weeds where no one saw her relaxing on the chair. Loretta reached into her pocket and felt for her earrings. Secure. Next, she dipped her hand into her Gucci bag and pulled out a pack of Virginia Slims and a Zippo lighter.

The fingers of her right hand fondled the loose, unlit cigarette. Loretta placed it in the side of her mouth, flicked the lighter, and lit up. The Zippo lid snapped shut like a cocked pistol.

She breathed in a line of smoke that curled down her throat; the once-familiar taste warmed her inside and sent a rush of nicotine to her bloodstream. Her head bent, she stared at the cigarette in her hand as it rose to her face like a little bird. Her arm trembled, and her nervous fingers fluttered, causing hot ashes to fall to her lap and burn a hole in her Anne Klein suit. It didn't faze her. She continued to smoke like she was swallowing a secret.

The warm October days and cool nights reminded her of summers as a child in the South. Like a bloodshot eye, the sun sank further beyond the Atlanta skyline, leaving a slight chill to the Georgia evening air. She felt the temperature drop as her world turned from the light and fell into darkness. A flood of memories raced the nicotine to her brain. Loretta rocked the chair back and pressed her shoulders against the van, stealing the trapped heat. Her head tilted back, stretching her neck taut; her eyes drifted shut.

Last night's revival reached a pitch not even the ministry team could recall. The presence of God created a stampede to the altar, interrupting the praise and worship service. Sinners needed neither song nor sermon to persuade them. People stood or kneeled on every square inch of the auditorium, some with hands lifted and others holding tight to the back of the pew in front of them. A significant number, men and women alike, spoke in tongues.

The healing line formed, stretching from the platform to the rear of the church and around the sanctuary. Old and young lined up to relay their afflictions to the woman of God. To have Loretta's anointed hands touch them. An act of faith, believing for their miracle.

A young girl, possibly fifteen or sixteen, appeared in the line. Loretta stood speechless before her, observing the girl's beauty and long red hair. Her tattered jeans, tattoos, and several piercings in her eyebrows and nostrils were evidence of the life she lived. The girl asked for deliverance from drugs and alcohol. A dedicated choir sang softly in the background, and every head bowed. Eyes closed, the mass of humanity grew quiet, believing Loretta possessed the ear of God.

The girl's hair reminded Loretta of her own once upon a time. She told the young woman if she hid any cigarettes on her to throw them to the Devil. The girl reached into her back pocket, pulled out her Virginia Slims and a shiny new Zippo, then tossed them to the floor. As if possessed by an archangel, Loretta commanded her, "Young lady, the Lord has delivered you tonight. Let her go, Satan! Sister, never smoke again. You won't need them. In Jesus' name, I command the demons of nicotine, drugs, and alcohol to flee from you and never come back! Ask

Jesus into your heart, dear girl; ask Him to become your Savior."

Loretta laid her hands on the girl's head, and she fell back. Two male ushers caught her and lowered her to the floor. The wild congregation mounted to mob frenzy, shouted praises to God, and clapped without ceasing.

Loretta raised her hands and pranced around the girl, shouting, "The Holy Spirit revealed to me a black ring around her mouth, a black ring of smoking and sin, and now it's gone! Raise your hands to the Lord, Saints of God. Another soul saved from the flames of hell." Loretta danced on the altar in praise to the Lord. "This is your hour of deliverance. God is in this place. His angels are here, people. They're walking up and down the aisles. Jesus has entered the building. Reach out and touch the Lord as He passes by."

No one but the hardest of hearts remained in their seats. The place shook and trembled in the holiness of it all, ablaze with His glory.

Loretta watched it all closely. Suddenly, as if bitten by a rabid dog, she let out a shrill cry to suppress the darkness shooting out of her heart, but it spilled over as a fearsome, piercing wail. A stream of tears and sobs shook Loretta until her body landed on the floor where the tattered and tattooed girl once stood. Her Assistant Evangelist, Rusty Walters, explained to the alarmed congregation that the Lord was moving in His often-mysterious way through His servant, Loretta Lynette.

But Loretta knew better. Her sins had found her out. After years of denial, grief sent her face down on the floor. No one knew how badly Loretta wanted her own deliverance. More than any sinner who sat in her service and experienced the convicting power of the Holy Ghost. Loretta longed for something she felt she could never have. But before her ushers managed to pull her off the floor, Loretta retrieved the lighter and cigarette pack beneath her and shoved them into her suit pocket.

⁓⁓

Loretta sucked hard on her cigarette one last time; the tobacco cracked and popped. Her ten minutes were up. Stretching out, her long legs found the edge of the asphalt next to the church van. She kicked off her shoes and wiggled her toes in the red dirt. She wanted to disappear like the threads of smoke in the air. A long sigh escaped her lips, ending in a deep, guttural moan.

"I can't do this anymore."

~ Essie, 1983 ~

When they built Aunt Sye's house, they squeezed it between a creek and a tiny general store she and Uncle Royal managed on the edge of town. Granddaddy Aikens died, leaving equal shares of the land and store to his children, Sye, Noble, and Paul David— my daddy. After Uncle Royal earned a purple heart in Vietnam, Sye convinced everybody the best job for Royal was tending the store from his wheelchair. So, Daddy and Noble sold their parts to Aunt Sye.

I spent the hot summers on Sye and Royal's front porch with a cold cola between my knees to cool off. Air conditioning remained a luxury they could not afford. Every evening, Uncle Royal rolled his wheelchair out onto the rickety porch with a glass of iced tea and a damp towel to cool off the back of his neck. He rolled his own smokes to keep the bugs away.

Dusk came early enough, along with the mosquitoes, a dimming of the heat, and the first fireflies of the evening. But the sunset made the world soft and carefree. Most nights, people in Selma tuned their radios to the strains of a country song, a fiddle, and a mournful whine. Our house was no different. Music added a simple delight to the world in which we lived. The tinny echoes of old-timey music playing on Sye's kitchen radio identified us. They gave us a sense of who we were. I'd scoot my fanny up against the aluminum siding next to the screen door and listen to Patsy Cline cry along with the steel guitar while eavesdropping on what talk there was with one passing neighbor or another.

Ray Keith was Aunt Sye's baby. Ten years older than me, my cousin loved fast cars and pretty girls. His mullet haircut threw Royal into regular conniption fits, instigating lewd comments from Daddy and Uncle Noble. Fag hair, they called it. Pussy hair.

Ray ignored them. The whole town, especially the girls, knew Ray because of his John Mellencamp hair, tight blue jeans, and rolled-up T-shirt sleeves. But more than anything, Ray Keith liked to piss off his daddy and crank up the volume on any rock 'n' roll song. As expected, Uncle Royal hollered loud enough to wake Lazarus a second time. "Shit-fire! Turn off that damn devil music!" I'd giggle because he'd say it about any music that wasn't country or bluegrass, especially rock 'n' roll and TV preachers. Royal hated TV preachers.

Aunt Sye said a few years back, she drove Royal home from a doctor's appointment, and out of the blue, she stopped at a tent revival and wheeled him in. She said it was the last time Uncle Royal went to church and for me to keep quiet about it.

It fascinated me to the point of asking him, anyway.

"Danged woman evangelist, it was. They're all a bunch of looney tunes, money-hungry crooks—bah! Thinking they know better than the good Lord Himself. I wouldn't give you a danged dime for the whole lot!"

I never brought it up again. I figured Sye had her reasons; she never pushed religion on him after that. Aunt Sye attended First Methodist, but kept evangelism out of the house.

Every night I waited on Sye's porch for Daddy to come home from the Esso station. He'd bought it before I was born. Noble rebuilt carburetors and rotated tires while Daddy, a bit more refined than Noble, dealt mainly with the customers, pumping gas, changing oil, and selling candy bars and Cokes. Sye said Daddy finished high school, but Noble dropped out in the eighth grade. Though half the town of Selma stepped softly around the Aikens brothers, my daddy and uncle were gentle and sweet with Ray Keith and me.

Daddy, Uncle Noble, and I lived in the apartment above the gas station. Daddy slept in the larger bedroom; my twin bed barely fit in the other. When Noble was home, he slept on the pull-out couch. We ate at Aunt Sye's until I was old enough to cook. Aunt

Sye and I did the family laundry in a Hotpoint wringer washer every Saturday on her back porch, saving Noble and Daddy's grease-covered overalls for the last tub of dirty wash water.

Slow to rise to her brothers' shenanigans, Aunt Sye protected and put up with the men in her life. She treated Daddy and Uncle Noble like little schoolboys whose behavior was more comical than worrisome. Worse, she encouraged it by frequently bailing them out of unfortunate circumstances.

Like Elvis, both Daddy and Noble kept their youthful faces. Even Noble, with two deep purple scars on his cheek from a broken beer bottle and a stacked deck in a game of strip poker. The three women he'd met at Pokey's Pool Hall turned out to be wives of men who worked at the mill, and that's all they cared to tell me about Noble's scars.

Daddy and Noble did everything they could to forget the hand life had dealt them. Rowdy and playful, or as Sye said, "full of shit and vinegar," they'd terrorize the locals until somebody called the sheriff, who locked them up for disorderly conduct. Either drinking and shooting bottles off fence posts—disturbing the peace at two in the morning—or racing their pickups down the middle of town at midnight, drunk as skunks. Take your pick. But my aunt bailed them out every time. She'd come home, yawn, kiss Ray Keith and me good night, and haul herself off to bed.

The 80s were just the tail-end of the 60s as far as Daddy, Noble, and Sye were concerned. Not much changed in their world.

I turned nine on Ray Keith's eighteenth birthday—the night he lit out after Janey Gay and followed her to the coast after a nasty fight. When Aunt Sye found out, she made Uncle Royal call Daddy and Noble, and all three piled into Noble's truck and went after Ray. But it was too late. Janey Gay suspected Ray Keith loved her, and she made him chase her to prove it. He chased her all right—to the New Bern Justice of the Peace and into a Super 8 Motel. By the time Uncle Royal found them naked in the sheets,

Daddy and Noble were too drunk to care and found the whole thing amusing.

Daddy and my uncles rented the room next to Ray and Janey Gay for the duration of their wedding night and proceeded to howl and torment the newlyweds until Ray Keith punched a hole through the wall. Noble and Daddy took off the next day, leaving the happy couple to take Royal back home and continue their honeymoon in Ray Keith's bedroom.

Some days, it plain pissed me off. I'd hear about the fun after it was over. I'd sit and twist my hair into knots, wishing I'd been born a boy. But I stayed out of the way and remained invisible. It kept my hide from being tanned. I did a good job; they ignored me most of the time.

Until that day I started asking too many questions about my mama.

I asked four people who gave me four stupid answers. My mama's name was Elle. Not E-l-l-i-e or Elly with a y. Just Elle— one syllable, they said. Neither Sye nor Daddy spelled it for me, pretending they didn't know how. But I'd seen it spelled E-l-l-e in one of Janey's Glamour magazines, and I pictured my mama as one thing only. Glamorous.

I never saw a picture of Mama, her handwriting, or a piece of anything belonging to her. The only thing I had to prove she existed was myself. Someone had wiped all evidence of Elle from our apartment and Sye's house before I learned such a thing as a mama existed and that every kid in my neighborhood owned one but me.

I used to stay awake and pretend my mama liked to curl up next to Daddy in bed. That I heard her through the walls, speaking sweet words into Daddy's ear while he complained and watched Johnny Carson. I even imagined them having sex, like most kids who occasionally hear their parents' stifled moans. I tried to smell any perfume she might have left on Daddy's old clothes or blankets, but it was long gone by the time I thought to act like a hound dog.

My mama was a ghost who appeared, bore a baby for Daddy, and then returned to her spirit world. I didn't understand why she didn't love me enough to stick around, and it was clear nobody in the family cared to divulge that information. The family kept Daddy's secrets. But they had to give me some kind of answer when I kept on asking—and asking. And didn't stop.

One day, exasperated, Aunt Sye grabbed my head and pulled my dark red hair away from my eyes, pushing it behind my ears. Then she ran her thumbs over the few freckles on my forehead. "Little girl, the night your mama gave birth to you, the moon turned cold and putrid looking, infected-like, needing to be lanced and left to bleed all over God's heavens. It gave me chills, I swear. The way you are now, asking things you'd be better off not knowing. Why can't you leave this alone, child?"

I didn't say a word; I just looked hard into her gray eyes that matched the streaks in her hair. More than I wanted to eat, play, or sleep, I wanted to know about my mama. And Aunt Sye knew it.

She sighed heavily and thought for a moment. "I suppose you're ready for the truth. She was an escaped convict, honey, and when the sheriff caught her, she bit him and gave him blood poisoning. She's in prison now, where she belongs. Paul David never should've married her. I told him to throw her in the nuthouse. Leave it be, Essie. Quit asking questions."

But I knew Aunt Sye brought me into the world, and that I was born in her bed. Sye said Bridie Mae, her friend from church, worked at the courthouse when I was born. When Sye and Daddy went to report my birth, Bridie Mae recorded it as <u>Mother's First Name—*unknown*: Last Name—*Aikens*: Sex Of Baby—*Girl*: Name—*Estelline Phoebe Aikens*: Born—*July 6, 1974*: Weight—*7 pounds 5 ounces*: Length—*19 inches*: Father—*Paul David Aikens*</u>. Stamped in bright red letters across the top of the Johnston County Records, LEGITIMATE BIRTH told the story in two words. Aunt Sye handed me the certificate, hoping to shut me up.

But not long after Sye's miserable explanation, I heard Noble whisper to Daddy the car they bought Bridie Mae the week I was born still ran like a top, and he wondered how much more free gas she was entitled to get.

When I confronted Uncle Royal, he wheeled his chair up to the kitchen table to peel me an apple. I figured that way he wouldn't have to look at me.

"Your mama, huh?" He started at the top of the apple and worked the knife back and forth, stripping the skin like he skinned squirrels. "Well, little lady, best I can say is, Paul David met the trifling pissant woman during a Gospel Sing in '73 at the First Baptist Church in Raleigh. She seduced him in the parking lot right after the Oak Ridge Boys sang *Jesus Is Coming Soon*. But the next year, your daddy caught her making her own fireworks following the Fourth of July picnic with some drunken salesman from Bernie's Used Car Lot. Right next to your daddy's gas station in a '70 Ford Thunderbird with dealer plates. Two days later, your mama gave birth here, at our house. Paul David sent her packing the day after. By God, it was the best thing your daddy ever did."

I liked Ray Keith's story best. I remember the cigarette flicking up and down in his teenage mouth when he spoke. He told me my mama was too young to have a baby, and that she cried for nine months and then lost her mind. Ray said even though he was only nine years old, he remembered she screamed for two days straight, giving birth to me, and that Royal closed the store for fear of losing his customers.

"She's a mentally deranged woman. Ran buck naked out of the house the next day, I seen her," Ray Keith said.

I liked to think of my beautiful mama running naked through the streets of Selma and of Daddy and Noble running after her. I imagined she was part Indian, running back to her tribe. Or a mermaid, and needed to return to the sea before the full moon. I'd dream up anything, imagine any wild story to keep from thinking she didn't want me.

I finally got up the nerve to ask Daddy. He sat me on his knee; I was still nine. He hugged me first, like he always did. Then he cleared his throat, coughed once, and said, "Us being Methodist and all, we didn't see God the same way, your mama and me. Raised Pentecostal Holiness, she was one of them Holy Roller types. She didn't like my drinking and carrying on with your uncles."

Daddy said she never loved him, not in the way she should have. After a few beers, he spilled the rest of his story, saying he met her at a local revival and got saved just for her. Two days later, he asked her to marry him. She gave birth to me nine months after that. But the next morning, she was gone forever. "In ten months' time, she had come and gone out of my life. And yours, Essie. She wasn't a forgiving woman," he said. "She called her brother, an uncle you never met, and he picked her up from Sye's house the day after you were born."

Daddy never did say whether or not Mama married him. But he said she was pretty, and that's all I'll ever know. Because when Uncle Noble and Daddy got drunk and flew off the bridge over the Cape Fear River in Noble's pickup truck, the truth of who my mama was, died with them. I not only lost Daddy, but I also lost all hope of knowing my mama. I knew Aunt Sye and Uncle Royal were bound to carry Daddy's secret to their graves.

I turned ten the day I stood by Aunt Sye at the double funeral. Losing both brothers in one day liked to kill Sye. At the graveside, she folded me into her arms, left her frosted lipstick on my cheek, and said, "Damn them both."

Half the town paraded through the house that afternoon, filling up on ham, black-eyed peas, corn casserole, and fruit salad. I hid in my room to avoid pitiful stares from the ladies of the Methodist church. Later, Aunt Sye opened my door and held out her arms. As I walked into her embrace, she sighed. "Well, girl, all I have left of Paul David is you. I guess that'll do until you bury me next to them ornery brothers of mine." Then she did the unexpected. Something I had never seen her do before. She cried. I waited until she finished, then I went into the kitchen and poured myself a bowl of Cheerios.

Aunt Sye and Uncle Royal sold Daddy and Noble's gas station, paid off their debts, and the rest went into a savings account for me. All fifty dollars of it. Time stood still for the next five years.

~ Essie, June 1989 ~

The day after Ray Keith joined the Marines, Janey Gay realized she was pregnant. The family, what was left of us, revived itself again. Everybody thought it'd be good for me to move in with Janey while Ray finished his service to Uncle Sam. Their little apartment in town wasn't any bigger than Daddy's. Janey dolled up the back porch and made it my room, which she thought of turning into the nursery after the baby came.

The June night before Ray left for Parris Island and ten weeks of boot camp, Janey Gay cried her eyes out. Her pregnancy had recently blossomed over the edge of her pants. She begged Ray to change his mind. The rumored war in Iraq loomed large over our heads.

Ray Keith's tears were new to me. He tried explaining to Janey that joining up was his only way out of the poorhouse and living like his parents. Ray refused to take over his daddy's dead-end store and said that he was done driving a Cheerwine truck. He also said Janey's job of waiting tables at the local Barbeque Pit was not a career in the making.

Ray was right. We all knew it. There was no money for college or to better himself as things stood. He tried hard to comfort his pregnant wife. "I have to find a trade, finish school—make a good living for you and the family. The only option is my Veteran benefits. We have to do this, honey. I'll be back in no time."

Between Janey's sobs, I heard him say something about buying the dream house she'd always wanted. But it didn't ease her tears; she bawled into the night.

I cried too. Alone on my bed, listening to all of it, missing Daddy, worrying about Ray Keith and Janey Gay. I also asked

God to find my mother wherever the unforgiving woman might be living.

~ Atlanta, Georgia, October 1989 ~

Loretta pushed her ten minutes to twenty.

Leading evangelical ministers said the Lord ordered Loretta's steps. As she climbed into the church van with the keys inside, she wondered if God was ordering these steps. Starting the vehicle, Loretta slipped on her sunglasses, and drove out of the parking lot.

Loretta lit another cigarette with one hand and gripped the steering wheel with the other. The mega-church revival and every obligation disappeared right along with her. She paid no attention to the road or her next move. Her thoughts turned to her brother. If only Teague were alive. "What good is all that money when you're miserable as a polecat?" His lectures burned in her memory over and over. "Hypocrites are like flies on a dead possum. They reproduce more nasty flies." She hated when he said it, but Teague was right: she was a fly-producing hypocrite.

She'd been horribly ashamed of her illiterate family and all but disowned them. The Hollingsworth brothers were born with bulging foreheads, thick lips, and pale green eyes, almost yellow. Red hair, cowlicks, and bad skin afflicted Loretta's sisters. There wasn't a high school graduate among them except Loretta. Each one dropped out of school after the eighth grade to farm tobacco. Her brothers lived like a pack of crazy dogs that caught a whiff of a bitch in heat but were too lazy to do anything about it. And only Teague cared about her. The only person in the world she trusted.

Even as a child, she struggled to find a way out of no way. Loretta turned eight when she discovered her dead parents in the backyard—both shot through the head. In a jealous rage, Loretta's mother shot her husband once in the heart and twice in the head, then turned the gun on herself. Afterward, Loretta drifted from one older sister's house to another.

Her break came a few years later in the form of a grandfather she never knew she had. The old man offered money for college, and only for college, to any of his grandchildren. One grandchild took him up on the offer—Loretta. She moved to Tennessee and attended beauty school, where two regular wash and set clients, administrators at Lee College, offered her a position. Night shift on the janitorial staff. Broke and ambitious, Loretta cleaned women's restrooms until she eventually saved enough to attend Seminary, graduating third in her class.

Due to her meager circumstances, her ministry grew slowly. Then she met Evelyn Roberts, who took one look at her and quoted the scripture in Esther Chapter Four, "And who knows but that you have come to a… position for such a time as this." She invited Loretta to speak at a women's prayer group on the campus of Oral Roberts University. God's pure anointing filled the place. A word of knowledge came forth out of Loretta's lips. The evidence of that word produced miracles. Barren wombs conceived children. Blind eyes opened. Arthritic hands were instantly made straight, and a prosperity message for women like none other spread like an arsonist's fire through a lumberyard.

Overnight, speaking engagements and invitations to preach in churches throughout the country filled her calendar. For the first few years, Loretta refused to paint her face like a common floozy and risk eternal damnation. She wore her hair throughout the seventies and early eighties, reminiscent of a style predominant in her 1972 high school yearbook: long, straight, and tucked behind her ears. Preaching in starchy, long-sleeved blouses buttoned to the top under white robes, regardless of the lack of air conditioning, Loretta believed in suffering as much as holiness.

Then she met Tammy Faye Bakker, who set Loretta's feet on a new path. Suddenly free from the bondage of dowdy-looking women, Loretta engaged in a complete makeover, bought a new wardrobe, learned to sing contemporary Christian music, and discovered she loved big, flashy jewelry and designer clothes. Her ministry exploded into a mega-ministry.

When she appeared on Trinity Broadcasting Network, her following grew to evangelistic proportions, rivaling those of Lester

Sumrall, R. W. Schambach, and Marilyn Hickey. God blessed her, yet it did not fulfill her.

Now, years later, she struggled to hear God's voice. The more extensive her religious empire, the bigger her problems and the more money she needed to make it all work smoothly. Her staff depended on her for their livelihood. The stress of it all woke her at night. Loretta longed for sleep to consume her, like immersing her body in a deep tub of warm water. Desperate, she found no peace in the scriptures, her colleagues' advice, or the occasional hidden cocktail.

Early in her ministry, she closed her eyes and waited for the anointing to fill her bedroom. Even when she inhaled, the strength and knowledge of God satiated her body. Then the unthinkable happened: that sacred anointing never came; even getting out of bed was a chore.

Loretta found solace in a small wooden box tucked inside her dresser drawer. Someone carved *Gatlinburg, Tennessee*, into the lid of the cheap souvenir made of cedar. A keepsake Teague gave her as a present the year she graduated from Lee. During quiet nights, she'd pull out the yellowed envelopes, read the letters, and stroke the lock of hair. Her heart broke again and again. But it was too late. She'd made a fortune and won the hearts of Christian women worldwide. Thousands looked to her for a word, a miracle, a blessing, when she couldn't believe for her own. She had faith for the entire world but none for herself.

As Loretta watched the moon break through the clouds over Atlanta, tears left mascara streaks on her swollen face. Definitely the hypocrite her brother called her; she lost herself in the past and the road ahead. If she were lucky, she'd be at the beach by morning.

~ Essie, October 1989 ~

It rained in Selma the Sunday afternoon we headed toward Cherry Point in Janey's Ford Pinto. The October sky turned gray and weepy, the Southern pines dripped, and raindrops dappled shimmery puddles on lawns and roads—not a pretty day by most people's standards. But the rain was also gentle and well-behaved, making driving easier on wet highways.

Months previous, I took a shortcut to Cherry Point with a friend from school and her father. She wrote the route number for me in homeroom, swearing to God the shortcut lopped off an hour of our trip. On the map, 90 miles west-southwest of Cape Hatteras, Cherry Point sat at the foot of the Outer Banks. Getting to the beach lickety-split was fine with me. I loved the ocean, and Janey promised we'd sit with our feet in the waves before heading back.

"Hey! Look at that billboard," I said and pointed. "Ain't that the woman evangelist on TV? She's coming to town in January. Should we mention it to Uncle Royal?" I giggled, knowing the answer. "Loretta Lynette. Do you think that's her real name?"

"Probably not; you know them televangelists. They're like actors or Las Vegas showgirls. Everything about them is fake."

"You think?"

"Sure. They're all in it for the money. None of them make good parents."

"Why?"

Janey screwed up her nose. "Can you imagine how messed up their kids are? Always itching to live like other kids. Besides, I heard even the Methodist preacher can't make it to his son's baseball games. Too busy with one church committee or another. Me and Ray—we'll raise our kids in church, but I want us to be good people first. Like Sye and Royal."

I swallowed hard. "My daddy was good people; he was just a little wild, that's all."

Janey sighed. "Sure, Essie. That's all. Just a little wild."

There wasn't much to say after that.

We rode in silence, jamming to a Randy Travis cassette tape. When I shoved in Clint Black, I noticed Janey holding her belly and then rubbing her head. Whatever was happening, I hoped it'd wait two more days until we were back home, where Aunt Sye could take over. Sye had nearly spit when she saw our suitcases. But she knew better than to stand in Janey Gay's way.

I tried to break the silence between us. "Maybe if it's a boy, he can be the pallbearer at my wedding."

"Ring Bearer."

"Oh, yeah. Right."

Janey massaged her stomach again. "What road d'you say we needed to turn on?"

"Route 58, all the way to the coast. Turn right at the building with the big Yoo-Hoo sign."

"Okay, I see it. Ray will meet us in Morehead City if his staff sergeant gives him a pass, and then he'll take us back to the base for a tour. If he can't get a pass, we're supposed to drive to Havelock for the night and meet him on base in the morning."

"All I know is I want shrimp for dinner tonight." I expected Janey to agree. She loved seafood as much as I did. But I worried, watching her face turn white as the maple tree in our front yard. The one Aunt Sye attacked with a paintbrush every spring.

Janey put her hand to her mouth. "I'm sick. I need to pull over."

"There, pull over there."

Janey parked the Pinto on the gravel shoulder. She threw open the car door and bolted behind a thicket of briars and underbrush. The low-wrenching sounds of her lunch coming up made me gag. When she staggered back, drained and wiping her mouth, she reminded me of the day I came down sick with the stomach flu, and Aunt Sye handed me a trash can to puke in while I parked my butt on the commode with the runs.

"I wish I could drive," I said. "Maybe we should turn around."

"How many times do I have to say it, Estelline? No!"

The sun appeared from behind low clouds. Its rays pierced the pine trees' coarsely woven tops as it sunk into the landscape and sparkled off Janey's tear-stained cheeks. After an hour on the shortcut route, the pavement ended. A dirt road loomed ahead of us. Janey stopped.

"God, Essie, you sure this is the way? What's that sign say?"

I poked my head out the window. "Hofmann Forest. Give me the map."

"We must've taken a wrong turn." She handed me the atlas. "Look, a truck!"

"Roll your window down; make him stop," I said as the asparagus-green panel truck rattled toward us slowly. A plume of red dust kicked up behind it. Janey waved her arm out the window to flag down the driver. A man with dark eyes, pitch-black hair, and a straw hat stopped and nodded politely. An old woman with no teeth, deep wrinkles, and black dots for eyes sat beside him, chewing her cud. Or so it seemed.

"Sorry to bother you," Janey said. "Is this the way to Morehead City and the coast?"

"Si. The coast. Go that way," he replied, pointing to the road behind him.

"Thank you, thank you very much." Janey smiled and watched the truck drive in the direction we came from.

I felt lost. My stomach filled with butterflies. "Did he even know what you said?"

"Well, we got to assume he did, don't we? I mean, we've come this far." Janey started the car and drove in the direction the man pointed. She weaved in and out of huge potholes filled with rainwater. Tall pines and rows of harvested fields banked the muddy road for miles, but it was suddenly squeezed between acres of forest and wetlands as far as we could see. Janey switched on the car's headlights. "Does anything look familiar?"

I didn't want to say it. "No. I don't remember this dirt road."

"Then we need to turn around. I haven't seen a house since we left the interstate. I need to stop and pee."

"Look out! Janey, stop!"

A deer darted in front of the car, and for a moment everything moved in slow motion. I stared into its eyes and had the feeling it knew me. The Pinto swerved sideways, sliding the back tires into a deep pothole and slamming the frame hard on the road. With a jolt strong enough to rattle our teeth, we found ourselves stuck in mud and debris.

Janey's motherly nature kicked in as she grabbed my arm. "Are you okay?"

I nodded and wiped at tears, hearing Ray Keith yell inside my head; *this is your fault!* We could've been eating at Crabby Mike's, had I not tried to show off and take us on a damn shortcut. Instead, we'd lost our way in the middle of—God only knew.

Janey tried to rock the car, but the tires only spun in the mud. We weren't going anywhere. Then she let out a muffled grunt of pain between clenched teeth. What looked like pee ran down her pantyhose to her ankles.

"Help me out."

"Are you sick again?"

"It's worse than that. Don't cry. That doesn't help us now. And stop blaming yourself, Essie. We shouldn't have come. This is my fault, not yours. I'm the adult here or supposed to be. I had to try, you know? It's my fault. I had no business listening to a fifteen-year-old who doesn't drive and thinks she knows a shortcut. Oh God, I'm going to make a terrible mother."

"I'm so sorry." I squeaked out my words as more tears clogged my throat and made tracks down my sweaty face.

"Please, Essie. Stop crying and help me out of this car!"

The car's front end tilted slightly upward, and I saw one of the front tires had gone flat.

When I opened Janey Gay's door, her hands wrapped around the steering wheel and squeezed hard. Then, as if kneading a gigantic pile of dough, she groped at her enormous stomach and bit her lower lip, stifling an instinctive moan. Clearly, neither of us had the strength needed to push the car out of the quarry-sized mud puddle.

I pulled Janey out by her arms. She immediately hunched over, grabbed the door, and breathed in and out like she'd run a marathon. "Here's the situation. I'm sure I'm in labor; I think my water broke. I—I think." Her words strained and weak, she handed me a tissue. "Wipe off my legs before the mosquitoes find me. My pains aren't too bad, but I've no idea how much worse they'll get and how quickly they'll go. You've got to flag somebody down. We need help. I'll crawl back in the car, in the back seat with my pillow, and try to slow this down—if I can. Hell, I don't know what I'm doing; I'm running on instinct. Don't walk back the way we came; there's nothing for miles. We know that already. Walk in the direction we were heading. Maybe we're closer to civilization than we know. This road has to lead somewhere."

"I won't—I can't leave you—"

"—Yes, yes, you can. You don't have a choice—ohhh—" Janey buckled over and clutched her stomach again. "Damn, that one hurt." She inched herself down the side of the car, and I tried to help her. The back seat of the Pinto had to be the most uncomfortable place in the world to give birth. Time to run for help, not walk.

"You hold on! Keep your legs together. I promise I'll return as soon as I can!" My tears dripped onto her arm as she reached for me.

"Essie?"

"Yes?"

"Hurry."

I nodded, handed her the car keys and her purse, then grabbed the yellow plastic flashlight from the glove box before closing the door. I yanked off my sandals, threw on socks and sneakers, and took one last look at Janey, leaning on her pillow in the back seat. She spread her bent knees apart, searching for comfort. I placed my entire hand flat against the window as if to say, *don't worry, I'll get help*. She reached up, pressed her hand against mine on the other side of the glass, and then looked away. The pain on her face melted my fear. I took off running in the direction Janey told me to go.

There was nothing; nothing but insects, a dirt road, and the threat of rain.

~ Escape to the Beach ~

Loretta knew every state police cruiser between Atlanta and Raleigh would be on the lookout for the church van. Possibly Sam saw her drive out of the lot. She headed east, yearning to dig her feet into the sand. But miles later, the car headed due north to the Outer Banks, and places where she grew up, faint memories of a life she wanted to relive. A life where nobody knew of her importance to evangelicals around the globe. A town where she could walk at a leisurely pace down any street. Pop in the grocery store on a whim for coffee, milk, and eggs. Get her hair done without incident—and not a soul ask for her autograph or prayer.

She reached inside her bag to feel the smooth wooden box hiding the biggest secret of her life. A secret significant enough to destroy her as a minister of the Gospel and her entire ministry. A secret concealed from unforgiving Christians the world over.

Staying clear of main roads, Loretta passed through small towns and obeyed the speed limits, determined to avoid drawing attention. But she observed off-the-beaten-path areas with a more critical eye than in her past. Rural communities she hardly noticed in over fifteen years. One town after another, where folks steeped like old tea bags in their humdrum lives.

Loretta mumbled at the sight of roadside produce stands, flea markets, and general stores selling Moon Pies, three for a dollar. "Town this deep in the shithouse has nowhere to go but to God." Her words stunned her. *What a horrible thing to say.* She'd forgotten about small-town living and existing by the seat of your pants. Hanging on until payday, hoping to find a few extra quarters in the couch for a hamburger.

It all flooded back, but reality took over in the midst of remembering, and she wanted to drive back to Atlanta. Make up a lie like the one Aimee Semple McPherson told. Maybe a story of escaping an abductor and if she could manage a minor wreck, not hurt anybody, bruise herself up a little; perhaps they'd feel sorry for her and let the whole thing go. Any way she looked at it, she was in serious trouble—stealing the van, skipping out on a healing service in a mega-church like Church of the Savior.

At a stoplight, she stripped off her suit jacket and pulled on a T-shirt somebody from the church's youth group left in the van— JESUS FREAK in giant red letters. She lit another cigarette and drove by tiny Baptist, Methodist, and Nazarene churches with no marker out front. Loretta shook her head, finding numerous church signs disturbing. Quoting jokes instead of scripture.

Driving past the next religious billboard, Loretta slammed on the brakes. *The sins of the fathers are visited upon their children.* She pounded her fist on the steering wheel. Although Loretta despised most men, she hated her father the most. One big son of a bitch who used his charm to attract women. Gullible women obsessed over him to the point of madness. Whining like puppies to have their bellies scratched, among other things. They fell in love with his swagger and whatever money he pulled out of his pocket. He didn't come home much, but when he did, he'd make another baby with her mama, another red-headed child with pea-green eyes and acne. Children, he didn't know what to do with. The man never cared much about anything; he treated his kids like a pack of wild dogs and his wife like a whore. Loretta couldn't blame her mother for what she did. She had fantasized about killing him herself—with worse than a bullet.

But Loretta would have died for his attention. Born at the tail end of his brood, she remembered Teague said their old man probably didn't know she was one of his; there were so many kids in the house.

Over time, Loretta learned how to channel her decades of frustration and neglect into a talent for acquiring admiration. Even God's. Her faith unwavering, she'd flash her eyes along with her million-dollar smile, and the deaf heard whispers in the wind. The lame danced on the altar. The mute joined the choir. As a result, she raised money for ministries and missions in less time than it took any male televangelist to make a buck. The camera loved her, and she freely gave Academy Award performances behind hundreds of American pulpits before going international through the media of television. She was the country's evangelical sweetheart, the Christian woman's idol and best friend, and the conservative voice for women of the Republican Party—a spokeswoman for the Pro-Life Coalition in Washington, D.C.

A high-priced publicist carefully planned her itinerary, manipulating it to make her a spiritual superstar. Loretta received invitations to nearly every evangelical event, mega-church, and Christian Women's group from Bangor to Palm Springs and Seattle to Miami. She had gained the whole world, but lost her soul along the way. Lost it in the memory of a young lover and a pregnancy nobody but a few poor people in North Carolina knew about. It plagued her, day and night, for years. In the end, gnawing guilt defined her life. She'd begged God for forgiveness, but the road kept leading her back. Back to a family and a moment she knew she must face in order to stand herself one more day.

~ Essie ~

Sharp as a sickle, the moon darted in and out of bloated black clouds. The tears and snot I didn't wipe on my sleeve, I swallowed. Walking for over two hours, I saw nothing but darkness and shadows. My flashlight grew weak, and I wanted to scream, to pray. But I didn't know how.

Silent streaks of silver split the clouded sky in the distance next to the dry one hanging over me. I studied the storm, hoping it wasn't heading my way. Forcing myself to move forward, I tried to stop worrying about anything other than Janey.

But there were no cars. No lights. Just me. A girl alone in the dark. Trudging down a dirt road. In a forest, no less. The Twilight Zone kind of night that makes most folks nervous, even in the safety of their homes. I hadn't a clue where I was. Only that the destination stretched beyond the reach of my eyes, leading to exhaustion. The night sagged in the humid air, prickling my skin with the coming storm. A hoot owl, with wings spread wide, flew into long-slung trees. My ears closed to its frightening questions, "Who, who will save you now?"

I shifted into a faster stride. Fireflies blinked their fleeting beacons, like the opening eyes of hidden creatures to see a human fumble her way in the dark. At the end of a clearing, tall oaks loomed toward me, hoping to snatch me by the neck. When the dirt road turned into asphalt, I felt a slight sense of relief. Still, no car approached. It was nearly eleven o'clock by the moon's dim light and the light on my Timex. Janey had been alone for the past three hours. My legs ached, and my feet grew colder and wetter inside my shoes. But I refused to stop or turn around. I kept my eyes on the road as I marched toward help or Judgment Day, watching the crackling glow of lightning closing in.

Moments later, I rounded a corner to see headlights cut through the thick darkness, blazing down on me. Yanking off my sweater, I jumped and waved like a crazy person, not entertaining one thought of serial killers or a car full of drunken men. This was the first car I'd seen since the panel truck with the old couple pointing us in the wrong direction. I had to make this person stop and help me. Or die trying.

~ End of a Long, Dark Road ~

Loretta had been so careful not to be found that she'd lost herself. She thought she knew all the back roads in and out of the Carolinas—at least she used to. Especially those leading to the coast. But driving through the worst thunderstorm she'd seen up close and personal since living in the area, it was no wonder she found herself in a forest, on the road to—she had no earthly idea. And she needed gas. It'd been years since she'd been responsible for her gas gauge. There wasn't even a service station to pull over and ask for directions.

She eased the matronly van to the side of the road, her radio tuned to the Gospel Hour, supplying the ideal rapturous accompaniment for her trip to the Carolinas. It was the perfect prison break, a breath of freedom to do and act how she wanted and not a soul to sit in judgment. An opportunity to right her wrongs.

But with the dark night came the fear of being discovered. She would've turned around and headed straight back to Atlanta that second, except for a young girl in the middle of the road waving her arms like a lunatic.

Lord, save me from calamity or help me save this soul from worse.

~ Essie ~

The van slowed to a stop, and I saw it was a woman. Relieved, I flung the door open, breathless, throwing all caution to the side of the road. She was pretty, a Jesus Freak. Or so said her T-shirt. A faint thread of hysteria grew in my voice. "We've had an accident! My cousin's having a baby in our car. Oh, God. She's alone in the back seat!"

"What? Slow down, honey. You say you're out here all alone?" The woman driver turned off her radio and looked at me suspiciously, like I was lying—or something worse.

"Ma'am, I'm sorry, but there's no time to play twenty questions. You've got to help us. My name's Essie, and my cousin is in terrible shape; she's about to have a baby if she ain't had it already."

"I'm gathering that. She's on this road? In the car?"

A larger sense of relief surrounded me like a warm hug. "We ended up in a deep mud puddle. Janey Gay's water broke. Oh, God—"My tears dripped down my nose, to my lips, and fell off my chin. I wiped my dirty face with the back of my hand. Mosquitoes feasted on my legs, and I began to scratch like a dog.

"Hold on, honey. Grab a tissue out of that box."

Wearing shorts, a tank top, and a thin sweater, I didn't know how chilled I was until I felt the heat inside the van. In what seemed like minutes compared to my long walk, the white Pinto with Janey's head in the window came into view. The woman nosed the coasting van over to the road's shoulder and stopped behind our car, leaving the headlights on. Both of us hurried to the Pinto. Inside, with her legs still bent, Janey Gay appeared fragile-looking and barely taller than a twelve-year-old, moaning and pushing on her stomach as if she could shove out the pain if she pressed hard enough. Despite the cool night air, her thick glasses had fogged over, and sweat poured down her face and neck. The sting of labor siphoned the color out of her skin. Her tangled dark hair fell in pain-soaked curls around stark white cheeks. I lifted my head to wipe my tears and glanced at the pale moon breaking through a dark cluster of clouds. Raindrops dotted my arms and legs.

The woman with big, round circles for eyes smiled at Janey. "Hey there, sweetie, what's your name?" A flush deepened the dimples on her cheeks.

"I told you. Her name is Janey Bertram," I said.

"Essie! Mind your manners!" Janey pulled off her glasses, and her eyes sparked at me. "It took you damn long enough. I'm sorry, Ma'am. My little cousin's worried about me."

"She should be. When did your pains start?"

"After lunch. I thought we could make it to Havelock; my husband is stationed at Cherry Point. We were taking a shortcut when my car landed in this hole. Now it won't start, but I don't think we can push it out, anyway. You're the first person to come down this road in hours. My doctor said I'm not due for three weeks—"

"—If he was any kind of doctor, he would've insisted you stay off those swollen feet. Well, let's get you to a hospital. I doubt we'll see many cars on this road. How did you say you ended up here?"

I wiped Janey's glasses and handed them back to her. We looked at each other, and another tear rolled down my cheek.

"Was my fault," I said. "I thought I knew a shortcut."

Janey drew her legs back up and clutched the seat; her knuckles went white. Her face pinched, and she squeezed her eyes shut. "They're about ten minutes apart, Ma'am, but they're killing me. I don't understand. I'm not due for another three weeks," she repeated.

"Babies come when they want," said the pretty woman. Then she looked at me. "I'm sorry. I didn't catch your name in the van."

"Essie," I said as her attention returned to Janey. Reaching into the car with her long arms and beautiful hands, she rubbed and patted Janey's knees to comfort her. A different class of people than Janey and me, or anybody I knew for that matter, she had the prettiest red nails I ever saw on a woman.

Getting a better look at this stranger who no longer seemed strange, I stared at her hair, the color of red plums. Same as my own. I'd always hated my hair color, but suddenly I liked it. Resembling Reba McIntyre from the side, she seemed to beam like a light in the dark. I admired her makeup and her thin lips lined in red and the gold cross hanging around her neck. Her silly T-shirt nearly covered her skirt. Staring at her face, I saw mascara tracks down her face as if she'd been crying. Then it hit me; she hadn't told us *her* name.

"We've told you who we are; what's your name?" I watched her hesitate, almost like she hadn't planned on telling us and didn't want to say.

"Loretta. Loretta Lynette."

I touched her shoulder to get her to look at me. "Now I know why you look familiar; I saw your billboard on the interstate. You're the evangelist!"

"Yes. I'm afraid I am. I apologize for meeting you under these circumstances."

Janey pulled herself upright when she heard Loretta's name. "What's somebody like you doing out here?"

"It's a long story. Right now, you need medical attention, and we can talk about me later. Essie, go to the other side, get in behind her, and help push her out. Try to stand and walk, Janey. I'll open the back of the van and clear a spot where you can lie down."

Janey looped her arm around my neck, and we scooted out and stood in the grass. Inching our way to the van, I watched Loretta toss boxes of what looked like Sunday school papers and Bibles on the side of the road.

"Not much room in there, but you can stretch out. You think you can climb in?" Loretta asked.

"I believe so," Janey said. She whipped her damp ringlets around her face, doubling over again. Her glasses fell off and her curls stuck to her eyelashes. More water poured down her legs and into her shoes.

"Oh, God, Janey, please be alright—please, Oh, God—"

"—Estelline! Calm down. You're no help to me like this. Find my glasses."

Loretta grabbed a roll of paper towels from the back seat. "Good Lord, get those pantyhose off her. I'll start the van and be back to help her in."

While I shoved Janey's glasses back on her head and worked at pulling the now ripped-to-shreds and goopy pantyhose off her legs, Loretta hopped into the front seat and slid the key in the ignition. The van started, coughed, then stalled. She tried again, and it started again, but soon sputtered and stopped. On her third try, it clicked, then—nothing. She turned around and looked at us for a moment; I'm sure she didn't know what to say.

"It seems I'm out of gas."

My face flushed hot. I bolted to the driver's window. "Out of gas? We're stuck out here with a baby on the way, and you're out of gas? How could somebody like you be out of gas?"

Janey doubled over. I think the fear she'd felt, alone in her car, hit her hard again because I heard nothing from her but a terrified squeak. It seemed she'd lost her voice.

Loretta shook her head and shrugged. "I'm sorry. I didn't realize I was low on fuel until I found myself on this road. I'd have been stuck out here too." She opened the door and followed me to help Janey into the van. "Look," she said. "Nobody is going anywhere until morning. There's nothing around for miles. Maybe we'll see another car. Maybe by morning, someone will drive by. Even if we pushed your car out of the hole, you said it won't start, and if you haven't noticed, both tires in the front are flat. In the meantime, we need to get comfortable; we may be spending the night and delivering a baby before help can get to us. I see three gallons of drinking water in the back and some Styrofoam cups. They must use this van for Sunday school field trips. There's a first aid kit under the seat. You've got a blanket in your car; I see two more here. Let's pray and ask God to help us."

"You pray; you're the expert." I refused to look at her. I wanted to spit—at myself, at God, and at this stupid red-headed woman with no gas in her van.

⌒ℓℓ~

A half-hour later, Janey Gay lay in the back of the van, clutching her pillow and blanket. Her pains subsided somewhat. Loretta and I sat in the front seats. There was no need to bother Janey until she needed us. Loretta handed me a can of Diet RC and an apple. Scared and starved, I was glad to get it.

The night air grew colder. My watch blinked the time. Two a.m. I felt Loretta staring at me. We fell into a companionable silence full of questions neither wanted to ask. She appeared distracted by the dimple on my cheek as she touched one on her own cheek. A large mole stood out on her right arm, just like mine. She was beautiful, even though she *was* Aunt Sye's age, possibly. But she was even prettier than her billboard picture.

I looked up at the sky. "That's strange. The storm's blowing over."

"What did you say your name was?" she asked.

"Gosh, you don't have much memory for a preacher. My name's Essie, for the third time."

"No, your cousin called you something else a while ago."

"Estelline. My name is Estelline Aikens. Janey calls me Estelline when she's mad at me."

I watched Loretta pull her blanket around her neck, turn her head, and stare out the window. "I knew some people named Aikens once," she whispered. "Where do you live?"

"Selma. You?"

She shivered hard enough for me to notice before grabbing a tissue and dabbing at her heavily made-up eyes. Her voice cracked, and she gave me a feeble smile. "Well, I live all over. Evangelists travel a lot. But my home is in Little Rock, Arkansas."

"You like being a preacher?"

"Have you watched me on TV?"

I giggled. "Sorry, no. My Uncle Royal thinks you're a phony, and he makes me turn off the TV. We don't go to church much. Just my Aunt Sye. I don't think it makes us bad people, though."

"No. Neither do I. But what do you know about televangelists, Essie? I mean, have you thought about what we do?"

"Sorry, no again. You preach a lot, I guess. I am curious. Are you like a movie star?"

Loretta chuckled. "Long ago, they used to treat us like rock stars. I suppose some evangelists would still like that. But, no, the only star in my world is Jesus. We live in a time when televangelists rule the airwaves with their networks. Still, for some people, we're just another stop in an evening of channel surfing. They've forgotten the time of years past when revival meetings were as exciting as the circus coming to town. The premiere woman evangelist in the old days was Aimee Semple McPherson."

"Did you know her?"

"No. I've been told I'm a lot like her, though. Those days are long gone. People expect more out of me. But—" she sighed, leaning against the headrest, "I'm about to slow down. Live in the real world for a while."

"That's why you're out here all alone?" The night air blew in the cracked window and across Loretta's face.

"Yes. I had to stop. I had to—find—something," she whispered and then closed her eyes. "To go higher with Him," she pointed to the sky, "I must find closure about an event that occurred years ago. I was just a young girl."

"You ever been in love?" I asked. I figured she meant a lost love with all her talk about finding closure. A romantic notion in my mind, at least.

"Yes, once. A long time ago."

"What happened?"

Loretta sighed. "One night, he came to my place and smelled like betrayal. Then I caught him the next night in the act."

My turn to sigh. "Most men cheat, don't they?"

Janey groaned from the back. "Not Ray Keith!"

Loretta reached over the seat and stroked Janey's brow. "Hey, little mama. You're supposed to be asleep. Any more pains?"

"Just twinges, nothing so severe I can't stand it."

Loretta's eyes lit up. "I forgot; I've got a box of Moon Pies in my bag."

"Oh, man, I'd love one," I said.

Janey rolled to her other side. "None for me, thanks."

We ate in silence, Loretta and me. Sleep settled on my eyelids, and I blinked to stay awake. It helped to know Janey rested in the back. I felt warm beside Loretta. Peaceful. "Thank you, Miss Lynette; I don't know what would've happened had you not come along, despite you running out of gas." My voice possessed all the grace of a strangled bullfrog.

"You're welcome, but I believe you should thank Jesus, not me."

Her statement struck me as an insult. "You think I'm a sinner?"

"Have you accepted Jesus as your Savior?"

"I believe in Him. I think I got saved once at Vacation Bible School."

"If you did, then you'd know it."

"How do you know when you're a Christian?"

"You love Christ, follow Him, believe in His miracles, you're used according to His divine will."

"How does anyone know God's will?"

"For me, it was the opening of many doors. He made my path plain, and I walked where He said to go. I can hear His voice and relay it to those in need. He uses me because I yield to Him freely, where others do not."

I snorted so fiercely that the RC Cola I'd just gulped shot out of my nose. I coughed and gagged. "That's about the dumbest thing I ever heard. What makes you so much better than me? Hmm? Why can't God talk to *me;* tell *me* His will?" I laughed and wiped my nose on my sleeve.

"He can, but most people don't have enough faith, or they live in fear. Many refuse to be open to the Holy Spirit, don't believe, or listen."

"Well, I'll tell you, Miss High and Mighty Preacher Lady. You're no better than me, Aunt Sye, or my cousin Janey back there, who got knocked up by her stepfather and had an abortion when she was sixteen before Ray Keith married her. The way I see it, we're all a bunch of no-good sinners, and we do the best we can along the way. And if God wants to talk to me, I think He knows where I damn well live."

Loretta wiped at her eyes again. "Maybe you're right, Essie. Maybe I'm all wrong," she said with an apologetic ring. "How about when your uncle isn't around? You ever turn on the TV and watch someone preach and pray for the sick?"

"Nope. I figure, if there is a God who created the earth and the moon and the stars, and He decides to use somebody on TV to deliver a message to humanity, that person sure as heck won't show up in a cheap suit and a bad hairstyle. Oh, I'm sorry. I don't mean you, of course."

Loretta laughed. "Now, that's one I haven't heard. You make a good point."

I laughed too. It felt good, so I kept asking questions. "Where did you grow up?"

"Near your area, actually."

"You say you know some Aikens?"

"Yes."

"You know any of my family? Noble, Sye, or my daddy? His name was Paul David."

"Yes, I knew them. Any more questions?

"Is that your real name? Loretta Lynette?"

"Yes, first and middle."

"You got a last name? Have you ever been married?"

"I use Lynette as my last name; my last name was Hollingsworth. Funny, I've never told that to a soul. You're the first. And the answer is *no* to your second question. I've never been married."

I asked no more questions. Loretta's answers came to me straight and smoothly. We looked into each other's eyes, and then she reached up, lightly touched my cheek, and smiled. "You best try to sleep. We'll have to get help at first light, and like I said, we may have to deliver a baby."

I decided to ask one last question. "Is Janey in danger?"

"I don't know. But I'll pray God be with her and her baby."

"Thank you," I said and yawned. "I'm sorry if I insulted you."

"Not at all."

I opened my sleep-sticky eyes to morning's foggy light seeping through the front window of Loretta's van. She was gone, but Janey woke wide-eyed, gasping for breath. She rose on an elbow and appeared startled.

I reached for her. "Are you okay?"

"I got to pee, bad. And I think my pains are back and worse than last night."

"Hold on. I'll help you squat outside the van."

"Where's Loretta?"

"I don't know. I woke up, and she wasn't here." Stepping outside, I felt like a dry little weed must feel when the rain comes. A fog had settled over the road, but the dampness felt good on my body.

"Oh, Essie, this baby's coming!"

"Damn it! Where's Loretta?" I helped Janey Gay stand on the side of the road, first leaning on me, then on the van. She tried to pee, but there was nothing, just lots of pressure. She walked back and forth a little, hoping to ease her pain.

I slipped around the side of the van and tried to start it, hoping by some miracle, gasoline had appeared in our tank. That's when I saw headlights barreling toward us through the fog. The ambulance and its flashing lights were a welcome sight.

She'd left me after I'd fallen asleep. Loretta walked seven miles back to a farmhouse she remembered passing in the storm. The old couple recognized Loretta and allowed her to use their phone. An ambulance followed a police car that picked Loretta up first before finding Janey and me alone, frightened more than ever. Janey's pains had dwindled down to three minutes apart.

A kindhearted policeman filled the tank in the van with two gallons of high-test, pumped the gas pedal, and started it. The ambulance sped away to the nearest hospital with Janey moaning in the back. I grabbed Janey's suitcase and mine out of the Pinto and loaded it into the church van. Loretta and I smiled similar smiles, hearing the policeman report on his radio he'd found the missing celebrity preacher. Then I realized. She had run away from God.

The officer removed his hat as if Loretta were royalty. "Ma'am, I'll escort you to the hospital before we move on. They've cleared me to take you through South Carolina to the Georgia line. The Georgia state police will take you the rest of the way to Atlanta."

"Thank you, officer." Loretta looked at me. "Ready to go?"

The authorities allowed Loretta to take me to the hospital. They were obviously sympathetic; after all, she was nobody's prisoner.

We left Janey's car behind in the mud like an old sow. I watched it in the rearview mirror. As we drove away, weaving in and out of potholes on that god-forsaken dirt road in the Hoffman forest, I hoped to never again lay eyes on that Pinto. Or the road it sunk in.

Loretta and I remained quiet, racing to the hospital. She dropped me and all our luggage off at the door by the emergency room.

"Aren't you coming in?"

"No. You'll both be fine now. I have responsibilities. I need to get back."

"But I need to ask you more questions—about God and all."

She took my hand and placed a folded piece of paper in my palm, closing my fingers around it. "This is my private phone number; don't give it out. Call me; let me know if it's a boy or a girl. Let's stay in contact. I'd like to know you better, Essie. Will you give me your phone number? And address."

"Sure." I scribbled it on a paper towel and then asked the question that teetered on the edge of my tongue all morning. "I've got one last question."

"Okay. Better make it quick; the hospital may send security after me if I don't move this van soon."

"Did you know my mama? Her name was Elle."

She smiled wide and ran her hand through her unwashed hair. "Looks like the press has got wind of where I am; I see a reporter making a beeline across the parking lot straight for us." She reached out and pulled me into her arms, breathing in my scent, burying her face in my hair and neck. This was more than a hug; this was a lifetime of love flowing from her arms and into me. She kissed my cheek, her tears wet on my face. I wrapped my arms tight around her, not wanting to let her go.

"Yes, I knew your mama. I have something for you," she said. She opened the back of the van, slid her hand into her leather bag, and then handed me a box made of wood. "This is yours. You take it home and look at it in private. We'll meet again someday." Fresh tears glistened on her cheeks. Then she kissed my forehead and rushed back into the van.

I felt a great loss, like I'd lost my daddy all over again. I watched as she drove away behind the police escort, her arm flung out the window, waving to me.

The reporter ran after the van, his strapped camera bouncing off his back. "L! Stop! I'd like to ask you some questions. L, please stop!"

For a moment, I thought I heard him wrong. The next second, I was chasing the reporter.

"Hey! Mister! What d'you call her? Hey! Stop! Please—what, what did you call her?

"Weren't you with her?" he asked. "Who are you?"

"She stopped to help us; our car broke down. Please, what did you call her?"

"Don't you know who that is? That's Loretta Lynette. That's L."

He must've seen the confused look on my face.

"She's called L by her close friends. Okay, sure, the press found out, so we all call her L. Like the letter L. Didn't you know that? Where have you been, little lady?"

The corners of my vision blurred, and my eyes filled with puddles of tears. "In a world of sin, I guess." I held my box tight with both arms and walked on clouds into the hospital. It all made sense. They called her L. Of course, Elle was L.

After an hour of phone calls to Cherry Point and then to Aunt Sye and Uncle Royal, I sat in the waiting room while Janey Gay gave birth to her little boy. Ray Keith arrived sometime later after Sye and Royal greased the nursery window with their noses.

Thankful the police found us, everybody about hugged the goody out of me. Sye was too occupied with her new grandson to stay mad at Janey or me. Even without discussing it, Janey and I agreed to keep silent about Loretta. I bent over and kissed Janey's cheek as she held her baby boy. She waited until the family left the room.

"You know who she was, don't you, Essie?"

"Yes. You going to tell Sye and Royal I know the truth about my mother?"

"No. They'll find out soon enough. You mad at them for keeping it from you?"

"I don't know how I feel. I can't think further than you, Ray, and the baby."

"You'll handle it when the time comes. At least you know who your mama was."

"No, Janey. I know who she *IS*. She's not dead; she's alive. I don't understand what happened or why, but I will someday. Right now, all I know is she came looking for me. She loves me, and I can feel it. And that's all I need to know."

Days later, after we settled Janey Gay and the baby at home, I found the courage to open the worn wooden box. The scent of cedar and perfume floated out, and I missed her for the first time. I pulled out a stack of letters and arranged them in order of the postmark. Yellowed and brittle, the letters were in Daddy's handwriting. He had mailed them to her, along with my baby picture and a lock of my hair.

I opened the first letter and began to read.

L,

I know you won't write to me, and I understand. But I plan to send you a letter every week. I hope this one finds you well at that fancy college. I know why you can't be with us, your grandfather being a former Tennessee Governor, and I know he wants more for you than I can give you. Things would be different if you had just said you'd marry me. Someday I hope you allow me to explain about Connie Jo. I'm so sorry you caught us in Bernie's Thunderbird. Damn it, L. I wish you'd believe how sorry I am.

I promise I'll be a good daddy to our little girl. And if you still want to keep the baby a secret, my family won't tell it. I suppose your family doesn't know about little Estelline, except for Teague.

I'm thankful you at least gave me a post office box address. You said you'd return after college, but my heart breaks when I look at our daughter. She looks like you. Estelline learned to roll over in her crib yesterday. She keeps Sye busy. I don't get to see her much, with all the work at the gas station and keeping Noble in line. You don't want to be married to a heathen. But I miss you, L.

If you're ever in town, please call me, and we can meet somewhere private. I'd love for you to see our baby again.

All my love,
Paul David

Now I had all my answers, the second miracle of my life—the first one that Loretta found me. There was nothing left to know. God brought her back into my life. She would find a way to redeem herself and make me a part of her again.

A pair of sparkly earrings hid under the stack of letters, and I decided to keep them a secret from everyone.

I stared at the telephone. My hands shook as I picked up the receiver and dialed the number she gave me. When I heard her voice on the answering machine, all I could do was—cry.

The Homestead

THE HOMESTEAD lends itself to the supernatural. Spiritual to its core, this tale of hearth and home came to me during a nightmarish time in my life. Needing peace, I found it in THE HOMESTEAD.

Decades ago, an elderly lady named Edna inspired me in many ways. Remembering her fondly, she developed into one of the characters. I wrote several drafts of this simple old story. But it never spoke to me and said, "done." Not until I renamed one particular character. When I changed the name of Edna's husband to Leo, I finished the story within hours.

Afterward, I sat at my desk and laughed—because, in real life, Leo *was* Edna's husband.

I think she was trying to tell me something.

*I*n 1852, Halston Wenger carved his homestead out of the far most majestic region in the Blue Ridge Mountains. He nestled the house amidst acres of pine and plowed fields at the base of Stone Mountain. Decades later, seven generations of the Wenger family had lived on the land, raised their children, and farmed the eighty acres. When they died, they were laid to rest in the family cemetery under a large, shady grove of pecan trees.

Wenger blood and sweat were as much a part of their homestead as the dirt under their feet. That strange and infinite bond gave them strength and faith—in the unbelievable.

The ancient farmhouse cooled and creaked as the grandfather clock struck eight. Outside, fireflies danced in the dusk. Noah Wenger strummed his guitar and rocked back and forth in time to his music. His left leg rested outstretched on the swing while the other remained planted on the porch. Muscle-bound from years of plowing, planting, and harvesting, he could not hide the tenderness in his voice. *"Blessed Assurance, Jesus is mine..."*

Edna tapped her foot and nodded to the beat of her favorite hymn, entertained by the dance of fireflies. A gentle breeze carried the scent of overturned earth from a nearby field as her mind traveled back into the dim mists of time.

Leo—riding high on the John Deere, his overalls soaked in sweat and dirt and the stench of cow manure; how she missed that awful aroma. Even at an advanced age, Leo towered over most men. Strength abounded in his large, leathery hands. To Edna, her husband was like the landscape. He would go on forever. But his heart exploded in his chest, and grief consumed her from that day until now, like blistering heat on parched ground. At ninety, she no longer blamed God for cheating her. For rapturing Leo and leaving her behind.

"*... oh, what a foretaste of glory divine...*" Her son's baritone voice, mixed with the sweet chords of his guitar, interrupted Edna's thoughts. Opening her eyes and breathing deeply, her spirits sank like the sun. The deep despair of loneliness had taken its final toll as the brilliant orange heavens over the homestead faded to glitter on dark blue velvet skies.

⸺ ∼ ⸺

"Mama, let's go in. It's getting chilly, and you'll catch your death." Noah's voice trailed as he meandered inside and switched on the porch light.

Her tiny feet shuffled across the porch. Noah held out his hand and took her by the elbow. Edna's back curled like a cashew, withered and salty, but she didn't need him to help her to her room. Still, it felt good to be loved by her son. She hobbled past family photographs hanging on the rose and vine-papered hallway walls, remembering each devoted face.

"Mama, Dana's working late. Want me to fix you a bite to eat before bed?"

"Not tonight."

"You sure?"

Her sunken lilac eyes teared in response.

"Want me to sit a spell?" he asked.

She laid the palm of her wrinkled hand on her son's rough cheek. "No, wait for your daughter to come home and fix *her* something to eat."

Noah sighed, then lightly kissed her forehead. "Okay. See you in the morning."

His patient smile warmed her. Reaching up to touch his face again, she returned his smile. The bedroom door closed behind her, and she waited until Noah's heavy footsteps faded. Edna shuffled to the window. The lace panels billowed as cool air drifted through the screen. It drew her attention to a lone firefly flickering in the darkness of her room. She stood for a moment, mesmerized by its simplicity. Slipping into her nightgown and the warmth of her bed, Edna placed her hand on her broken heart. She'd languished enough. *Enough already.*

Weary and ready for bed, Noah flicked a wooden match with his thumbnail and lit the gas stove for a cup of tea. His gaze fell on his worn overalls. Clean enough to sit on the upholstery, he dropped into his chair at the table and rested his head in his hands. Lately, he rode the worry wagon. His only child, tall, stunningly handsome, and strong-willed, was the spitting image of her grandfather. She was Leo, inside and out. Noah had hoped for a son. Instead, a little girl cried in his lap the day his wife skedaddled back to Boston.

He had encouraged Dana to take the job at the mill, hoping she'd find some kind of living off the farm. Although he needed her help, he hired migrants instead of watching his daughter wear out before her time. But in the past two days, she'd made herself clear. Working inside a cotton mill's weave room drew a meager living, and she hated it. She quit. The farm, her first love, had called to her. Her determined voice rang inside his head. *Only thing I love more than this land is you, Daddy. And Grandma Ed.* Farming flowed in her veins as naturally as the spring water spilled out of the rock by the corncrib. It was time to accept it.

Dana's last night at the mill left her tired and irritable on the drive home. Each stoplight seemed to last forever. As her Pontiac crested the hill toward home, she stared in disbelief at flames licking the night sky. Her foot slammed the gas pedal to the floor. "No! God, No!"

Barreling up the drive, Dana sensed the unbearable anguish of loss build within her like a pressure cooker. Gravel pinged her car as it collided with Noah's truck. She'd barely felt the crash, and it didn't matter. Dana flung the door wide and flew into her father's sooty, black arms.

Noah wilted; his words stumbled out of his mouth. "I—I couldn't get her out."

"Who, Daddy? What are you saying?"

The terror on Noah's face said it all. "I couldn't get Mama out!" He fell to his knees. His glazed eyes mirrored the flames as tears dripped to his torn and muddy overalls.

Dana stood numb as one in a dream, watching it all.

Mose Johnson, a neighbor, directed fire trucks into the yard, then rapidly moved cows to the pasture as sparks drifted dangerously close to the barn. But when the front porch buckled and the old tinderbox house exploded into a raging inferno, Dana crumpled into a heap of molten grief on the ground. The cost of the fire would plague them forever. Photographs, books, and keepsakes from seven generations burned to ashes in a few brief minutes. But the actual loss, Dana knew, was of one tiny woman. *She was never meant to burn, not now or in the hereafter.*

Like the blackened windows of the fire-ravaged house, Dana's eyes opened with the first smear of foggy dawn. Rising from the rocks where she had fallen, she strained to see through the mist. Scanning the surrounding area, someone had covered Noah with a quilt as he slept under a massive hickory tree. Staggering toward the burnt-out shell of the old farmhouse, Dana pressed her hand to her aching heart. Her head pounding, she approached the smoking embers of the front porch. Stumbling through the obliteration of what was left of their home, she shivered. The flames haunted her. And yet, amidst the waste, a tiny firefly appeared, as if surveying her loss. Blinking through the smoke, Dana watched the firefly encircle her, land on her breast, then fly away, vanishing in the fog.

Maneuvering through the rubble, she stepped over smoldering remains of furniture, appliances, and melted memories. The pungent smell of ruin floated into her nostrils, and she prayed to wake up. It had to be a nightmare. Dizzy and searching for a way out, she discovered another firefly circling the smoke as if clearing a path. Dana followed and watched the firefly disappear in the mist, but not before finding herself standing on pieces of charred boards and cinder blocks. An overwhelming urge to shake her fist at God gave way to the remaining parts of their back porch collapsing under her. Stunned and sore, she grabbed hold of a scorched porch post and pulled herself up. But as she brushed away debris, a woman appeared several feet away, walking at a fast clip through the fog.

Dana stood and shouted, hoping to catch her attention. "Hello!" But this woman did not respond. Assuming she was a neighbor from the next farm coming to help, Dana thought little about her until a tall man emerged at the misty pasture's edge, and the two embraced.

She picked up her pace to observe them more closely, but suddenly the fog thickened, and she lost sight of the pair. Jogging in the pasture's direction, she glimpsed them again in the haze standing at the top of the hill. Determined to catch up to these wayward strangers, she nearly tripped over a hay bale as they turned and waved.

The words spilled out of her mouth. From somewhere in her Sunday school youth, the power of suggestion became a blazing reality. *I will give you beauty for ashes. The oil of joy for mourning. A garment of praise for despair.* The surrounding field took flight. Millions of fireflies filled the air, blinking and blinking the fog away, enveloping the couple in brilliant light. Young and beautiful, Edna and Leo had crossed the great divide. Dana's tired eyes glazed over with tears.

She began to run. "Grandma! Grandpa! Wait!" But the couple didn't seem to hear. Hand in hand, they turned from her and walked over the small hill in the pasture toward the grove of pecan trees, disappearing in the bright morning sun that cut through the fog.

When Dana reached the top where her grandparents had stood, they were nowhere in sight. She fell to her knees. In her misery, two fireflies lit on her arm. She watched them flitter to her shoulder as rolling tears washed fresh tracks through the dirt on her face. The fireflies flew away when shouts from the barn startled her.

"Over here! I found her! Here!" Mose waved his arms and howled like a hound dog. Dana jumped to her feet and bolted down the hill toward the barn. Noah, in a sprint, arrived at the site and fell into charred grass beside the body of the mother he loved.

Mose had covered Edna's lifeless body with a blanket. "She got out, Noah," he said, laying his hand on his neighbor's shoulder.

Dana fell to the ground beside her father. Noah looked into his daughter's swollen red eyes. "She's truly gone."

Dana threw her arms around his neck. "She's not gone, Daddy. I saw her. And Grandpa. Up there." Dana pointed to the hill in the pasture behind them. "They found a new piece of land to homestead."

In that instant, the sun's rays poured through breaking clouds illuminating the grassy knoll where eternity begins for members of the Wenger family, and fireflies light the way.

Old Time Religion

In 2004, The Paper Journey Press in Wake Forest, North Carolina, first published **OLD TIME RELIGION** in the anthology, *Original Sin: The Seven Deadlies Come Home To Roost.* Under the sin category of gluttony, this story won its special place in the book.

Described as funny, dark, and the most disturbing in this collection, OLD TIME RELIGION touches on many sins. Combining the dark side of religion with the true blessings of salvation is difficult to maneuver in any piece of literature. But isn't that the world in which we live? Actual events inspired this story because, as I have often repeated—there is a fine line between truth and fiction. The question is, can you distinguish between the two?

*I*n 1966, Pastor and Evangelist Earl Angle preached to his Gastonia, North Carolina congregation four times a week and held soul-saving tent revivals across the south. Finagling supper each Sunday with select members of his hometown congregation, Pastor Earl paid particular attention to single mothers and widows with children. Said it was his solemn calling to tend to the fatherless.

Ralph Edwards, a deacon, cornered his pastor in the vestibule before service. Besides reporting names of new members, he mentioned Millie Culver's man no longer lived in the home. "Left her high and dry, he did. Them poor kids of hers. All alone with no daddy. Of course, you must know Millie's father died last year and willed her all his money."

"No. That so?"

"Why yes, and the woman can cook. Land sakes, her pies won blue ribbons at the county fair three years in a row."

With great interest and mounting sympathy, Earl turned his consideration to the Culver family. His bug eyes followed Millie and her children as they entered the sanctuary, and he contemplated the possibilities.

Millie had indeed practiced the fine art of Southern cooking. She set the table and sighed deeply, surprised Pastor Earl asked to be received at her supper table again. At first, his persistent requests for her strawberry pie flattered and amused her. But in the past year of obliging her pastor with homecooked meals, a suspicion gnawed at her innermost thoughts. Annoyed by his constant insistence on eating at her table, she questioned whether her pie or some other need brought him to her house on the second Sunday of every month.

Pastor Earl preached against the sins of adultery and divorce. But Millie never hid the breakup of her marriage. *So why me?* Although few women divorced in the South of the 60s, Millie's was civil. And even more unusual, she agreed to share custody with Tom on the first and third weekends of every month. Still, her pastor's personal attention troubled her. And she distrusted his intentions. As much as she desired a position of importance in the church, she possessed no romantic interest in this rotund man.

❧

"Peggy weren't but three when we divorced, and Kyle was nine," *she told her pastor the first Sunday he sat at her supper table.*

Millie pushed her blonde ringlets off her clammy forehead with the back of her hand. "I never loved him, and he had a wandering eye." She glanced at Earl as he forked fried potatoes and onions into his mouth. "He loved Constance Littman, not me." She sighed and passed him another chicken leg. "Tom always preferred brunettes. Dated me to make her jealous. 'Cept, I got pregnant. Poor Tom, we knew it were a mistake. But I was a sinner, and my daddy didn't want reproach on our family, so I married him. Weren't but sixteen myself."

The pastor kept his conversation at the table to a minimum until he emptied his plate. "Missus Culver, far be it from me to cast the first stone, dear lady. Your children are blessings from Gawd. Pass them biscuits round 'eah again."

Millie felt the need to testify further. "But I was lost, and now I'm found. I just want to raise my kids right. Can't fix what's already been done." Passing the biscuits, her eyes filled with tears. She realized Earl was far more fixated on her food than her pain, as he had nothing more to say.

After supper, instead of driving home, the bloated pastor maneuvered to the Culver family's front porch hammock for an afternoon nap. The front porch thermometer read 102 degrees. The brutal summer heat stifled the lush southern landscape, and every creature moved in slow motion. Especially Earl.

◦~ℓℓ~◦

After a full year of Sundays, this day was no different. "Momma, why's he coming to supper again?"

Millie listened to Peggy whine, knowing she disliked Earl, especially how he looked at everybody with one eye motionless while the other rolled toward the sky or the ground. The neighbor kids stayed away when Pastor Earl came to Sunday supper, which made for a dull day as far as Millie's daughter was concerned.

Weary of explaining the family's monthly ritual of playing host to their pastor, Millie brushed and braided Peggy's hair. "Young'un, he's our guest one Sunday a month. Besides, the Lord's Day is a day of rest. We do church and supper, and that's it. No TV, no games, and you can't run 'round here in a bathing suit when our pastor visits, you understand me?"

"But it's hot, Momma. Please let Tammy come over; we like jumping through the sprinkler."

"This ain't the day to show your legs to company. You're seven years old, girl: time to grow up. Go on now and get your brother. We'll be late for church." Millie ended the conversation by lightly swatting her daughter's backside with the hairbrush. She watched Peggy slide her hand down the hallway wall. *Lord, that girl can't be a lady, no matter how many whippings she gets.*

◦~ℓℓ~◦

Bypassing the blessing, Pastor Earl shoved collard greens into his mouth until Millie interrupted his third bite with, *"Dear Lord, we thank you for our food..."*

She had thawed an extra pack of chicken legs and fried more potatoes than usual. The pastor loaded a considerable amount of collards next to his chicken, potatoes, and gravy, leaving room for pickle relish and stewed corn to spill over the sides of his plate. Peggy handed him an extra napkin and saucer for biscuits and apple butter.

The Culvers watched in amazement, once again, as the ravenous pastor piled his plate twice and then a third time. When he washed down the last two pieces of pecan pie with an entire pitcher of sweet tea, Millie decided that if she ever wanted leftovers in her Frigidaire again, she'd have to stop his gluttonous freeloading.

⌒ele⌒

Peggy Louise picked at the dirt between her toes and glimpsed up occasionally to watch a string of drool slide down Pastor Earl's chin and land on his red satin tie. Standing to cool off from her cramped toe-picking position, she fanned flies away from his sleeping body, a sweltering heap spilling over the edges of her momma's hammock. Beads of sweat glistened on his forehead and his nonexistent upper lip.

Peggy sighed. *That pig must weigh 500 pounds.*

Squatting on the porch steps, she wrapped her arms around her legs. Disgusted with the fat lump of lard sleeping in the hammock, she considered poking at Earl's fleshy jowls. But sure as shootin', her momma would blister her butt if she woke him from his customary Sunday siesta.

Earl had thrown his soiled linen jacket over the porch railing. His white shirt, now wrinkled and wet, heaved up and down around his massive stomach while he snored. She figured if she loosened his tie, he might breathe easier. *Then again, maybe he'll strangle.* "Let him," she said.

His snoring, drooling, and passing loud and lethal amounts of gas were more than Peggy could stand. With her shoes in hand, she ran off to find her brother. Kyle had to see the sleeping pile of poop on their front porch, and maybe he would find it as sickening as she did.

The tool shed door stood wide open. Kyle huddled in the corner, reading his Spiderman comic. Peggy approached with her usual caution so as not to piss him off. "Kyle, come see. Ol' Earl's done passed out in Momma's hammock again."

"Leave me be, and who cares if he's in a food coma? Let him die. I hope he does."

"What's the matter with you, goober?"

"Nothing. Let me be. And for your information, I ain't going back to Momma's church again. Ever! She can whip me 'til I bleed; I ain't going. Now I told you, get out of here!"

Peggy had never heard her brother talk like that. "I'm telling Momma," she hollered, skipping to the tire swing.

"Good!" Kyle said, slamming the shed door.

Millie dried the last serving bowl and placed it in her cupboard. She untied her apron and wiped away more stray hair. Summer's heat had grown unbearable. Window screens swayed inward as fans rattled, pulling at humid air that had no desire to be moved. She peeked through the screen door and shook her head at Earl, sweating bullets in her hammock again. *I'll have to hose it down tomorrow.* Millie stepped out the back to avoid waking him and stopped dead in her tracks. Something didn't ring right. *Did he wink at me during supper? Or Kyle?*

At thirteen, Kyle suffered from puberty and mood swings, but today he seemed more touchy than usual. She found her son where Peggy had left him earlier.

"Where's your sister?" Millie asked.

"Didn't know it was my day to watch her," he said.

"Young man, do I need to discipline you on the Lord's Day?"

"Sorry, Momma."

She stared at the top of her son's head. "Might as well spill what's bothering you before it's time to return for evening service." Millie watched him take a deep breath.

"I ain't going back to church."

"And why not?"

Kyle stood. Almost her height, he hesitated, then met her eye to eye. It unnerved her. "I don't believe like you do. I think Daddy has the right idea. Love God, be a good person, and you'll still go to heaven without having to attend church and be a hypocrite."

"Who's a hypocrite? Me?"

"No, Momma. Not you."

"Who then? Who's the hypocrite?"

"Can't say."

"Why not?"

"You won't believe me."

Millie lowered herself to the cool tool shed floor and motioned for her son to join her. "Is it Earl? What's the matter? What'd he say, Kyle? Tell Momma. I won't be mad. Just tell me the truth. I'd believe you before anyone in the wide world."

Kyle's words spilled out, along with his tears. "Me and Pastor Earl, we was sitting on the porch today while you and Peggy made supper. I tried, Momma. I tried to be nice to him, like you told me. He asked me to come sit by him. Said he wanted to show me a magic trick. Told me to close my eyes. So, I did. He kissed me, Momma. He kissed me on the mouth. Hard. I wanted to puke my guts out."

Millie reached out and encased her son's face between her small hands. The agony of his revelation tore at the core of her maternal being. Anger toward her pastor mounted to fury. Tears pooled in her eyes when she spoke. "Kyle, baby. This ain't Jesus' way, and he don't make men do this to little boys. You don't have to worry about not going to church because I ain't going back there either. We'll find us a new church, even if it means being holy at home."

Now she understood why Earl insisted on visiting only on the Sundays she had the children. It wasn't her he cared about. Or even her cooking. He wanted her son. Like a mother bear, Millie's rage grew hotter than the oppressive summer sun. Rushing toward her front porch hammock, she saw that Earl had rolled onto his side, his backside exposed. Rounding the corner at a fast clip, she kicked his enormous bulging butt as hard and as far as her foot would go. Millie lunged at him like that momma bear, scratching him, pounding him with her fists, slapping and spitting, exploding in ferocity born from the heartbreak of it all. She screeched, "Get off my property!" Any witness would've sworn she had lost her mind.

Startled, Pastor Earl rolled out of the hammock and landed on the porch floor. "What's gone on 'eah?" he yelled. "Why you do this, Missus Culver? Why?"

Millie gritted her teeth, then spit. "You sonofabitch, you molested my boy! You lustful sonofabitch! You kissed him, he told me, and I want you off my property now, or I'm calling the sheriff! Don't you ever come back!" She pummeled him again with her fists. "Me and mine will never step foot in that blasphemous church again!"

Their pastor grabbed his coat from the porch railing, hurried down the steps, and ran to his Cadillac. "You tell anybody 'bout this, Missus Culver, and I'll see you lose those brats. You 'eah me?!"

"Burn in Hell, Earl Angle, you fat bastard! Burn in Hell!" She chased him, throwing rocks at his car as he escaped.

Millie's legs shook, standing in her driveway. Crying and bewildered, she crossed her arms against her body, holding a bruised hand, and turning slowly. Peggy and Kyle stood frozen on the porch, their eyes wide and mouths open like hungry pups. When she unfolded her arms, they ran to her. Millie embraced her children as if she had snatched them from the claws of Satan himself. She stumbled back to the porch but collapsed short of the steps. Kyle attempted to help her stand, but they all landed in the dirt, holding each other as if their world had turned upside down.

Millie knew her daughter had heard the whole fighting match. The pain in her heart transformed into a sick and fiery pile of guilt. *How did I allow this to happen to my children?*

Peggy's tiny arms encircled her mother's neck, then reached for her brother.

When Kyle patted her injured hand, Millie's heart broke. Unable to control her sobbing convulsions, she pulled him close.

"Momma, please. Mom, it's okay. Please stop crying." Surprised at her son's smile, she kissed his forehead. "I didn't know you had it in you," he said. "You beat the tar out of him! You whipped his ass!" Kyle wrapped his arms around her shoulders. His eyes brimmed with tenderness and tears that cut her to her core. "Don't cry, Momma," he said and smiled again. I guess Jesus *really does* love me. Just like you."

The following Sunday, Pastor Earl Angle made his usual grand entrance. His congregation stood and applauded as he strutted to his pulpit and wailed, "Gimme that old-time religion; it's good enough for me! Yes, Gawd, I 'eah what you're trying to tell your children tonight. You reap the seeds you sow, dear people. It's time to plant your financial seeds. Who's got twenty dollars to give to Jesus tonight?"

Pastor Earl searched the congregation and found the family he'd invited to church sitting on the front pew. He smiled and nodded, delighted in his soul-winning ability. He had contacted the recent widow after reading Tuesday's obituary. Howard Dunning had suffered a heart attack, leaving his wife, Betsy, a cook at the local diner, and their three young sons.

Pigment of My Imagination

It may surprise you that the protagonist in **PIGMENT OF MY IMAGINATION** is a man. But he's definitely *fried*, and the woman he loves is out of reach. In his feeble attempt to rescue her, he is inadequate at best.

I sliced this story from the TELEVENGE trilogy during one of its many drafts. Ken Kopper moved me as a soft-spoken man with a conscience. He begged me to develop him into his own narrative, and I gave in. I'm glad I did. I love these characters. Their desires are timeless, as are their messages—good or evil. The story deals with sensitive issues of race, regret, and longing for something you can never have.

~ **November 1974** ~

Ken Kopper opened the Kopper Kettle Diner for breakfast. After placing the *Open* sign in the window, the front door's pull shade slipped out of his hand, rolled up, and smacked the top of the window at the exact moment a ladder flew at his face from the other side. Glass shattered on the sidewalk and the diner's gray and white tile floor. It sounded like a bomb. Startled, Ken hopped away from the door to avoid injury but fell backward, knocking the brass coat rack behind him to the floor. Another bomb.

Corbet Butcher dropped his toolbox to the sidewalk in apparent shock. Two men, one on each side of the busted door, stared at each other—speechless. Corbet's runaway ladder would cost him this time. Ken shook his head, watching his friend tiptoe closer to the door and peek through the jagged hole.

The glass cracked under Corbet's boots, his face red in embarrassment. "G-Godamighty, Ken. I-I-I'm sorry. It slipped, d-didn't see it s-slip—Golly."

Ken pulled himself up to the nearest booth and rubbed his bad leg. "I'll deduct it from what I owe you."

"Uh-that'd b-be fine, m-my fault. Got a broom?"

"I'll clean it up; just repair my blasted sign." Ken picked a piece of glass out of the heel of his hand. His temper in check, as always, he limped to his supply closet for a bucket, a broom, a dustpan, and a Band-Aid.

Corbet stood five feet eleven inches with square shoulders, stringy dirt-brown hair, and a right blue eye. The left one was blind and clouded over, but also blue. His speech impediment annoyed most folks. So, Ken usually did Corbet's talking for him.

People assumed Corbet and Ken were brothers, their resemblance eerily similar. Loyal friend and customer, Corbet arrived daily with news and opinions of local current events. But on that chilly morning, he wasn't a patron. Ken had hired him as a handyman. The sign over the diner needed work. Two bulbs burned out. One under a *P* and the other under the coffee cup. The only part of the sign visible in the dark was the steam rising out of the cup. Open until two in the morning, the diner attracted second shifts from the local newspaper and Baptist Hospital. Ken wanted his sign fixed.

After duct-taping thick plastic over the hole where the window had been, Ken called Eugene Guthrie at the local hardware. Eugene hooted, hollered, and belly laughed into the phone. "You hired that dimwit? Whoo, wee! That's a good one, Ken. Sure, I'll drive over after lunch to fix you up. That redneck idiot! Why the hell did you hire him? Blind in one eye and cain't half see out of the other. Oh—my, that's a good one—sorry, I cain't—stop laughing!"

Ken held the receiver away from his ear while Eugene kept on. "Ol' Corbet cain't change a damn light bulb without shutting down all of Winston-Salem! Whoo, that's ripe—good one. Lord, Ken, he ain't no handyman—he's a nut! Oh—me!"

"Come fix my damn door, Eugene!" Ken slammed down the phone.

⁓ℓℓ⁓

The glass scratched at the sidewalk as Ken swept it into a pile. He ignored Corbet on the ladder, tearing apart his sign. Ken figured it might get fixed without further incident if they didn't talk.

Corbet shook his head. "You hear 'b-bout all the t-t-trouble in Brown Town on account of that c-colored man, Lightner, b-being elected Raleigh's mayor? First time in this s-state. Never thought I'd see it in my lifetime." He dropped a new light bulb that popped like a firecracker when it hit the sidewalk. "Shit." Corbet fished another from his toolbox.

Ken swept it up with the rest. "Don't fall, Corbet. Don't even talk right now. Fix the sign. And quit calling the east side of town Brown Town. Good God, get over it. I'm sick of it."

"What?"

"Just fix the goddamn sign and get down!"

"Sorry! I'm real s-sorry; d-didn't I-I t-tell you I w-was s-sorry?"

Ken sighed. "Yes—yes, you did." Wiping his hand on his flannel shirt, his Band-Aid rolled off. He hesitated, but he had to calm Corbet down. "Apology accepted." Examining the cut, it appeared deeper than he first thought. Blood dripped onto his jeans and boots and dotted the sidewalk. He needed stitches. He slid the broken glass into the bucket and watched Corbet slump over the ladder. Ken cleared his throat. "There's coffee and a ham biscuit when you're done. On the house." He couldn't chew out his friend. They were like brothers. About every other month, Corbet stayed in Ken's apartment when he got evicted from his own.

Glad it ain't too cold today. Closing the bandaged door, Ken hobbled into the kitchen and stitched up his hand. After opening a bottle of Mercurochrome, he dabbed the wound with a stinging icy swab. His hand throbbed, but Ken wrapped it tight before limping over to fire up his grill. He chuckled despite the pain. "What a gimp I must look like."

Ken refused to go off on Corbet or anybody else. His old man had exploded on humanity every chance he got. Ken wanted no part of that now. But he knew Corbet was right. Every White person in Winston-Salem called the east side of town Brown Town. The term originated long before Ken was born, and everyone called it Brown Town as if it were its given name.

Trouble brewed near File Street at Bluey Jones' juke joint. It'd been breaking news the past three days since the state elections.

The jury still held out on how the South of the 70s would continue to uphold Civil Rights laws.

When Vince Kopper was alive, he hung a confederate flag on the wall over the booths of his diner. It didn't matter to Ken's dad what occurred at the Woolworth counter in Greensboro. His diner was off-limits. Vince kept his sign in the window. NO COLORED.

~ July 1962 ~

"You know I fought with Patton. Ken's going to Nam." Vince Kopper announced it to his customers like it was a rite of passage to manhood.

"I heard things are heating up over there," said a customer.

"Yeah, but it'll make him a man. Teach him a few things about life. You forget the women you've bedded, all the places you've been, but by God, you never forget your war. Best part of my life."

"Mine too, Vince."

"Me too."

"Damn straight."

"Make him a right smart man, Vince."

Ken huddled behind the swinging door to the kitchen, listening to their war cries. It didn't matter to his dad that the military had started shipping soldiers back in body bags or reported them missing. Ken picked up the phone and called Corbet. He wasn't afraid to die; he just didn't want to watch anyone else do it.

Vince wiped the Formica counter with a greasy rag. "No son of mine is a coward! No, sir. We come from a long line of patriots. I'm taking him and Corbet to the Army recruiter tomorrow morning."

Ken stepped out of the kitchen and stood beside his dad. Customers greeted Ken as if he'd already come home a war hero. The elation on Vince's face lit up the dining room.

"You must be proud, Vince."

"You bet. Wish his mother could see him."

It was the last time his dad put his arm around Ken, hugged him—and even kissed him, in front of a row of five decorated veterans sitting on bar stools, drinking cups of coffee, smoking unfiltered Camels, sharing war stories, battle scars, and old tattoos.

That night, Ken and Corbet decided to get drunk one last time before morphing into mighty men of valor.

Ken approached his dad months before, explaining to his stone-cold face that he wanted to go to college, be a social worker—help people. Dreams that struck his dad like a punch to the kidneys. "There's a lot of social injustice; I want to make a difference, go to law school—"

"—Law school? Why the hell do you want to be a bloodsucker? And you can forget social work. Social worker means *Communism* in my book." Vince pounded his fist on the counter. "No son of mine's some *Commie lover traitor*! Forget it!"

"But—"

"—One more word, and I'll beat it out of you with my strap!" The old razor strap hung on a nail in his dad's bedroom. He'd belt-buckled Ken's backside for less sass than this. His dad's response didn't surprise him. A veteran of the *big one*, Vince had fought the Nazis. Communism, Socialism, Marxism, and Fascism all meant the same thing to a man like Vince Kopper. He was more scared of *catching* Communism than typhoid, the measles, or venereal disease.

Vince claimed the day his son was born, he shot out of his mother like a cannonball. That the infantry was his destiny! From that day, Vince planned Ken's military future down to the minute. And so, for his dad's sake, for Vince to hold up his crew cut head around his crew of regular customers, Ken lived to please his dad and agreed to join the Army after graduation. Ken knew nothing *he* wanted mattered.

But the blessed event of Vince turning his son over to Uncle Sam never happened. The car accident had seen to that. When Ken woke up in Baptist Hospital, the pain of rejection and defeat spoke loud and clear in his dad's eyes. Instead of returning home with war wounds, a purple heart, and honor, Ken convalesced in shame, his leg broken in three places from a fast Chevy and four cases of Pabst Blue Ribbon.

Even though Corbet lost sight in his left eye after his head busted through the windshield, Vince never forgave Corbet, either. He swore Ken and Corbet slammed into the tree on purpose. A desperate and convenient excuse to never face the guns in a Vietnamese foxhole.

Ken recuperated in the tiny apartment above the diner and asked to learn about the restaurant business to ease some of his dad's blatant disappointment. But the two barely spoke afterward. Nobody won in the end. Vince never got to brag about his son shooting gooks in the trenches. Ken never went to college, never married, never saw the ocean, and never did anything after that but try to make his old man happy.

⌒ele⌒

"What the hell are you doing?" Vince wrapped his leathery hand around his son's neck and yanked him into the kitchen.

"Sir?"

The fire in his dad's eyes sent chills down Ken's spine. Vince flashed yellowed teeth, and his mouth was rigid. Pulling Ken by the back of his flannel shirt, he hissed, "You heard me. We don't serve niggers in here!"

"The man just wanted a glass of water and a sandwich. He paid me and left a nice tip, for Christ's sake."

"Jesus Christ ain't got nothing to do with this, boy. Why did you let him sit at my counter?"

"Dad, I don't get it; he's a man, just a man, like you or me."

"He's a goddamn nigger! Don't you ever, *EVER*, allow another nigger in this diner, you hear me? Was anybody else in here? Did anybody see him come or go?"

"No. The place was empty. Why do you care? It's skin pigment, Dad, and that's the only difference between him and us. Skin pigment. Why do you imagine the worst about everybody with black skin?"

"A pigment of my imagination. Is that what you think? Bullshit." Vince plopped down at his makeshift desk in the kitchen corner. "I have to make me a bigger sign!"

Ken sighed and shook his head.

"Don't you disagree with me, boy! They're more different than you know. It's time you came to one of my meetings."

Ken forced a couple of swallows; his throat had gone dry. *Why didn't God delete skin pigment altogether?* He drew the line at his dad's *meetings*. "We got customers." Ken dragged his bad leg out to the counter. The subject of his dad's *meetings* never came up again. Ken decided he'd rather wreck another car and ruin his other leg than become what Vince was. A proud veteran, a prominent business owner, a member of the Klan.

The day his dad died, Ken yanked the confederate flag off the wall and replaced it with the stars and stripes handed to him at graveside. Then he limped to the diner's front window, grabbed the NO COLORED sign, and drove the ten miles back to Magnolia Acres Cemetery and the graves reserved for military. Wilted flowers in plastic baskets rested haphazardly around fresh red dirt piled on Vince's grave. The funeral home hadn't even taken down the tent. Ken shredded the sign over his dad's final resting place. The pieces blew into the cracks and crevices of earth, grass, flowers, and the new headstone marking Vince Kopper's remains.

~ February 1975 ~

When they built the Kopper Kettle Diner in the early 50s, they wedged it between the Western Auto and the Glass Slipper Beauty Shop on 2nd Street. It stretched wide enough to seat twelve at the counter and deep enough to fit two rows of booths along the windows. A large pass-through to the kitchen allowed Ken to work at the grill and watch his employees and customers simultaneously.

Turning the sign from *Closed* to *Open*, Ken poked his head through the doorway to catch the first warm spring breezes but spotted Merida Holcomb in her red, white, and blue voting dress instead. He noticed she wore it three days in a row after the November elections and had it on again. She had traveled door to door with her petitions and worked hard for Black voter registration.

Merida made a beeline out of the Rexall across the street and headed toward the diner. She lived in the apartment over the drugstore and cleaned most of the retail shops and businesses on the block. Next to Corbet, she was Ken's best friend, if he could say he had one. He imagined Vince rolled over in his grave every time Merida waltzed into the diner.

Quite possibly, she was his mother's age, though he was never sure and wasn't planning to ask. Her laugh chimed like bells, up and down the scale. Plump and tidy, she'd taken care of him, cleaned his apartment, and washed his one load of laundry each week in exchange for a free meal now and then. When Vince died, Merida noticed the sign gone and toted a macaroni and cheese casserole across the street. That was the day Ken and Merida became friends.

The morning sun shone on her face as she bounded through the door. "Kenny boy, I came home late from Bible study last night. Osa got to talkin', and you know how she do go on. Well, Osa's boy drop me off and waited 'til I got up the stairs and into my place, 'cause we seen some White man snoopin' 'round on the street. I peeked out my front room window and watched him cross over to the diner. He took a long look in the windows, real suspicious like. He been 'round town b'fore."

Ken laid a tray of mustard and ketchup bottles on the counter and nodded to Sophie, his waitress, who had walked in behind Merida. "Lots of people snoop around town after dark."

"This was different. A car pulled up fast to the curb, and he hop in. A bunch of mens hid inside. The streetlight showed 'em. Be careful, Kenny. You know they still mad you didn't join up with your daddy."

Ken smiled, mildly amused at Merida's ramblings. "There's no more Klan."

"Tha's what you think. Tha's what they want everybody to think. By the way, I heard Mavis is comin' home. Her Aunt Lula say she be here a while. Maybe she go sing at the church. I'll tell her to stop by and see you."

"Thanks, but I doubt Mavis remembers me."

"Sure, she do. She ate at your diner every day with her friend after school." Merida slid off the stool and dashed toward the door. "Gots to run; I be deliverin' your laundry this afternoon."

Ken didn't get the chance to say thanks. She walked faster than any woman he knew. She'd always said a tribe of wild Baptists raised her, and she wasn't kidding.

His heart warmed, remembering Mavis, and he smiled. Born to a White father and a Black mother, Mavis had suffered undeserved hardships. That much Ken knew of her. Staring at the floor as if searching for a face in a dark pit below him, Ken recalled he had not shed one tear since his dad's death. *So many times, I wanted to ask her on a date. I would've loved to have given you some sweet brown grandchildren, you self-righteous bastard.*

⁓ＥＬＥ ⁓

Early morning's low light brought in the day's first customers. Corbet, naturally, and Eugene Guthrie.

Eugene's craggy face and twice-broken nose became the butt of jokes around town. Small and stocky, his narcissism and spooky affinity for hardware got on Ken's last nerve. Eugene seldom used hardware; he only liked to sell it. Sarcastic and quick-witted in a dark, sharp-edged way, he was prone to anxious twitches and restless shrugs and licked his fingers after a meal. Rapidly balding at forty, Eugene's dome poked through his few comb-over strands. With a coffee cup in one hand, his free hand fidgeted with his bow tie, then palmed a greasy shock of graying hair off his forehead. His brown eyes darted around the room before he spoke. "Corbet, you been busy? You make enough money to pay your rent this month?"

"I-I'll have you know, Eugene, I m-m-make out fine as a handyman. I do g-g-good work."

"Yeah. So I hear. You did a hell of a job on Ken's front door."

"D-don't start with m-me, Eugene. Me and K-Ken are s-square."

Ken picked his pencil from behind his ear to take their orders and sensed Corbet's need for him to agree. But as usual, Ken kept his thoughts and comments to himself. His quiet nature developed from years of refusing to be like his dad, causing him to lose a few customers, primarily those who knew and loved his old man.

"What'll you have, Eugene?" asked Ken.

"KKK omelet, whites only," he said.

Ken ignored him. "Ham, eggs, and biscuits; your usual."

"Right," he snickered, trying to get a reaction from Corbet.

Corbet hunkered down over his coffee and opened the newspaper. He hated Eugene.

"You folks get up on the wrong side of the bed? It's a joke!"

Ken hollered through the pass-through, "Not to you, it's not!"

"You're right about that, Ken, my boy. Says somewhere in the Bible, in the Book of Tribulations, I do believe, about the difference in the races."

"Not in my Bible," said Ken.

"Since when, Eugene, do y-you read the Bible?" Corbet asked.

Ken didn't feel like arguing. He left the two stooges to finish their breakfast, said he had paperwork in the back, and to check with Sophie if they needed anything.

"Thanks. Thanks a lot," Sophie whispered as she sliced pie for lunch.

Ken had listened to Eugene and Corbet bicker back and forth enough over the years to fill a book. Recently, he'd heard Eugene had become more of a brazen bigot than usual, ignoring any Black person who walked into his establishment. He figured one of these days, the trouble in Brown Town was sure to land on every street in North Carolina because of people like Eugene.

But Ken also recognized Eugene as a bully who lived to torment Corbet. Simple-minded and slow, Corbet repeated things he heard and read, never knowing what they meant. He wouldn't have made it through school if Ken hadn't helped him. Corbet pored over the newspaper, word for word. It made him feel smart, at least. Neither friend nor foe to the Black man on the street, Corbet spoke to anyone kind to him. For all the reading he did, Corbet Butcher was plainly ignorant when it came to people.

Customers straggled in and out all morning. Weary of it all, Ken wanted to sleep. Sleep and dream of Mavis. His leg gave him fits, his head pounded; his heart longed to be touched. In truth, he never had an opportunity to fall in love with Mavis. A good ten years older than her, he didn't stand a chance. Especially since she moved to New York City after graduation to become a famous singer. She was worldly; he'd not traveled out of North Carolina. Her voice was angelic; his twang curled his tongue so bad no visiting Yankee understood him. She was Black, *and* she was beautiful. He'd not had a date since the accident. Nobody looked twice at him except for the occasional hooker running into the diner to escape the rain. And he limped—constantly.

Ken flipped a few pancakes on his griddle when he heard a customer yell at Sophie,

"Hey, you serve shit on a shingle?"

"You see it on the menu?" Sophie could sling hash better than anybody. She'd worked for Ken as breakfast and lunch help for the past two years. Another waitress took over during evening hours. Sophie slid the order in the window. "Eggs over easy."

Ken took a quick peek at the customer on the stool next to Eugene. Definitely a loudmouth, he had squeezed into a powder blue polyester blazer and sported a yellow tie to match his blonde flat top. He talked football to Eugene as if he coached the Vikings.

"Yeah, I've crunched a lot of cartilage in my day," said the loudmouth.

Sophie poured him another cup of coffee. She returned to the kitchen to fill her tray with an order and said, "Yeah, and he ought to clip his nose hairs."

His deafening, non-stop, play-by-play rundown of the Super Bowl cleared the booth behind him. Two elderly ladies shot him with looks of disgust, swinging their pocketbooks out the door. He lit a cigarette and pounded the counter, amused at his jokes.

His fork fell on the floor, and he yelled at Sophie again. "Hey, sweetie, get me another fork."

She slammed one down by his plate.

"Testy little thing, ain't she?" He laughed, watching her walk away. "Damn that receiver. *I* could've caught that ball! It just slipped through his hands, poor bastard."

Strangely enough, Ken had seen him somewhere before. The sizzle and smoke from the griddle and the noise of the diner impaired him from hearing the rest of the man's conversation with Eugene. He noticed their talk intensifying. They'd gone from discussing football to something more serious.

"Ken, see you tomorrow." Eugene waved and left his breakfast companion alone at the counter.

Ken nodded, then hobbled over to clear Eugene's dishes.

The loudmouth's beady eyes shrunk to tiny dots. "You own this place, boy?"

"Yeah. And I'm not a boy."

He pinched his cigarette, took a long drag, blew the smoke straight up as if it would hit the ceiling, then sipped his coffee. "I hear you've got a checkered past."

"Who are you? What do you want?"

"They call me Bull. I hear you're a nigger lover."

"Why don't you pay your bill and leave, Bull. Now. I think that'd be a good idea."

"Fine." He stood to leave. That's when Ken noticed it, a pin in his lapel. The red circle, the white cross. "You shamed your daddy, boy. I'd be careful if I were you."

Ken counted five new customers that day, all with the same pins on their lapels. Merida was right. The Klan was alive and well, living in Winston-Salem and eating in his diner.

At two-twenty in the morning, he crawled up the steps and fell into bed. Eighteen-hour days, seven days a week for the past ten years, his inherited diner would kill him, too, in the end.

Ken passed his hand along the other side of the bed, registering once again he was alone. Another part of his brain recognized he was an early riser, and it was time to get up.

His joints creaked and popped, threatening to drown out those of his metal spring mattress. Easing himself upright, he threw his legs over the edge of the bed and massaged the stiffness out of his knee, then reached across the chair beside the bed and snagged his watch from its place. Five-thirty.

Ken filled the bathroom sink with steaming water, then lathered Gillette Foamy on his face while examining it and his wild hair in the mirror. Lines had formed in his cheeks, along with two-day-old razor stubble around his lopsided smile. His eyes had always been blue. They gleamed back at him from beneath a heavy brow; the new wrinkles at the corners reflected his careworn life that seemed to grow deeper the past few days. A thick, muscled neck flared into broad shoulders, outspanning the edges of the mirror, sloping down to a chest made powerful from lifting heavy trays and using a wheelchair before learning to walk again. He'd be thirty-one years old next week; he looked forty and felt fifty.

Unfolding his straight razor, he scraped away his night beard. Dawn crept through the curtainless window. It had rained; puddles formed in the street. A man walked his dog; a jogger ran past and jumped over sidewalk litter. A siren blared in the distance. The same sounds and sights every morning.

The emptiness of the past ten years since his dad's death had found him lacking and lonely. Though Ken didn't consider himself old in years, further inspection of his hair showed the first signs of gray. Dark shadows from little to no sleep circled his eyes. He had zero sense of fashion, charm, or etiquette and no concept of how to act around pretty women. Especially one he liked. Time hadn't stood still waiting for him to catch up, fall in love, start a family, or take a vacation. He felt his life slipping away. He had to find himself. Or die trying.

Ken's hand trembled slightly, filling his cup with more coffee. The pain in his leg wasn't any worse than before, simply different. It was Sunday, the heathen hour. The hours between ten and noon, before the holy rollers let out of church and the restaurants fill up. A time when heathens can get a good seat—don't have to wait in line. But there was never a wait at the Kopper Kettle Diner. Not anymore.

Whistling with the radio, he startled when the front door's bell jingled. In walked a pregnant Andie Oliver and Ken's secret flame, Mavis Dumass. His eyes burned a path from her big green eyes to her unbelievably full lips, down to the hollow of her neck where they rested on the see-through blouse that left little to the imagination. Her golden-bronze smooth skin and delicate but tall frame glowed like the woman Mavis was.

Before shuffling out to greet them, he stopped whistling. *Girls hate older men and their vibrato whistles.* A couple of high school girls mentioned it once. When he'd served them their cheeseburgers. While whistling.

Ken shoved his pencil over his ear and ignored the pain in his leg. He smiled wide, then led them to a booth that faced the street. "Glad to see you both; been a while—hey, Mavis."

"Hey, Ken. Good to see you, too."

The girls slid across the wooden benches opposite each other and simultaneously wiped crumbs from their respective sides of the wooden table. It was a piece of their past, and they fell into it like a pair of old shoes. Worn and comfortable. They knew the menu by heart. They'd studied together there, ate the cheapest items on the menu, and drank fifty-cent cups of coffee. Ken recalled how Mavis always asked him to help her with math, and Andie called him Koppy.

"Didn't know you were expecting, Andie."

"Yeah, Koppy, in a month." She patted the top of her baby-filled belly. "New menus?"

"Nah, just cleaned off the old ones. I'll get y'all some sweet tea."

"That'd be great," Andie said.

Reluctantly, he walked away but strained to listen to their conversation.

"Lawdy, Andie. Ain't had me a mess of barbeque since the graduation party your mama gave me before I left town."

"Go ahead, indulge. You'll puke it up later."

Mavis cackled, "In that case, I'll get the slaw and fries on the side."

Andie and Mavis had been friends all their lives. That much Ken knew, and he knew Andie had taken some heat during high school as a White girl with a Black best friend. He'd heard Andie's daddy marched in Washington with Dr. Martin Luther King. One of the few White men who dared. Vince Kopper had discussed it at length with his customers and refused to serve Andie's family at the diner. It still embarrassed Ken, and he remembered the incident like it happened yesterday.

The door's bell jingled again. Ken looked up and squinted; the sun's rays poured through the front windows, highlighting floating dust. Two regular Sunday customers, Melvin Johnson and his wife, Beulah, strolled in. Sophie grabbed silverware and two plastic-covered menus and led them to the booth opposite Andie and Mavis.

Middle-aged with slicked-back salt and pepper hair, Melvin nodded to Ken. His maroon double-knit polyester pants seemed tighter than usual, and his white shoes matched his leather belt. Melvin's typical Baptist ensemble. Ken smiled at Melvin's pocket protector filled with ballpoint pens, always arranged in his left shirt pocket, while his New Testament sat in his right pocket. Nothing changed. Even his wife. Dowdy and tasteless, Beulah wore the same cheap gold-tone shoes and navy cotton dress to his dad's funeral. Ken noticed the couple glaring at the girls in the next booth. Andie, clearly a pregnant White woman, laughing and carrying on with a stunning Black woman who obviously had money and dressed accordingly.

Baptist man spoke up, "Was a time when they didn't allow Negras and prostitutes in this diner."

Ken watched Andie and Mavis freeze in their seat, apparently unsure they had heard him correctly. But Ken heard the old racist just fine. Pissed off and dragging his bad leg, he hobbled over to the back of the booth where the couple sat. On top of the previous morning's threats by a flatulent flattop blowhard, he refused to tolerate hatred in his diner. Not one more day. He'd listened to it all his life; it was time to speak up.

Ken rested one arm on the booth behind Melvin's head, leaned on it, and said, "True enough, Melvin. Years ago, when you and my dad wore bed sheets on your heads and burned crosses in folks' front yards, only White people were allowed in this establishment."

Sophie walked over to freshen their coffee and to listen to Ken.

"But my dad's dead, and I've owned this diner for nearly ten years. One day I had a nasty car accident, you remember, I almost lost my leg. I'd be dogged if I didn't need some blood because I nearly lost all mine. Got me a rare type and only one colored man came to my rescue; he gave me some of his blood. Since that day, I understood that the same color of blood flows through all people's veins, and their money is as good as mine or yours. Besides, these two ladies have eaten at the Kopper Kettle since they were too young to drive."

Ken shifted his weight off his bad leg and leaned on the other side of their booth. "War's been over nearly a hundred and some years; ain't likely the South will rise again anytime soon. So, if you and your missus don't like the patrons in my diner, I suggest you haul yourselves to the McDonald's down the street."

He started to walk back to the kitchen, but stopped and rubbed his last comment in the old bigot's face. "Lord, Melvin, there's Black folks at McDonald's too. You may have to eat at home to keep away from them." Ken cleared his throat and motioned to his waitress, "Sophie can take your order."

Ken turned and winked at Mavis and Andie. Mavis stood, applauded, and whistled. Andie saluted him from her seat. Melvin Johnson stood and threw some change on the table for their coffee while Beulah scooted across the booth seat. Filled with obvious indignation, they hurried out.

It surprised Ken when Mavis bounded through the kitchen door. "Ken—hey, thanks. Looks like your dad died at the right time; I might never have been able to eat here."

"True enough," he said. "But times are changing."

"Ain't changing fast enough." She reached out and touched him on his chest. "You've touched my heart, though. I've never known any White guy to do that. Except for my daddy. You're a brave soul." She smiled, then stepped back and looked around as if shocked to find herself in the kitchen. Then she winked at Ken, turned, and walked back to eat lunch with Andie.

He sighed. *No, not brave. If I were brave, I'd ask you out. And I'd be a lawyer or something other than this.*

But Mavis was right about a few things. Ken learned years ago, White folks in small North Carolina towns still flew confederate flags on the courthouse steps and in their front yards. In rural areas, where people lived in dilapidated mobile homes and decorated their porches with refrigerators, old couches, and collarless dogs, Black folks still refused to drive through those areas, especially at night. Mavis was safer in New York City. For the first time, Ken was glad she'd moved above the Mason-Dixon line.

Sophie yelled back to the kitchen. "Ken! It's Mavis Dumass on the phone."

His heart raced. *Why would she call me?* "Yeah, hey, Mavis," he said, resting the phone receiver on his shoulder and wiping his hands on a towel.

"Ken, I need to ask you a favor."

"Sure. Shoot."

"I need a private booth Monday morning at nine. I'm meeting a certain man, and he won't see me unless it's in private. Can't be in the main eating area."

"I suppose you could use one of the two booths in the back I usually hold for any overflow. Course, ain't used much lately."

"Thanks. You're a doll."

Yeah, I'm a doll. I'm giving the girl of my dreams a private booth to meet another man.

❧

Mavis arrived early, thanked him again, then stuck a twenty-dollar bill in his shirt pocket. He handed it back to her. "Ain't something illegal going on here, is there?"

"No," she giggled. "I'm meeting a well-known preacher this morning, and he doesn't want anyone to know he's here with me. Got it?"

"You having an affair?"

She gave him a soft hoot. "No. Nothing like that. We don't see eye-to-eye on a few things, that's all."

"I'll leave you alone. Sorry, I had to ask."

"I'd ask too if this were my place. Thanks for the booth. I need to keep it private and hope you won't say anything when you see who it is. By the way, he'll arrive at the back door. Will you let him in through the kitchen?"

"Sure. But don't make it a habit. Meeting men this way, I mean."

"No problem. I'm on my way back to New York soon."

"Sorry to hear it."

"Really?"

Their eyes met, and for an instant, he almost said yes. But he smiled instead and set a pot of coffee on the table.

He watched her pour a cup; her hands shook. She pulled out her lipstick and a mirror from her purse and checked her face. When she worked her lipstick back into the tube, she seemed annoyed. Her mysterious preacher was late. She laid a napkin on her lap.

Ken hesitated, then asked, "You okay? Anything I can do to help?"

"No. Just—whatever you hear, please keep it to yourself."

"You know me, Fort Knox Ken. Andie still attend that House of Praise church?"

"Yeah."

"Isn't that the crazy televangelist, Reverend Artury?"

"Yeah." Mavis stared straight ahead.

"Okay then. I'm here if you need me." Ken wasn't sure Mavis heard him. She stared, trance-like, at the wall as he limped back to the kitchen.

Sophie seated customers in booths and at the counter. Someone dropped their knife and hollered for a clean one. The smell of bacon and sausage frying floated through the diner while Ken filled breakfast orders. His customers appeared oblivious to Mavis sitting in an obscure booth in the back, and he jumped when he heard the knock at the back door.

Reverend Calvin Artury stood there somewhat relaxed and out of character in dark sunglasses, jeans, a ball cap, and sneakers. A thin tuft of hair stuck out of the top of his plaid shirt that opened to the third button. If it wasn't for his gold watch, pinky ring, and the gold Cadillac parked in the alley, he looked like every other redneck who walked into the diner.

Ken pointed to the back room. The Reverend's cologne lingered in the kitchen, overpowering the smell of grease on the grill. Ken watched the odd way the televangelist strut up to Mavis, startling her as he slid into the booth.

Wonder what it's all about? He watched them talking, neither one smiling except in disgust.

Limping in, Ken didn't so much as blink an eyelash at the Reverend. Mavis ordered a big breakfast for herself. Ken turned to the preacher.

"Just coffee, thanks."

"It's a shame," Mavis said. "Ken here cooks a mean omelet."

"No, thanks."

Ken winked at Mavis and headed back to the kitchen. He had barely turned around when he heard, "Will he keep his mouth shut?"

"Who, Ken? He's a good ol' boy. Believe me, you can trust Ken Kopper. I assure you he hears lots of stuff in this diner, and the man's as safe as Fort Knox."

Ken told Sophie he'd bus the tables. In truth, he wanted to keep an eye on the back room since the conversation between Mavis and her minister friend seemed heated.

Serving Mavis breakfast, he kept his composure and poured the Reverend more coffee. Reverend Artury's eyes blazed hot as Mavis peppered her eggs and buttered her biscuit.

"Calm down, Cal," said Mavis. "God doesn't want you found out. It wouldn't sit well with all the people He's honestly trying to save. Lots of good folks out there seeking a true God. Not the kind you're selling."

The Reverend reached across the table and took hold of Mavis' wrist as she lifted a forkful of eggs up to her mouth, causing them to fling back on the table.

Ken grabbed the Reverend's arm, breaking him loose from Mavis. "Back off, mister," he said, still pretending not to know Artury's identity. "Say what you come to say and get out."

Reverend Artury peeled off his sunglasses and glared at Ken. His ice-blue eyes bore into Ken's as he jerked his arm from Ken's grasp.

"It's okay," Mavis said. "I'm alright."

Ken turned to leave, hoping Mavis finished her meeting without further incident. At the same time, he tried to shake the mind meld. Still, he stayed within earshot, keeping watch over Mavis.

As soon as the Reverend walked out, Mavis bolted to the toilet. Ken cracked the door open, listening to her wretch. He followed as she staggered back to the booth. Mavis pushed her food away and rested her head on the table.

"You good?" Ken cleared the table around her.

"Yeah. Give me a minute." She pulled a twenty out of her cleavage and handed it to him.

"Keep it," he said. "Breakfast is on me."

"No, actually, it's in your toilet. Sorry. Food's great; it's the company I keep."

"I didn't hear much. You looked whipped."

"Not quite. Not yet."

"You sure there's nothing I can do? Don't know what this was all about, but maybe I could help."

Mavis raised her head. "No, nothing you can do. Sorry to drag you into this. Please watch your back."

"I ain't afraid of guys like him."

"Listen to me, Ken. Obviously, I've made him angry. You saw him—here—with me, and I've also made him nervous." Mavis wiped her mouth again with her napkin. "I know things about him, and for all he knows, I've spilled my guts to you."

"Ain't he supposed to be a man of God? Why should I be afraid of him?"

"Because—because he's no man of God. He's a Godfather."

Ken chuckled. "In Winston?"

"Yeah. In good ol' Winston-Salem. The perfect cover. A Southern Godfather in a Mafia of holy men."

~ May 1975 ~

Summer heat brought young men downtown, cruising muscle cars through the streets, their eight-track tapes cutting mixtures of rock and country through the air.

Peach-tinted shadows fell softly through the diner's windows. On that late afternoon, only the refrigerators hummed in the kitchen. The dining room sat empty, and someone had nailed a For Sale sign on the front door. Upstairs, the sun's rays warmed Ken's apartment. City air filtered through the window screens, bringing the sound of loud mufflers, louder music, and the smell of exhaust.

"Who's there? Golly, you scared the crap out of me. Who— Who are you? What do you want?"

"Ken Kopper, thus saith the Lord, your Day of Judgment has come."

The gun fired twice. He lay on the floor, blood spilling from his chest and mouth. It pooled around his head. His vision blurred, his breath labored, and he tried to talk but only gurgled his final words. "I'm n-not Ken—"

Nobody heard him.

～✐～

Merida crossed the busy street, dodging fast, shiny cars— convertible Stingrays, souped-up Chargers, and throaty Camaros. She almost dropped the basket of Ken's clothes. Her Baptist bun nearly came undone, shaking her head in repulsion at young White boys wasting time and their daddy's money. "Humph. Gas goin' up to fifty-five cents a gallon, I swear, no respect."

Merida found the diner's back door unlocked. Climbing the steps to Ken's apartment, she mumbled on every step. "I swear! That boy do live dangerously. He leaves his door open in a neighbor- hood full of dope pushers, muggers, and homeless folks!" After setting down the laundry basket, she poked her head into the tiny living room.

The noise in the street drowned out Merida's screams.

～✐～

Ken stood with his bare feet in the salty waves. He'd driven to South Carolina and Kiawah Island non-stop. His last-minute resolution to leave town was an impulsive decision he had never made. It excited him, exhilarated his soul to leave the state, and set eyes on the ocean. Determined to change his life, he traveled to the Atlantic to find a new home. Start over. Of course, he would return, settle his affairs, and bring Corbet to Kiawah with him. They'd buy a place near the beach and rent boats to tourists. Find a house with a front porch.

Ken imagined him and Corbet enjoying future sunsets in rocking chairs, doing things old men do. *Corbet will like it here.* All he had to do was sign the papers and hand the keys to the diner's new owner. Pack his things; pack Corbet's things. And leave. Never look back.

A pretty woman with her jeans rolled up in ankle-deep water walked by him.

"Hi," she said and smiled.

"Hello," said Ken.

Yeah, Corbet's going to like it here.

Beach Babies

The story, **BEACH BABIES**, swam around in my brain from the day I met the late Bobbie Sue Rossi, my mother-in-law. A woman from the South, she showed me the true meaning of unconditional love. Her heart included a deep ocean of treasures and memories, and her stories only enhanced many of my own. Bobbie and her twin, Bertie, lived their childhood and early adult years in High Point, North Carolina and worked in the hosiery mills. For me, the recollections of her life were like striking gold. As a storyteller, I discovered a mentor.

This particular story came to me as I stared at an old picture, which is now the cover of this book. Bobbie Sue Rossi was not a heroine; neither is she a legend. She was simply a woman who survived enormous odds. I identified with her in more ways than she ever knew. Making no excuses for our behavior or even our mistakes, we shared many secrets. Her courage will go on in the lives of the women she touched. And so, I dedicate this story to her memory.

~ May 1945 ~

*B*ertie hated Mama. She hated her for her backhanding and beatings and for allowing boarders to sneak into our beds while we slept. Nighttime raids, we called them.

I hated her too, but not as much as my sister did.

Crawling into my bed, Bertie curled up like a cat near a fire and bawled for a good hour. I gave her my best devil-be-damned smile. "Time to get the hell out, Bertie. You with me?"

She jerked her head up and glared at me. Drool slid out the side of her mouth as she spit her words. "Hell's bells! I was ready to leave here five years ago, the day after our 12th birthday, and I still got scars from that beating." Her nose dripped, and I handed her a rag.

"Yeah, I remember. It was such a *happy* birthday. The bitch threw Daddy out of his house not five minutes after we blew out the candles on the first birthday cake we ever had. I say he figured life as a hobo and riding the rails was far easier than living in her nuthouse."

"Mama says he's in prison."

"Could be. We'll never know for sure." I sighed and kicked the quilt off my legs.

"Why'd Daddy leave us, Bobbie? Why'd he let her run him off?"

My sister's question stung me like she'd snapped a rubber band at my head. Daddy left in a hurry, with only the clothes on his back. We were told Erwin Doogan hopped on a train to Knoxville and never returned.

"Men do funny things when they're scared shitless. I think the Depression broke him. Mama never loved him. Maybe she threatened him. Held a gun to his head. I doubt we'll ever know. Not as long as we're here."

Bertie gnawed on her pinky. Even at seventeen, she chewed her fingernails. "But Mama don't want us either. Except to cook and clean, among other things." Bertie rested her head on the pillow and turned over onto her back. "The war's almost over; I hear they're hiring at the mill."

"No, Bert. We got to go. As far from Mama as possible. Hosiery mill ain't far enough. I'll find us a place." A tiny seed of trust slipped from her hand into mine. I watched her stretch and yawn. She closed her eyes. I yawned in return, then opened the windows further, hoping for a cool breeze. After turning my pillow over to the cool side, I pulled my nightgown off my legs. I couldn't get comfortable. Sitting up, I dangled my feet over the bedside, listening to Bertie, ever so quietly, cry herself to sleep.

The old house creaked and sighed, settling in for the night until, finally—blessed silence. The place boarded ghosts, as well as guests, and I imagined those murmurs and moans were the whispers of dead relatives. I held myself still for the moment, even going so far as to hold my breath. The lonesome sound of a single car on a deserted street and a train whistle in the distance broke the night's stillness. I tried to forget the ghosts. I didn't need more spooks in my life.

I slipped off the bed onto cool floorboards. My thoughts ran too wild for sleep. A shiver ran up my back, but this coolness was comforting, reminding me my heart still pumped blood. I was alive. And where there's life, there's hope. I padded down the stairs, stole a cigarette from Mama's purse, then slipped out the back door. I needed the night air.

Cordella Doogan, our mama, ran Doogan's Boarding House on Russell Street in High Point. A big Victorian with lots of closets and places to hide. It belonged to our daddy's family, but they were all dead or crazy as loons, so Mama took it over after Bertie and I were born. Running her decrepit hotel got us through the worst of the Depression, and it kept Mama from working in the mill.

She swore she'd not end up like Granny, trapped in a hosiery mill sewing the toes on socks. Mama wanted nothing to do with cotton and would've preferred not to wear it, except there was little else to choose from in 1945, especially when people considered you less than poor White trash. That's what Bertie heard the girls at school call us when we turned our backs.

With the mounting stress of a fledgling business, Mama's abuse increased in our advancing teens. Like indentured servant owners from the not-so-distant past, she unnaturally assumed it was her right to do with us as she pleased. Twice, we ran away with no plan of where to go or how to get there. And twice, Sheriff Cuddy, a friend of Mama's, found us and brought us back. Each time, the punishment got worse. After our last jailbreak, the sheriff said he'd happily take us to reform school. No season went by without a stinging ass and a bruised face.

Over the years, I grew accustomed to waking in the dark to Bertie's sobs. Her nightgown ripped or messed up by an invasive houseguest groping at her breast. Mama threatened us with the strap and hard labor if we didn't keep our mouths shut.

I smoked my stolen cigarette outside by Juba Lee Truvey's trashcans and her dog. Watching the fat mongrel chew on one of Juba's ham bones, I stopped in my tracks. Our neighbor's old bitch dog snarled with each step I took toward her tar-papered doghouse. She reminded me of Mama. Holding on to the scraps of life, showing her teeth should anyone try to take them away.

I scuttled back to the kitchen. Mama's roll-top desk squatted like an old wash woman in the corner. Opening the drawer where Mama kept her record books and house receipts, I rummaged through the mess until I found what I was looking for. Her address book. A few pages were smudged with a red stain from spilled cherry pie. I recalled the night Daddy wrote his sister's name in it. *Ruby Doogan.* Daddy's pie had fallen off his fork; he always got nervous picking up a pen.

Staring at her name, I suddenly understood why he had written it down. Someday Bertie and I would need to find Ruby. Daddy didn't write much, having a sixth-grade education, and he barely scribbled his name. But I made out Ruby's address just fine. I tore out the page, stuffed it into my nightgown pocket, and tiptoed upstairs.

I tunneled under the sheet and put my hand on her shoulder. "Bertie, you awake?"

She opened her sleep-filled eyes. "I am *now.*"

"I'm declaring our own D-Day. This Sunday, after church. Viola will drive us in her car. She's always bugging somebody to share the drive so she can visit her boyfriend at the beach. We just won't come back with her. Not to High Point, and they can't force us back. We'll be eighteen in three months. I think we can stay with Ruby."

"Daddy's sister, Ruby?"

I caressed her dark curls and snuggled up to her back. "That's the one. She's the only relative we got left, other than Daddy."

"Maybe she won't want us, Bob. I mean, hell, we haven't seen her—in what, twelve years! Long before Daddy skipped town."

The night air stirred the treetops near our room. Juba Lee's dog barked in her backyard.

"You think Aunt Ruby knows where Daddy is?"

"I don't care where *he* is," I said. "We need a place to stay—real jobs. From what I can recall, Ruby was dumb as a tick on a toad but sweet. She'll let us stay if we pay our way."

I hid Ruby's address under the mattress, remembering the last time we saw her. Bertie nearly drowned in the ocean and never ventured near water again. I swam as far out as possible until my toes couldn't touch the bottom, and the waves almost rocked me to sleep.

Bertie blew her nose again and then cuddled her pillow. "So, where does she live?"

"She lives in the same old house near the ocean, if Mama's address book is right. She's probably still cleaning motel rooms at Carolina Beach."

Sleep evaded me. My brain fired in all directions, keyed up with plans to escape Mama's prison. I lay there thinking about Bertie and me, hoping to make a life for ourselves. The truth was, I worried more about Bertie than myself.

The word *opposite* might explain us. I was a towhead blonde with freckles, pallid and plain. Bertie had a body that caused men to walk into walls. She redefined beauty. An inch taller than me, her burnt-brown locks never needed the hundred bobby pins I stuck in my hair every night. I had a wide nose. She had skinny arms. Bertie grew painfully thin over the years, and though I took pride in my slim hips, my belly bulge gave me fits. Bertie only spoke if spoken to. I never shut my mouth. She seldom cussed. My *f-bombs* were legendary.

I loved boys, lots of boys, especially Hank Williams. Bertie never confessed to a crush on a movie star or famous country singer. My Dixie-cup breasts were a constant source of jokes and humiliation. Bertie's melon chest was ready to be picked. She was content to stay home, flip through magazines, and learn new recipes. I stole time away from Mama to ride in cars with boys, sneak off to picture shows with boys, and dance until dark. With boys.

The natural redness of Bertie's lips blushed like she'd chewed at them for hours. Mine were plump but colorless. But our eyes were identical. Chocolate brown with yellow flecks. When Daddy smiled and said, "They're the color of rum," Mama snorted a sarcastic snicker.

"They're plain shit-brown like yours, Erwin," she said. Bertie swore someone had left her on our doorstep. She looked nothing like Daddy or me. Or Mama. Finding our birth certificate proved once and for all Bertie and I were twins.

It didn't surprise me when my sister quit school in '43. Hand-me-down dresses from Juba Lee's daughters did Bertie in, but not as much as restroom comments at school. Every morning, Rita Hayworth look-alikes squirmed for a spot in front of the mirror. Applying thick coats of beet-red lipstick and pulling bobby pins out of their hair, it was a wonder they made it to class before the second bell. "Looks like somebody made the Doogan twins new dresses!"

"Lord, no. Those came from the church bazaar; My cousin, Mary Margaret, threw those dresses out two years ago."

I didn't care what the girls at school said: I had determined to finish my classes. Be somebody. But all Bertie wanted was a man to take care of her. As much as she hated Mama, Bertie was more like her than she knew.

I graduated with the class of 1945, but we made no fuss about it. I didn't want Bertie to feel bad, and Mama—well, she couldn't have cared less.

I looked at the alarm clock. Five-twenty. Swinging my legs over the bedside, I threw back the twisted sheets and tried to shed the residue of a restless night. I had slept maybe three hours. It didn't matter. Starting breakfast for seven people required getting up at five thirty. But I needed to pee and didn't want to stand in line.

Tied into the kitchen plumbing, our commode sat on the back porch. Tar paper over plywood surrounded it for privacy. A three-foot square sweatbox in summer, we all but froze in winter. The only thing making it better than an outhouse was not having far to walk, and we could flush it. Too many times, though, we waited behind one of Mama's houseguests. Mama provided a bowl and pitcher in everybody's room for washing, but we all shared the toilet.

I wiped maggots off the seat with Sears and Roebuck catalog paper and sat. Just once, I wished for a roll of toilet paper. I'd pestered Mama to build a bathroom, but I knew her backward frame of mind and how she clung to old habits. She argued that most worldly improvements were frivolous, and she couldn't afford anything more modern than the toilet she squatted over.

Mama insisted indoor bathrooms were nasty. But we were tired of unnecessary hardships. A woman shouldn't have to freeze to death or wipe maggots off the seat before relieving herself. I longed to bathe in a porcelain tub with a lock on the bathroom door. Flushing the American Standard commode, I determined Bertie and I would someday take a step up in respectability and culture and live in houses with inside bathrooms. Own bathtubs with porcelain handles, rolls and rolls of toilet paper, and big fluffy towels.

A fist banging on the other side of the door interrupted my fantasy. "Hey! I'm paying to use that toilet!"

I didn't light a match. I hoped my stink asphyxiated him.

Mama refused to take in over three boarders at a time. Always men, of course. And unless a woman arrived with a man, she turned them away. We provided breakfast and dinner with the cost of the room, which had to be paid upfront. She'd been stiffed too many times and learned the hard way—about everything.

Bertie and I slept in the attic, but sometimes, when the weather was unbearably hot, we sacked out on cots shoved into the corners of the screened-in back porch. A chance we were willing to take, depending on who the guests were for the week. Cool porch air felt far better than the sweat-drenched sheets of our sweltering loft.

Usually, around two in the morning, Mama showed up, reeking of sour men and hard liquor. Her voice thick and slurred; she'd kick our bed. "Bobbie Sue, wake up. Somebody here wants to see how pretty you are—be nice to him." Then she'd walk off with an extra five dollars in her pocket and leave us for whatever happened next. I learned to shut off my mind, but Bertie—Bertie couldn't. She broke down nearly twice a week.

I finished setting the table. It was Wednesday. Meatloaf, mashed potatoes, lima beans, and biscuits with peach jam. Sweet tea and coffee. Banana pudding for dessert. Bertie and I took turns serving and clearing. That week, guests checked in on Thursday for a three to four-day stay, all in town for the Southern Furniture Market. The Market closed in 1941 because of the war, but Mama kicked up her heels in 1945. The High Point furniture industry was back in business. Mama loved city people. Merchants who spent money drinking gallons of sloe gin and bourbon—and tolerated her cackle.

During Market Week, she babbled on like a love-starved hen about her few days on the Vaudeville stage. Mama crooned to old records and pranced around the parlor, her scarf floating in and out of the air between the menfolk. Imitating Mae West and singing off-key, her screechy soprano voice made Juba Lee's dog howl. I laughed so hard I got sick. Her mid-life thickness, stuffed in her best red dress, waltzed in front of men too drunk to care.

Bertie scowled and declared she made a fool of herself and us. I agreed, but it felt satisfying to poke fun at her. Even if Mama looked like an overgrown tomato with matching red lips and a huge ass, she was entertaining. She usually picked one man and stuck to him like a bitch in heat until the end of Market Week. He kept her high on Wild Turkey and love and usually booked an extra day or two until tiring of her—or until his wife called. Whichever came first.

It was about then that I started hiding out for the night, sleeping outside or in Viola's car. But Mama always came looking for me. If she couldn't find me, she'd beat on Bertie, and Bertie couldn't take much more. She grew weaker by the day. I knew I had to save her. Save us. So, I stopped hiding at night. I toughened up, refused the latest advances on my body, and took my beatings from Mama. I tolerated Mama's strap because I knew Bertie could not. Red welts on my legs and ass didn't stop me from finally making a deal with Mama to lay off Bertie. "Just use me," I said.

Mama looked at me like I had three eyeballs, refusing to discuss it. The sober Cordella Doogan portrayed herself to the world as a loving mother, a successful businesswoman, and a good Christian neighbor. "I pay the bills," she said. "You live in *my* house. Eat at *my* table. Do as I say or pay the consequences." The subject was closed.

I grew to hate her as much as Bertie hated her. But I didn't want my hate to send me to Hell. Our preacher pointed out that a person sometimes traveled over a lot of ground before arriving in Hell—or Heaven, for that matter. If hating Mama would send my soul to Hell, my only hope was to escape. Leave and never come back. Travel over that ground before I died.

On a Saturday afternoon in June, Mama's best friend, Juba Lee, waddled over to our kitchen and announced the new preacher for First Pentecostal had arrived. She'd heard he was young, fresh out of seminary, and unmarried. Mama said *she'd* heard he possessed stammering lips and looked forward to watching them quiver. Juba Lee agreed and said she'd also heard Reverend Jenkins was every bit as good-looking as Billy Graham. That made Mama smile. She loved having a leg up on her Baptist friends.

Later that day, Mama hitched a ride into town with Juba Lee; she had to get a permanent wave special for the occasion. Bertie and I had always planned to hightail it out of High Point after our eighteenth birthday. Who knew God would give us a break three months ahead of schedule?

We declared our day of deliverance. Sunday after church.

The line behind us snaked out to the parking lot with church members ready to make their first impressions on the new man of God at First Pentecostal.

I stared into his Sinatra-blue eyes. *He couldn't be any older than twenty-five. Twenty-seven tops.* We didn't see many good-looking young men in town. Uncle Sam had sent them all to Europe or the Pacific. I wondered why he wasn't married; until I shook his hand. It felt like a large moist mushroom. He wasn't bad to look at, but obviously, women made him nervous.

"You're twins?"

"Only when we're together," I said. "When you see us apart, we don't look alike."

He glanced at my sister. "You're right. You don't look like her. So, who's Bobbie, and who's Bertie?"

My sister pointed at me and giggled. "She's Roberta. I'm Alberta; call me Bertie."

Reverend Ross Jenkins was a looker. As Bertie shook his mushroomy hand next, I breathed him in. He smelled of peppermint and witch hazel aftershave. The Reverend had a dimple in his chin like William Holden, and for a wild second or two, I considered touching it and asking him how he shaved in there. His hair held the presence of all colors, black with reflections of red, and his eyes were kind.

With a sorry shake of her head, Mama shoved us forward. "Go along, girls. Juba Lee saved us a seat down front." She wanted her ten seconds with the new preacher.

"Lord, what bee is in that woman's britches this time?" Bertie whispered.

"A Bee-attitude. Blessed are the poor, for they shall inherit the kingdom or a spot on Carolina Beach; take your pick."

Bertie smothered her laughter all the way to the altar.

Mama fanned her face with her funeral home fan and winked at Reverend Jenkins. The same fan she stole and stuffed in her purse the day Juba Lee's daddy died. She waved the pleated cardboard slowly under her chin. The funeral home advertisement side faced out. *Death, Where is thy sting?* Bertie and I caught a whiff of her whiskey breath with each twist of her wrist. A sickly sweet, smoky odor, much like baking pies in a hot kitchen on a humid day. A smell that also carried a vague threat. You could never tell what a woman with that kind of breath might decide to say at any moment.

Juba Lee and Mama bookended Bertie and me in the pew. Mama on one end and her friend on the other, my sister and I were like fried apples between two soggy crusts. Juba Lee's dull brown hair sprouted coarse grays over the tight bun at her neck. Despite the heat, she had wrapped a shawl around her fleshy frame, resembling a tightly wound serpent coiled like a copperhead.

The First Pentecostal Church congregation seemed to hang on Reverend Jenkins' every word. More shouts and affirmations of *Amen, brother*, than I ever heard. At some point during the sermon, I stopped staring at him and listened. His voice pulsed with animation and fervency as he obviously strived to make a good first impression of his own.

"Exodus twenty-two tells us, thou shalt not suffer a witch to live! What is a witch today, you ask? Fortune-tellers! Psychics and Gypsies!" He preached louder than thunder, raising his arms and shaking his fists. It was a well-rehearsed and choreographed speech, and I had the feeling he didn't believe it any more than I did.

I nudged Bertie. "Let's get our palms read next week."

She giggled until the organist finally plopped down at the Hammond. Reverend Jenkins wiped the sweat from his brow. We stood at ten minutes to twelve and turned our hymnals to page fifty-four. The Reverend could not only turn a phrase but also sang like Bing Crosby in a minister's robe. Mesmerized, I stayed longer than I intended.

"I am bound for the Promised Land, I am bound for the Promised Land... oh, who will come and go with me, I am bound for the Promised Land."

Eventually, I looked at Bertie. "Time to get out of Dodge."

She cut her eyes at me, nodded, and nearly yelled her response. "Let's go!"

Mama heard. She yanked me down to the pew, her hand a tight grasp on my arm. "Where the hell do you think you're going?"

"Oh, who will come and go with me, I am bound..."

"You can't stop us." I twisted my arm out of her grip. "We're packed. Viola Truvey is waiting outside."

She slapped my cheek. Folks in nearby pews stopped singing and turned to watch.

I peeled her dishwater-damp hands off my arm again and gritted my teeth. "We'll be eighteen in three months, and you can't bring us back this time."

Bertie grabbed my hand. Together we crossed the line of lost innocence and stepped all over Juba Lee's serpentine body, getting out of the pew fast.

"...for the promised land."

The singing stopped; the sanctuary fell dead silent—the attention—on us.

Mama stumbled into the aisle behind us and screamed. "Come back here, Bobbie Sue! I'll snatch out your arm and beat you with the bloody stump!"

I stopped at the back double doors, turned, and shouted into the filled-to-overflowing silent sanctuary. "Time to find new girls for your whorehouse, Mama! Hope you pay them more than you paid us!"

The bell tower at First Pentecostal Church tolled twelve as we bounded down the front steps and into Viola's waiting Chevy. We barreled out of town, north on Main Street toward Greensboro, then on to the coast and our destination—Carolina Beach.

After a quick stop for supper, I took the wheel from Viola and drove all night. Juba Lee's oldest daughter and our friend had turned twenty-two the past spring. Viola worked at a furniture factory and met a young man at a party who lived and lifeguarded at Holden Beach. Helping us escape our prison gave Viola the nerve to break out of her own—living with Juba Lee. I told Viola if her mama kicked her out for helping us, she could stay with Bertie and me for a while.

Heading east, away from the Piedmont, tobacco fields, and crowded cities, we journeyed on quiet roads spread out flat and dark under countless stars. My excitement escalated. With one hand loose on the wheel and an elbow poking out the open window, my hair whipped around my head in a yellow swirl. I stopped only once to pee and gas up. Bertie and Viola slept all the way to the beach. Not me. The wind of freedom on my face ignited something inside, and all I could do was sing in silence.

We dropped Viola off at her boyfriend's house. He agreed to drive Viola to Aunt Ruby's on Friday, where she could pick up her car and return to her job in High Point. Without Bertie and me. Mama was sure to interrogate Viola as to our whereabouts. I supposed Mama might send the sheriff after us again, but we were prepared. Bertie and I could hide for three months if we had to. But I also knew Viola despised our mama. Her silence was another risk we were willing to take.

As I crossed the bridge over the Cape Fear River, I knew I was searching for something but it wasn't the sea. Bertie and I celebrated our fifth birthday the last time we saw the ocean. As young as I was then, I had found God in the waves, the salty wind, and the sky that touched the water on the horizon. I lost Him living in High Point. Maybe I was hoping to find Him again.

Around us, a storm broke. Fat raindrops splattered on the car's roof, gaining crescendo. With each wind gust, the trees swayed and shook. As the sky opened up and the heavens cried, the lash of water whipped through the windows. The car provided little shelter from torrents of rain as we rolled the windows up.

"Windows are fogging over; we might as well stop for the night," I said. Without Viola, we each had a seat to sleep on. My watch said three in the morning—too early to barge in on Aunt Ruby. I parked behind the Five and Dime next to the birdbaths and porch swings and sprawled out in the front seat; Bertie curled up in the back. I fell asleep to the whirr of a stiff wind and, finally, a calming rain.

At seven, I woke my sister. I'd been awake to watch the sunrise. The aroma of sea and summer heat struck my nose like a gentle slap, and I tasted salt on my tongue. I unfolded myself out of the car, stretched, then walked to the beach. Peering out across dunes running up and down the long sweep of sand, I felt wrapped in a silken cocoon of euphoria. A cry of relief broke from my lips. Blue skies, billowing clouds, and the sun hot on the top of my head, I wanted to shout my freedom to the world. A soft breeze rustled nearby palmettos. I was ready to work on my tan and let the ocean's song lull me into a stupor.

"Did we bring the baby oil and iodine?" I handed Bertie a warm Coke and a pack of Saltines through the car window. It was the best breakfast I could come up with.

"We need a job, not a tan."

"I need a job, a tan, and a man. And not necessarily in that order," I said.

Bertie pulled herself out of the car, and we meandered to the Texaco station on the corner. I asked a woman who talked like Carmen Miranda for a key to the restroom and directions to Lake Park Boulevard. "Is down that way," she pointed.

It looked like any other neighborhood except for the palm trees and sandy soil. I drove slowly so Bertie could read the house numbers. It cowered alone at the end of the street in all its rundown glory. Exactly where we had left it. On a flat, treeless lot, overgrown with sea grass and dying evergreen shrubbery.

Ruby's house was little more than a shack on stilts with a shaky front porch extending the entire length of the house. A rectangle of four small rooms laid end to end. From what I remembered, she had planned to build a bathroom off the back. I fantasized for a moment and felt bubbles around my neck.

Grainy brick-red tarpaper covered the outside, and a few thick sheets hung crooked. The last time we visited Ruby, Bertie and I had just lost our first tooth, and she gave us each a nickel. She'd spent all her time taking in laundry and working at the Starfish Motor Court. She babysat for a neighbor when she wasn't cleaning toilets and stripping beds at the motel.

I also recalled Ruby as a tiny woman with dark brown hair braided down her back and always wearing shorts or overalls. I never saw her in a dress. But she had a pretty face, with a broad nose like mine. I wondered if she had changed much in twelve years.

A pair of beagles howled from the tops of their doghouses as soon as we came within view. I couldn't imagine why she kept hunting dogs at the beach. Years ago, Daddy had built Ruby a barbeque pit and rack in her backyard. She labored over pork butts on the weekend and sold wrapped sandwiches at the beach. Mama hated barbeque and said it was the poor Southern man's meat. I loved it. I found Aunt Ruby's little enterprise fascinating and hoped she had continued it. Maybe she'd consider expanding her operation with Bertie and me around.

Walking across the porch, I nearly tripped over an old kitchen chair resting beside a leaky icebox. The chrome chair had almost rusted in two. Its vinyl seat, ripped and faded, had worn through with its horsehair stuffing sticking out like small explosions. I imagined Ruby never cared much for pretty decorated houses with prissy front porches.

Even if the place were clean inside, it was anybody's guess whether Bertie would commit her backside to any of Ruby's furniture. I, on the other hand, made myself comfortable anywhere. Possibly living next door to Juba Lee and her filthy house made me careless about falling into the mangiest-looking chair or couch, stained with God-only-knew-what and smelling to high heaven. But for Bertie, cleanliness was her greatest virtue, and she was bound to work herself into a fit cleaning Ruby's house like she'd cleaned Mama's.

Someone had stuffed the rusty screen door with little tufts of cotton, blocking a few holes to keep out the bugs. When I pulled it open, it fell off the hinges.

"You think she lives here? Maybe she's moved."

"She's here. I smell bacon. Listen, Bertie." I put my ear to the inside door. "It's the Grand Ole Opry on the radio."

I knocked. The front door squeaked open slowly. Ruby tossed her graying braid across her shoulder. Her milky white skin appeared soft as velvet, and the smell of Tabasco sauce and vinegar drifted through the doorway. "Well, land's sake, if it ain't the Bobbsey twins."

I shot her a quick smile. "Hey, Aunt Ruby. Can we come in?"

She nodded, then motioned for us to enter. Her slight hug felt like the soft nudge of a butterfly wing striking against my breast. The odor of cigarette smoke in her hair overpowered any barbeque aroma in the house. Ruby had little life left in her; we had come just in time. After twelve years, she startled me. I remembered her frame as small but Ruby had become frail, even though her mental faculties did not seem diminished.

"Damned lung cancer," she said as she lit a cigarette.

When Ruby talked, every word crawled out as if she were waking up or falling asleep. Bertie and I figured her medicine had taken its toll. But if her speech was slow, her body was even slower. Arthritis had settled into every joint. She seemed uncomfortable in an upright position, always searching for some way to prop herself up. Gravity proved too strong for her. Layers had fallen away. Aunt Ruby had retreated on herself the way a plant curls up in the autumn of its life to prepare for the cold.

Ruby Doogan bore no children and spent her life savings on doctor bills. She never married. To her, love meant falling off a building and trusting a devoted man to catch you at the bottom, or at least possess the decency to call an ambulance. Her only possibility for a husband had split town before she landed. Frankly, she wasn't chancing another leap of faith. She'd paid off her shack and acre of land, working endless hours for one motel and then another. In time, she retired and then got sick.

Finding Ruby gave me a sense of divine intervention in our unfortunate circumstances. Although my mortal soul hung in the balance due to my lack of belief and ignorance of scripture, I had no doubt His hand was on the situation.

As it turned out, we all needed each other. In the time it took to eat our first meal together, our lives changed forever. Bertie and I began to live again, but as for Ruby, she was approaching the full circle of her life, returning to what she was at the beginning. A beating pulse inside a trivial human body.

~ July 1945 ~

We found life quite tolerable at Ruby's. Living in five *small* rooms instead of ten large ones took some time to get used to. But for a while, our time was our own. Bertie and I cleaned, scrubbed, and repaired the long-neglected house. Ruby had added a bathroom with a tub, for which Bertie and I were grateful. A tiny piece of Heaven.

Back in High Point, a busy Russell Street ran in front of Mama's boarding house. But on Ruby's stretch of sandy beach, seagrass butted up against a short driveway, a narrow gravel road, and a boardwalk leading to the sea.

Early one sultry morning in July, Ruby found a spurt of energy. She rolled her sleeves high above her elbows and placed pots on the stove before surprising us with, first, a palm reading for both of us, and second, "We're having company for dinner," she said and winked.

Bertie and I giggled. We had talked about getting a palm reading from the first moment we sat at her kitchen table.

"You feel good enough to make dinner?" asked Bertie.

I kicked my sister under the table. "Next question, who's the mystery guest?"

Ruby ignored our interrogation and proceeded to get rid of us for the day. "Feed my dogs on your way out." She handed us bowls of leftover breakfast scraps. "Them's good watchdogs. Lets me know when somebody's coming. Now go! You'll see Madame Tuleh's Palm Reading sign on the boardwalk," Ruby said. Then she shoved us out the door.

For the first time in our lives, we stepped outside wearing makeup, shorts, and midriff tops. Hand-me-downs from Ruby. Though Mama's wicked deeds hid behind the walls of our house, she kept our dresses and her own respectable—shunning the very appearance of evil. But there we were, strolling the boardwalk without a dowdy dress to cover us—our bodies exposed. Two girls exchanging religious rags for a new look—a fresh start.

"I feel naked," Bertie said.

"You look great. Mama would die, wouldn't she?" I laughed. "No more cotton dusters, sister."

"The entire Pentecostal congregation will disown us."

"I think they already have. Who cares? Look where we are, Bertie. On Carolina Beach. We live here." I kicked off my flip-flops and ran into the sand. Twirling and kicking my feet like a child, I felt ocean breezes whipping around my legs and sunrays kissing my body. Sweat dripped down my back, but not the same sweat that popped out of my pores in Mama's sweltering attic. No. This was a healthy sweat. The kind that made me feel alive, not drained of energy, but boiling over with life.

"At least you have a job!" Bertie yelled.

Out of breath, I returned to where she stood on the boardwalk. "Do you ever look at the bright side?"

"What's the bright side?"

"Forget it."

I wanted to hit her. We had escaped the hell of our childhood to live on the beach, and Bertie still couldn't be happy.

"Bobbie, I'm sorry. It's better here than with Mama. But I'm tired of sitting around the house with Ruby, and there's not much to do other than wrap barbeque sandwiches twice a day. I want a life."

I shook my blonde curls at her. "I don't consider my job at Clyde's Dry Cleaners a career in the making, and they run me ragged."

"Still. It's an actual job."

We stood in front of Madame Tuleh's sign, weather-beaten by the salty air. "We're here. Let's see what our future holds and have some fun for a change, alright?" I looked at Bertie with a silly grin and gave her a light punch in her arm. She hung her head, embarrassed by her complaining, then batted her lashes back at me and smiled.

"Okay, sorry again."

"You're such a shitbucket sometimes, you know?" I kissed her cheek.

Bertie pushed the door open, and a brass bell jingled. The shop appeared smaller than it looked from the outside. Painted navy blue walls with a moon and stars stenciled on a black ceiling, the place felt magical. The crude wooden floor creaked and groaned beneath us. Sickening sweet air reeked of something that burned my eyes, and behind an antique desk, tattered burgundy velvet draperies sectioned off a private room. When they flew open, I sneezed as dust particles glittered in the musty air. Then Bertie sneezed. But our mouths dropped open when a half-dressed older man scurried out in a hurry, attempting to button his shirt.

"Madame Tuleh must have all *kinds* of customers," I said.

Bertie sneezed again, but she got my sarcasm. She wiped her nose, hiding her giggle behind her hankie.

"Hellooo, I'm Madame Tuleh; you must be—no, don't tell me—you're Ruby's twins!"

Before we spoke a word, the fortune-teller took Bertie's hand and closed her raccoon eyes. I almost laughed at her heavy black liner and lashes. Dark blue shadow arched over each eye; she was a strangely stunning woman. Like the whores on the boardwalk late at night.

"I sense peril. Your aura disturbs me," she said to Bertie. "It's illuminated." Her voice sounded throaty and hoarse, her accent—peculiar, like Greta Garbo. "Dark, very dark. It sparkles with turmoil." Her earrings swinging as she shook her head, Tuleh motioned for us to follow her. "You must allow me to help you out of harm's way, child. Before it's too late," she added. "Please. Make another appointment for more readings. I do it for half price."

I watched Bertie's eyes widen. Afraid she believed her, I interrupted.

"My turn, Tuleh. My name is—"

"—I know your name," she said. "I make tea. You wait here."

I stifled another laugh. But Bertie didn't move a muscle and stared straight ahead. I nudged her with my elbow. "I hope Ruby didn't break the bank for this," I whispered.

"She's creepy." Bertie's nervous reply concerned me.

"It's a scam, Bert. We're here to have fun, but this is just a scam. Let's play along. Okay? We've always wanted to do this."

Slowly, like Aunt Ruby, Tuleh floated to the back room with a large leather book riding on her hip. I imagined it was her book of spells. I watched her fill a teapot with water. Tuleh's gauzy blouse stretched tight across her large breasts. Her tiny waist accentuated large hips resembling two watermelons shimmying under a skin-tight black skirt that dragged the floor. Her blue-black hair flowed like a river down past her butt, appearing to have never been cut. Fascinated by her eyelashes as thick as spiders, I also decided she wore the brightest red lipstick on the plumpest set of lips I ever saw. The color matched nicely with her red and orange print shawl draped over her shoulders. Silver earrings dangled from her ears as she brushed back thick tresses with chipped-red fingernails. Tuleh reeked of garlic, onions, and Evening in Paris perfume; my stomach turned sour, and I hoped her tea tasted better than she smelled.

In minutes, she motioned for us to join her in the back room to sit on a ratty couch. I knew all Bertie wanted was good news. Tuleh positioned herself opposite us in a worn rocker with her teapot balanced in her lap. She gave us each a cup of tea that tasted like dishwater and then dumped the cups upside down on a plate. "Ah," she said to Bertie, poking a finger into the leaves. "Find husband, and bad luck is gone."

"I don't have a boyfriend," Bertie said.

Tuleh shrugged. "Then you have bad luck." Bertie didn't need a fortune-teller to tell her that.

Tuleh poked around in my cup next. "You, my dear, you are star in God's Heaven."

I rolled my eyes. "What does that mean, exactly?"

"It means you are stronger twin. You will lead others to righteousness. Your determination to finish school, and graduate, where your sister did not, it make you a great woman, loved among many."

I laughed at this, thinking about the bottle of Wild Turkey and the pack of Chesterfields I bought with my last paycheck. But Tuleh, it seemed, took her job seriously. Her face was impassive as she picked up Bertie's hand again and turned it this way and that.

For some crazy reason, I felt uneasy. Like she'd seen something scary in the lines and creases.

Bertie must have felt it too. "I'm afraid we're on a time schedule, Madame Tuleh. We've got to get back to help our aunt with dinner. Thanks for the reading. It was—uh, fun."

I sensed Tuleh knew Bertie no longer cared to learn about her bleak future. Tuleh smiled, told us to say hello to Ruby, and that she'd award her a free reading if she sent in one more customer.

Walking home, my attempt to break the silence between us fell on deaf ears. "What a snake charmer," I said. Bertie said nothing. I made fun of Madame Tuleh, speaking with a sultry foreign accent and swaying my hips to make her laugh. Finally, she gave me a weak smile but still said nothing. Sometimes Bertie's quiet nature drove me crazy. "Why didn't you tell her about your boyfriend?" I asked.

"Why? So she could tell me I'm about to lose someone I just met? No thanks. I don't need to hear that. Besides, he's not a boyfriend. Not yet. We're—just going out. That's all."

I stopped, planted my feet in front of Bertie, and forced her to look into my eyes. "Everything she said was garbage. It's a quick way to make a buck. Quit being so damn negative all the time. Hey, maybe *we* ought to read tea leaves. What do you think? Be her competition!"

"Not interested," Bertie said, stepping around me. "But tell me something, Bob. How did she know you graduated, and I didn't? We never told Ruby; Ruby hasn't talked to Mama in years. How did Tuleh know that?"

My feet froze in place. "Good question," I mumbled.

Ruby served sausages, which had split their casings to season fresh cabbage wedges floating in a fragrant broth. A roasting chicken, browned to perfection, fell quickly into serving pieces as she wielded her knife. She checked the sideboard where an apple pie waited alongside a basket of fresh cornbread. A pitcher of lemonade sat on the table, along with butter and a jar of peach preserves she'd made the past summer.

"How was Tuleh?"

Bertie acted like she didn't hear her and dug into the preserves.

I pulled out forks and spoons to set the table. "She seemed fine to me. She said to say hello."

"That's not what I'm asking. How was your reading?"

"Typical. We're both about to be millionaires and live in California. Bertie's engagement with Dean Martin will be all the rage. They'll have lots of babies, and I'm destined to find the cure for cancer."

"Do it soon, will you?"

My heart went out to Ruby. Finally, somebody cared about her; she wouldn't last long enough to enjoy it. We'd watched her decline from the time we arrived. A kind soul about to fade on the Carolina beach horizon. And no matter what Tuleh the gypsy said, I didn't believe a word of it. If anyone deserved a bright future, a chance to get the life they genuinely wanted, it was Bertie.

Wisps of Ruby's hair worked loose from her braid, gluing themselves to the back of her neck, slick with sweat; her huge green eyes shone with unshed tears as she gazed out the window, wiping her hands on a dish towel. Ruby's nervous expression told us our mystery guest had arrived.

"Okay, girls, dinner's almost ready. I hear my dogs. I think you need to welcome our surprise visitor." Ruby smiled, deepening the lines around her eyes and highlighting the wrinkles next to her lips.

I stepped onto the porch and watched a car stop in the driveway. The window rolled halfway down, and someone tossed out a lit cigarette. When the door opened, and Daddy stepped out, tall and handsome with a clean shirt and combed hair, I nearly fell over. He looked like Jimmy Durante in tan pants and a pair of brown and white spectator shoes.

I screamed. "Bertie! It's Daddy!" I flew down the steps and into his arms. Bertie followed but reserved her excitement, offering only a slight smile and half a hug.

"Yesiree, it's my girls!" His arms felt massive and warm around me. But when he opened the car door and pulled out a birthday cake, I saw his eyes glaze with tears. "I figured we could try this again," he said.

Bertie said little at our dinner celebration. That night, while she tossed and turned in her sleep, I crawled out of bed and sat at the cracked-open door, eavesdropping on Daddy's conversation with Ruby. I knew there had to be more than the stories we'd passed around the dinner table, along with the cornbread and lemonade.

Daddy spoke softly in a deep, baritone voice; I pictured his dark razor stubble shadowing his chin, his shoeless feet crossed and parked on Ruby's coffee table, his toes wiggling in his brown and white argyle socks.

He had been in prison; that part was true. He'd come close to murdering one of Mama's drunken boarders who freely and mistakenly admitted he had taken liberty with Bertie and that Mama had set the price at five dollars. It took all of his self-restraint to keep from twisting the guy's fancy shirt collar tighter around his fat neck. As it was, he nearly killed the man. Daddy put him in the hospital with a concussion and three broken bones.

Unfortunately for Daddy, the man turned out to be a state official, a representative from Raleigh passing through.

Daddy cried into his big hands. "I knew Cordella abused the twins, and I couldn't stop her. I should've killed her. Hell, I ended up in prison, anyway. She testified against me—said I lied about what that bastard did to the girls."

"It's over, Erwin. Those years are behind you. Bobbie and Bertie are here now—with me. You see them when you want. They'll be here after I'm gone. I'm giving them this old house. Are you heading back to High Point after you leave here?"

"The boarding house in High Point belongs to me, and I'm selling it. I've got a place in the mountains. When I divorce Cordella, she will have to buy me out or move on—like I've had to do. I found a little town I like, near the Blue Ridge. Sweet people. I've learned a trade."

"Nah, you don't say?"

"Yes, Ma'am. Can you believe it?" I heard him slap the table. "Learned how to build houses. Work with wood. I got my eye on a piece of land. Maybe later, I can send for the girls if they ain't put roots down here. They're welcome to stay with me; make sure they know, Ruby."

He was gone in the morning. Eerie and quiet, the house felt depressing without him. Bertie wasn't surprised he'd not said goodbye. According to her, no man had the courage to say it. And if they came back at all—it was too late to say anything.

As the wind carried in a storm off the ocean, the men from the funeral home carried Ruby's coffin and struggled to keep the flowers from falling off the top. Bertie and I followed behind. Women from the local Baptist church filled a few seats at the memorial service where Ruby was a member but never attended.

Bertie had found her. Her arthritic fist, dangling over the side of the couch, clutched a recipe for fried apple pies. Bertie placed Ruby's fist on the small mound of her chest, where it lay with the other one like two lumps of dough.

The pastor spoke empty words over a body he barely knew. No one cried, and no one said they were sorry.

"At least she had us a while," Bertie said.

I nodded. "There should've been music."

"Goddam," I heard Bertie mutter.

"Goddam," I agreed.

~ August 1945 ~

In three months, Bertie fell in love with Air Force pilot, Court Callahan. One afternoon, she arrived home feeling hot and sick. Besides the bright flush on Bertie's narrow cheeks, she looked much as she had when she finished dressing that morning in the new pink sweater Court bought for her, a vivid contrast to her worn daisy print dress. Bertie stared into the mirror as if she'd forgotten what she looked like—glossy black curls, rum-brown eyes, an impatient look of expectancy. With a twisting pang of recurring loss, she repeated Court's letter he'd written to her just before he left Carolina Beach for Fort Andrews.

"I love you, Bertie. You have"—she stopped, her breath caught in her throat, *"the love of adventure. I didn't believe you existed. Now I know you do. Someday, Bertie, we'll be together. The two of us, forever."*

He'd kissed her, she'd said. A kiss that held a promise of joy unspeakable.

"And full of glory?" I smiled.

"Oh, the half has never yet been told," Bertie answered. *"I'll be back. Count on it.* He said that, Bob. He promised."

The light and bloom of the afternoon sun had settled in her eyes and cheeks. She looked feverish. My heart broke for her. I knew she'd count the days until she heard from him again. A slight undercurrent of jealousy pulsed in my veins. Loving a man like that, or the pain of missing him, I envied her.

Bertie took to her bed and lost herself in the story of their first date. She lingered on certain words and wiped tears away on others. They kissed on a long, desolate stretch of sand with seagulls stealing their Ritz crackers. Their hands moved beneath each other's shirts; their hair made stiff from seawater and salty air. They'd made love in the waves. "It was," she sucked in her breath and cried, "the most precious moment of my life." She stood on wobbly legs and walked to the radio. Her hand rested on the dial. *"I'll be seeing you in all the old familiar places…"* echoed through the house. I wanted to absorb her pain. It was as if she were alone in the world. Instead of turning it off, she turned up the volume and listened to the entire song. As it ended, Bertie switched off the radio and crawled back into bed.

She fell asleep in my arms, clutching his letter. The ink had stained her palm like a faded tattoo. His words of love slipped from her limp fingers and fluttered to the floor. I covered her with Ruby's old quilt, picked up the letter, and laid it on her dresser.

Bertie deserved him. He was her first love. I'd met a few lookers, but it always ended after the first date. I remained busy with my job at the cleaners while Bertie stayed close to home and made barbeque sandwiches. We didn't travel much past the boardwalk, the grocery stores, or the Baptist church. Bertie had settled into a routine, but I was still searching for adventure. It struck me that Court got that part wrong.

I considered a quick trip to Madame Tuleh again, but our money was too tight for excursions. We didn't hear from Daddy—or Mama, or Court, for that matter. We had no phone, and our nearest neighbor complained if he had to deliver a message. So other than our radio, movie magazines, and a local newspaper, we were cut off from the world.

I glanced at the newspaper on a sun-drenched morning before leaving the house for work. Noticing the date, August 6, 1945, I realized it had been over three months since we arrived at Carolina Beach. No matter how hard I tried to slow the hands of time, the days disappeared in a gust. But then the headlines screamed across the airwaves and newspapers. "U.S. Drops Atom Bomb; Hope for Earlier End to War." Frightened at the state of the world, I thought of all the young men I'd known in school and the few from church—most never returned from the war. It seemed like every family on Russell Street had lost a son, a brother, or a husband. Those who came home were never the same. I diverted my thoughts to Court. How handsome he looked in his Air Force uniform. I prayed for his safety, then shook myself because it was my first time praying for anybody in years. Even for myself.

But Court didn't come back. We spent money we didn't have on telephoning the Air Force base. In the end, we heard his plane had crashed into the Pacific.

"The densest material on earth is a broken heart," Bertie said. "People usually make do with the hand life deals them. But it has dealt me a heart of stone. I can't see or feel my future anymore." Bertie crumpled Court's letter, shoved it into her sweater pocket, folded her arms, and fell into Ruby's tattered easy chair.

It woke her early. The whirr and roar of a low-flying plane spiraled across the house. Bertie's eyes flew open, enormous fear-filled puddles of tears. Sucking in air between clenched teeth, she stumbled out of bed. I watched her from my room. The tendrils of the nightmare clung to her, like the hair stuck to her face. She clamped her fingers over her lips to keep from crying out until I rushed to her side. Wrapping her in my arms, hearing the panic escape as one long pitiful wail; it broke me. My tears mixed with her own, holding her face to mine. Gradually, the familiar surroundings brought the world back into focus.

"It was a dream," I whispered. "Just a dream."

She waited for the relief those words had brought her in years past, but it didn't work this time. Life's nightmares were Bertie's realities. After months of struggling to put years of Mama's abuse behind her, and suddenly losing Court, those nightmares haunted every second of her existence.

For days, I sat helpless as my sister wandered through the dimness of the living room to the kitchen and back, rubbing her eyes, wishing she could sleep. She worried about everything; eventually, she never left her bed. She had tried to accept Carolina Beach as her new home. But Bertie never felt she'd had a home. A house and children with Court were simply fantasies—dreams.

Bertie had spent her only moments of happiness with the man she loved. Those few sacred moments were all he had given her.

The love of her life was dead. A life that had known so much loss. She adored Court's smile when he said her name. With his intelligence, wry humor, and innate thoughtfulness, Court wasn't like other men. Bertie never again expected to be thrilled when a man entered a room. She dreamed of him every night, and each dream became worse. Bertie's head was ringed in a vice of pain. I gave her aspirin every day, but it didn't help. She'd said her bowels were sick as if her very intestines were corroded and rotting. Lying in a bed that smelled of damp linen and desperation, Bertie resigned her young life to bad luck and one nightmare after another.

On a Tuesday morning in late November, Bertie peered out the window at the darkening sky over the ocean. "There must be a storm coming in," she said. I made coffee, but she refused a cup or any bite of breakfast. She sat at the window instead, staring at the sea as if waiting for Court to walk out of the waves. Storm clouds gathered as tears fell off her chin. Distant thunder and lightning rolled and cracked across the sky, and I saw her shiver, still fighting remnants of constant bad dreams.

Suddenly, Bertie struck her face and chest with both fists. She wanted to pummel her body, blacken eyes that had seen too much, stop a heart that had loved and hated too much. She screamed that the pulse in her head beat so violently she couldn't stand it. I grabbed my sister and held her. It was all I could do. The thousands of words I'd spoken to her heart in the past few weeks went unheard and unchecked. I knew I had to get help. I was losing her.

When I awoke the next morning, our home was silent as a grave.

Bertie was gone. I ran through the house, up and down the street and boardwalk, and finally, to the beach. A group of locals had gathered around a body that lay still on the sand, and I knew it was her. I staggered through the crowd and looked into the sorrowful eyes of a stranger who had tried to revive her. As frightened as Bertie was of water, she had walked into the sea. I fell on top of my sister, crying salty tears that mingled with the seawater beading up on her body. She was out of her pain. It was my turn to lose the love of my life.

~ July 1946 ~

The year passed by in a blur. Buying booze on the boardwalk was easy, and the bars and stores served anyone who appeared old enough. Ruby always said Carolina Beach was a drinking town with a tourist problem.

I turned into a younger version of Aunt Ruby, working all day at Clyde's Cleaners and all night at Midtown Motor Court. I needed diversion; they needed a night clerk. Busting my butt kept me from the house, memories of Bertie, and the vodka bottle. If I ended up with time off, I drank until I passed out in my sister's old bed. Too young to die and too pissed off to walk into the sea. Cheated out of happiness, I had lived a lifetime before turning twenty. The world's war was over, but mine had just begun.

Making enough money to purchase a few new outfits, I decided the time had come to be the whore Mama raised me to be. My new red skin-tight skirt with a kick-pleat in the back hugged my round rear and matched my body-hugging sweater. I dressed it with a string of Bertie's fake pearls and matching earrings. Slipping into four-inch heels, I hung my pocketbook in the crook of my arm, painted my lips, lit my cigarette, and swung my hips to the nearest bar.

Women rarely visited Skipper's Bar and never on a Sunday. It was the kind of bar a woman, looking for her husband, sent her kid in to drag him home. Dozens of eyes flashed at me through murky shadows. I walked, unconcerned, across a sticky, liquor-stained floor. The click of my heels echoed off the wood-paneled walls. A few men dropped their stares back into their drinks, but most kept their sloppy gazes helplessly fixed on my backside.

Determined to be a sophisticated whore, I asked for a Fuzzy Navel. "It's that peach-colored shit," I explained to the bartender.

"Oh," he nodded. "Our drinks don't come in colors or fruit flavors."

"How about a Slippery Nipple?" I asked and winked.

"How about whiskey?" He suggested.

"Give her a beer," a familiar voice told him.

Slowly turning my head to the end of the bar, I squinted to see through the cloud of smoke and through my failures, fiascos, and of course—the ghosts. "Court?"

"Skipper's house whiskey tastes like it could strip the varnish off wood," he said.

I froze. It *was* a ghost.

"Hey, Bobbie Sue. Mind if we talk?"

Too startled to offer any objection, I nearly fainted.

He moved to the stool next to mine.

For a moment, my words wedged in my throat. "We thought you were—d—"

"—Dead?"

"Yeah."

"So did Uncle Sam. It's a long story. How are you, Bobbie?"

"Fine. I guess I'm fine." In shock, I somehow managed to give him a quick hug. Rotating my bar stool, I needed to see him straight on. Watch his eyes. Hear his story.

He spoke of being shot down into the cold water of the Pacific, found unconscious, and transported to a wounded battleship that limped into a port in Guam, where he was hospitalized and remained in a coma for over two months.

"When the doctors released me from the hospital, the Air Force flew me to D.C. I discovered they had told Bertie I was dead. I wanted to return to North Carolina for her, but I called your neighbor to take her a message before I arrived, not wanting to scare her. He told me what had happened." Court shrugged his shoulders and sighed. "I came anyway. To grieve, I suppose."

The truth spilled over in his tears, embarrassing him.

"I've been to her grave. Then I realized I needed to see you, too. Tell you how sorry I was. I loved her, Bobbie; I really loved her. Her passing—it broke my heart."

Clearly as tormented as I was by the unexpected blow of losing Bertie, Court sat silent for a moment. I sipped my beer to calm my nerves and felt a line of foam across my upper lip. I wiped it away with my thumb. He had just come in from swimming in the ocean. His hair was still wet, and there were small damp patches where his skin pinked through his cotton shirt.

We sat and talked about Bertie into the late afternoon, and I agreed to meet him for drinks again the next day.

"You look good, Court, for what you've been through."

"Thanks; although the hearing in my left ear is shot, I'm limping like an old man, and I've put on some weight. But on the positive side, I've still got 20/20 vision."

"Here's to good vision," I said, holding out my glass.

He clinked his against mine.

I took another gulp of beer.

"You know, we're a couple of losers when it comes to finding happiness," I said.

He nodded. "Here's to finding happiness."

We clinked glasses again.

I took another gulp of beer. This time, Court reached out and wiped the foam off my upper lip with *his* thumb.

He dropped a few crumpled bills on the bar. I downed the rest of my beer, and we slid off our stools. Court followed me and whispered over my shoulder. "Did Bertie ever tell you how we met?"

I uttered a slight giggle. "She said you stared at her when we were sunbathing on the sand. That you followed us home like a love-sick schoolboy. Like we were a couple of beach babes." Court moved around me to open the door. Standing in a silhouette of soft daylight, he smiled a smile I remember to this day.

"I *was* following. But not to meet Bertie. I was following *you*."

I think my chin dropped to my chest. I backed against the door jamb. "But—"

"—I ran into Bertie the next day on the beach; this time, she was alone, and I bought one of her barbeque sandwiches. Everything happened from there. I fell in love with her. How could I not? But *you* were the beach baby I wanted to meet."

Court stamped a quick kiss on my forehead. His hand slid into mine, pulling me out of the bar behind him. The sun blinded me; I couldn't see a thing. I lifted my free hand to shield my eyes as he led me and I thought of the old hymn, *Where He Leads Me, I Will Follow.* The whole meet-cute thingy scared me. My sudden desire to find Jesus again also frightened me.

Court and I met every day after that for weeks. Guilt plagued my every waking moment, and I felt I had betrayed Bertie. On August 1st, I stood at my sister's grave and asked her to forgive me for falling in love with Court. The following day, I found the letter he had written to her in a drawer of her things I couldn't part with. I showed Court the letter, and we agreed Bertie loved us enough to forgive both of us. But suddenly, I knew in my heart she would want *me*, rather than another woman, to have Court. So, I allowed myself to be taken over by him. Entirely.

We were married on the last day of August in 1946.

~ June 1952 ~

Beachfront property, unbeknownst to me, was a valuable asset. We sold Ruby's old shack and acre of land and bought a small house near Wilmington. An expert in investing and saving his pennies, Court took advantage of the post-war land development boom. In a matter of months, we broke ground on a new house with the biggest bathroom I had ever hoped for.

In time, I grew restless and decided to go to college. I graduated near the top of my class. Then I shocked my husband when I asked him to join a new church with me. Later, we both walked hand-in-hand down the aisle and dedicated our lives to the work of God.

Next, I surprised myself when I said I wanted to attend seminary. But I went just the same, with Court's full support, and he sent me to the best. To Harvard Divinity School.

The day I graduated, I recognized a familiar face smiling at me in the audience. She had cleaned herself up and lost weight, but she was there and as bohemian as ever. *Tuleh, of all people, to seek me out and attend my graduation.*

I recalled her ancient prediction—that I would lead many to righteousness. When I looked for her afterward, someone said she'd returned to Carolina Beach. I tried to locate her days later. She had locked her shop and put a sign on the door: *Out Of Business.* The merchant next door said the authorities had deported her.

Mama died in '48. After the boarding house sold, she moved in with Juba Lee, who wrote a letter explaining Mama had contracted pneumonia and died in her sleep. That was best. I never saw her again after the day Bertie and I left her standing alone in the church, screaming bloody murder. But I didn't hate her anymore, either.

Daddy passed on, too. He willed me a parcel of land in Sparta, North Carolina. Court and I moved to Sparta, to the Blue Ridge. We built a church there where I preach to a small, devoted congregation. Court hailed from Boone originally, so it was like going home for him. Several generations of Callahan relatives were buried near an old homestead, which sits on two hundred and fifty acres of mountain property near Boone.

But the best part has been the birth of our son, Matthew. My son will have a blessed childhood. And my prayer for him is to someday find the love of his life.

My road has been a complicated one, long and sometimes treacherous. I have traveled from a godless existence to one filled with the Holy Spirit. From childhood molestation to experiencing the true meaning of love. From abject poverty to the comfort of having more than enough. From the dark nights of loneliness into the light of family and friends. From the deepest of sorrows to the highest of joys. From death into life. What Satan stole from me, God restored—seven times over.

On many Sundays, I lead congregations to righteousness. I fulfilled a harlot's prophecy. I relate to the destitute, to the homeless, to the unloved. I teach others to give love and to receive love. I minister to women on the edge who have lost everything, including the ability to reason, and those who cannot forgive. And though I fall short occasionally, God has seen fit to make my path a plain path. This is my destiny, my journey.

I carry on without her. Despite her death, I still see her in all the old, familiar places. But through the years, nothing will take her out of my heart; she was part of me—every day. She still is. My Alberta Lou. My Bertie. My beach baby.

Coal Dust On My Feet

I was born a coal miner's granddaughter, which inspired the story **COAL DUST ON MY FEET**.

Widen, West Virginia, a coal town that haunted my childhood, was once involved in a reign of terror that is said to be the most prolonged and violent coal strike in American history. As a child, I was privy to bits and pieces of these stories.

A land not settled or tamed easily, this state produced resilient and proud citizens. West Virginia coal miners and their children did not romanticize their lives. They survived them.

Some of the country's most fierce and rugged lands exist within these rolling Appalachian mountains, hills, and valleys. There are no expanses of level ground. Anyone driving Interstate 77 through West Virginia can testify to its extreme twists and turns.

Due mainly to the terrain, the outside world only existed in an occasional radio program or newspaper article, even as late as the 1950s. Time stood still in the hollers and mountains around Clay County for many years. Life for my grandfather centered on his family and his job, mining coal for the Elk River Coal and Lumber Company.

Visiting my grandfather's company house in Widen, which still stands, I developed a powerful curiosity about the place I knew as a child. Over months of research, I discovered deep family roots in the area. My grandfather played a part in the Strike of 1952, siding with the company loyal to him through the Great Depression. Unfortunately, his family split their loyalties; some with the company and others with the miners.

This story includes actual places and people. Jack Hamrick, Ed Heckelbech, Bill Blizzard, Charles Frame, John Lewis, Jennings Roscoe Bail, Governor Marland, and Joseph Bradley were people who either lived in or near Widen and were associated with the coal strike. Otherwise, the plot and remaining characters are fictional, created from my imagination purely for storytelling. But the violence from September 1952 to Christmas Eve 1953 is legendary, and those killed and maimed live on in their family's memories to this day.

Cousin against cousin, father against son—and the union, though it failed to break the back of the company, changed things. Eventually, the company closed its doors. In its heyday, 3,000 people lived in the coal town of Widen. Today, there are less than 200. The town folded up except for the post office and a few who refused to leave.

Woven from threads of family history, COAL DUST ON MY FEET is a tale of love and betrayal, forbidden passions, long-buried secrets, and one woman's struggle with her heritage and her God—and the ancient bridge where the real and the supernatural meet.

~ Widen, West Virginia, September 1952 ~

*N*o one knew how long the strike would last.

Bullets whizzed past Thirl Nettles' head. Bolting for cover, he leaped into his 1940 Plymouth sedan. His right leg throbbed with a red-hot searing pain all the way up into his groin. Only moments before, he'd left the League of Widen Miners meeting, strolled past the tipple, and whistled his favorite song, *Walking The Floor Over You.*

"Thirl! You okay?"

"I've been hit!" He slid down on the seat and pressed his hand on the wound, the inside of his car spinning around his head.

"Hold on!"

The pain shot through him like nothing he'd experienced before. Not just a pain—an explosion like a live grenade thrown into his body. It couldn't be contained. It spread and expanded, searching for ways to escape the confinement of his skin. His flesh vibrated with it.

Hearing his heartbeat in his ears, he glanced down at his legs. Dark, warm blood soaked his pants. For a moment, he was sure they were his dad's legs, the day they carried his dead body out of the Macbeth mine explosion. Thirl lay motionless on the seat as more rifle fire struck his car until dark was the only hand he had to hold before he passed out.

Dawn arrived, sifting its dull light through DeDe Nettles' lace panel curtains. In the front room, the coal stove grumbled, and ashes rattled into the ash pan. The morning grew miserably cold. Raw and damp. The damp that eats into your bones and sucks out the marrow. It had rained for two weeks straight. Buffalo Creek ran high, its steep banks muddy and slick.

Thirl opened his dark eyes to find a blurry Doctor Vance hovering over him and the other side of the bed smoothed by his wife's small hand, her pillow tucked tight under the chenille spread. Groggy, Thirl recalled the shooting and tried asking who came to his rescue, but the room swirled around his bed. Hearing the doctor's voice fade, Thirl succumbed to the darkness again.

Doctor Sherwood Vance, a wide, solid stump of a man, boldly bald and nearsighted behind wire-rimmed glasses, mainly muttered to himself but partly to DeDe.

"Bastards—lowlifes. Miners, they call themselves, but they have no loyalties, not to their town, country, or even each other. They call themselves godly men, but they'd sell their souls for a wooden nickel and a plug of tobacco." The good doctor worked the bulge of his jowls while changing Thirl's bandages. "They talk like politicians, up one side and down the other. No respect for the League trying to make life better. What do they expect when somebody, like Jack Hamrick, goes berserk in the mine! He deserved to be fired!"

DeDe unfolded another blanket and pulled it over her husband to keep him warm. She had combed back his oiled hair and washed the coal dust from his face and body the best she could. He'd kept a trim figure all these years despite his diet of fried potatoes, sausage, and squirrel. And daily helpings of molasses and biscuits. Like most men who worked in a coal mine, the man ate for enjoyment.

DeDe watched their son, James, pull his legs up to his chest and sink into the bottom of his dad's bed. He stared at the blood on the floor. At nineteen, he stood tall like Thirl, sharing his unreadable dark blue eyes and constant smile. But where his dad's hair blended into the mountain's brown clay, James inherited her burnt red locks, often appearing as if they'd been dipped in honey when the sun hit at the right angle. She hugged her son's shoulder, pulled off his cap, and kissed the top of his head.

Until that moment, she had no strength to ask questions. Her immediate concern was to assist the doctor in keeping her husband alive. But rage bubbled under the surface of her constraint, searching for a way out of her mouth. She wiped the sweat from her forehead with the back of her wrist and followed the doctor into the kitchen to prime the pump and heat water. Tears dripped down her cheeks, watching Doc Vance lean into the sink to scrub her husband's blood off his hands.

All the nights DeDe lingered in her kitchen while Thirl washed up after work, they troubled her now. Every evening he stripped to the waist, never minding the mine dirt that covered him like shoe polish. Dipping over and over in water to his elbows, he turned the water black, scrubbing with a wire brush and hard granite-like soap, nearly removing the flesh from his arms. She thought she'd never again see the correct color of his skin. Permanent coal dust had collected in the wrinkles on his face and the creases in his neck. To DeDe, her husband's hands looked like a black bear's paws.

Of course, she'd heard him brag, more than once, that he'd never lost a finger in the mine. She also knew he regarded non-life-threatening professions as jobs for women or over-educated men. Thrown into a world between Heaven and Hell, Thirl walked to work every morning while DeDe watched from the front porch. She'd heard the Catholics had a name for it. But unlike everybody else who lived in a coal town, her husband remained content in the place he stood—never expecting God to give him more. Even if he deserved it.

A sob caught in her throat, and her voice and stare were equally painful. "What happened, Doc?"

Doc Vance dried his hands on a clean towel. "Thirl stood in the room when Harry Gandy fired Jack Hamrick last week. You know Jack and Opal? I believe they attend your church."

"Don't recall his face. I know his wife." She wiped tears with the cuffs of her blouse, then motioned for him to sit at the kitchen table.

"The way I heard it, Hamrick went plum crazy last week when asked to work in a trackless section of the mine. Management wanted to try out a new machine. Hamrick flew into a rage, shouting and screaming, 'The job's not safe! You'll kill the men!' Damn fool, took a pop bottle, broke off the end, and slashed an inch-long gash in his supervisor's cheek. Took me an hour to stitch him up. You got any coffee?"

"I'll make some," DeDe said. After rinsing out cups, she filled the coffee pot with water and Maxwell House and then turned the electric stove on high. While it perked, DeDe scrubbed found blood off the table with rough sweeps of her arm. Her elbows pumped sharply as she sniffed more tears back into her head.

Doc Vance removed his blood-spattered glasses and wiped each lens slowly. "I wasn't there when Gandy fired Hamrick. But I walked into Gandy's office tonight after the League meeting. Thirl had just left. Nobody expected miner retaliation. After all, it'd been a week since they'd fired Hamrick—but Jonas Zirka, a troublemaker in my mind, got everybody stirred up. When problems come to the mine, and things look bad, one man always thinks he's got all the answers and will take command. Usually, that individual is crazy. This time, it's Zirka. Hamrick needed firing. But Zirka's gonna use it and some other lame issues to bring in the Union again. Lies are an infectious disease. Zirka contracted it from some fat cat in the United Mine Workers. Anyway, I heard the gunfire. So did Gandy."

DeDe stormed back into her husband's sick room and glared at her son. "Get a message to Mister Gandy. Make sure he knows it was your daddy who's been shot. Use the phone in his office to call the sheriff."

"Ain't no use calling the sheriff, Mama. They done formed a picket line at the top of Widen hill. Doc's right. Zirka's behind it. All that noise last night, those car horns blowing and moving through the streets—the strike's on. I was with Savina last night. When I took her home, it was Odie who told me 'bout Daddy. I wanted to go straight to the sheriff. But her daddy said the law won't come unless somebody's dead 'cause Widen is all private property, owned by Joseph Bradley. Odie said he's going to side with the men. Go on strike." DeDe knew her son saw no point in holding back the truth, even from a woman.

"Then you get a message to Savina's daddy. Tell Odie he best remember who helped him with his farm last year when Josephine died." She gave her son a maternal once-over that made him instinctively straighten up from his slouched position on the bed.

"Yes, Ma'am. Next time I see Savina."

"Your girl, Savina, she's welcome here, James, but Odie won't allow your skinny Company butt on his property. Not now."

"No, Ma'am."

She watched James lower his gaze to her bare feet and chipped toenails spattered with blood. DeDe turned to search for her shoes, remembering Thirl's promise to take her to the church sing next week in Gassaway. She'd planned to wear shoes with her toes sticking out. Two nights before, she held a bottle of red nail polish in front of Thirl. "Real pretty," he'd said.

Doc Vance carried two cups of coffee in from the kitchen. With his elbows fanned out and his eyes on the coffee, he glided up and handed her a cup, stiffly easing himself down on the chair beside her. They continued the vigil beside Thirl's bed, watching his chest rise and fall with each breath as if, at any moment, the body would change from a wounded man to a corpse.

"Odie ain't too bright," said Doc. "The man has only two more years of work to gain a pension but decides to strike. Told me he ain't paying fifty cents a month to that no 'count Company League. Damn black throat. The pension eligibility rules require twenty years of service, of which Odie already has eighteen. The man's throwing away $1,200 a year for life to save twelve dollars. I swear, he sleeps with his head up his ass!"

James sat staring at the wall, his thoughts tumbling over one another in no particular order. An hour after Hardrock Dodrill and Boney Butcher called Doc Vance, drove Thirl home, and then carried his bloody body into the house, James assigned himself guard duty over his dad's bed.

Dazed and irritable at five in the morning, James stood, stretched, then aimed his numb body to the front room, where he fell into his dad's favorite chair, facing a magnificent ten-point buck's head hanging on the wall. A buck they'd hunted for two years until Thirl bagged him last Thanksgiving. His dad killed it, and he sketched it. James had collected his charcoal drawings from the time he was old enough to hold a pencil. His mother stored them in her chifforobe but hung a framed sketch of the live buck on the wall next to its dead head.

James rested back against the old chair, drifting between sleep and memory. Turning his head, he leaned into the scent of his dad's hair tonic and lye soap buried deep in the leather. He saw himself as a child, lifted onto his dad's shoulders in the Thanksgiving Barn. He recalled his dad's coal-crusted hands thumbing through the Bible on Sundays, his mother insisting he sit still on a hard church pew, and how he sat between them on that pew, playing with the flexible watchband peeking out from under his dad's sleeve. How the gold had worn off, and how it pulled at the hairs on his dad's arm.

He remembered his dad sucked peppermints and whistled when he drove. On his dresser, he kept a pickle jar full of change. Each night James listened to the tinny pings of nickels, dimes, and pennies as his dad emptied his pockets into the jar. The sounds of his childhood as he drifted off to sleep.

His mother had educated him on the importance of coal and how it kept food on their table and heated every home in the country during winter. "Why, without coal and the miners who bring it to the surface," she'd said, "America is no better than some dying country in Africa with starving children." James waved to his mother every morning, stopping at her flower garden—a giant truck tire laid flat and painted white. James had positioned it next to the dogwood tree in the front yard, a tree she'd insisted his dad plant the day he was born.

Now, the world had changed overnight. Reliving the past twenty-four hours, he remembered arriving at the mine, walking through wisps of smoke left hanging in the air—the last puffs of his dad's cigarette. "Tell your mama I'll be home late; I have a League meeting after my shift," he'd said.

His dad was fine then, and now he wasn't. *How did it get this far?*

James had dressed for work like he did every morning. The men who worked that shift called it *morning*. But it was still night to James—dark, cold, and silent. He heard the click of his dad's boots pacing the kitchen floor while he waited for his lunch bucket. His dad's muffled voice and his mother's as they said their goodbyes—sounds that haunted him now.

Together, they walked out of their soot-coated house and crossed the front yard. He and his dad were no different from dozens of other men, crossing their own front yards, wearing hard hats with lamps attached to the front, and carrying lunch buckets the size of toolboxes. A mass of miners chewing plugs of tobacco to lubricate their throats against gritty coal dust.

A first-shift supervisor, his dad worked for Elk River Coal and Lumber for as long as he remembered. He'd said mining provided a good living and would do the same for James. Proud to be a miner's son, James followed, as expected. He'd worked the mines from the day he graduated high school, never revealing his plans to leave Widen and the life he knew. As far as his parents were concerned, he was born a miner for the Company.

His dad squeezed his arm every morning without saying a word. A quick grasp just after turning the key in the ignition, keeping his eyes straight ahead. He'd never talked about their work or the dangers of it. His grip was a fast second of assuredness that everything would be fine—today. It was their unspoken secret, one they shared man to man.

James couldn't recall how long he'd been sitting there. He just knew his head ached from lack of sleep, and his stomach growled from lack of food, but he stood and walked three steps to the gun cabinet. Selecting a twelve-gauge shotgun from the rack and a box of shells from one of the bottom drawers, he shoved three shells into the gun's magazine. After jacking a bullet into the chamber and engaging the safety, James paused, peeled off his Elk River Coal and Lumber Company cap, and tossed it on the buck's right antler. Grasping the shotgun in both hands, he kicked open the front door and slipped out of his mother's line of sight.

Doc Vance checked Thirl's pulse and then packed his medical bag. "Keep that wound clean and dressed. Send James to the office if you need me. Your lucky husband should be fine. Shove these pills down his throat for the next few weeks. We'll watch for infection. A few more inches and that bullet would've severed a major artery."

The old doctor hadn't stopped talking since he arrived minutes after they laid Thirl on his bed. "The League of Widen Miners is a legal bargaining agency for Bradley's employees. That committee came together to create the Company's welfare plan for its workforce, and I helped to put it in motion. That League is a fine group of men as God ever made. Sure, the Company formed the League, but it offers medical and retirement. Don't those fool strikers remember the mine stayed open two and three days a week during the Depression, even when other mines shut down? Don't they remember that?"

"Lord, Doc, they've been trying to strike here since I was a girl. You're really worried this time, aren't you? How long do you think this one will last?"

"How long's hard to say. As long as it takes. As long as the United Mine Workers provide their strike fund. John Lewis and Bill Blizzard are behind this one again, bigger and better organized than the last strike. I'm afraid it'll get more violent before it's over, as long as the miner's morale doesn't crack."

DeDe set her coffee cup on the table by Thirl's bed. "I believe I've told you I'm not from Widen. My family came here from Matewan to escape that town's reputation, violence, and death. Daddy died here, in Widen, from black lung back in '44. Mama, well, she passed from black lung too. From thirty years of washing Daddy's clothes." DeDe smoothed the front of her bloodstained blouse, her stare drifting through the windows and then back to Thirl. Her voice remained strained but soft. "My daddy believed Joseph Bradley owned the safest mines in the state, so we moved here. But the mines will kill us all, eventually."

Every man in her life had been or was a miner, including her son. They all learned the speech patterns of the coalface. The walls spoke to seasoned miners in response to the slightest tap of a pick or a shovel. Sighs, hisses, pops, squeaks, groans, crackles, gurgles—each sound warned of underground water, a weak wall, or a methane leak. Her father once told her that if the mine choked and found itself about to crumble, it shuddered first, then screamed like a terrified woman.

But to DeDe, a prolonged strike was as dangerous as a cave-in. "I've seen the killing a strike will bring. I'll protect my own."

Her face was already beginning to sag, her carefully groomed hair was already beginning to gray, and her eyes were already receding into a calm, dark indifference most people saw as insight. Makeup and skincare did not fit into her budget. DeDe looked down at her bitten half-moon fingernails, then twisted her thick copper hair into a knot and anchored it with a comb and pins at the private part of her neck.

She stood and retrieved her pocketbook from the closet.

Everybody in town, including the good doctor, knew she kept a gun in her purse. She walked back into the kitchen, gripping it against her chest, and Doc Vance followed on her heels.

"DeDe! Now you listen to me. I won't have you or any other woman in this town in harm's way. You let the men handle this. The Company recruited its own force. Thirteen good and loyal men, I've heard. Sworn in as deputies by the County Sheriff to guard the town. Stay out of it, DeDe; I mean it." Like two grimy nickels, his eyes glared as sternly as his warning. "You tell the rest of the women to stay close to home and keep their young'uns in the house after school. I've always been fond of your family. Why, it was just yesterday, I delivered James in this house."

"Yes, you certainly did. Actually, it was nineteen years ago. And you stood by us when we buried a stillborn son five years later. I've had enough heartache, Doc."

Doctor Vance nodded, avoiding her eyes, then gathered his jacket and medical bag. "You know management's secret weapon when there's a strike? It's the women. Mama goes a few months with only gut paste gravy and biscuits to fix for supper; the old man's hanging 'round the house drinking and yelling because the kids're sick and crying. Dirty clothes are lying everywhere, and he's gone most evenings to a Union meeting or finishing his shift on the picket line, coming home tired, cold, dirty, and stinking of liquor. Drives every woman I know crazy. They'll settle because their wives'll make them settle."

DeDe nodded in return. She picked up his hat and led him to the door. As the granddaughter of a Baptist minister who mined West Virginia coal at the turn of the century, she figured that might count for something with God. DeDe smiled deceptively and handed the doctor his hat. "Vengeance is mine, saith the Lord of hosts."

"You just remember that," he said as the screen door spanked shut behind him.

DeDe Nettles was a pistol. She carried a .38 Smith & Wesson at thirty-nine years of age and could shoot straight. When she slipped it into her apron pocket, it felt heavy, like a ball and chain. Stifling a yawn, she shuffled out the back door for fresh air. Stretching and leaning over the railing, hearing—she wasn't sure. "Raccoons trying to get to the chickens." Whispering to herself, she wasn't sure if she shivered from the stiff wind or the voices blowing in from the yard. "The whole world's gone crazy." DeDe quickly spun back into the kitchen and locked the door behind her. It was the first time she'd turned that lock since she'd married Thirl and moved into the house on Nicholas Street.

After pouring another cup of coffee, she needed the comfort of her chair. A Christmas present Thirl brought from Charleston on the train years ago. The same year he purchased their first refrigerator and added the bathroom to the back of the house. She had placed the overstuffed velvet beauty next to his leather monstrosity.

DeDe smacked the back of the chair before she sat. An impulse from living her whole life in a dusty coal town. She recalled the first time she sat in that chair, shocked at her reflection in the window, laughing that she looked like a redheaded kewpie doll. But now, life's sorrows stared out of her lashless brown eyes. Up close, her skin revealed a vague meshwork of lines and wrinkles, like an orange peel. DeDe had witnessed firsthand the hardships of mining life on women, and she was no exception. Every miner's wife she knew aged quickly.

For all her religious dreams, visions, and premonitions, she headed the women's Bible study group every week, specializing in prayer for miners' safety. Petite but often the most prominent presence in the room, DeDe's physical size many times went unnoticed. Some folks said she had the *gift*. Her grandma had it, and so did her mama. An uncanny ability to see and hear what ordinary folks did not. Deanna Nettles kept her personal thoughts to herself and was never prone to gossip, but when she spoke, folks paid attention.

Still, she shot a perfect game of pool on any given Saturday night, arriving on time for Sunday school the following morning after collecting every child for miles. It amused Thirl that his wife testified about sanctification like she invented it. But no one questioned DeDe's devotion to her husband, her son, and her God.

With as much commitment and passion as Joseph Bradley when he built his coal empire in Widen, her loyalty lay with her family, not the Company. Bound to protect her own, DeDe did not mince words. Her soft smiles became few, reserved mainly for James. The whole of Widen knew she loved her boy, and that James was her prize possession.

DeDe's hand slipped into her pocket; her fingers clasped the cold metal of her gun. With her other hand, she reached out to the table beside her, lifting the tintype of her grandfather, turning it in the dimly lit room, tilting it this way and that, gauging the severity of his lifeless face. He was God's minister, yet she wondered if he heard the mine scream before his head snapped toward the explosion and the rumble of the fireball—before he was incinerated. Or maybe he never saw it coming. Perhaps tons of earth buried him without warning. Maybe thousands of pounds of rock and boulders crushed his bones, split open his organs, annihilated his senses, and wiped out his life before he understood what was happening. But she doubted it.

The coal town sprawled over the bottom of the holler some sixty miles northeast of Charleston, the state capital. The narrow county road to Widen coiled over and around every hill and gully, eventually turning into a broken dirt road with ruined shoulders and potholes. At the top of the steep slope that dropped into town, a posted warning read, HILL, until somebody scratched it into the word HELL.

At the bottom, insignificant Company houses sat back from the road at the mountain's edge. Occasionally, a larger house broke the chain of smaller ones. Not the typical plaid grids of flatland towns, Widen's twisting octopus of streets swirled through the valley. Although the valley sprawled wide, as they usually did in that part of the country, only one road and one railroad led in and out of town. Deafening coal and passenger trains rode the rails and filled the valley with screeching brakes and shrill whistle stops.

A loose-plank bridge near the Grille Canteen and Pool Hall rumbled like thunderclaps each time a vehicle drove over the creek. Depending on the weather, the fast-moving stream collected beer bottles, candy bar wrappers, and cigarette butts. Paved streets belonged in cities like Charleston and Huntington. Slag, coal, or dirt had covered Widen's roads since its conception.

The town lived and breathed coal. The Company's huge gob piles, ominous heaps of mine waste with their guts ablaze, filled a person's nostrils with the pungent odor of struck matches. Some over thirty feet high, the graceful slopes of loose coal and sulfurous dirt glowed a muted orange.

The tipple's steam rose like the breath of a monster. A place where miners screened and loaded coal into railroad cars, the tipple demanded the town's attention and tribute. Its silo, locomotive shed, and repair shops hugged the Company's railroad yard that Joseph Bradley bought and paid for. He owned the tipple and nearly every business in between, including 310 dwellings. Bradley owned Widen. But it was first and foremost a coal mine, and the people who gave their blood and sweat to it seldom left town.

The trees may not have been straighter in Widen, the grass greener, the sky bluer, or the mountains more purple and majestic, but when the mine produced, it often seemed so. On warm summer mornings, the locals told their children and each other that God covered His black gold with these hills, this place—first.

But those stories ended. During the first weeks of September, after the strike shut down the mine, the town's inhabitants remained behind closed doors, clothed in fear. The school closed, the Grille closed, and even the post office closed the day after the strikers dug in and parked their cars, sons, and guns at the top of the hill. The road into Widen.

Inhaling the rugged land of his childhood, James watched Odie Ingram skirt the timber at the far end of the east pasture, mounted on a young, edgy bay colt. Huge maples, oaks, and hemlocks towered over everything, standing still in full foliage on the mountain behind his farm.

Odie worked hard in the mines, and he worked his horses hard. Always welcome on the Ingram farm, James had no idea what Odie might say now that they were on opposite sides.

James stood at the gate and leaned his shotgun against the fence. He knew most of the boys he'd gone to school with sided with the strikers, and he wasn't taking any chances. Boys like Cole Farlow, known for his hot head and short fuse. Cole spouting off that he'd shoot a kiss-ass Company man faster than a nigger-lover—those words stuck in James' craw like a tough piece of meat he couldn't swallow.

If the strikers had tried to kill his dad, they'd shoot at anybody. James respected his dad's position. He'd never side with the Union. Even if he shared a few Union sympathies, his love and loyalty to his family far outweighed any feelings for or against the Union.

But beyond his duty to honor his parents, he loved Savina with his soul, and today he intended to explain that to her father—hoping to keep his place in Odie's house as his future son-in-law.

James suspected Odie liked him well enough, but he'd made it clear—Savina could not marry until she turned eighteen. It was her daddy's stubbornness, Savina had said. James, in an attempt to be amiable, respected Odie's condition. But deep down, James doubted Odie would give his daughter away. James anticipated an eventual elopement. Many couples in Clay County married early, but Odie had an innate fear of living alone since his wife died, so James agreed to wait, hoping time ease his anxiety.

Odie rode high in his saddle, appearing taller than he was. Through the mist of daybreak, the dreamy scene played like a Western picture show. In the distance, on his favorite colt, Odie checked the mares for signs of illness or accident. The horses fanned away from Odie and the colt. Quick in the morning chill, the mares puffed funnels of breath and shook their heads at the inconvenience.

Never fond of the Company he worked for, Odie mined coal for one reason and one reason only—to pay off his farm and to raise quarter horses. Odie rode up to the barn, then jumped down and hitched the colt to a post, nodding to James. But when Odie ambled toward the back of the house instead of the gate, a chill ran the length of James' body.

Gazing up at the dreary sky, James dreaded confrontation almost as much as mountain winters. Still, he knew he couldn't stop conflict with Odie any more than he could stop the strike. And winter was on its way. The leaves were changing, like the rest of his world.

James walked toward the peeling, sagging farmhouse. A pack of spittle-flinging dogs barked and paced back and forth on the front porch. Chickens roamed freely. Savina quit trying to fix up the place after her mother died. The house had vomited its insides over the yard. Rusted bedsprings, a bloodstained mattress, dented pots, trashed books, unopened mail, empty Pennzoil cans, bald tires, corroded truck parts, and the stench of wet newspapers.

Odie kicked the screen door open and lifted his gun from his side. Gray drizzle blotted his skin as he stomped to the bottom porch step. Mud and manure covered his boots. His mouth spasmed at the corners, and he pulled twice at his ear with his free hand. Their eyes met with awkward glances. Odie's teeth clamped shut, and he stared at James with the eyes of someone who thought he was about to be told a fact he already knew.

James recalled what his daddy said about Odie. That he changed amazingly little over the last thirty years. Except for the paunchiness around his middle and the hair loss, he remained the same friendly boy he'd gone to school with. James considered the fact that his daddy didn't really know Odie.

"Morning, Mister Ingram. Savina in the house?"

"I figure she's down by the crick."

James nodded and headed in the creek's direction.

"James!" Odie cocked his rifle.

James froze, feeling Odie's fiery stare burn the back of his neck. He turned around. "Sir?"

A twelve-gauge aimed at his head revealed Odie's message before he spoke it. "I don't want you coming 'round here anymore. I don't want you seeing my Savina again."

Until that moment, James was unafraid of Odie's intimidation. But his attempt to keep him from Savina left him weak-kneed. "I have a right, Mister Ingram. I have a right to see her. We agreed."

Odie's blue eyes blazed, considering James' declaration. "Comp'ny men have no rights on my property."

"Mama thought you'd feel that way. Said to tell you to remember who helped you on the farm last year when Josephine died."

Odie lowered his gun by only an inch or two. "I don't need reminding. You tell your ma—Thirl and me are even. Ask Boney and Hardrock. Ask them who drove Thirl's car to the Grille last night. With him in it, passed out and bleeding like a stuck pig. I don't owe your daddy a thing, boy. He helped me when Jo died, and it was me who saved his life last night."

James opened his mouth, but nothing came out. Except for his eyes, Odie was a colorless man. His pale skin, gray hair, gray face stubble, and gray cigarette smoke swirling between his fingers matched the grayness of his voice. Pockmarks and scars marred his face. Small cauliflower ears poked out from the sides of his head. His left ear lobe, which he tugged whenever he felt uneasy, oozed with an open sore, and his nose lay flat against his face—the result of shoeing an uncooperative horse. James believed despite Odie's unattractive features, coarse speech, and rough manners, he possessed a sixth sense to observe the world around him, like a wolf in the wild.

James stuffed his hands in his jacket pockets and shrugged. "You and my daddy been mining together since you were my age."

Odie cleared his head and throat, coughed, then spit a plug of phlegm at one of his dogs. "Boy, you ain't telling me what I don't know. Your daddy and me spent years together in them deep, dank holes in the ground. Going in before sunup and coming out after sundown, Lord knows we never saw daylight for weeks. That cage dropped us like rocks hundreds of feet into them black holes. We'd walk to the tipple together with our dinner buckets every day, giving the Comp'ny another day's labor, never knowing if we'd come home."

Odie dropped his gun to his knees. "Anybody ever explain the definition of slave labor to you, son?" Odie flicked his cigarette to the ground. "It's coal mining. Men who work a job where they risk their lives every minute and at the end of the pay period owe more to the Comp'ny store than they made. Debts don't die with them, either. They're passed on to their children. It's time the Union comes in, makes things better, work less hours, stricter safety rules. You heard Zirka. Time to let some of the younger fellers in on them committees. You need to join us, James. Time *we* make some decisions."

"Daddy said Joseph Bradley has the highest safety standards in the state. He kept the mine open during the Depression so the men could feed their families. Daddy said Bradley pays as high as Union scale."

"Your daddy has his opinion about Bradley; I have mine. Bradley owns the damn bank. He owns us, boy. You think about that. We can't take a shit unless Bradley approves it. Now I'm telling you to get off my land. You best hope the Union gets into the Comp'ny; then maybe we'll talk again. Otherwise, Savina is off limits to you, son."

❧

"Deanna? Where are you, honey?" Thirl twisted his head, his eyesight blurry in the dim light of his bedroom. He dreamt of himself lying in a coffin with pennies on his eyes. That the undertaker placed the wooden box on sawhorses in their front room. He stretched his arm down to his leg—*still there*—trying to remember what happened, feeling like someone had sawed him in half. Thirl had prepared for a mine disaster all his life. He wasn't prepared for a bullet.

From his bed, Thirl focused on the burning coal in the stove. Like the red eyes of a black dragon squatting in the front room, blowing hot breath into the house, the dragon sat defiantly on its asbestos-sheathed-in-tin mat, waiting for an opportunity to strike. Thirl closed his eyes again. They felt hot. His mouth felt hot. His body—felt sick.

"DeDe, you in the kitchen?"

He sensed something staring at him and turned his head slowly. On the bed beside him laid his wife's sock monkey. It had always made him laugh. He tried to smile, but the pain wouldn't allow it.

Daylight faded, and the room darkened into a roundness, like standing in the bottom of a well—or a mine. Managing no more than a hoarse whisper, only the tear tracks on Thirl's gritty face hinted at his agony.

"Deanna?"

DeDe kept vigil for three days, more in than out of her tiny bedroom. Preparing the oven for cornbread, she'd heated bacon grease in her iron skillet before pouring the batter. James would be home soon to check on his daddy. No one had eaten a bite the past three days until she pulled herself away from Thirl's bedside to cook something besides the pinto beans simmering on the stove. A food offering from her neighbor, Pearle.

Hearing her husband stir, she crept in and pulled the string to the ceiling light. A naked bulb, painting the walls a feverish glow that failed to reach the corners.

"You're awake." DeDe put on a smile she pulled from her sleeve and sat on the bed's edge. She wiped his brow with a cool cloth. "Here, take this pill. Doc Vance said it'd help. Someone shot you, but I suppose you know that."

Thirl fought an impulse to gag. Choking, he attempted to swallow the large pill.

"Sorry, darlin', but Doc said—"

"—Don't care what Doc said," he gagged again. "I can't swallow pills. Never could. You know that. And turn off that damn light bulb."

"Don't get pissy with me," she whispered. "I don't want to be a widow just yet, so if you don't mind, you'll swallow the pill whenever I give it to you."

DeDe stood and turned off the light. The glow from the front room seeped into Thirl's bedroom as she lit a kerosene lamp, placing it on a small table by the bed. Its light barely touched Thirl's head. But she sensed he preferred it.

Thirl sipped at the water glass she held at his lips, then asked, "How bad is it?"

"You'll live. But you're going to limp awhile."

"I mean the strike."

"Strikers cut off the town at the top of the hill. James says he's not sure yet if there're enough men to keep the mine open and how many of them live out of town."

"Tell James to stay away from the line; it's dangerous."

"Hush, now. You need to rest." She wiped his head again. DeDe felt his strength fading fast. "James is a man now and knows how to care for himself. You taught him well."

"No, honey, if he's got any good in him, it's from you."

DeDe wrung out the cloth in a chipped spatterware bowl. "Odie threw him off his farm."

"So. Odie's striking. I figured as much."

"It was Odie who saved your life. Drove your car to the Grille away from the danger. Hardrock and Boney were closing up the place. They brought you home. You'd lost a lot of blood."

"Odie was my best friend once."

"I know."

"I should've taken you and James to Oregon. Bought some land with my cousin after the war. I've wasted my life, DeDe." His eyes flashed a determination not to cry.

"We don't waste life, Darlin'. It wastes us."

~ October 1952 ~

Finding a few hundred of its workmen still available, The Elk River Coal and Lumber Company, which remained wholly shut down during the first week of the strike, resumed limited operations. But resumption brought Ed Heckelbech, UMW organizer, to the picket line, and the violence began again. Jonas Zirka and his pickets commanded the only road into Widen. They continued to cut off non-strikers who lived outside the town. All traffic in and out ceased.

As a warning to the few Company men who attempted to drive through the picket line, strikers shot out their tires, yanked out the driver, and dynamited their empty vehicle. If a man tried to cross the picket line again, a dozen strikers picked up the vehicle, shook it, and then rolled it with the driver inside, this time down Widen hill.

Odie stood on the picket line more than was required. Most nights remained quiet. Several times, though, he had thrown rocks and bricks at cars, and he'd been involved in rolling Delmar Tuller's car down the hill, but the scab limped away. Fruitless efforts to call the law proved that the state troopers sided with the strikers. Each time law officials arrived at the top of Widen hill, they'd tip their hats to the picket line, shoot the breeze a while, and head back to Charleston to report no disturbance. Company-paid armed guards prevented the total takeover of the coal town, but suspicions grew about how long that would last.

The strikers' most significant victory resulted on the day they stopped a train and forced the passengers to unload. Odie wasn't near the car where he'd heard Zirka struck a man and shoved him at gunpoint off the train. Nevertheless, Odie stood shoulder-to-shoulder with the rest of the picketers as they dynamited the railroad trestles at Sand Fork and Robinson. He'd been part of the crew, uprooting telephone posts, cutting a quarter mile of line into short pieces, and successfully isolating the town. Odie watched Widen citizens go hungry for the first time in over a decade. The strikers had effectively placed a chokehold on the town, and it wasn't bound to stop anytime soon.

Stepping on generations of leaves, Odie perched himself on a log with a straight shot into the switch house. Switch houses controlled electric circuits in the mines. Posted Company guards prevented entry of saboteurs, but clearly, a war now waged on the mountain. A war with no help from the law for Bradley's Company. Union votes, not Company votes, had put the Attorney General and Governor into office.

The strikers met to toss around ideas about how to keep the mines shut down. Cutting the electricity was Odie's idea. Contemplating his aim, Josephine's words shot into his mind like a silver bullet meant for his heart. *She loves the boy, Odie. I weren't but her age when I married you.* He'd worked his wife into an early grave and then spoiled his only child because of his burdening guilt. He'd allowed Savina to go off with James whenever she wanted. But he *needed* Savina at home now. The place fell apart without her. Thoughts of keeping Savina away from James plagued him more than the strike. He couldn't be with her every moment.

Odie was aware Savina had missed plenty of schooling the past year, and there'd be no going back to school for her until the strike was over, and maybe not even then. She had new responsibilities, bigger ones than books, learning, and frivolous high school activities.

From the surrounding hilltops, rifle bullets went whining into the switch houses. Odie fired his last shot, taking out the electricity in the mine and cutting all power into the town. He reached into his pocket for his tobacco pouch. Thumbing a plug into his lower lip, he hid in a rhododendron grove until darkness covered his trek back down the mountain.

"You're from that little shithole town, Widen, right?" The man bagging several carts of groceries eyed the two men in front of him warily.

Harry Gandy, Joseph Bradley's assistant and operations boss, and Red King, a loyal Company man, found an old logging trail over the mountain and got to Charleston to buy food, filling Harry's car to the brim.

"Yeah," said Red. "We're from Widen."

"What're you doing, buying groceries here?"

"We're on vacation. Thought we'd stock up on the way to the beach." Harry tipped his hat and snickered as Red paid the bill.

The carload of provisions had to be unloaded at the first blown-out bridge by a human chain, like a bucket brigade, passing the contents from hand to hand. They filled a railroad motor coach that was fortunately left in operating condition between the two blasted bridges.

They repeated the same process at the next destroyed bridge before the daily shipment finished its journey into town. At both transfer points, men worked while protected by Company guards. Harry Gandy continued to sneak in groceries for weeks. Unloading, passing bag after bag, and always under the watchful eyes of a man with a high-powered rifle.

Thirl stood with his crutches under his arms and grinned while the non-strikers filled wheelbarrows and sacks with meals for hungry families. Taking nothing for himself, he thanked God for the vegetable garden his wife insisted on growing every year. A garden that overtook most of his backyard. And he was grateful for the fruit cellar she'd made him dig years ago. He'd been quarrelsome and nearly refused. *I've dug enough dirt for Bradley; I don't need to dig it in my yard.* It shamed him to think how contrary he'd been. She always knew things he didn't.

Thankful for the hog she bought and butchered every year, Thirl appreciated that his wife also kept chickens in a coop behind several feet of chicken wire. As far as he was concerned, chickens were on a level not much higher than rats. He preferred deer meat and squirrel, but the store no longer stocked eggs. Able to collect them from her hens each morning, he'd stopped complaining.

Chocked full of jams and jellies, pickled beans, tomatoes, and corn, a pantry packed with pride and home-canned goods, DeDe had turned their house into a small eatery. She fed those most desperate. Her breakfasts of bacon, eggs, and biscuits with sorghum molasses filled the bellies of many Company men and their families over the next few months. Forks scraped against plates, and the clinking of glasses sounded like angels singing in the rafters.

Every morning, the smell of coffee drifted into his bedroom, along with the mournful songs of the Carter Family on the radio. Every sight, scent, and sound signaled to Thirl how lucky he was to have her. She looked fetching, even propped up against the refrigerator with her arms crossed, watching people eat. He sipped his coffee and gazed at the freckle on her forehead beneath the zigzag part of her hair. Her countenance melted him, making his chest and brain like corn mush. As the day wore on, the sensation hardened to a prickling along his spine, then to a low hum in his abdomen. He'd thought about her cooking, and he thought about her naked—in equal amounts of time.

She was his gift from God. Because she knew things. Odd things. More than a few times, his wife had told him of a coming flood or the imminent death of a healthy neighbor. She'd predicted the famine the year before it hit the mountain. But the day DeDe dropped her dusty beans on the porch because she'd *seen* Josephine fall dead in her kitchen, gripping her heart over five miles away, Thirl never doubted her again. And yet, he often wondered if she knew how much he loved her.

~ January 1953 ~

Winter came and stayed. Whiteouts followed snowstorms, each day gray with a fierce wind from the North. The deserted hollers of man and beast stood empty as wasteland; creeks morphed into perilous piles of ice, and air as brittle as kindling burned inside every nostril. Coal trains stopped because of the cold, as well as the strike. Water pipes cracked; nothing moved. All of West Virginia froze over as snow piled up, unsympathetic to the needs of people.

A hazy sun rose over another clouded sky while a charcoal film blanketed the snowscape. January drifts banked windowpanes, leveled streets, and faded the mountaintop above Widen like smoke. When the last storm petered out, the town lay steeped in fog—the ground-hugging kind that follows snow in valleys where coal towns nestle between mountains. Fog alone did not deter the citizens from carrying on with their lives, but fog with snow was something else. A person stayed inside, worn down by cold trips to the outhouse and restless sleep. Beneath this rag-and-bone sky, only the looming violence of strikers cast a shadow. Snow smothered every inch of ground where the land bordered Buffalo Creek.

James followed a deer path over the mountain. Rabbits scattered into thickets of rhododendron. Bobcat tracks pocked the drifts. He threaded his way over and through mountain trails with less difficulty than a sliver of soap through his fingers. Her love pulled him like a solar eclipse—breathtakingly beautiful, spellbinding, blinding him to her daddy's contention. Blessed with a young man's body, James knew coal dust had yet to bite at his insides, and he intended to keep it that way. In the meantime, passion and pleasure waited for him at the end of his path in a feather bed, in a secret place where they could be alone. A place where they'd made a pact to meet one night a week.

Savina told Odie that Hephzibah Kelly needed her help. Odie never checked on her for that one night, especially in Colored Holler.

Warm and dark, the little cabin smelled of wood and pine. Once occupied by escaped slaves, it had remained shrouded under thistle brush, pine boughs, and rhododendron for the past hundred years. Jabo Kelly told stories of how his inherited small farm had laid hidden in the federal state hills long before Widen and its coal became an idea in the mind of a young man named Joseph Bradley.

Surrendering to his wife's nag, Jabo allowed the two young lovers to use it. The Kellys loved Savina, who had claimed them as her best friends. Nobody but Savina ventured into Colored Holler. Mama Ola, Jabo's mother, had tended to Savina's sick bed months before, bringing Hephzibah with her. The women became friends and allies. An unusual relationship in Widen, which Odie Ingram tolerated and for which James was forever grateful. A relationship only a few families in Colored Holler knew about.

Savina scrubbed the cabin until her hands bled. Highpockets and Percy, Jabo's sons, assisted James in repairing the place for the better part of three weeks, turning it from a shack into a one-room hideaway complete with a working fireplace, feather bed, table, oil lamp, and a straight-back chair.

Careful to avoid being followed, James wended his way up a steep and snowy hill, eyeing the thicket of pines holding the cabin in its midst. He stood quietly for a moment, breathing deeply, his breath pluming in the frigid air. Picking up his heavy snow-packed boots, one after the other, James stepped into a blanket of white powder now three feet deep. Smoke curled out of the chimney; she was already there. Savina's footprints, followed by her dog's, left a trail for him to follow. James opened the door as Rascal barked.

"Hush, boy—it's me—shut up, boy." The old beagle panted and whined; his tongue, as pink as raw bacon, hung out of his mouth.

James stomped slush from his boots and walked over the threshold, tall and strong, like an oak tree covered with snow. Breathless, his nose dripped, and ice had crusted his hair. His cold cheeks turned red as maple leaves in autumn. James felt his chest and stomach constrict in a slow concussion of affection at the sight of her. She had told him he always rushed her and pushed her into bed. His plans to keep the conversation light and move a little slower faded with each glance at her face. Smiling, James removed his coat and boots, then set them near the fire that warmed the room and cast a throbbing crimson glare on the bed.

Her words fell softly on his heart like winter snowflakes. "I hope you're hungry," she said. "There's fresh bread and butter I brought from home. And candy bars. And I threw a couple Cokes out back in the drift."

His love for her kicked him hard in the chest, and all he uttered was a squeak.

Savina stood by the fire, wearing the thin gold band she'd pulled out of its hiding place. A wedding ring he'd bought her from the Sears and Roebuck catalog she wore only in the cabin. Her faded dress hung below her knees, and the pink of her elbow showed through the hole in her sweater. But James imagined she could wear a feed sack and be beautiful, except most of her dresses weren't much better than the one she had on. His mother offered to take her shopping in Summersville on more than one occasion, but Savina refused. It wasn't her apparel he cared about, anyway. After they married, he'd ensure she had better dresses than the threadbare garments she owned.

Savina's face flushed from the fire. Tears started in her eyes, but she blinked, and they disappeared. Still breathless, James cupped her chin, pulled back her hair, and lifted it to kiss her bare neck. He'd never seen a prettier round, soft face. An angel face with a perfect nose and smooth cheeks, big wide blue eyes like her daddy's, and full lips that melted him with her kiss. Her light coppery hair, a shade lighter than his own, glowed near the fire like a new penny.

The top of her head barely reached his armpit. The first time he laid her naked on a blanket in the woods, Savina's adolescent body splayed out tiny and shapeless on the ground. He had made love to her at sixteen. No hips, bony legs, and breasts the size of fried eggs. But her breasts and hips had seen the light of womanhood, rounding and softening in the two years since meeting at the cabin. James looked forward to her eighteenth birthday. In five months, he would remind Odie of his intent to marry his daughter no matter how the strike turned out.

Savina slipped out of her shoes and socks and sat on the floor. She propped her feet on a dry log, pulling her knees up to her chin. Her dress rode up, exposing her white panties that glowed in the dim orange light of the fire. James sat beside her, crossing his legs, trying not to touch her. Without warning, her hands unbuttoned her dress.

Next to the heat of their blazing fire, the two wordless lovers stepped out of pools of clothes left on a makeshift wood floor, springing for the warmth of the bed and mounds of quilts.

James' hands skimmed over her face. Her nails dug into his back and urged him closer. He found he could not think at all. His body, long and lean, moved over her petite frame. This was not their first time, but his need for her was as continual as the snowfall outside the cabin's window. In a moment, her whole body urged him to find her. As light as the promises he whispered, his touch found the place he searched for. She followed his lead through the moment, and by the time their limbs tangled together, James could not recall even one fornication scripture.

Covering her mouth with his own, she arched into him and closed her eyes. James moved as if nothing existed but the darkness of the cabin. Then, just as he could not hold on any longer, he forced her to look at him. "Nothing will ever keep me from you," he said.

For the rest of the evening, their bodies lay woven together, moving to the rhythm of their own love song. Savina's smile touched him. She had lost every inhibition her world had bestowed upon her while they created a life together. A life existing only in secret. As she fell asleep in his arms curled up against him, he memorized how she held her mouth, the way her dimple twitched when she slept, and the perfectly straight part in her hair. Her scent lingered on his skin, and James knew any prolonged separation from her would be unbearable.

A full moon rose from behind the ridge, its light casting shadows of trees on the snow. He held her delicate hand up to a pink sliver of moonlight falling diagonally across the quilt, illuminating the slim gold band. A reason to smile. Someday, he'd call her wife, and she'd wear the ring in public. He held it against his lips, forgetting everything but Savina and the path to Colored Holler.

Early morning clouds broke open to a clear sky and bright sun. The snow melted, dropping in clumps from bent tree limbs as the soothing sounds of water trickled in the creeks again. They lay under the warmth of quilts for some time, spooning and drowsy.

Savina inched back the covers and slid out of bed, carefully walking around the few floorboards that moaned. She positioned two logs on the empty grate, then pulled a quilt off the bed. Curling up next to the hearth, she poked at the red coals.

James watched her, hoping the sparks ignite the log. Finally, his quiet voice tipped over her shoulder. "Stop thinking; it gets your mind all tied in knots."

She jumped. "Oh—you scared me. And I ain't thinking."

"All liars will burn in the lake of fire; ain't that what Pastor Jessie says?"

"In that case," she said, "we're both gonna fry."

He tried to swallow around the knot lodged in his throat. The truth sat in his stomach like something indigestible—a stone, a nickel. "In a couple months, this'll all be over, maybe sooner. We'll be married and on our way to Ohio. I can land a job with one of the Akron rubber companies. We'll come back to visit, you and me and our young'uns. It'll work; you'll see."

Doubt flickered across her face.

James crawled out of bed and stoked the fire hot so Savina could dress and not freeze. She was always cold, and she hated winter. After pulling her sweater over her dress, Savina stepped into a pair of leggings made of thick wool and lined with flannel. She sat back on the bed and smoothed her dress over the Confederate gray fabric.

"What are you laughing at?" she asked.

"Where'd you get them things?"

"They were Mommy's. Stop laughing. They're warm."

"Sorry."

"No, you're not."

He squatted in front of her at the edge of the bed, his limbs hinged like grasshopper legs. "They remind me of how old-fashioned you are."

"I thought you liked that about me."

"I do. I love that about you." He took her hands and kissed them, then sang two lines of her favorite hymn, *"Some bright morning when this life is over, I'll fly away, to that home on God's celestial shore, I'll fly away…"*

She stood and pulled his head into her breast. "It's better when your daddy sings it."

"Lady, you ain't marrying me for my singing." He kissed her one last time. "I'm late, and I have to go." He stood, pulled on his jacket, and watched her twist off the gold band. She hid it again under the stone beside the hearth.

James slipped his hands into his gloves. "There's a meeting at the Grille this morning, and Daddy wants me to go with him. Wants to make sure I'm not swayed by the strikers."

"When's it going to end?" Savina tucked her scarf inside her coat and pulled another over her head as James held the cabin door open for her.

"Not soon enough. FBI says the Union is violating the civil rights of miners. They say it's a federal offense to hinder anybody from their work. I heard they told the strikers to get themselves a lawyer."

Savina pulled on her own gloves. "Daddy said some men are asking for their jobs back. But I say the strike ain't about to end as long as the UMW gives the strikers free groceries. Only about fifty men left at the top of the hill."

"The worst fifty," James said.

Savina shrugged. "Daddy's just blind," she said. "He'll come around soon as we're married. He won't want hard feelings between the families. 'Specially since he and your daddy are old friends." She giggled. "James, what are you doing?"

"Making a snow angel. That's what you are, Savina Ingram, soon-to-be Nettles. A snow angel." He had fallen back into the drift by the cabin's door, his legs and arms moving like a cartoon character in the snow.

A second later, she joined him, flapping her arms and legs up and down, creating her snow angel. Revived by the cold, Rascal barked and jumped over them and through the drift.

Laughing, James pulled her up. He looked down at the snow where their bodies had laid side-by-side, perfect angel depressions in the earth. Savina stepped over them with the utmost care, and seeing how careful she was, he stepped over them, too, then pulled her into a hug. He hugged her while their bodies, encased in packed snow, turned cold in the frigid mountain air.

~ April 1953 ~

Soaked in the color of old bones, the sky refused to reflect springtime temperatures. Smaller trees, bare of bloom, huddled beneath their blanket of fallen leaves. Gray maples and elms on the slopes around Widen topped themselves with tight red buds. From a distance, they stained the hillsides a raw dark pink.

Thirl recovered slowly over the winter, but his limp dictated a need for a cane as he returned to work after Christmas. Picket lines dwindled, and the terror eased, spreading into the surrounding countryside. But the morning after Odie's barn caught fire and burned to the ground, Savina showed up at DeDe's front door, looking for James.

"We lost two horses and our cow. Somebody blew up Daddy's tractor, too. They excused Daddy from the picket line for the week.

I need to get home before he realizes I'm gone. Lord, he's taken to carrying his gun ever'where, even to the outhouse. He guards our farm like some ol' chicken sitting on her eggs. I doubt he'll sit with the strikers at the top of the hill now. No time for it. He's sure some poacher's out to kill the rest of his horses and burn down the house. He comes looking for me if I'm out of sight for long."

James ran his hand through his auburn hair, tarnished by a double shift of coal dust. He kissed her softly, and her mouth tasted of milk and berries. "I can't stand this anymore. Why can't we be together like we planned?"

"Won't be for a while. Not 'til this damn strike's over." Savina said. "He knows when I leave for Colored Holler and when I'm supposed to be home."

James realized his mother had overheard their conversation as she opened the screen door precisely when Savina finished her last sentence. With a tall glass of lemonade in one hand, she closed the door behind her with the other.

Cuddled up on the porch swing, James nudged Savina. They both sat up straight as DeDe placed the refreshment for Savina on the railing and smiled.

"Thank you, Missus Nettles," Savina said. She eyed the glass but pulled her heels up to rest on the swing instead, wrapping her arms over her knees and smoothing her skirt to her ankles.

James watched his mother open the door to go in, then wheel around quickly, as if she had something in her mouth she had to spit out. "Why are you going to Colored Holler, Savina? If you don't mind me asking."

Savina and James looked hard at each other, but she blurted out her answer before he thought of what to say. "Old Mama Ola and her daughter-in-law, Hephzibah, are my best friends." Savina reached for her lemonade and sipped before carefully stepping over her words. "Hephzibah cleans the Bradley's house over in Dundon and washes Mister Bradley's laundry. Mama Ola's son, Jabo, he fixes things 'round the house for Mister Bradley's wife. Jabo retired from the mine last year with thirty years' service."

DeDe nodded. "How does she get over to his house? I know Jabo doesn't drive."

Savina scooped a mosquito off her arm and rubbed it between her palms. She hesitated, avoiding DeDe's eyes. "Ever notice how mosquitoes are like little butterflies, so dainty and easily broken?" She took a deep breath. "Mister Bradley's man picks her up. And sometimes, I ride along to help. Every other day or so. Jus' to make a few dollars. Help Daddy make ends meet."

"Oh," DeDe said, turning slowly to walk back into the house.

"She won't ask how you got to be friends with Hephzibah or Mama Ola," James said.

"She will eventually." Savina stood to leave. "Most folks in Widen stay clear of Colored Holler. Your mama's no fool, James. She'll want to know."

~ Tuesday, April 14, 1953 ~

DeDe awoke, ran her tongue behind her teeth, and tasted bitterness. A bitter sorrow, like chicory that melts on the tongue, unpleasant and turning it dark with despair. Another storm moved into the valley. The wind whipped pine branches back and forth, scratching across her bedroom window. She hated wind with no rain. At least the rain washed the air; this type of wicked wind had picked up coal splinters and hurled them at her skin. She felt an uneasiness in her spirit, and the top of her head tingled.

The scent of Thirl's Vitalis on his pillow roused her smile. Out of habit, she moved her hand along the other side of the bed, feeling only lingering warmth on the empty spot. He was always first out of bed. She hugged the abandoned pillow to her chest and inhaled the scent of his hair, letting herself drift a while longer.

On mornings like this, she was grateful for the bathroom Thirl built. DeDe reckoned outhouses were only good for knowing your neighbors' bathroom habits. Hearing Thirl maneuvering his stiff leg through the kitchen, she raised herself on one elbow and saw him limp into the tiny bathroom. When he filled the basin with warm water to shave, it was time to get James out of bed, or they'd both be late.

DeDe prepared both lunch boxes in the cold kitchen for her men and filled each Thermos with boiling coffee. After stirring the coal stove in the front room, she heard the first drops of rain pinging the windowpanes and then the knock. Peeking out the window, DeDe's heartbeat quickened at the sight of two men standing at her door.

They knocked again, hard and fast. Someone yanked open the screen door, causing the spring to emit a startled twang. Whoever stood on the other side clearly wasn't worried about disturbing the household.

Thirl poked his head out of the bathroom—shirtless, wiping the remains of shaving cream off his face with his towel. DeDe heard him pulling on his pants, his belt buckle jangling. "Who is it at this time of the morning?"

"Company men, I'm sure." DeDe opened the door and found Dewey Wilson standing behind Jugg Pyle. The wind flung rain on their faces like cold spit.

"Morning," said DeDe.

Dewey nodded. "Thirl inside?"

"Getting ready for work. You need to talk to him now?"

"Yes, Ma'am," said Jugg. "We—"

"—Ain't got time for pleasantries." Dewey interrupted with an icy stare. "Didn't come fer no tea party. Gotta talk to Thirl."

"Hold on, *gentlemen*. I'll get my husband." DeDe opened the door wide and led them to the kitchen. She knew Thirl had dressed while keeping an ear on his visitors. James hadn't stirred from his room. After a quick knock at his door, she kept her tone quiet yet firm. "Get up, son; we have guests."

A groggy voice squeaked in the darkness. "Who is it, Mama?"

"Company men here to see your daddy. Get up now. You're both late as it is."

Thirl eased his way into the kitchen to find the men at the table with their hats in their hands. "You fellas want some coffee?"

"Ain't got time for coffee," said Dewey.

Jugg stared at Thirl's clean face, rubbing the stubble on his own. "Some of the men had a meetin' at the church early this mornin'. We knew you wouldn't want no part of this, but me and Dewey thought we'd at least let you know on account of you bein' shot and for all your misery."

"Just tell him, for Christ's sake." Dewey blew a wrathful breath from his nostrils while his huge brown hand thundered down on the table. "It's like this. From the start, the Comp'ny admonished us to avoid any action construed as retaliation against the strikers. But we're tired, Thirl, tired of turning the other cheek. You know it weren't Comp'ny men that burned Odie Ingram's barn. Strikers did it to their own to make us look like a bunch of vigilantes. So, here's the deal. Bosses don't know yet, 'cept you. A group of men is driving a bulldozer up to the head of Widen Road. They plan to plow the striker's headquarters off the hill. We're through with 'em. We want to get back to work. Comp'ny is losing money, which might destroy the town if the strike continues. We ain't safe in our own homes. Time we did somethin' besides sit by and let them take potshots at our cars and families. Tub Perry's got a dozer he used when he worked on the roads. He's on his way now."

James bounded out of his room, his shirttail hanging, one boot on and holding the other. "Y'all can't do that! Somebody's going to get killed!"

"Son! Calm yourself. Get some breakfast." Thirl threw a glance at DeDe.

She rested her hand on James' shoulder. "You men ever lost a loved one? Have either of you buried a dear soul in the ground besides your parents? I'm not prepared to lose my husband or son because you boys want to act like a bunch of John Waynes and plow the strikers into the dirt."

Dewey Wilson spit a stream of tobacco juice into the pop bottle he pulled out of his coat pocket. A steel-eyed glare was his only response.

Jugg, the town's undertaker for the past ten years, quoted from the book of Job, "The Lord gave and the Lord hath taken away."

"I prefer Deuteronomy," DeDe said, looking hard at both men. "*I* will render vengeance to mine enemies. Vengeance is the Lord's work—not ours!"

With the speed of an old-timey gunslinger, Dewey yanked an ancient gun out of his other pocket and spun the barrel, his aim crooked, and his eyes loose-closed. The tip of his tongue stuck out of the corner of his mouth. Pointing the gun toward the window, his finger tightened on the trigger. "I'm ready to help the Lord; what about you, Jugg? You need to calm your wife down, Thirl; this talk is between the men here."

DeDe picked up a dishtowel and pretended to clean off the table. "And who do you think suffers the most? The men?"

"Dewey, put your gun away. My wife is privy to all I know. She has a say in what goes on in this house, gentlemen. I believe she's fixed breakfast for your families a time or two. And if you want to discuss business in my wife's kitchen, you'll have to listen to her."

Jugg nudged Dewey toward the door, nodding to all three of the Nettles family. "We're sorry, Ma'am. We jus' wanted to let you know what happened at the meetin'. But you cain't stop it, Thirl. It's already started."

Dewey slipped his gun back into his coat pocket, spit in his bottle, and shoved his hat on his head as he stormed out.

"Good thing he ain't a Union man." Jugg's nervous chuckle brought no reaction from DeDe or Thirl. "I apologize for Dewey; he ain't been himself lately. Strikers rolled his car down the hill last week. He'll settle down. I don't see this as an act of violence, jus' us peaceful men bein' fed up. That's all. Rest easy, Ma'am. Ain't gonna be any killin'."

"And a cat's butt ain't puckered," said DeDe, throwing her kitchen towel on the table and leaving the room.

Strikers had set up their field station in the middle of the Company road at the top of Widen hill. Benches made from scrap lumber and old automobile seats ringed a cluster of fifty-gallon drums. Fire barrels, the strikers called them.

As men for the Union scattered right and left to safety, the bulldozer tracked into their camp, pushing the barrels, benches, lunch boxes, and accumulated trash across the road and over the lip of a deep gully.

Whooping and hollering, Dewey, Jugg, and a hundred Company men drove back into town, honking their truck and car horns and lighting firecrackers as if they deserved a parade. Celebrations vibrated all over town, from one end to the other. Folks walked out of their homes that evening, gathered on porches talking and feeling free to move about as if it were D-Day all over again.

"They're rejoicing for the wrong reason." DeDe rocked back and forth on her porch swing. "Strike's not over." She sighed, weary of the argument, and felt her back ache between her shoulder blades. "Battle's just begun."

Her neighbor, Pearle, squatted on an apple crate and broke pole beans. "If you ask me, I'm hoping that's the end. I ain't been to Strange Creek to see my grandbabies since this thing started last year."

The people of Widen allowed their children to play in the streets once more. A few boys carried baseball bats and gloves toward the park. A young girl rode her bike toward the Grille.

DeDe sensed the tingling in her head again—and thunder rolled in the distance.

~ Saturday, April 18, 1953 ~

"Can we come in?" the woman said with a sheepish smile. "It's rainin' fit to start the second flood out heah."

DeDe took a minute to recognize Hephzibah Kelly and her husband, Jabo. "Of course. Where are my manners? I wasn't expecting guests. Today being Saturday, the men out doing whatever it is men do on Saturdays." She smiled.

Hephzibah returned her smile, but Jabo held a steady gaze into the house.

DeDe held the front door open while her unexpected guests pulled open the screen door.

As tall as a poplar tree, Jabo stooped over to walk through the doorway. DeDe watched his eyes register the scope of the room and its contents. "Sho is uh nice place y'all got heah."

DeDe wasn't sure how to respond. "It'll do until we get our mansion up yonder."

Neither Hephzibah nor Jabo registered a grin or acknowledged they'd heard her. They stared at her furniture, the buck's head on the wall, and the linoleum on her kitchen floor.

"Well, please, come sit at the table. Would you like anything cold to drink? It's getting warmer. Summer's 'round the corner." DeDe's instant politeness smoke-screened her quest to find out about a person. Her eyes sparked with curiosity the second she spoke to anyone, glaring into their spirit and soul. Within minutes, she had strangers pegged. It scared the hell out of James but fascinated Thirl.

Leading the way to her kitchen table, DeDe motioned for them to have a seat. She didn't remember Hephzibah being so pretty. Her hair shined dark as a crow's wing, smoothed back but frizzed out around her forehead. Her licorice-smooth skin contributed to her looking younger than her years. A blue cotton waistless dress hung from her shoulders to her knees, and she had rolled her stockings to her ankles.

Jabo nodded, "A drink of water be nice, thank you, Missus Nettles—"

"—Oh please, call me DeDe." Fetching glasses of cold water, she felt unsettled and assured at the same time.

"Miz DeDe, we came heah 'cause we good friends of Savina. Your James and Savina aimin' to marry, and I knows that ain't no secret."

"No, but I believe it'll happen later than sooner, with the strike and all."

"True, Miz DeDe. Tha's fuh sho." Jabo shook his head wearily. His gray hair curled in tight clumps around his ears. A frost of unshaven stubble smudged his chin, and the soft blue of his eyes glowed to the point of grayness. Veins ran along the top of each thick bicep. His pants hung loose and rumpled.

Hephzibah eyed her husband, turned her gaze to DeDe, and spoke softly. "You knows I work for Mist' Bradley."

"Yes, I heard that."

"I try to stay outta the White man's business, and I do. But Jabo and me love Savina like our own. And we love your boy, too, Miz DeDe. He's a good boy, and Savina says we can trust you."

"Thank you, Hephzibah. How long have you known James?"

Jabo stared at his wife. "Oh, well, me and James shoot the breeze sometimes when the women folk visit after they finish work over at the Bradley house."

"Oh."

Hephzibah smiled. "I'll state the reason for our call. Jabo do it better, though. You tell her. You tell Miz DeDe what you heah."

Jabo slid down in his seat, steepled his fingers, and looked across the table to the wall. "When ah retired last year from the mine, Mist' Bradley offer me a handyman job at his house. Fixin' whatnot 'round his place. Big place, you seen it?"

"No, I've heard it's lovely."

"Yes'um. Anyway. Ah was layin' a new rug in they dinin' room two days ago, and ah heah Mist' Bradley talkin' on the phone. Miz DeDe, Comp'ny men ought not to make the strikers mad. Shouldn't have bulldozed 'em off Widen hill. They started a war. It gone be a bad one. Strikers took over the garage in Dille as a new headquarters and made it a cook shack too."

DeDe grabbed her throat, and her eyes filled. "What else do you know, Mister Kelly?"

"Only reason Ah'm stickin' my ol' neck out is 'cause Savina love James. She love her daddy, too. Hephzibah and me jus' want your family be safe. Tha's all."

"Anything else?"

"Someone at the FBI owes Mist' Bradley a favor. He calls Mist' Bradley from time to time. Sent two deputies—askin' the strikers lots of questions. Pretty rough stuff, what they say to each other." Jabo paused and lowered his voice.

"Mist' Bradley say, iffen he found a way to split 'em up, make all Widen men see the Union's jus' a bunch of lef-wing troublemakers, don't have their best interests at heart, well, then, this strike be over in a week." Jabo paused again and stared out the window this time. "Ain't gone happen, tho'."

"And why not?"

Jabo straightened in his chair and leaned into the table, his voice almost at a whisper. "Mist' Bradley say, Union sees his Comp'ny as a test case. A win in Widen means they win the whole state. So, the strikers, they dug in for the duration. As long as it takes. 'Specially now, since the Comp'ny men shove pickets off the hill. Union men got the strikers all keyed up. They be cocky as hell. Strikers think Mist' Bradley gone throw in the towel, give 'em whatever they want. Mist' Bradley say he never give in. Probably be some men gettin' hurt or worse."

"Mist' Bradley, he is right. 'Cause later, ah heard two Union fellas walkin' in the woods near my place. They been collectin' guns and lots of 'em. They laugh and say they gone shoot dead the first man who drive through the picket line this week. They say this town could be havin' a few funerals soon."

"Why didn't you tell this to Mister Bradley?"

"Ah jus' a handyman, Miz DeDe. We don't speak much. Like ah say, ah don't stick this ol' neck out for jus' anybody. Still, it gone on too long. Comp'ny mens, they cain't take they family in and out of Widen. Been months for mos' of 'em. Only day Comp'ny people able to leave town was Election Day. Thank the Lawd, nobody got killed that day."

"Worse part, Savina's daddy, Mist' Odie, he sent word to Mist' Bradley at the house today. He say he die before he work in non-Union mine again, and he take a few Comp'ny men with him."

DeDe leaned back in her chair, crossing her arms. "I've been sitting here thinking, I'm calling all the women for a special prayer meeting. It'll be at my house this Wednesday evening. Every woman, whether her man is Union or Company, they're in need. Hephzibah, you and Mama Ola are welcome to join us."

Hephzibah's eyes grew wide with a hint of surprise. "That'd be nice, but I don't know how the White ladies in your church, in Widen, take to coloreds invadin' they prayer meetin'."

"You have as much right to divine protection as the rest of us. I want you here, praying with us."

Jabo chuckled. "Oh, we protected. We do like the Hebrews. We sprinkle the blood over our door, tell the Angel of Death to pass over this house. It work too. You should try it." He pushed his chair back from the table and grinned as one does when disclosing an unsettling secret. "The rich man thinks we's niggers, Miz DeDe. They call my home nigger holler. But all Widen is nigger holler. You and your kind, as well as me and mine. You jus' got a little more jiggle room, tha's all."

DeDe caught Hephzibah's eyes roaming around her kitchen. "We're not rich, Mister Kelly. Nobody in Widen is rich, except Mister Gandy and, of course, Mister Bradley."

Hephzibah stood and pushed her chair into the table. "Jabo don't see what I see. They's not rich, either. I sees they socks, they underwear, and I wash they clothes, and I sees how Mist' Bradley worry over his bills. Some days don't even get home 'til way late at night. And his wife is sick. Always a guard protectin' his home with a gun. Nah, he ain't no rich man."

Jabo held out his hand. "Was nice talkin' to you today. Ah hope we didn't put you out none."

DeDe smiled. "I enjoyed the company." His touch was warm, firm, and yet gentle. A double-handed shake. She recalled how preachers always grabbed your hand with *both* of their hands, one squeezing your palm and the other squeezing your wrist. "You're a minister of the gospel?"

"Yes'um. How you know that, Miz DeDe? Lawsamercy," Jabo chuckled. "Ah preach every Sunday in our church up the holler. Come visit sometime?"

DeDe's eyes glazed with tears; her mouth quivered for words. She'd never received an open invitation from a colored church, nor had she expected to attend a service surrounded by Negros. But there was always a first time. "Yes, I'll be glad to visit when the strike ends. Thank you for your kind comments about my son and for warning us. I hope my emergency prayer meeting will reach God's ear."

"Ah be bringin' Hephzibah and my mama on Wednesday long 'bout seven. They's prayin' women. Prayer warriors. It be after dark, that way nobody sees. That be fine with you?"

"Come as soon as you like." DeDe's eyes met Hephzibah's. The two women embraced. Another first.

~ Wednesday, April 22, 1953 ~

Opposing sides filled DeDe's house quickly. Women who were sympathetic to the Union and Company women who wanted the strike to end exchanged a few polite nods, stares, and smiles. The ladies, lacking for words, gathered in opposite rooms of DeDe's house—Company women in the kitchen and Union women in the front room. Despite warmer weather, tension chilled the air. Some hadn't seen or spoken to each other in months. DeDe suspected each woman planned to speak their mind, even if their voice shook.

It wasn't until Ossie Casto, a bitty, elderly woman, stood and sang *Oh Promise Me* that giggles erupted throughout the house. With flesh the color of toadstools and an eroded memory, Ossie thought they'd gathered to pray for President Roosevelt. But it broke the tension. Stifled words, longing to be said, spilled out of every mouth, and the rooms converged. Long hugs, apologies, and borrowing a handkerchief or two—DeDe heaved a sigh of relief and put her purse away. The healing was long overdue.

Opal Hamrick arrived late. A wide-bottomed, hard-looking woman of forty-five or so who carried a lime Jell-O mold on a plate. Her husband, Jack, remained on the strike line despite being fired by the Company. Opal hugged DeDe so hard her hair had to be combed again.

Tessa Butcher, Boney's wife, waddled through the front door nine months pregnant with her fourth child. She hovered her backside over Thirl's chair to sit, her bare legs swelling above tight ankle socks. A welcome distraction, Tessa's affliction and possible remedies held the interest of every woman in the room.

They searched for ways to divert themselves from the past months of living in a war-torn town. Sylvia Dodrill complained she'd lost her shape with her last child. But Fleeta Thigpen disagreed, stating the only thing wrong with Sylvia was faded yellow hair clinging too close to her skull. The Digg sisters, Lottie and Goose, busied themselves in DeDe's kitchen, making lemonade and cutting the crust off cheese sandwiches. Tootsie Barrow told Imogene Sanders who complained of a headache, that she might feel better if she put on some lipstick. And Edith Holcomb, a heavyset woman with thin legs and broad feet, exchanged recipes with Margie Tuller, who walked five miles to the meeting because the strikers had rolled her husband's car.

Pearle Gibson arrived late with her Bible-toting Aunt Hattie Mae. She walked over to DeDe and immediately knit her brows together. The old woman gave DeDe's hand a gentle squeeze. "The Lord holds a flashlight as we walk through the valley of the shadow of death, dear. He helps us find new life in the midst of the valley."

Clearly embarrassed, Pearle grabbed her aunt's arm and pulled her to a seat in the corner. She mouthed *sorry* to DeDe. But DeDe smiled. She smiled because it was all she could do; she chilled for a moment as Hattie Mae's words shook her to the core. Immediately, DeDe turned her attention to the other women to rid her mind of the old lady's words and remind herself that the room wasn't cold. In fact, she had opened all the windows. The temperature had broken records that late April evening. The heat and humidity in the room caused some to stand and catch a breeze while their dress hems lifted in the hot air like a sigh in church.

But the women grew quiet and Christian love faded when DeDe opened the door to let Hephzibah and Mama Ola step inside. Wearing church dresses and holding their Bible in the crook of their arm, they nodded a polite hello to the room. Not one woman's chin quivered. More than a dozen pairs of inquisitive eyes glared at DeDe's visitors.

DeDe didn't hesitate. "I invited Hephzibah Kelly and her mother-in-law to visit with us this evening. You all know Mama Ola." Mama Ola's wide smile showed a mixture of gaps and brown teeth. Her white hair glistened against her dark brown skin.

"I prayed hard about it, and I believe God laid it on my heart for them to be here. We are all women, women of faith, women who want an end to the strike, but above that, we are women who know how to love. Women who want our families safe. These women do, too. And they have voiced their love for my family. I am proud to have them in my home tonight. I want you all to welcome them."

DeDe's words dashed against her teeth; her pleading glance fell on Opal, who chewed her gum in short, irregular snaps. If Opal showed acceptance, the rest would follow. Opal stood and walked over to Hephzibah. "Your boy, Highpockets. He did a fine job building my hog pen last summer. Got good manners. It's nice to meet you both. C'mon ladies, meet DeDe's guests."

Breathing deeply, DeDe felt a breeze against her now sweaty back. She pulled her sticky blouse from her skin and stood still to let the air dry her clothes. While the rest of the women surrounded her two new friends from Colored Holler, welcoming them in the name of the Lord, she asked God to lead, guide, and direct because, as it stood, they needed more than cheese sandwiches and Jell-O to get through the evening.

The social hour passed. DeDe intended to devote the next hour to the scriptures, reading, and praying. She scarcely found her voice as she preached. "I'm reading today from Ephesians, the sixth chapter, verses ten through seventeen. Scripture that Pastor Jessie read last Sunday. I believe it's appropriate for this evening."

"Finally, my brethren, be strong in the Lord and in the power of his might. Put on the whole armor of God, that ye may be able to stand against the wiles of the Devil. For we wrestle not against flesh and blood, but against principalities, against powers, against the rulers of the darkness of this world, against spiritual wickedness in high places. Wherefore take unto you the whole armor of God that ye may be able to withstand in the evil day, and having done all, to stand. Stand therefore, having your loins girt about with truth, and having on the breastplate of righteousness; And your feet shod with the preparation of the gospel of peace; Above all, taking the shield of faith, wherewith ye shall be able to quench all the fiery darts of the wicked. And take the helmet of salvation, and the sword of the Spirit, which is the word of God."

Darkness from outside permeated the room, even with DeDe's single lamp on her bookcase. Night sounds of frogs, crickets, and an occasional dog's bark suddenly ceased as if on cue.

For the moment, the air around them felt heavy and dead. The screen door to the porch fluttered in place, and DeDe's white chiffon curtains at the windows blew gently inward, billowing like angel's wings as if some supernatural being had glided into the room. Lottie put a hand to her mouth. The breeze stopped, the women froze, and their fanning ceased. Nothing moved, not even the wind.

The singing filtered slowly into the room. As if a choir floated up Nicholas Street, a soft carol of voices intending to escalate in strength and grow louder, recognizable—a chorus, a mass of voices singing in a heavenly language. The sound grew as if someone had turned up the volume on a radio. It drifted through the doorway, and as it did, a light came with it, filling the place. It expanded and appeared to seep into every mind and heart. And then, just as it came, it descended out the west window, as if someone opened a vacuum and the singing was sucked out.

No one spoke for a period of unknown time as every watch on every wrist stopped. Even DeDe's mantel clock ceased to chime the hour. Sounds of murmured praise came first. Speculations emanated from every corner—Did you hear it—Yes, what did you hear—What was it—A choir—No, it was angels—Yes, angels singing—Do you believe in angels?

Hephzibah whispered to Opal that tongues of fire hovered over each woman in the room. Opal reached for her hand and smiled. "I seen 'em too."

Sylvia and Tessa believed it was the radio next door and an electric surge. Lottie and Goose cried. The women, in one accord, sang quietly. "Praise Him, Praise Him, Praise Him in the mornin', Praise Him in the noontime, Praise Him when the sun goes down…"

The preaching and prayer meeting lasted well into the evening. One by one, the ladies bid their teary goodbyes. Pearle pulled DeDe aside after most had gone, and a few waited for their rides. "Was it a sign? A good sign or a bad sign? What'd it mean?"

Hattie Mae didn't hold back. "It was a sign of the second coming."

"Oh, hush, Aunt Hattie! You don't know that." Pearle shook her head at her elderly aunt.

"Maybe not. But I know somebody's coming," she said.

Hephzibah looked at Mama Ola. "What you think, Mama?"

The old Black woman stared at DeDe and grinned. "She know. She know what it was."

Pearle's hand, still on DeDe's arm, trembled. She asked her again. "What do you know, DeDe?"

"I know it's late. Thank you all for coming."

~ Thursday, April 23, 1953 ~

"He must be a new hire!"

"Let's roll him!"

"Teach him not to take *our* jobs!"

The 1947 Ford truck bounced and crashed through a different grove of trees and brush. Removed from their previous headquarters, the striking men found a steeper embankment than the Widen hill to roll cars. Each Company man the strikers rolled had narrowly escaped with his life, and many nursed wounds months later. Fresh scars and broken bones were not an uncommon sight in Widen. Doctor Vance treated a new patient in his office nearly every week from a fight or a vehicle shoved to the bottom of a gully.

Jonas Zirka bounded toward the truck to scare the man inside with a few potshots and to get a good laugh while he watched him run like a coward into town. The same as he'd done time and time before.

After a thorough search, he yelled to the men at the top of the hill, "You see this feller get out of his truck?"

"No, where'd he go?"

"Nobody here! Not a trace of him. Nothin' in the truck to say who he was."

Agitated and humid, the air felt rough like tree bark in the lungs. Coal dust filled the afternoon sky as static disrupted the radio's Mom and Dad Speer gospel hour. An early afternoon storm rumbled in the distance. Inside, the house grew dark. DeDe lit two kerosene lamps with flames like shivering butterflies. She thought of Savina.

The prayer meeting phenomenon had kept her from sleeping until morning. Drowsy, she rested her head against her chair. Thunder rolled again, nudging the storm closer to the valley.

Drifting into a nap, DeDe jerked awake during a strange dream when she heard the knock. She moved slowly, as if wading through waist-deep water toward the door. Her hand turned the knob, but she stopped as the sound startled her, like a seal had broken open. DeDe surprised herself when she pulled the door wide without first peeking through the window to see who stood on her porch. Smothering a yawn, she nodded at the strange creature, smiling back at her. "May I help you?"

"Howdy-do, Ma'am. A woman in town pointed me to your place. I'm looking for Odie Ingram's farm. Do you know Savina Ingram and where I might find her?"

Despite the smell of the oncoming storm, DeDe inhaled the wood smoke of his voice, followed by the fragrance of apple blossoms floating through the screen door.

Her tone, soft and clear, held a slight touch of fascination. "I know her, yes. May I ask who you are?"

He grabbed the rim of his brown felt hat and tipped it. Nodding his head curtly, he said in a rugged voice, "Sorry, Ma'am."

His apology drew a small smile from DeDe.

"My name's Herald. Herald Wingate."

An odd-looking man, thin, tall, and handsome in an out-of-the-ordinary way, he seemed friendly enough. His colorless eyes, long elfin nose, unshaven face, and muscular hands appeared pale against his ragged and dusty clothes. Tattered pants ended at scuffed leather boots. High cheekbones suggested Cherokee blood, but his presence stood out like offensive profanity against the budding pink roses in her flowerbed behind him. Something comparable to finding lice on a little girl's head.

"I'm an old friend of Savina's mother."

"So, you're from—"

"—Bethlehem, Ma'am."

"Oh, yes. I remember now. Jo lived in Pennsylvania before she moved here with Odie. 'Bout the same time Thirl and I moved to Nicholas Street here in Widen."

"That's right. I promised I'd check on Savina now and then. I knew Missus Ingram suffered from a heart condition, and I'd had a few conversations with her. She didn't wish to leave Savina alone to care for Mister Ingram. But these things can't be helped sometimes."

He pulled the brim of his hat down low enough to hide his strange-looking eyes. Long, dark hair grazed the shoulders of his blue wool jacket with holes in both elbows.

DeDe recalled the Depression years when her mother befriended many a man on foot in Matewan, either with his family or alone. Ragged men, poor men—her mother fed them and sent them on their way with a sack of salt pork and biscuits.

Suddenly she found herself standing in the middle of her front room with a stranger, without knowing how she got there or why she felt no alarm. "Would you like a bite to eat? There's leftover ham from breakfast, and I can fry you a couple of eggs."

Removing his hat, he smiled and said, "That'd be nice, Ma'am. I thank ye kindly."

She pointed to the bathroom. "You can wash up in there."

DeDe cracked two eggs in the skillet and listened for her guest to return to the kitchen. She propped her purse on her cutting board, just in case. When he emerged, his hands glowed raw and pink from the scrubbing he had given them, and he smelled like lye soap mixed with apple blossoms. He nodded and sat at the table, his left hand resting against his leg with the palm turned out, and a New Testament held loosely between his thumb and two fingers.

"Smells mighty good, Ma'am." He ate leisurely and articulated his words like music, his voice echoing through the house. For the next hour, Herald Wingate pulled spiritual topics of conversation from thin air and made DeDe a verbal bouquet of Biblical subjects irresistible to her. She'd never met anyone who knew the scriptures like this man.

DeDe stood near the stove, assessing the dusty, bedraggled stranger. The first stranger she couldn't peg. Her back remained straight, but the tight knot of hair at her neck quivered with indecision. Was he who he said he was, and should she tell him where Savina lived?

~ Sunday, May 3, 1953 ~

As the night faded and the morning sky drowned the stars, Thirl passed the biscuits to James and heard the screen door stretch on its rusted spring.

"DeDe home Thirl?"

"No, Pearle. She leaves early on Sunday. Teaching Sunday School this morning."

"Oh, right. I suppose she told you about our prayer meetin' last week?"

"Sure did."

Pearle turned to leave. "Guess you know then; God talks to the women in this town."

Thirl smiled at James across the table. "Your mama tell you anything about this strange new fella, Herald Wingate? I heard he's been spotted several times around town in the past week. Seems only the women have met him. Word has it he's a guest at the Ingram farm. An old friend of Josephine's. You meet him?"

"No, Daddy. Ain't met him, but I'm sure Odie wouldn't let him stay unless he knew him. Kind of makes me a little uneasy, though."

"Why's that?"

"Savina said he preached at their prayer meeting last week. Even been up to Colored Holler, telling the women to pray for peace and safety. To reach out to God, trust and obey Jesus. He said Widen is on the verge of destruction unless the women pray harder. Unless they tarry before the Lord, all the men, except Pastor Jessie, are bound to suffer. That the men have made a mess of things. 'Cause they don't pray at all."

"Next time this Herald fella comes to the house, I want to see him."

"If you *can* see him."

"What do you mean?"

"Hardrock said Sylvia stood out in the yard the other day, gabbing up a storm. Right into the air. To nobody. So, he asked her what she was doing. She said, 'Talking to Herald Wingate. What—you think I talk to trees?'"

~ Thursday, May 7, 1953 ~

Savina fed the chickens in the yard, listening to Herald Wingate's voice drift across the air and into her ears like music.

Suddenly, a shudder ran down her back, and her lips lost all color. "What did you say?"

Sitting on an overturned bucket, he had left muddy footprints up the steps to her porch. Holding his Bible in his hand, he pointed toward Dille. "I said your father is in danger. There's a group of Union sympathizers at the cook shack, and your father is one of them waiting for the next shift of Company men driving into Widen. This violence must stop, Savina. God is not pleased."

Chickens pecked at the ground around her. "How can *I* stop it? Why don't you stop them? How do you know?"

"I heard voices while I prayed in the woods yesterday, and only prayer can stop this. I came here, to Widen, for three reasons: to preach to open hearts and minds—turns out that's the women. Secondly, to check on *you* as I promised your mother, and third, to warn your father. My work is done; it's time to take leave." He closed his Bible and stuffed it into his coat pocket. "I advised your father not to go to the cook shack today. He told me to mind my business and that it was time to vacate his farm. Savina, all you can do is gather with the women in town this morning and pray."

"But you just got here. Is it too cold in the barn? The lean-to is temporary 'til we can afford to build a new one. Daddy won't let strangers in the house. He always sends drifters to the barn to sleep."

"No, it was fine. Horses are pleasant company. I thank ye both for your hospitality."

"Please stay a few more days. I want to talk to you more about Mommy."

"Can't. I told you everything I know about your mother. You must be at peace knowing your mother resides in Heaven now."

"But you knew her from birth, didn't you? How old are you?"

His teeth showed through his grin. "Old enough. Too old."

A bittersweet smile eased across Savina's lips. "You sure don't look it." She emptied the chicken feed bucket and pulled her sweater closer to her neck, shifting her gaze to the lowering sky. Lightning flashed in the distance. "I think another storm is building over the mountain. I need to bring Daddy home. I can take you as far as the cook shack, Mister Wingate."

"You shouldn't go. Go to town instead. Pray with the women. Talking to your father has done no good. You'll not bring him home, Savina. Men are creatures of free will. But these men won't stop until they shed innocent blood—the town will not recover. I'm walking into Widen to say goodbye to Missus Nettles and the ladies gathering for prayer."

Before she spoke again, Savina's sorrowful eyes pleaded with him. "Please, Mister Wingate, meet with the Company men. They're good people. Tell them what you told me, and they'll help you stop this war."

"Like I said, my business here is finished. I must bid you goodbye now."

"Please don't go. At least stay for church on Sunday," she said, dashing up the porch steps and into the house. Savina grabbed her purse and her daddy's car keys and rushed back outside to tell him goodbye, but he had left no trace of himself. On the clean steps, in the empty yard, or in either direction of the road.

⁓⁓⁓

"Signs and wonders follow believers," Pearle said, raising her hand. "I believe I have a testimony."

The ladies assembled in DeDe's front room shouted—Bless God—Tell us, Sister Gibson—Yes, speak—Go on and testify, sister!

As DeDe lit the coal stove to warm the house from the morning's chill, she nodded for Pearle to begin.

"I believe in miracles, ladies. I believe God will end this strike. Soon. I believe He's given me the strength to endure until the end.

Union or non-Union. We're all God's children. I want to testify to the strength I've felt since the night we all heard the angels sing—"

"—We don't know exactly what that was, Pearle!" Sylvia Dodrill shook her head.

"Oh, ye of little faith!" The deep, male voice startled the women, causing each to jump and turn their heads to the screen door. No one had heard the slightest sound of someone walking up the clapboard porch steps. Herald Wingate stood on the other side, curling the brim of his hat in his hands.

DeDe rose to greet him. "Mister Wingate, you shouldn't walk up on people like that. Would you like to come in and join us?"

"No, thank ye. But keep praying, ladies; my time here is up; I must return home. I came to say goodbye and to warn you. There's a storm coming. And to pray for Savina Ingram."

DeDe felt her insides turn to mush. "Why? Herald, is Savina alright?"

"She's gone to warn her father. There's danger on the roads this morning, ladies. Remain here and pray through to victory. Call on the forces of Heaven to hold back the darkness that's coming—"

"—Stop! Don't scare us like this anymore, Mister Wingate! We've had enough." Sylvia stood and stomped her foot like a petulant child. "He's an old beggar who's waltzed into town, and you ladies think he's the voice of God!" Sylvia glared at him as she shifted from foot to foot. "Stop it! Stop scaring us. Go home to wherever you're from. Leave us alone!"

"Sylvia!" DeDe shrieked. "Sit down!"

A sudden wind kicked up, and the sky grew dark as a bruise beneath the skin. Lightning flashed, followed by rolling thunder through the holler.

"Sorry to bother you, ladies. Goodbye again." Within seconds, he tipped his hat, turned, and walked to the gate.

"Wait! Mister Wingate!" DeDe kicked the screen door open and ran down the porch steps, trailing him into the street. "Please forgive Sister Sylvia. Her husband's been sick with—"

"—Black lung. I know Missus Nettles. Mister Dodrill is dying. Somebody needs to have faith for him. His wife does not."

"Won't you stay a while longer?"

"Actually, Ma'am, I've got coal dust on my feet. It's time to shake it off. You've been kind to me, and I thank ye. Goodbye, now," he said, tipping his hat one last time. Leaving behind the scent of apple blossoms and the strange, soft, ethereal sound of a choir in the distance, Herald Wingate carried no pack, sack, or piece of luggage, and only the top of his Bible stuck out of his pocket.

DeDe stood solemnly, watching him depart swiftly down Nicholas Street and disappear at the corner. Her mouth moved, whispering a scripture that spilled off her tongue like bitter medicine. *"And whosoever shall not receive you, nor hear you, when ye depart thence, shake off the dust under your feet for a testimony against them. Verily I say unto you, It shall be more tolerable for Sodom and Gomorrah in the Day of Judgment than for that city."*

On their way to work in the pouring rain, a convoy of miners sympathetic to the Company and a few new hires passed the striker's headquarters. Someone hit the lead car in a blaze of rifle and shotgun fire. In the dull gray light of the cook shack, Odie hunkered next to Jennings Roscoe Bail, who fired his .35 caliber steel jacketed rifle at anything that moved. Pitted and pocked like an old bone, Jennings turned Odie's stomach sour. Watching him enjoy the fight, Odie swallowed bile and tucked his Colt Pistol under his belt.

Odie stood, backed up, and glued himself to the wall. "You hit him!"

"Son of a bitch! I sure did! Maybe I can get me another! Jennings shot again. "Hey, where you goin'? This's jus' like ol' times, shootin' at the Germans! Stay and have some fun!"

"You're crazy!" Odie slid back to the floor.

Jennings crouched by an open window, his coat flapping, his face pinched, mouth a tight, thin line. "Don't stand there like a damn idiot, Odie. You're a Union man. Don't tell me you're scared! Here." He held up another rifle, his knuckles white, and pushed it at Odie. "Use one of mine!"

It was on Odie's tongue to say he was a coal miner, and miners didn't shoot at people when he realized it was irrelevant and untrue. He'd done plenty of shooting the past few months, and every time he used his gun, he could've easily killed somebody he knew. Old friends. Family.

"I think I hit me another Comp'ny bastard! Don't run off, Odie. This's what we been waitin' for!"

Odie crawled to the door but not before tossing Jennings's rifle to the cook shack floor. Running toward the gully, Odie tripped and nearly catapulted down the same hill he had rolled a few cars. Panic vibrated in his head, and shouting and chaos echoed in his ears. His gut hurt. The killing wasn't his idea. Not really. He'd talked a big talk, but when it came to it, he ran—a coward. His eyes strained to see the men bolting for cover. But it wasn't until the smoke cleared through the trees that he glimpsed the lead car in the ravine, shot full of bullet holes.

It belonged to Charles Frame, a miner he played pool with at the Grille last year. The car had plowed head-on into the deep gorge. Odie charged downhill, tripping over tree roots and sticker bushes. Taking cover behind a thicket of pines, he hid as close as possible to Charlie's car.

A bullet hit the chrome bumper with a sharp clang. Odie's pulse quickened, and his breath caught in his throat. He steadied his hand, aimed, and shot back. He'd left the cook shack shelter, knowing his situation fully well. Ricocheting bullets might accidentally hit him from his own men, who now fired rapidly. Odie figured another ten feet and he'd help Charlie out of his car. A shot whizzed past and splintered the pine tree beside him. Darting to the car, he tripped and fell short of the door. Looking up, Odie turned sick again at the blood splatter on the broken windshield. He crawled the last two feet.

"It's all right," he shouted. "I'll get you to Doc's." From his crouched position, he did not know whether Charles heard him. Odie glanced up. Charles glared back at him, pasty white with his left eye open. He looked about thirty. Odie recalled Charles had three kids, and that Savina had watched his children in the past. Blood dripped from Charles' mouth.

"You'll be all right," Odie said again, more to himself than anyone else. But the moment he pried open the car door, shots rang out from above. Once again, shouting followed, then more gunfire echoed from the road and the cook shack. He remained curled in the dirt beside the car until the shooting stopped.

Finally, Odie stood and felt Charles' pulse. The miner's blood-matted hair clung to his face. He didn't move. Charlie lay dead at the wheel. Odie grabbed hold of the door and sighed deeply before reaching in again to close his left eyelid. Sickened at pools of blood covering the floor, Odie surmised a single shot killed him. The left side of his face recalled a handsome man. But the bullet had entered the back of Charles' skull and exploded at the front, destroying the entire right side. No expressions remained but the leftovers of surprise.

"Well, Charlie boy," Odie whispered, "I guess the only decent thing we did was kill you instantly. Don't look like you suffered." Still, he felt his stomach tighten, and he swallowed to keep from getting sick again. *Please, God, let it not be one of my bullets that's done this.*

Another volley of shots rang out from the road above, cracking above his head and embedding bullets in the surrounding trees. Odie felt an incredible sense of failure. Ignoring the gunfire, he shivered, staring at the dead man he once knew—a miner just trying to get to work. Odie looked back only once as he climbed out of the ravine.

Rain drummed down in opaque sheets. Savina squinted to see beyond the steady sweep of windshield wipers, barely keeping up with the downpour. As crooked as a snake's back, Widen Road ran alongside the creek. She kept reminding herself to use the clutch, knowing she'd catch hell if the car slid down the slippery bank into three feet of muddy water. But Herald Wingate's words of warning blared in her ears, propelling her forward.

Savina took the next turn slowly but slammed on her brakes to avoid hitting the man in the middle of the road. The car jerked and stalled. Turning the key, Savina glared at the image blurred from the pounding rain, pushed off the car's windshield by inadequate blades. Time stood still with the click, click, click of the wipers.

Savina shrieked more from terror than anger when a gun fired in time with the next click—into the radiator, killing the car. Throwing open the door, she stood in the mud; the rain soaking her. Looking down the barrel of a shotgun, she fought to keep her voice steady. "What are you doing?!"

"That you, Savina?"

"Good God, yes! What are you doing, Cole Farlow? Why d'you shoot my car?"

"I jus' came from the shootin' at the cook shack; I thought you was a scab. What—you gonna arrest me?"

"Who got shot, Cole? Who?"

"Don't know. Don't rightly care." He staggered a step or two and swayed, staring at Savina like a starved dog after a hunk of meat. The car hissed, and steam shot out of the grill and from under the hood.

Staggering toward her, Cole dragged his rifle behind him in the mud. A chew of tobacco swelled his lower lip like a bee sting. Alcohol clouded his eyes, and Savina smelled it through the rain.

"Well, well, well. If it ain't the purty little whore belongin' to James Nettles," he slurred. Cole's wide, bully grin burned a hole in her stomach as he swung his gun over his shoulder. "I heard you been spendin' time up in Nigger Holler. You cheatin' on James with some old nigger man? Ain't you and James sup'osed to get hitched soon?"

Yelling above the roar of the rain, she stepped backward and away from him, sliding in the mud. "What I do in my spare time is none of your business, and you know I'm engaged to James!"

"Too bad. Every man in Widen's got a hard-on for you. Maybe you need to spread it around some, 'fore you give it all to young Mister Nettles."

"Stop it! Enough of your foul mouth. Who got shot? Is my daddy okay? Have you seen him?"

"Seen a couple fellers with bullet holes through their damn heads. Must've scared the piss right outta their peckers too." Cole laughed and pulled a whiskey bottle from his pocket. "So, what the hell you doin' out here?" He unscrewed the cap and took two long gulps.

"Better question is, what are *you* doing here? What'd you do at the cook shack? You running from something? Did you shoot somebody, Cole? Tell me. Why you been drinking?"

He slid another step closer and dropped his liquor bottle in the mud. His clothes torn, Cole rubbed at his unshaven face, bleeding from deep scratches, like he ran through a patch of briars surrounded by barbed wire. "My, you're an awful nosy little gal." He took a quick step forward, lifted his rifle, and jabbed the barrel into Savina's chest.

Fear spread through her belly like a spray of ice water as his finger twitched on the trigger. "You need to go home, Cole. Go home and sleep this off."

Cole staggered. "Nah—I think I'd like a little taste of what James chews on." He yanked the gun back and jabbed it again, hard this time.

Savina stared down the sleek black barrel of an old hunting rifle used for small game and shooting cans off fence posts.

He leaned toward her over the gun that connected them like an iron bridge. "Why don't you and me get in that dead car's back seat?"

Savina put the tips of her fingers against his cold, hard chest. "Stay away from me, Cole, you hear? My daddy'll skin your hide while you're still alive. I'm walking back to town. You can crawl into Daddy's car and sleep." Savina pulled away slowly and turned around to head in the direction she came from. Panic seized her by the throat in the chilling rain, cutting her breath in two. Shaking, she slid in the mud and fell hard on her hip, but stood quickly and continued moving, cold mud covering the right side of her body.

The gun fired. Savina's head snapped sideways, her body rotated just enough to see Cole lurch, stagger, and then lean against the car, having shot his gun into the air. "Get back here," he said. "You always was a tattle tale little bitch." His eyes glowed bloodshot red through the downpour.

Savina turned her back and continued walking.

"I said get back here!" Another shot blasted somewhere behind her.

She kept walking.

Cole Farlow was a better shot drunk than sober. At the moment of impact, the third bullet burrowed through Savina's back and bulls-eyed into her heart as she fell into the mud on Widen Road.

Word spread quickly of the shootings at the cook shack. By noon, the mine closed again. Thirl left the house to meet with the heads of The Elk River Coal and Lumber Company and told his son to sit tight until he returned.

James shut the door to his room and turned on his radio since they had canceled his shift. He had no plans to meet Savina, so he positioned himself on the bed, finding solace in sketching pictures of Powell Mountain and how its trees appeared to huddle in velvet-green patches after a cool rain. How the clouds seemingly towed their shadows over its peak. Singing along with Elvis Presley or Chet Atkins, James sketched away the morning as heavy rain and wind rattled his window.

DeDe busied herself while attempting to shake the night's dreams that left her with an unwanted foreboding. She carried a broom and dustpan full of coal ashes outside, but the second Highpockets walked up her front porch steps, dread ignited like a small flame in the center of her stomach.

An hour passed as DeDe stood on the other side of her son's door and wept. Wiping tears from her face, she found the courage to knock.

"That you, Mama?"

The door creaked open. She avoided his eyes and sat heavily at the foot of her son's bed. "Oh, James," she breathed deep and searched for words. "There's been an accident. Doc Vance sent Highpockets to the house." Hot tears trembled on the white rims between her eyelids while misery clung to the corners like little bits of sleep. DeDe's face twisted as though she waited until that moment to allow herself a full measure of grief.

"What do you mean?"

"It's Savina." Her hands came to her face and covered her mouth. She inhaled sharply through trembling fingers and then closed her eyes as the tears fell. "Her car broke down, and she got out. They think she went looking for Odie. To warn him not to go to the cook shack. Cole Farlow. He shot her. His mama found him drunk in the back seat of Odie's car. He took off. Nobody can find him." DeDe had dreamed of Savina—her tiny body, bloody, slumped on the ground. Though she didn't want to believe it was anything more than a dream, it left a cold pain inside her now.

James let his gaze fall as he sat silently, his eyes seemingly focused on his hands and the tear that dropped to his lap. Standing, he reached above the bed for his rifle. "Where is she?"

"Don't, James! Don't do this. You can't take a life for this."

He started to leave the room, but halted at the door. "Is she dead?"

DeDe had nothing further to tell him except her damned dream. Another premonition. But it was too late this time, and it wasn't enough. "I don't know. She's at Doc Vance's office. Cole's mama found her, too, and took her to Doc's."

DeDe rose and drew closer to her son, attempting to hold him. For a moment, he wept quietly and thoroughly into her shoulder as she couldn't remember him crying since he'd been a small boy— long shuddering inhalations and then a gentle high keening as his held breath rushed out. He pulled away, his voice barely a whisper. "I'm going to see her." He looked back. "Tell Daddy I love him."

Her eyes pleading, she sensed a sorrow she'd not felt since the day they pulled her grandfather out of the mine in pieces. "Stop, James! Come back this instant! You can't raise her up; only God can do it! Only God can do it!" DeDe followed him, grabbing his coat and clutching his arm as large tears coursed wildly down her pale cheeks.

James escaped the grip of her fists and drove off in his truck. DeDe fell to the road, the coal cinders cutting into her knees, the mud sucking the life from her body, the sound of her son's cries still in her head and piercing her heart.

Time passed in slow motion once again. DeDe pulled herself up at the gate in a drizzling rain. Through the mist, Thirl's car raced up Nicholas Street, nearly taking out a fence post before screeching to a complete stop. Rushing to her side, Thirl threw his cane to the ground and reached for her. "I heard."

DeDe allowed herself to be encompassed in her husband's arms, comforted, but then pushed him away, pawing at his shirt where she had leaned against him, wanting to speak but not finding the strength.

"How did it happen?" he asked, his voice gentle. "When?"

She seemed stricken again at the question. Her eyes swam and grew larger, but she held on and spoke softly, "Savina set off this morning to find Odie. Oh, God." DeDe held tight to Thirl as if she might faint or be sick. "This afternoon. In the rain. Her car broke down. Highpockets said they think Cole Farlow shot it in the radiator. He was drunk and—" Laden with grief, DeDe's body slumped at the gate again, too heavy for her legs to hold. Thirl eased her into the yard and down to the grass, where she sat and held fast to her husband. Gulping for air, she managed to squeak out her words. "Cole shot her in the back. She's at Doc's. James said he had to see her. But I know he's gone to find Cole, Thirl. He's going to kill him—we got to stop him—"

Before she finished, Thirl had swung himself back into his Plymouth, barreling back to the middle of town, to the clinic, and to find his son.

The smell of death and remorse—sweet and pungent, seeped from the cracks between the floorboards of Doctor Vance's clinic.

Savina's body made a small lump beneath the sheet like a bundle of firewood. James picked up an unresponsive hand. It lay motionless in his palm. He stared at it with blinding compassion and a grief that cut him to the bone, never to heal. After talking to her like people talk to their babies in the womb, hoping she heard him, he bent down and kissed her lifeless cheek. Doc Vance had washed the mud off her body, but her hair remained damp. Dirt and blood had formed a crust along her hairline and the corners of her mouth. The table felt moist but with the stench of an overused dishrag. Someone had thrown her bloody clothes and shoes into a corner. She deserved better than this.

Doctor Vance stood obscurely by the bed. "She's in a better place, James. You must be strong for her."

The words stuck like a knife in his gut. He swung around and stared at the doctor. "You don't know the half of it," he cried.

"You'll recover from this, son. You have to go on."

"To what? Die in the mines like the other crazy men in this town? No thanks, Doc." His cheeks glossed wet with tears; he turned back to brush her hair from her face. "We was leaving. We had plans. But they're all wasted. All wasted."

The state police arrested 52 strikers that evening, incarcerating all, including one woman and two small boys, in the county jail at Clay. Bill Blizzard protested, but for the first time, Governor Marland ignored his call. The police confiscated a twenty-gun arsenal at the cook shack, and issued warrants for the arrests of Odie Ingram and Cole Farlow, who remained at large.

The evening light lingered long enough to not need headlights. James drove along the washboard road with ease. He knew every pothole.

Coasting his truck past Cole's house, James stared back at the men gathered on the porch, casting wayward glances. He figured they were kin. Cole's dad had died during the invasion of Normandy. Cole lived with an eccentric mother and grandmother; both had refused to leave town after the war.

The path to finding Cole was an easy one. From the time Cole turned sixteen, quit school, and started work in the mines, James found him predictable. Cole's mother, however, was not. James stood in Cole's house the day she stumbled in, screaming drunk, reaching into her son's shirt pocket to yank out a wad of cash, then slapping his face before disappearing for the week. Her drunken exploits spread all over town like a house on fire. She had hooked up with a politician from Charleston. When Cole found her at a roadside motel, naked and beaten, Cole nearly killed the man, which landed him in the county jail for a month. But that didn't stop Cole from finding trouble at every opportunity. "Bad seed," Doc Vance called him, stitching closed the deep cut over James' eye from a punch Cole threw over a lost game of pool.

As boys, they played in an abandoned mineshaft on the opposite side of South Mountain, dug by the sweat and blood of turn-of-the-century miners. Unlike Joseph Bradley's newer coal mine with its main shaft near the tipple and its underground maze of tunnels running sixty miles from Clay to Nicholas County, the deserted cave hid behind bramble, brush, and hundred-year-old trees.

At fifteen, Cole built a moonshine still close to the opening of the old mineshaft, and James donated ingredients from his mama's fruit cellar. When Thirl discovered James' latest exploit, he immediately introduced both boys to the wrath of God. The rod was not spared. Neither boy sat comfortably for a week. Despite warnings to never venture inside the dangerous mine again, it remained a place of risk, excitement, and exploration for Widen boys.

The night of their high school graduation, James and several boys from the class asked Cole to join them. Filling a washtub with ice and beer, they carried it into the cave and spent the night drinking, playing cards, and smoking packs of stolen cigarettes while pretending to be men.

Driving in the dark, James' eyes stung as he wiped at tears with his bare hands. Recalling Cole's life, James determined that had it not been for Savina, he might have ended up like Cole. Alone. Aimless. Destined to grow old in Widen and die in the mines.

Before leaving Doc Vance's office, James heard the rumors. Authorities rounded up every striker involved in the cook shack shootings except Odie and Cole. But James knew what the authorities did not. As a seasoned hunter, Odie had acquainted himself with every mountain track and trail in the state. With access to a good horse, Odie, no doubt, had gone into hiding, never knowing about Savina.

As for Cole, James knew his hiding places.

Pulling his truck up to the mouth of the mineshaft as far as it would go, James stepped out into tall grass and weeds leading to cut timber logs framing the opening. He switched on his flashlight and pulled his shotgun off the front seat. The wind blew colder after sunset, but the rain had ceased. James shook visibly, but not from the night air or from fear. Ravaged by grief, he felt insanity leaking into his pores like that raw, cold rain. Rage twisted tight around his head as if caught in a vise, squeezing out all reason.

"Cole! It's me, Cole. We need to talk!"

James pushed through briars, finding light from a small fire casting shadows on the mine walls. He tossed his flashlight into the weeds. Cole crouched like a feral cat against a pile of rusted metal. The remains of their moonshine still had crusted over with several years' worth of dirt. Despite its age, the recipe dangled from ancient wires hanging from the ceiling. An empty whisky bottle lay on the ground. Coatless and covered in dried mud, Cole's lifeless green eyes fixed on James.

James found his voice. "It was an accident, wasn't it? You didn't mean to kill her. Tell me that. You owe me that. Tell me you didn't mean to kill her."

Cole stood, stepped toward him, and smiled a ragged gap-toothed grin that was both knowing and mean. Another half-empty bottle of whiskey dangled from his right hand. "I don't owe you jack shit." Chinless, with an enormous Adam's apple and sideburns like Elvis, Cole stood a good foot over James. His foul 100-proof breath reeked as putrid as the damp mine.

Cole dropped his bottle to the ground, shook out a Lucky Strike, lit it, and blew a stream of smoke toward James. He had tucked in his stained T-shirt and rolled another cigarette pack into his right shirt sleeve. Blue jean cuffs turned up around his muddy work boots hung just above his ankles. Strings of oily black hair dusted his shoulders in different lengths. His big, round ears stuck out, making him appear almost comical. Almost.

Sweat rolled down James' cheek. "Did you do it on purpose? Did you touch her?"

Cole flicked his smoke into the dirt and stared, shooting James a don't-mess-with-me smirk, the drink long gone to his head. He snarled like a rabid dog. "I shoulda shoved her in the back seat 'fore I shot her; now I'm gonna fuckin' kill you!"

A war scream pierced the darkness and echoed through the mine. Dust flew into the air as James dropped his rifle in the dirt, hurling himself at Cole.

James got him first with a left hook. Cole wheeled around and came back, driving a vicious blow into his nose. It sent James reeling. He felt the crack and went to one knee, his eyes welling up and a fountain of blood erupting from ruptured vessels. It poured like a faucet thrown on. James wiped the blood from his face. It dripped from his hands as his nose seemed to disappear into its cavity.

The blood appeared to unnerve Cole. He froze while James crawled up the rock wall to steady himself.

Through eyes blurred by tears and blood, James caught movement coming toward him again. Struggling to hold on to his bearings, he crouched low, preparing for the strike, but ducked farther down as Cole's fist landed above his head into the rock. He saw it sent a bullet of pain up Cole's hand and arm.

Despite Cole's agony, he swooped in from above and rushed James once more, whirling his pained fist squarely at his head. Fighting back a sudden wave of nausea from a pungent mix of tobacco, alcohol, and Cole's unwashed body, James forced himself to push off with his feet, turning his body slightly, catching the blow in his right arm instead of his face this time. He somehow snaked his arm around Cole's, his hand winding up on Cole's shoulder. James sidestepped Cole, making full use of their combined momentum, allowing Cole to trip over his feet and tumble to the ground.

A sickening pop echoed off the mine walls, followed instantly by Cole's hideous scream of pain and rage. James maintained his hold on Cole's arm, forcing it farther back, then letting him fall into the dirt. Squinting through swollen eyes, James bent over Cole where he lay, face down, moaning and clutching his wracked shoulder.

James mercilessly hooked the toe of his boot under Cole's armpit and rolled him over onto his back, resulting in another pitiful cry. Staring up with eyes that glowed a savage inner fire and unquenchable pain, Cole used his legs and good arm to skitter away. James stalked after him, adding fear to the hatred that glared back at him. Cole's attempt at escape was cut short as he rammed into a wall of railroad ties.

Eyes darting from side to side like a cornered fox, Cole accepted escape was not to be found. Fumbling at the top of one boot with his good hand, he produced a Bowie knife from its sheath, satisfaction replacing some of the fear. Undeterred, James drove forward with a purposeful stride, dodging a feeble swing of the blade but tripping over Cole's deliberate swipe with his feet, landing flat on his back in the dirt. Cole rolled, stood, then placed the heel of his boot squarely on James' stomach, just below his rib cage, the knife at his neck drawing blood. James grimaced and let out another gasp of pain.

But the pain from Cole's arm caused him to stagger backward a little, lifting his boot from James' chest. James heard the wheezing sound of air being forced back into his lungs. Cole lurched forward again; his hand flashed out from behind his back, trailing after it a reflection of the metal that swung toward James in a sweeping arc. James flinched instinctively, but his blurred vision hampered his reaction, too slow to save him from the unexpected attack.

James rolled, but not far enough. This time, he felt the jolt, then the sting. A sharp smell cut through his swollen nostrils, a damp stain grew across his arm, then his whine pierced the cave's dead air. Cole, fighting against his own pain, rocketed through the air again and stabbed ruthlessly at an unsuspecting James, this time slicing his cheek open with the tip of the knife.

Half crawling and half falling, Cole stabbed at him again but missed entirely and bowled over from drunken exhaustion.

James rotated to his hands and knees, breathing fast and hard. His head wanted to explode from the pain, his arm throbbed with his heartbeat, blood soaked his coat, and he felt vomit stirring inside. Picking up a rusted pipe near the fire, he struggled to his feet and swung at Cole's head, hitting him square in the mouth. Smacking against the mineshaft wall, Cole's lips burst open, shooting blood to his face and sideburns and soaking his shirt.

"Yer fuggin dead," he muttered, spitting a tooth into the dirt. A wicked smile twisted on Cole's mangled lips, causing James to wince, which tugged at the flesh and bone of his busted nose. Through the slits of swollen eyes, he saw the terror and shame holding Cole in their grip. Cole swung the knife loosely in his hand.

James took a breath as if to say something. Still, words seemed inadequate and insufficient to account for the years of humiliation Cole lived with daily from an overbearing whore for a mother and taunting men from the mine. A cry from a distant holler rang in James' ears and pulled at his heart, and he raised his hands; sanity replacing adrenalin.

"Cole—stop—enough."

"It'll never be 'nuf." Cole lunged with the knife again, trapping James against the twisted metal of the old still. The strength poured out of James' injured arm; his futile attempt to fight off his adversary made Cole laugh. "Yer just like her. She walked off, refused to fight me, and paid fer it."

Cole pricked the knife's point through James' shirt and into his chest, emitting a lewd chuckle as if surprised at the ease with which the sharp blade penetrated. James' eyes popped wide as the knife entered his body. Driving the knife deeper, the blade biting through to the bone, Cole shoved harder until it plunged deep into his enemy's lung. James coughed and gasped. Blood oozed from his mouth and chest wall.

Without a word, Cole yanked out the knife and backed up. Stumbling toward the dying fire, he bent down with his uninjured arm, picked up his whisky bottle, and took a long swig. He swayed back and forth, feeling his way along the rock wall until he tripped over James' rifle on the mine floor.

Through the swollen slit of one eye, James watched him. After finishing the whiskey in the dirt, Cole stood and walked back to pull the truck keys from James' coat pocket. Staggering to the mine opening, Cole let out a lewd snort, looking back only once before starting James' truck and disappearing into the dark.

James heard her voice; Savina, he was sure of it.

Blood seeped from every orifice. He tried whispering her name, but his lips only motioned what his voice could not speak.

He stopped his breath. Not breathing came as a relief from the shortened, labored gasps of his last minutes. Was the voice real or imagined? *Savina.*

Weightless and floating through vast expanses of darkness to a pinpoint of light, he knew her voice. *Savina.* It was the last thing James heard as the fire died in the cave.

~ Friday, May 8, 1953 ~

DeDe sat on a log in the cemetery near the old church. Rain fell pitilessly, and the trees offered little protection, almost as if someone had poked a hole in an overhead green awning.

It wasn't a cleansing rain, and she knew it wouldn't renew her. Instead, she expected it to wear her down, obliterate her features, and allow her to dissolve back into the earth like warm rain on snow.

Leaning forward, she crossed her arms on her lap and hung her head low as fat raindrops turned her auburn hair into a twisted brown mop. Her thick yellow housecoat clung to her thin body like a wet rug, and her feet bled from coal cinders and mud as she cried huge heaving sobs.

DeDe felt certain Thirl would find him safe. Drunk, maybe. But not dead. Her head pounded from endless weeping and a restless night's sleep. But when Thirl returned at dawn with Pastor Jessie, neither uttered a sound. The devastation and grief in her husband's eyes told the story. DeDe instinctively knew. Still in her robe, she bolted from the house as a woman who lost her mind. Careening down the street to no place in particular, her march ended at the cemetery behind the church, staring down the hole dug for Savina's funeral.

Rain poured from an angry sky once more. DeDe rose on shaky legs, knowing Thirl stood behind her. His natural compulsion to follow her came as no surprise. Breathing deeply to collect what strength remained, she turned and narrowed the distance to her husband with two steps. Pounding her breast with her fist, emphasizing each word, she spoke in a voice betrayed, "God has allowed my child to be stolen from me. He has deceived me!"

Thirl caressed her face in his hands. His voice, low and hoarse, pierced shadows of death lurking to find her. "You don't mean that, Deanna. If anyone knows of God's love, it's you." His arm steadied her, and his kiss on her forehead spoke of a higher love she would have to trust more completely in the days ahead. He led her to his car and gently put her in.

Morning's light remained ashen and murky. The old Plymouth's defroster sputtered and coughed against the fogged windshield. As Thirl and DeDe arrived home, the storm subsided, breaking into streaks of bright sun that lit the dogwood leaves in the yard. They sparkled like tiny flashlights attached to every branch. *Flashlights through the valley of the shadow of death.*

That's when they appeared: The people. Half the town scattered across lawns and roads.

They got in their cars and drove to Nicholas Street or opened their doors, forgetting to close them, and walked into her yard and her neighbor's yards, standing—silent. On her small lawn and front porch, they all held some part of themselves: an arm pressed to a chest, a hand up across a forehead. Union sympathizers and men and women loyal to the Company together for the first time since a gunshot maimed Thirl last September.

Edith Holcomb wore only one shoe. Tessa Butcher clutched her newborn to her chest, her other three children strung behind her as she darted across the street. By mid-morning, an additional twenty or so draped themselves across the Nettles' porch and every available chair inside the house, including the kitchen table— sniffling into handkerchiefs, wiping tears.

Opal Hamrick's booming voice broke the silence when she entered the yard. "Goose Digg told me, but I couldn't believe it!" Some tried to guess where the Farlow boy hid out. A few men passed around opinions about which paths he'd take over the mountains.

Thirl spoke in spurts, barely audible. "There's been enough killing. Leave it alone, boys. This is in God's hands. The sheriff's been called."

A breeze blew in the windows whenever anyone opened the front door. The room became a sea of floating white chiffon lace—surreal and ominous. The clergy from area churches descended. Pastor Jessie, with his wife and two daughters in tow, organized food, spoke to Jugg about the double funeral, and started a prayer circle.

DeDe dried off and changed her clothes, but her face never dried completely. Continually wet with tears, it felt chapped and raw to the touch from so much wiping.

The world fell silent in trickles until Dewey Wilson ran across the road in his stocking feet, his shadow flung out in front of him, painted long by the early sun. He arrived at the front steps heaving for breath, a newspaper in his hands. "They're callin' for an end to the strike!" He gathered his paper into fragile leaves of print, his socks soaked with morning dew. "Where's Thirl?"

Lottie Digg, a nervous, pinched woman in a blue housedress, stood on the porch, her hands around her Bible. "Where d'you think he is, Dewey? He's in the house with DeDe."

Dewey bolted inside and laid the paper gently in Thirl's arms. "This won't ease yer pain none, but it looks like the strike might be over. It's over 'cause this town's finally come to its senses. This town and them vultures in Charleston. James had to die for it to happen, but it ended it." He turned to DeDe. "I'm sorry, Deanna. I'm sorry your boy had to die for all of us."

She nodded in appreciation of Dewey's words. "A small comfort," DeDe said. "I sort of understand how God must've felt." Her voice drifted into each room of her house as everyone stopped to listen. "Please. Let's remember all the families that lost someone they love. I hear the Frame family is burying Charles today. So many mourning families in Widen." Her eyes filled with tears as she hung her head again.

Later, the house filled with another shift of neighbors who brought more food—fresh eggs, a roasted chicken, pots of beans, pies—gallons of tea. The preacher led many in prayer, then asked Lottie to read the Psalms. Her gentle voice wavered slightly, but after each reading, she asked the same question. "Pastor Jessie, how is any of this God's will?"

Thirl wandered to the backyard to smoke with some of the men, his face calm, almost blank. DeDe roamed the peopled rooms of her house, from the bedroom to the porch to the kitchen and back again, wishing each neighbor find a reason to leave. But she didn't have the heart to tell them to go. Grief had settled over Widen like a heavy winter fog. Not one family escaped the misery and sorrow they brought on themselves.

Still, DeDe needed the house to herself at five o'clock. The agreed-upon time for the undertaker to arrive with James' body. Set up his coffin on the sawhorses already sitting in her front room. She longed for the quiet of that moment, with no one questioning her rush to bury him beside Savina the next morning. She'd had enough questions. Comments. Condolences.

DeDe peered through her rusted window screens at the hazy backyard filled with people who weren't good at much. All they knew was mining. Nobody had gone to college. But the town had one talent: faith. Raised in the shadow of this great faith, in the vast floodplain of belief, they believed in the power of Jesus Christ. The same yesterday, today, and forever.

To DeDe, Jesus was more real than the people of Widen. She often heard His voice as she walked a path to the store or school. He was her comforter, her most intimate friend. As far as DeDe knew, Jesus was a Jew who wished He were a Baptist. To say you didn't believe in the existence of God and His son was like saying you didn't believe in cornflakes or sunsets or that the earth was round. But in the last few hours, His voice had gone silent.

DeDe escaped to the bathroom to sit alone on the floor. Afternoon sun strained through the window, the light bouncing off the chrome tub handles and shimmering across the porcelain, filling her small bathroom with an underwater radiance. Like somebody had taken the needle off the record, the music she'd heard her whole life, the music that played all around her, just stopped. A stillness of supernatural proportion. She'd never experienced such silence. DeDe rubbed her ears, thinking perhaps she'd gotten something stuck inside, maybe water from the rain that morning. She shook her head back and forth. But there was nothing. Just a ghostly quiet. And sorrow. She'd had no premonition of her son's death. She felt betrayed.

⌒⟶⟵⌒

Jugg Pyle, Widen's undertaker, and four other miners carried James' casket into the Nettles' front room. As Jugg closed the casket's lid for the night, DeDe hoped Jugg thought about the morning he and Dewey stood in her kitchen and argued with James about shoving the strikers off the hill. She hoped they *both* thought about it good and hard.

"I'll be by in the morning to prepare for the funeral procession," Jugg said.

Thirl nodded, shook Jugg's hand, and closed the door behind him. DeDe watched her husband fall exhausted into his worn leather chair, angling his elbows on the arms. Thumbing through his Bible, Thirl's tears fell on the fragile pages crackling in his grip. His eyes appeared to absorb each paragraph quick and eager for answers to questions he didn't know how to ask.

At midnight, DeDe sat with her arms outstretched on the kitchen table, staring at a blank wall. *How can I be childless, God? Childless women own more than one church dress; they buy pretty shoes and wear stain-free clothes. They smell of perfume, not fried bologna sandwiches or dirty diapers. Their stomachs lay flat, and their breasts are small and manageable. They shop in Charleston and make appointments for permanent waves. Childless women live in tidy houses with clean walls and floors and hang little towels in the bathroom. I never cared about all that. I lived content with the one child You gave me. Now You have taken my only son! How do I live with memories of his life and his*—for a moment, she lost her words and her sanity—*incredibly horrific death! Tell me, God!* She gritted her teeth. *How do I live with that?*

DeDe pulled her arms back and placed her hands in her lap and her head on the table. The emptiness of it all caved in on her until she heard the knock at the back door and sighed. "No more, not tonight, and not at this late hour."

But Thirl had already opened it, finding Odie Ingram standing on the back porch in the dark, his hat in his hand.

~ Saturday, May 9, 1953 ~

She'd survived the night. DeDe rose slowly, feeling the creak and snap of each vertebra. Sleeping in James' bed, or trying to, she wanted to smell him, feel where he had been only hours before. Dreams of him as a baby, crying at her feet, toddling behind her as she hung sheets on the line filled the few hours of sleep she got.

Swinging her feet over the side, the sole of her foot landed on one of her son's drawings sticking out from under the bed. Savina. James had not shown her this picture. There was a curious look in Savina's eyes; she looked strange. Different. DeDe noticed the date. July, the year before. She carried it to her chifforobe and placed it with the rest of his sketches in the box. She'd bury them there until she could bear to put them in a scrapbook.

"Bury," she said aloud. The word stuck in her throat.

DeDe wasn't a stranger to burying a child. But she had not known her stillborn son, and this was different.

Holding a cup of coffee in one hand, she slid the other along the top of the closed casket placed carefully in the irreparable break in her heart. James had slept his last night in their home. How could she find the strength to pull her blue funeral dress over her head and face the crowds again? How could she lower her son's body into the ground and keep on living?

DeDe stumbled into the church, watching Pastor Jessie greet people with a double-handed shake.

"You and Thirl need anything, anything at all; you call me, hear?"

DeDe smiled weakly but said nothing.

She walked to the front pew and looked into the sleepless face of Doctor Vance, his glasses foggy from humidity and tears. She sat next to him. Hands clasped together, twisting in her lap, she avoided his gaze.

"He was a dutiful son."

DeDe cleared her throat. "Thanks, Doc. I just want this day to be over."

He leaned toward her. "But you can't let grief consume you, Deanna."

She nodded. "People give in to grief the way they fall in love. Grief will be my constant companion for the rest of my days." Doctor Vance squeezed her hand, then moved over one space so Thirl could sit beside her.

The crowd grew quiet, except for a low volume of dissension as Odie Ingram walked to the altar where his daughter's casket lay next to James'. Odie stood disheveled in a wrinkled suit and placed one hand on each coffin. His shoulders heaved up and down until Thirl stood and guided him back to the front pew for the eulogy. Tears coursed down Odie's cheeks, unchecked. The crowd of mourners murmured among themselves over such a blatant display of forgiveness.

Aging years since DeDe had seen him last, Odie seemed frail, hairless, and embryonic. His old-man shoulders, thin and lifeless, moved beneath the fabric of his jacket, grabbing hold of James' casket and hoisting it to his shoulder. DeDe prayed for Thirl's bad leg when he raised Savina's casket to his shoulders. Sixteen men in all carried Savina and James to their final resting places. Sixteen men who were neither Union nor Company that day.

Odie had appeared on their back porch to ask his friends for forgiveness and grieve with them. Thirl contacted the sheriff and requested that Odie attend his daughter's funeral and get his house in order. The Nettles took responsibility for Odie, promising the sheriff he could arrest Odie at his farm on Monday morning. Thirl made another promise to his old friend. He would sell Odie's farm for him and put the money in a fund for miners' children.

Thirl, DeDe, and Odie were miners' children who became miners. It was only fitting they carry one another's burdens and share in each other's sorrow on the day they buried their children. Buried them under a Golden Delicious apple tree in the church cemetery, two rows from a tombstone barely readable. *Herald Wingate, Born 1884, Died 1909, Friend of C. G. Widen, town founder.*

~ Sunday, May 10, 1953 ~

Odie spent the last night on his farm, collecting essential papers and a few pictures of Savina, placing them in the middle of his kitchen table to be found easily. In the crude barn he'd built after the first one burned, Odie cleaned the stalls and said goodbye to his small herd. He fed his dogs, chickens, hogs, and horses, placing feedbags where DeDe could reach them without too much trouble. Hanging his head and dragging his body through the house, he gathered Savina's belongings and the few clothes he owned and put them into two boxes for the Baptist missionary fund. Finally, he collapsed into a chair and stared into a blazing fire until morning.

~ Monday, May 11, 1953 ~

Outside, the low light of dawn came quickly. The sun won its battle, and storm clouds departed, leaving behind ragged wisps of black and gray, streaking the blue sky like soot on a clean sheet.

Odie had one last mission. His car totaled, his truck confiscated by the authorities at the cook shack, he relied on his bay colt to help him fulfill his last duty to his friends. Seizing the reins, Odie swung up onto his horse's back, knees tight around the animal's barrel of ribs. The horse uttered a great whinny, tossed his head, and broke into a lope across the hill. Odie wiped tears from his eyes with his coat sleeve and headed for Colored Holler.

The sound of a horse brought men and women out to their porches in the holler. Nappy-headed children peeked through windows. Smoke floated out of every chimney. When the horse stopped in front of Jabo's house, Mama Ola clopped out on the porch, her shoes too big, her apron too small, her eyes sharp and assessing.

Odie tipped his hat. "Ma'am." He remained on his horse. "Mister Kelly awake?"

"Nawser, you g'wan now. Git. We don't need no trouble up heah."

Hephzibah stepped out on the sagging porch and wrapped a shawl around her mother-in-law. "Jabo's in the house. He be out directly. We grievin' too, Mist' Odie."

"I know. You loved my Savina, and I appreciate what you did. What you all did for her. You know what I come for?"

"I knows why," said Hephzibah. "You ready to tell the Nettles the truth?"

"I am."

Jabo walked out with his rifle. "You do this, Mist' Odie, you do this right, or ah swear ah hunt you down mysef."

"I promise, Mister Kelly. I promise to make the Nettles' world a little happier today. I'm going to prison, probably for the rest of my days. You'll have no fight from me, Sir. Was my bullet that killed Cole Farlow two nights ago, and I will pay for that, too."

Jabo nodded and stepped toward Odie. "Come inside then."

DeDe filled her washing machine with boiling water from the stove like she did every Monday morning. She'd considered sleeping the day away under a pile of blankets. Except something forced her slow and heavy body to roll out of bed early. The sunshine, perhaps.

Sheets and towels went in first, then underwear, socks, Thirl's T-shirts, colors, and lastly—Thirl's work clothes. The same washload line-up every week for decades.

Sorting piles on the floor, the pungent smell of coal rose from the bottom of the clothes basket. Her hand shook, lifting out the last piece. Overalls belonging to her son. She shoved them into a paper bag with no intention of washing them. DeDe set the bag in his room and closed the door behind her. She wanted the room sealed off, kept as a tomb. *What would we ever use it for, anyway?* DeDe forced her mind to go blank, refusing to think of the fresh graves at the end of town.

Having time off from the mines, Thirl roamed the house and the yard, bumping into his wife at every turn. His mind weary, his hands empty—his heart needing a reason to beat, Thirl carried the heavy basket of sheets to the clothesline for DeDe to hang them. Needing to be near her, Thirl handed her clothespins until the first glimpses of the funeral procession for Cole Farlow moved up Nicholas Street. Recognizing the few cars following the hearse, Thirl walked back into the house and stepped out onto the front porch. His legs buckled under him. Falling to the steps, Thirl's eyes fixed on the motorcade rolling past his house. He didn't know where they were burying Cole. He didn't care.

The sheriff arrived early to arrest Odie at his house, but when he walked up the porch steps, he read the note tacked to the front door. *You can find me in town. At Thirl Nettles' house.*

Squeezing with his feet, he gave a little *hey-yup* and set the horse into motion after a quick nod goodbye to Jabo and his family. Odie headed to Widen, passing houses at a slow trot; it'd been years since folks had seen a horse in the middle of town.

DeDe heard the crowd's noise as she hung clothes on the line. It sounded like the whole town decided to stroll up Nicholas Street.

Thirl stuck his head out the back door. "Deanna! Come quick. It's Odie on his horse!"

DeDe wiped her hands on her dress and walked inside. Electricity prickled the air. Following Thirl as he limped through the house, DeDe hesitated at James' bedroom door. The top of her head tingled. Music welled inside her again, a sensation that carried a promise—like an unopened present. Moving forward with apprehension, she stopped at the front door. But the moment her foot crossed the threshold, grief moved aside as if binding chains were suddenly broken.

A horse pranced in the street by the gate. There Odie sat, high on that horse. His right hand wrapped around the chest of a smiling baby boy propped in front of him on the saddle. The baby looked to be about ten months old. DeDe ran to Odie, the truth revealing itself in the seconds it took to reach out with her arms. The Book of Life had never closed. Tears flowed as she laid her hand on Odie's leg.

Odie briefly gazed down at the boy, gently patting the child's cheek. He folded the blanket around him and allowed the baby to slip off his saddle, out of his large hands, and into DeDe's arms. He had James' eyes and Savina's mouth. And red hair. Lots of dark red hair.

"The most powerful force in the universe is gossip," said Odie. "Savina didn't want anybody to know, didn't want people pointing at her baby, calling him a bastard. Was my fault they didn't marry sooner. They'd planned to leave town next month, get married, and come back after some time had passed. Jabo Kelly and his family have been caring for the boy all this time; that's why Savina spent so much time there. He was born last July fourth."

Thirl walked up behind DeDe, placing his hands on her shoulders. As he reached over her to touch the child's delicate hair, Thirl smiled as the baby smiled; its toothless little mouth opening with a gurgle. With his finger, Thirl wiped drooling spit from the baby's chin.

Odie choked on his tears. "Thirl, meet our grandson. This here is Emery. Emery James Nettles. Son of James and Savina, grandson of Deanna and Thirl, and Josephine and—me."

Thirl unhooked a sack of clothes and diapers tied on the saddle. Odie laid his hand on Thirl's shoulder and nodded.

"We'll take good care of him," Thirl said, reaching out to shake Odie's hand.

DeDe's lips pressed against the baby's soft hair. Holding his tiny face to her own, she felt her tears flow as a silent police car nosed through the parting crowd and pulled up behind the horse.

~ Thanksgiving 1953 ~

The music dueled in the barn. Thanksgiving held a special meaning that year to Widen residents. Groups of men and women played fiddles, banjos, and mandolins. A few guitar pickers joined in. They danced and sang ancient mountain songs from their past and set rows of food for the town to partake in together, giving thanks for an end to the strike.

Thirl raised Emery to his shoulders. "Mamaw, you want us to bring you some cider?"

"No, you boys go on. I'll sit here a spell and listen to the music." She hesitated a moment. "Thirl?"

"Yes?"

"I want—I want you to know how much I love you."

He smiled down at her as he patted his grandson's legs hanging around his neck. "You're a fetching woman, Deanna."

She smiled back. He had been her rock, and she wanted him to know.

Observing her husband carry his grandson with the same love and affection as he once held James in the Thanksgiving barn, DeDe felt the pain of loss pull at her insides. She'd grown weak in mind. Mournful. Raising Emery only dressed her wounds with a Band-Aid. Losing James had taken more than a bite from her soul. Even Doc Vance worried about her. Part of his rounds to sick folk each week included a visit to the Nettles family.

Her foot tapped in time to the music. She pushed stray hairs back into place and closed her eyes, absorbing the low cry of the steel guitar.

"Nobody cares if you can't dance well. Just get up and dance."

She recognized him. Herald Wingate. DeDe turned toward the voice; her mouth open but silent.

He hiked up the same dirty boot on the bench beside her and rested his arm on his knee. "God will not let you suffer what you cannot bear."

"I can't bear any more." Anger filled her throat like she had choked on a piece of meat.

"He knows that. But you've got to find the strength He sent you to raise this young'un."

"What strength? When?"

"The night you heard the angels sing. That was for you, Deanna."

"Just who are you? Why are you here again?"

"He sent me to tell you. Who I am doesn't matter. Your suffering is over. You're to witness to those who still have some suffering to do."

"That's my purpose? To help others get through their suffering?" She turned away, indignant, and stared straight ahead to watch people dance.

"Yes, and to raise their child. They're watching, you know."

DeDe continued to stare ahead, ready to match him word for

word. "Who exactly is watching me?" He didn't answer. Jugg Pyle's fiddle moaned to the tune of *Angel Band* as the aroma of apple blossoms filled the room. She turned to speak to his face, but his face was gone, along with the rest of him. Nobody saw Herald Wingate that night, nobody but DeDe.

The Clay County grand jury handed up a series of indictments, from holding up the railroad and stealing dynamite to blowing up bridges and the murder of Cole Farlow. Found guilty of first-degree murder and given life in prison, Odie Ingram's trial headlined newspapers from Charleston to Washington, DC.

In November 1953, a federal grand jury in Huntington examined the evidence gathered by the FBI against the United Mine Workers. Many of Widen's striking miners found themselves doing time in federal prison. The United States Department of Justice regarded the indictment as the most significant attempt to deal with labor violence under civil rights statutes. Widen's reign of terror was over.

~ April 1954 ~

Spring came again.

Under the shadow of the mountain, in the town of their birth, the young lovers slept under the apple tree, side by side, in their graves. Near the humble walls of the little Baptist church, they lay unnoticed. Daily the tides of life went ebbing and flowing beside them. Every Sunday, throbbing hearts filed past where theirs rested. Every Sunday, Pastor Jessie searched the scriptures, but their eyes had closed until the day God descends with a shout. Every Sunday, the toiling hands of the Pastor shook those of his congregation while their hands ceased from labor, and a thin gold band lay forever buried in a cabin now abandoned. Every Sunday, weary feet shuffled into a sanctuary to rest from backbreaking work in the mines, but their feet had completed life's journey.

Every Sunday, the Pastor reached across his pulpit for the souls of his congregation, but their souls had walked to the light.

As Pastor Jessie concluded his sermon, his gaze fell upon Thirl, DeDe, and their grandson asleep in his grandmother's arms. He stretched his arms above his head, holding his black King James in his right hand. His voice bellowed, and he wept aloud. "The United States Government may have ended the strike, but Savina and James ended the hatred of family against family, brother against brother, man against himself. Their love was not in vain. God's ways are not our ways; His thoughts are not our thoughts. Who are we to know the plan of God? The violence and sorrow in Widen will not be put away and forgotten like an old picture book, but passed on for future generations to never forget what has happened here. This tale of woe is not the sole possession of one family but of every family in Widen. For we are all guilty. Let us pray and let us remember."

He played coal miner with his toy truck on Nicholas Street. On warm sunny mornings, anyone could find him sitting in the dirt, a little redheaded boy with brilliant blue eyes and coal dust on his feet.

Abigail Grace

Angels.

For years, I debated whether it was a subject I wanted to tackle or forget. After all, isn't the subject of angels overdone?

They're everywhere—on gravestones, mausoleums, and in cemeteries around the globe. Civilizations have written about angels in holy scriptures and religious texts since ancient times. They show up in novels, anthologies, children's books, and in seminary course work. Baroque sculptures and paintings of angels by old-world artisans are exhibited in museums and sell for millions on the open market. Angels appear on the walls and ceilings of basilicas, churches, and cathedrals worldwide. They're depicted in television, film, and video games as Marvel Comic-type characters in tights and capes. You can find them as cherubs with sweet round faces on top of Christmas trees or shelved in Hallmark shops as pudgy baby angels with wings. Retail stores carry cupid angels with bows and arrows and stuffed-toy angels dangle from mobiles over cribs. Overwritten. Overproduced. Overdone.

And yet, in my swamp of indecision, this story grew and molded over time. It weighed heavily on me because the truth is, I have more than a slight affinity for the supernatural. Especially angels. Not the sickening sweet angel of commercialism, but the real.

Some say literature seldom represents angels in the manner and for the purpose God created them. Challenge accepted. Placing my interpretation of a biblical angelic entity amidst the rough and soul-scraping world of coal mining, **ABIGAIL GRACE**, named for my maternal grandmother, was born.

And if you're wondering, this angel is not fried. But she knows women who are.

Above and below us, the West Virginia Mountains stood like a fortress against the outside world. The morning sun hung on a thread of pink and gold and flickered in the smoke-filled sky. My coat's ragged hem brushed the rhododendron and new-fallen snow, leaving a powder trail on the gob piles.

Close at my heels, Kat Dekker, in her well-worn boots, could not hide the sound of her breathing like a bull in the frigid mountain air. Beyond the distant ridge, smoke spiraled from the coal tipple. Kat could have walked to it blindfolded. She did not need my help. Late in January 1942, a month before her eighteenth birthday, I was aware Kat thought of nothing but her stepfather.

"Abigail—"

"—Kat?" I sensed it. Unbridled apprehension.

"Slow down," she said.

There was no time, and we both knew it. Instead, I picked up the pace. I felt Kat shouldering her burdens with heightened despair. One way or another, promises made in winter were broken by spring, leaving nothing but the dim scraps of a lost future and the relentless hope of escape.

Proving my loyalty from one disappointing year to the next, I had been Kat's only companion since the day she slid into a midwife's gifted hands. I continually marveled at my commission, as they seldom assigned them to angels like me. Interacting with Kat, at her age, as a kindred spirit and Guardian, I admit it was an unusual arrangement. A rare phenomenon. Miracle, if you will. I received no explanation why the Order of the Seraphim selected me, Abigail Grace, to fall into the arms of the Dekker family. In the years that followed, as the sun streaked the winter air with blood and brass, I soon discovered the reason.

Outside the mountains, the world was changing. The cold fog of war had rolled into Appalachia, pushing through its hollers and passages. But in the town of Clay, humans moved like the haints they believed in. Heads down, eyes averted, and constantly dodging the smell of burning coal beneath low-slung clouds. Their voices disconnected from their bodies, as fast as they appeared on the street, they vanished in the mist. There was little to celebrate. Happiness, like money, was hard-earned, and the people of Clay often confused love with obligation and duty.

For Kat and me, our similar appearance had its benefits. Those who caught sight of my fleeting shadow swore on their mother's grave they had seen Kat in one place or another. I thought it unproductive to use foolish appearances to confound the wise. Still, I found it amusing. Humans overlook the enchanted elements of the Bible, choosing instead to embrace the more believable parts. Powers and principalities are at the root of my existence.

I never wandered far from Kat's side. Tightly knitted as we were, we shared thoughts, words, and the misery of lost dreams. Yes, even Heavenly beings have dreams. And before you process my image in your head, I have no halo. No wings. No flowing robes. I do not glow in the dark. I am not that kind of angel. You all have one, you know. An assigned Guardian. But once out of diapers, few of you remain aware of us.

Forgive me. I am getting ahead of myself. On the day we rushed to the tipple, there was no time to think frivolous thoughts. My mission remained clear.

Plodding along to ensure safe passage, I took a shortcut, and being who she was, Kat followed my lead. Weaving through the trees, I ignored the iced-over path. Kat warranted every second of my concentration. But discerning the nothingness of her life as my failure, I forced myself to pay attention to the ground under my feet and our destination. Miners with a gallon of rotgut in their bellies were always toppling off one cliff or another. Men with hot tempers and foul mouths floating face down in the river less than a hundred yards from their homes; sometimes, I questioned why He gave men free will. It seemed like a death sentence to me.

Alas, dwelling on my frustrations with humans wasted time.

The morning fog swirled so that the pitted and motley face of the tipple emerged from the gloom like a medieval castle moving towards us. Kat shivered in the dawn light as we paced the edge of the lot, breathing in stops and starts until the third shift of miners stumbled from the mouth of the coal mine.

I watched Jubal Dekker's eyes search for Kat. His short walk over to where we waited took an obvious effort. His glassy eyes locked on hers. Blood swelled in his cheeks, and his breath labored; he stared hard, searching her face for the news she could not utter. Unfurling his fists and grabbing her hands, he squeezed until she winced. My arms longed to pull her from his grip. I wanted her free. Free as a slip of paper, floating to the ground and sliding beneath a chair or table. To never feel hunger, the emotion of the heart, or the raging pain of poverty. To protect her from a cynical stepfather and from becoming the empty-headed rag doll of her mother. But I seldom spoke near Jubal to cause Kat to answer.

Kat pried his grasp from her small hands, her eyes seeking mine. Jubal sighed deeply, his face creased and rigid. Under his hard hat, black dust mixed with sweat dripped into gray beard stubble. His chin dropped to his chest. Somewhere in Jubal's past, he had become a shattered man. He swallowed hard. "A boy?"

Kat nodded as I watched warily. A tear dripped from her chin to her boot.

"Whose fault was it this time?" he said from lips that peeled like old paint.

"Do not answer him," I said. "You have nothing to say he wants to hear."

Kat choked back a sob. "It was mine."

Jubal wanted that baby. That boy.

His fingers curled into fists again. The thorns in his raspy voice pricked the air. "Get in the truck," he said.

I raised my brows with a silent question. What will he do to her this time? A healthy girl, not his, and now two dead sons of his own; the constant low-level gloom inside the Dekker house had intensified to an unbearable crush on its inhabitants. A reminder of my inability to finish my work and save the one soul under my protection.

As glimmers of golden sun broke through the winter sky, we rode in tension as thick as mud to a tar paper and clapboard house where Emlyn Dekker lay stoic upon her bed. A slight woman with white-washed skin and a messy brown ponytail. The silence in her head blared against the emptiness of her womb and the merciless demands of a sadistic husband.

Amplified by the shrill whistle of the coal tipple sounding across the valley, the past loomed up, presenting itself inside that truck as a vision. And in the distance, a bank of snow clouds swallowed up the sun.

❧

From the beginning of time, the rugged Appalachian terrain hid its deep veins of coal. Boatloads of early immigrants had unearthed those long-buried secrets. Hearts and minds consumed with an insatiable need; men took far more than was theirs to take. As retribution, the mines blew now and then, burying men deep beneath the surface. Those same mines entombed Kat's father two days before she was born.

After the most recent cave-in, Kat stood spitless at the tipple, hoping the mine had also consumed her stepfather. But I had it on good authority that it did not, and she refused to believe me until she spotted the glowing light of Jubal's hardhat.

For weeks afterward, a bleak landscape plagued Clay with a churning fog, penetrating walls and dripping from rusted roofs. The night Emlyn birthed her third child, the moon disappeared, sinking the Dekker's world into a bottomless abyss. Dim bulbs flickered inside the house with every blast from the mine. The only hope of piercing the darkness fell to me, and the blinding snow drifted down mountain crevices to the creek that twisted through town.

My attempts to ease the contractions ended as Kat delivered the babe with incompetent hands. As she wiped her mother clean from the blood of another grueling birth, I waited for Emlyn to reach for her child. Her sallow face groaned, and she turned to the wall. Away from the quiet little boy, still slick and milky. "His wayward son," she said.

That is when I knew another Dekker infant would die, and I alone possessed no power to stop it. Faith in that household proved difficult to scrape together. Living in a coal town, no one blinked an eye at death. People expected it. Messy but predictable; harsh but inevitable, as there was always something worse than death. The horror of finding yourself nailed to the floor comes to mind.

The first time Jubal struck Kat, she was ten, and I saw as many stars before my eyes as she did. It was a hard smack, splitting her lip and causing her head to bounce off the wall. I begged for permission, that first time, to allow pox or polio to infiltrate his body. But all I heard was the hiss of a smoldering fire, the tick of a clock, and the sob of a child curled in the corner. Unanswered prayers are not only for humans.

Since early childhood, Kat never adjusted to the humiliation of a rough shove into a corner where a brutal hand hammered her dress or shirt to the floor. Other than a smack to her face or a belt crack on bare legs, it was Jubal's favorite mode of punishment. Sometimes he forced her to stay on that cold linoleum for days, throwing bits of food at her face, making her sit in her urine. Until Emlyn conjured enough courage, insisting he allow Kat to rip herself free.

You may wonder why I did not wield some type of *magic*. Why I did not call lightning bolts from Heaven, and why, in Kat's darkest hours, I did not transport her to another place and time. For the same reason, Christ did not call twelve legions of angels to deliver Him from human persecution. God's ways are not our ways. Not even the highest of the Heavenlies are privy to His thought process. And as I am not human, I will leave it there for now.

Most nights, Kat and I stacked our conversations to the rafters with the best ways to leave town. But my influence proved more difficult than expected. Kat remained for the sake of her mother. That much, I realized. Over time, I became desperate to further understand human despair, particularly that of women.

Battling the darkness that embraced humanity plagued me for centuries. Since the day a third of her kind plummeted from the Heavens, Edith Algiyah reared her demonic head the exact moment I had a situation in hand. I can attest female tormentors are the worst. I had been catching whiffs of her stench, and it troubled me.

Arriving home, Jubal parked his truck and spat. "Go on in. Stay in yer room."

Kat flew up the stairs and threw herself on the bed, crying hard enough to shake the posts. It was one thing to feel her agony; it was altogether another to watch.

I moved to the window. Whirling snow fell from an invisible sky as I prayed. Bracing myself, determined to wrench Kat from the enemy's snare, I set my face like flint. "Did God not tell us His grace was sufficient?"

Kat pulled herself up, thumbing tears from her eyes. "If grace belongs to God," she said, "then luck belongs to Satan. Because I have *none*."

Taking a firm grip on her shoulders with both hands, I felt less and less effective in my fight to save her. "You do not need *luck*, my friend. He promised to restore what the locust had eaten. Beauty for ashes, remember? Through it all, Kat, you *must* hold tight to the horns of the altar. To the promises of God. His, at least, are true."

The room vibrated with her anxiety, her misery, and she spoke sharper than intended. "Quit preachin', Abigail. I've heard it all. Every scripture, every promise. Biblical and otherwise. What do you know about it? How it feels. You're not like me. You have no mother with eyes pulled from the grave. There's no tight fist on *your* coattail!" Kat's voice slid across morning shadows, landing in my lap as if it were all that remained of her.

I had to agree she was right. Kat tilted her head in my direction, and though she was not looking at me, I saw the hint of a smile, and then, with her outstretched hand, she reached for mine. "I'm sorry, Abigail. I suppose even an angel can get on one's nerves."

Kat deserved more. The weight of my mission intensified and burned inside my chest. To lead her over the prison walls of Emlyn's self-preservation. Her mother's eyes had followed her since birth as if building a barbed-wire fence around her daughter. But Jubal had tied a noose around Kat's neck, yanking hard when he felt her pangs of wanderlust. The world was off limits. Nothing, not even her thoughts, escaped the dank hollers that haunted her.

Kat pulled her hand mirror out of the dresser drawer. It had been a while since we studied our faces together. So alike and yet so poles apart. Human and Guardian. A Messenger of the Divine and a coal miner's daughter, yet neither of us questioned our devotion to each other. Her discussions with anyone about my existence resulted in glaring stares of suspicion and apathy. I had walked with Kat through the streets of Clay, past fingers pointing at the idiot girl who spoke to disembodied voices in the air. In hushed tones of mockery and pity, they called her Crazy Kat, the hillbilly who sang with the wind and laughed at nothing.

I avoid human ignorance. It makes no sense to me.

Kat stared into her mirror. Her eyes were green as new growth, and her cheeks reflected a dusting of peaches fresh off the tree. But it was her hair that set her apart from girls in Clay. Girls with a greasy brown rat's nest plastered to their faces and neck. Kat's hair, like mine, flowed down her back. A river of honey with hues as rich as marigolds and sunsets. It flew free, never pinned up or pulled back. God's gifts to Kat were gems of beauty, endurance, and the ability to dream.

But when Emlyn pushed her last dead baby free from her body, Kat's dream also withered and died. And with it, her longsuffering.

That evening, Kat carried a tray of black coffee and a day-old biscuit into her mother's bedroom. Plopping it on the rickety bedside table next to Emlyn's ashtray, Kat cursed her fragile mother in an explosion of long-hidden infuriation. "Dammit, Mama! Please tell me where in the Bible it says if you can't cook, clean, or carry a thought in your head, the burden of your household falls to your daughter?! Why didn't you let me get the doctor, Mama?!"

Emlyn's eyes, the color of cold cement, only stared into her coffee. As if her daughter's words were nothing more than the cigarette smoke she exhaled, pale and meaningless.

As expected, Jubal reacted to the outburst. Pulling Kat away from her mother's bedside, he shoved her into the kitchen. Kat landed on the floor as Jubal set about hammering at whatever piece of her clothing his fist grabbed first. Several blasphemous words later, he stood and meandered to the table to open a tiny pine box.

Nailed to the linoleum, Kat bit at tears and stared at the back of Jubal's head. I knew she agonized for herself and the lifeless little boy in the box they would bury like a puppy found dead on the road.

Kat had asked God to forgive her for whatever she had done to deserve the task of midwife and the dread of living one more day. Instead, He exposed her to the full abrasion of Jubal's cruelty and the possibility of aiding her mother through another stillbirth. In Kat's prayers, she demanded a reckoning. One I could not give her.

At midnight, as the house chilled, Kat pulled herself free. Her dress mended, she crawled into bed, hugging her pillow and grasping my sleeve. What she said next spread like a bloodstain across the sheets between us. "I can't find my words, Abigail. I don't know how to fight him."

I pushed strands of golden hair from her furrowed forehead. I had exhausted myself of scriptures applied to her wounds like rags soaked in Mercurochrome. Kat bore the cross of an incapable mother, a deranged stepfather, and two shriveled baby brothers, purple and stiff. And she hated them all.

Even angels cry over shattered human hearts.

In the days that followed, bitter cold waited at the front door each time Kat stepped outside. A mixture of snow and rain combined with dead leaves and mud-packed roads. Unbeknownst to Emlyn, I visited her sleeping subconscious, diving deep into the cobwebbed corners of her mind, pleading Kat's case. Prophetic dreams are an effective means of communication and influence. Tried and true over centuries. Finally, Emlyn untied her apron strings and sent a letter to her sister in North Carolina.

On a bright and gleaming Tuesday, the response came. We held a secret meeting on the back porch, away from Jubal's prying eyes and jar of nails. Emlyn read Kat the letter. Her sister, Judith, had agreed to take Kat into her home. An empty bedroom and the chance to build a life awaited in Aunt Judith's bungalow. Kat jumped and twirled, reveling in the prospect, until I pulled on her reins. It was time to go to Mister Blosser's Grocery and Grill and send a telegram, making the necessary arrangements. And quickly.

Rubber factories to the north and the furniture industry to the south had stolen a small workforce from West Virginia, drawing families like bees to clover. The war effort offered a new world for escaping miners, and women were no exception. A life opened its jaws for Kat. No longer stuck in her teeth were the lies she told herself to remain in her stepfather's house. Her bruised body and besieged spirit never felt so much hope. She dared to dream again, to flee the cold, gray town that had consumed her since birth.

The next evening, a chilled rain fell over the valley, and a pale, transparent-looking moon struggled to shine through the drizzle. Kat shivered next to a weak fire as an oppressive breeze seeped through old windows and cracks in the walls. I had lowered myself to the chair beside her when the sound of Jubal's truck backfired and screeched to a stop. Hearing it, Kat's head snapped toward the door. A current of trepidation circled the darkness over our heads, and I stood to prepare for the fight I felt sure to come.

It surprised even me when Emlyn staggered into the front room, clutching her ragged robe about her neck. "I'll stop him," she said, her voice a soft whimper. It was like watching a mouse attempting to hold off a bobcat.

Kat bolted upstairs, but I remained steadfast.

Jubal kicked in the door. Tracking in mud and slush, he backhanded Emlyn where she stood. She stumbled, then dropped like a rock, covering her bleeding face with trembling hands. He had spent the day in the spring house. Drinking from the jug, not the spring.

"Get down here, gal!" Jubal's jackhammer command rammed into walls and doors, rivaling the darkness in intention. His weapon of choice appeared in his left hand; in the other, he held out a long, rusted nail. He tossed the hammer to the floor, landing inches shy of my feet. I recognized this rage. I had seen it thousands of times. But what he did not see was the twenty-foot black snake slithering between his feet and over his mud-covered boots. Edith never failed to find the right moment to challenge me.

"Kat, stay where you are!" My voice radiated as tiny flickers of light.

It is here I must tell you angels are not fairy godmothers. We do not wave wands, read minds, or intercept the plans of the wicked. We are messengers of God, sent to influence, comfort, and minister. And when permitted, offer a hedge of protection. Guardians like me engage in battle when the powers of evil show their most repulsive heads, not before and not after.

A cigarette flipped up and down between Jubal's lips. "What're you waitin' for, gal? Yer angel?" His crude laugh and snort ended as Kat crept into the room; the color drained from her face.

Once again, I bore witness to the ancient terror of Eve. It twisted like a viper around Kat, binding and turning her into sickening shades of green.

"You call me?"

Jubal's eyes widened. "Who else would I be talkin' to?" Gesturing with the tip of his cigarette to the hammer, he shouted. "Pick it up!"

Kat could not move.

He slammed the nail down on the kitchen table, took a long drag, and coughed. "I said, pick it up!"

Slowly, she pulled the hammer from the floor and placed it next to the nail.

Jubal squinted at the smoke curling out of his mouth. "Old man Blosser read me yer telegram. You think you can pull a fast one? You ain't leaving this house, missy. Not now. Not never. It's time you give me what yer mama cain't."

His words sat on Kat's shoulder, but only for a moment. Upon comprehension, Kat's knees buckled, and she grabbed the table to keep from falling.

I, too, understood the magnitude of his meaning. A smack to Kat's face and another rip in her dress were not enough for him. Not this time. Jubal's drunken determination became as clear as my witness to the Roman soldiers' intentions on Golgotha's hill. Having done all to withstand, I girded my loins and applied my breastplate. The second I readied the two-edged sword at my side, Jubal grabbed Kat's hand and jerked it across the table. Forcing it open, he drove the rusted flat-head nail through the center with one solid blow.

Kat's body reeled and folded forward, dropping into a chair. Her eyes closed, sweat beaded in tiny drops across her forehead. Blood streamed from her hand and over the table as the shock of

Jubal's icy steel hatred oozed up like bile into her throat. Forced out as one pain-filled cry, it sprang from colorless lips. "Whyyyy?!"

Deep in the middle of an Appalachian coal town, a rushing wind rolled through a tar paper and clapboard house, upended furniture, and gusted through rooms. It rattled the roof, then escalated to a violent shake that shattered windows and extinguished all light. All but that of a battle-ready angel and a dying fire.

Jubal froze, his dark eyes skittering.

As the breath of God blew inward, the divine storm raged, whipping my hair about my face and transforming my simple clothes into the brilliant robes of a Guardian given at my creation. Since the cross, those who drove spikes through innocent human hands have suffered His wrath. My mission was ending.

The veil lifted.

I turned my body from the shadowed walls and declared with the voice of Heaven's authority, "The burden of *this* Child of God is over! Release her!!" The sovereignty of His presence and the lightning flashes from my eyes demanded Jubal's attention. Drawn down by a divine hand far more powerful than himself, Jubal backed against the wall.

Beholding the supernatural consequence of his sin, Jubal's chin dropped and hung there, his body sparking with the terror he meant for Kat. My sword rang from its sheath. The force of it cut through the air, meeting with the head of the snake. Edith transformed. Levitating in her blood-red robe with bulging yellow eyes and flared nostrils, she toyed with her sword, poised for a fight she could not win. A guttural growl rolled out of her throat. I caught the fiery stink of Hell from her breath as she shrieked her final decree with the intensity of the demon she was. "Next time, Abigail. Until we meet again!" Like the blast of a mine, the force of Edith's hideous laugh ended with an explosion, leaving nothing behind but shoots of electrifying light, ash, and the stench of sulfur.

I sheathed my sword. Jubal's eyes bore into mine, staring at the illumination of God's power that now dimmed inside his house.

His mouth still open wide with a dry tongue that hung to his chin, he swayed as one in a trance. I wondered how long it would take before he blamed his drunken stupor for the spiritual warfare he had witnessed.

The bloodied hammer dangling from Jubal's fingers fell to the floor as he turned and found Kat at the table, eyes still closed, clutching her hand to her chest. A hand set free. A healed hand that no longer bled. He lunged and grabbed a fistful of Kat's hair, yanking her up and into his chest, her face inches from his own. That was when Kat found her words, each drawn out and punctuated with unmitigated power.

"LET … ME … GO!"

Jubal shook his head at Kat, unable to grasp her words. He struggled to speak, his tongue pressing hard against his teeth. He strained to push the foul oaths in his brain out of his gaping mouth. Each word died on the vine. In a sick instant, he grabbed the hand he had nailed to the table to examine it. As he did, his hot tears fell like melted iron to the center of Kat's palm. Wrenching her hand away, she screamed, but Jubal never heard a sound. He would neither hear nor speak again. Ever.

◦◦◦

The days passed.

A crow's 'caw' broke a deafening silence when Kat walked into the kitchen where her mother peeled parsnips at the table. A kind of sadness appeared on Emlyn's face, and her cheeks went slack. "I love you, daughter," she said, as if forbidden to say Kat's name. A neglected syllable of her past.

"I know."

Emlyn's hands dropped the knife into the vegetable bowl, and she paused, looked up, and smiled. "The Lord gives, and I'll be damned—He's taking my last one away." Her smile faded as though she were discussing the weather, her voice soft and polite. "Time for you to go." She glanced down at the worn linoleum between her shoes and then allowed her gaze to drift into the next room. The bedroom where her catatonic husband drooled on sweaty sheets and stared at nothing.

Emlyn stood and breathed into Kat's tangled hair, golden like the threads of the parsnips she peeled. Her words, smooth and round as river rocks, penetrated years of humiliation and vibrated with newfound strength. "The bus from Charleston leaves for High Point tomorrow evening." She pulled a bus ticket covered with dirty fingerprints from her apron pocket and held it to her heart. An embodiment of her love, the gift of freedom, and a promise kept. "Happy birthday, Kat. My sister's expecting you."

Abuse is abhorrent, but answered prayer is euphoric. A high-pitched sound erupted from Kat's throat like a gusher, as if she had never laughed before that moment. As if she raised her arms, she might fly away. *Oh, glory.*

A clear horizon loomed ahead. Despite the buckled pavement and winter potholes, the road pitched and rolled before Kat like a stairway to Heaven. An image of herself appeared in the darkness of the bus. An angel who looked like her. *You go where you are loved,* I said. *Time for me to go too.* I nodded toward the silent glitter of the sunset filtering through the window. *But He will never leave you. Never forsake you.*

Fading into the dim light of dusk, I smiled and blew her a kiss goodbye. Kat's eyes filled with the tears I knew so well. She reached out to touch my arm. An arm now unavailable to her human senses. She did not know it yet, but she no longer needed me.

Kat found not only her words but peace. The kind humans never understand. She became more than just another saved woman. Kat Dekker became a woman of substance. A force beyond adversity. Beyond failing. Beyond becoming her mother. On those dark nights Kat lay in my arms while brutally nailed to the floor, I reminded her what we are born into is not who we must remain. Through God's grace and unchanging hand, humans possess extraordinary abilities to walk in His footsteps; to change their adversities into advantages, and to stand against those who battle for their sanity. And their soul.

As a Guardian on this planet, I have carried millions of human souls through the barriers of time and space into the heavens. I am grateful I never had to carry hers. Kat's salvation is one of my greatest victories, and on the day she *crosses* the great divide, I will be there.

For a free eBook of **Televenge**, the first book in the
Televenge trilogy, go to: **getTelevenge.com**

An excerpt from **TELEVENGE:**

*He deserved to die. I thought about it a lot. During long nights
in the darkness of my car or motel room, I plotted his last breath.
Shoving anguish and torment so far down for so long had festered
like a rotting corpse until I no longer recognized myself. Years of
suffering at his hands produced the raw courage needed to put a gun
to his head.*

*I lit a cigarette and sat on sheets that reeked of body odor and
urine. Cleaning my .380 automatic, I decided they'd have to listen
after I pulled the trigger. Good behavior didn't mean squat until one
landed behind bars. My destiny was a prison cell and possibly Hell if
it existed. "Worth it all" were the only words out of my mouth that
day.*

*The Reverend expected my suicide, exhorting the ministry team
to pray, fast, and beseech God for me to open my veins and drown in
a pool of red unforgiveness. But he did not anticipate the vengeance
that pumped through me like a raging river. One more bridge to
cross and burn. My gift to the world was one less televangelist.*

*When did it all go crazy, you ask? Sitting here, telling you my
life's story, my mind skims across time like a water spider crossing a
pond. Back to 1972, when I was seventeen and pretty. And full of joy
unspeakable.*

Chapter 1

Daydream Believer

Andie ~ 1972

Never had there been a time when I was riper for love than the summer of my fourteenth birthday. I drew boys like beetles to magnolias. Nature, lust, puppy love; folks always had a name for it. But for a girl from Winston-Salem, it was the moment my hormones wept at the altar of my womanhood. I shouted, and my eyes sparkled with the covenant of God, embedding itself into the deepest regions of my heart. The gangly girl dissolved, leaving only a sanctified goddess, and in that instant—I met Joe.

Scanning the pews for a husband, I sat fixed in my seat at the House of Praise on the city's outskirts. I seldom missed a church service with my sister, Caroline, and our mother, whom we called Dixie. And occasionally, Daddy came with us when he felt the need. But from a tender age, I assumed angels kissed the sons of the righteous at birth because those upstanding families produced good husbands, fathers, and providers.

On my sixteenth birthday, Joe set our future in stone. He placed a silver promise ring with a diamond chip on my left hand. Dixie, who had also married young, permitted my chaperoned weekends in Salisbury, a town of Southerners with lineages back to Stonewall Jackson and beyond.

Maudy and Al Oliver welcomed me into their home. They had prayed long and hard for God to show favor to their three evangelical sons. Because of their fervent prayers, they believed Jehovah-Jireh blessed their eldest son with the talent of music, their middle son with the gift of intellect, and their youngest son with a church girl saved and filled with the Holy Ghost.

"Sleep well?" Maudy towered over me with wire-brush curlers wrapped tight to her head. Having made her prospective daughter-in-law a bed on the couch is exactly where she presumed to find me.

"Fine, thanks." But I hadn't slept at all.

Joe discovered an old mattress in the attic. He swore to God to love me forever, professing his promises in luminous moonlight streaming through open windows and reflecting off yellowed, peeling wallpaper. Brought up to believe in the word of a Christian man, I returned his promise—no matter our future, I'd love him until the end of my days. Rolling to my back, I pulled him onto my naked breasts, knowing someday we would recall our moment of commitment, of purest love when we had reached for the hem of God and vowed to become one flesh forever. I closed my eyes and made one last promise—to God. I would never love another. Ever.

The sizzle and aroma of fried sausage jolted my senses. I rolled off the couch, wrapping a nubby blanket around my shoulders. *I love you, Andie Rose.* Joe's voice penetrated my thoughts. Splashing cool water on my face, I wiped away the streaked mascara. The promise ring flickered in the mirror and in my eyes.

Maudy's voice rang from the kitchen. "Breakfast, Andie!"

I shivered. "Coming!"

He had held me until morning's first light, chancing discovery, not wanting to let go. He told me I was smart and pretty and sweet. He loved me, he said, and I again believed him.

Slipping out of his arms, I whispered against his cheek. "What will your mama say if she finds us?" Naked except for a pair of wispy blue panties, I stood in the steeply pitched attic and pulled on Joe's sweatshirt, daring to creep down the narrow staircase, careful not to wake the house. An hour passed when I heard him leave for work at the Esso station, and before I had a chance to respond to his kiss on my forehead.

Maudy knocked twice and hollered through the door. "Come get it while it's hot."

I shook myself free of the memory. "I'll be right out." Staring wide-eyed into the mirror, I felt a wild energy coursing through me like an electric current. It wasn't foreboding, doubt, or even the Holy Spirit. It was more like an unwelcome caution. My knees buckled, and I felt as if I might be sick. I sat on the bathroom floor, my head in my hands, and prayed for the feeling to pass. And then I smelled him. The remnants of Joe lodged in every part of me.

For more information or to purchase go to **GracelynRose.com**

Other books by this author:

TELEVENGE
Book One of the *Televenge* trilogy

AVENGE US ALL
Book Two of the *Televenge* trilogy

VENGEANCE IS MINE
Book Three of the *Televenge* trilogy

THE SANCTUM
A coming-of-age Southern tale dusted with magic
and set in a volatile time in America
when the winds of change begin to blow.